CONVERSATIONS WITH THE DEAD

HOUSE OF KANE BOOK TWO

*To Kathy
thank you so much
for your help?!
Philip M Jones*

Philip M Jones

FIRESONG ARTS, LLC
P.O. BOX 2164
HILLSBORO, OR 97123

ISBN: 0-9998128-3-1
ISBN-13: 978-0-9998128-3-9

Published by Firesong Arts, LLC
Changing the World, One Word at a Time
https://www.firesongarts.com/
Editing by Sandra Johnson
Cover Illustration Copyright © 2019 by MatYan

To Marvin and Peggy Jones

Your love and support have meant the
world to me.

What Readers Are Saying About
CURSED LEGACY

"Well written, a real page turner. Jones has the ability to draw you in and keep you wanting more!"

- Darci Naomi

"Genuine and realistic--an exciting read--and one you think about after you have finished story!!

- Terri Squires

"Such a good read. I love the use of magic and how well-versed Jones is with folklore. This world embraces light and dark with 3-dimensional villains and heroes who all believe they are using their powers for good."

- J Kovach

ALSO BY PHILIP M JONES

✳

HOUSE OF KANE SERIES

CURSED LEGACY

CONVERSATIONS WITH THE DEAD

KINGDOM OF ASHES*

(* FORTHCOMING)

CONVERSATIONS
WITH THE DEAD

CHAPTER ONE

The old brick walls felt as though they were closing in on her. The practice room was too close. Too small. Abby sat on the piano stool, trying to focus on her violin as her heart raced.

Two figures rested on the blood-stained carpet. "Mom? Dad?" Abby screamed. Hot tears ran down her cheeks before she fully realized what she was seeing. A pentagram with an eye in its center was painted on the wall in blood.

It's not real, she told herself. Abby blinked, trying to erase what she was seeing. Snap out of it Abby. It's just a dream. It's not real.

"Calm down, Abby," she whispered. She closed her eyes for a moment and took a deep breath. When she opened her eyes, she was in the practice room again. *A panic attack, Abby. That's all. It's not real. Calm down.* She repeated it like a mantra until the practice room felt less imposing.

It had been just under six months since she had returned from England; over a year and a half since her parents were murdered, and Abby was still plagued by these visions and nightmares.

"I don't have time for this," Abby growled. She took one more deep breath and plucked an A above middle C on the piano. Getting the note, she began tuning her violin. She listened and adjusted until she had found the pitch.

Abby placed the instrument in her lap and took up her bow, running it over the amber-colored resin. "This is good," she said, running her hand over the smooth wooden body of her violin. "This is real." She plucked the horse hairs and watched a small cloud of resin puff into the air.

"Shoot," Abby muttered. She stood, trying to brush away the white cloud of powder that had settled on her black skirt.

"Miss Kane?" There was a tap on the door. Abby looked up to see a plain-looking woman with a clipboard standing in the hall. She pressed a hand to her headset, listening, and then said, "They're ready for you."

"Thank you," Abby said. She stood with her instrument and paused a moment, lingering until the woman turned back down the hallway. "Invocus Aero," she whispered once she was sure the other woman wouldn't be able to see. She made a swiping motion over the white spot on her skirt, and the resin fell from her garment, disappearing against the tiled floor.

Abby hurried after the woman. She had to quicken her steps to catch up to the woman's brisk pace but easily followed her guide through the quiet back corridors of Benaroya Hall. They climbed a small staircase and stepped through a door. A heavy curtain was abruptly pushed aside, and Abby found herself standing on the stage of the grand concert hall.

The woman shielded her eyes from the blinding lights above and cleared her throat. Through the glare, Abby could just make out the forms of four individuals sitting in the third row.

"Abigail Kane," the woman announced before making her way into the shrouded audience.

"Miss Kane, thank you for coming. Tell us about your training," a man's voice called out from the audience in a thick German accent.

"I studied under Dr. Spellman as a student at Lancaster Preparatory Academy, here in Seattle, and then under Professor Goodwin at Armitage Hall in Oxfordshire, England," Abby responded. "I also received private lessons with Catherine Madrigal."

"Excellent," another voice called out from the audience. "How old are you, and where are you planning to study?"

"I'm eighteen, and I will be studying music at Oxford University starting next October," Abby answered.

"That isn't for another year, Miss Kane. What do you plan to do until then?" a third voice asked.

"I plan to continue my private lessons here and play with your symphony if I can," she added.

She heard a light chuckle pass through the group. "Very impressive, Miss Kane," said the first voice from the darkness beyond. "What piece will you be auditioning with today?"

"I've chosen Beethoven's *Violin Sonata No. 9*," Abby said, taking a deep breath to push through her nervousness.

"Please start when you're ready."

Abby placed the instrument under her chin and held the bow gracefully in her right hand, taking another deep breath. She hated the interview part, but this she knew how to do. She placed the bow on the strings and closed her eyes.

With a fluid motion, she began playing the piece she had been practicing for months. The violin was her first love, and the only real solace she had from the grief she was trying to put behind her. She let her heart move her fingers as she played. Her mind consumed the sounds of each note played in perfect pitch and let it resonate in her heart. There was a connection Abby felt between herself and the melody. It spoke to her like an old friend who knew her better than anyone else.

"Ms. Kane!" a man's voice rang out. Abby stopped and lowered her instrument. "Thank you, Miss Kane, we've heard enough."

Abby offered a confident smile and began to walk off the stage. She was not as sure as her smile would imply. When an audition ended that abruptly, it wasn't generally a good sign. "Thank you for your time," she said, with a slight bow.

"Miss Kane, one moment please," the German accent called out. A shadow stood and emerged into the light. A tidy gentleman wearing a sharp suit walked up onto the stage. He was maybe in his early sixties. His well-groomed, salt-and-pepper gray hair accentuated his business-like appearance, reminding Abby of her uncle Sebastian.

"I'm Kristoff Schreiner," he said, introducing himself.

"It's nice to meet you, Mr. Schreiner," Abby said and shook his hand.

"We would like to invite you to be one of our young solo artists for the holiday concert in December." The man smiled eagerly, waiting for Abby's response.

So fast! Abby's eyes went wide, and she had to clamp down her excitement before she made a fool of herself. *This is really happening? I can't believe it!* Inside she was screaming with excitement, but replied in a calm, even tone, "I would be deeply honored to play for you, Mr. Schreiner."

"You are a talented young artist, Miss Kane. I look forward to watching your career unfold." Mr. Schreiner smiled warmly. "I will be contacting you within the week. We'll provide the piece we intend to have you perform, as well as the rehearsal schedule and contact information for an accompanist you can practice with."

He reached into his pocket and handed her his business card. "If you have any questions, contact me."

"Thank you, Mr. Schreiner. I very much look forward to working with you," she said again.

Abby made her way back to the practice room. As soon as the door closed, she collapsed onto the piano bench. She let out a squeal that was much more in line with her youth than her previous control. *I can't believe it! This is what I've wanted for as long as I can remember!*

Abby couldn't stop grinning. She quickly put her instrument away before she hurried through the building and onto the street. Pedestrians flooded the sidewalks of the city, oblivious to her elation.

After a few moments, a white Lexus pulled up beside her. Abby flung the door open and threw herself inside. She grinned at her uncle behind the wheel. "They offered me a solo for the holiday concert," she shouted before she had even fastened her seat belt.

"Was there ever any doubt?" Sebastian teased. "You have talent, Abby, I don't think anyone has ever questioned that. Except you. When are you going to start believing in yourself?"

"I don't know," she said. "It's not that I don't believe in myself, it's just…" Guilt and shame washed away the color of her excitement as grief flooded her thoughts. "I guess I just always thought that when I got this chance, I would be able to share it with Mom."

She choked back the tears that were threatening to spill. It all felt different without her parents' support. She wanted nothing more than to have them beside her, beaming with pride. But now, without them… "I just feel like everything is going to get pulled out from under me." *Again,* she added silently.

"Oh, Abby." Her uncle reached over and grabbed her hand, holding it in his. "The last couple of years have been difficult. I know how much you miss them. But, you can't stop living your life because you're afraid of losing it. You know that isn't all there is to life, Abby. You just have to keep moving forward. I promise it will get better."

"When?" was all Abby said.

They drove in silence for a few moments. There was nothing else to say. They both knew it was still too hard.

Some days it was as fresh as if she'd found her parents two weeks ago instead of two years. She just wanted to be happy again–to enjoy this moment.

Abby stared out the window at nothing as Sebastian drove through the crowded streets. "I'm very proud that you even auditioned," he said quietly. "But I'm not surprised you were asked to be a guest artist."

"Thank you," Abby said, trying to smile in return.

The silence was more relaxed this time. Abby tried not to think about any of it, preferring not to get any more emotional than she already was. The endlessly warring grief, fear, and joy was exhausting, and Abby just wanted it to be over. "I just want to be happy again." She sighed.

"You will," Sebastian said with certainty. "I have a surprise for you this evening," he said, abruptly changing the subject. He had a suspicious glint in his eye that Abby couldn't resist.

"I thought we were having a family dinner this evening," she said in a bored tone.

Her affected disinterest didn't work on him. "Oh, yes, and there will be a special guest," Sebastian said slyly.

"Now you're simply being cruel." Abby laughed.

"Don't worry," Sebastian reassured. "I think you'll like this surprise."

Abby laughed. "I'll take your word for it." She stared out the window at the glass towers as they headed toward the ferry terminal. "It's not Grandmother, is it?" she asked after a moment.

"I said you would like it," Sebastian retorted with a chuckle. "I thought the two of you were getting along at the moment."

"She hasn't been so bad lately," Abby conceded.

"Vivian's always on her best behavior when she's up to something." Sebastian nodded.

Abby sighed. "You're too right. I'll take it for now. I don't know what she's conjuring, but I could do with a bit less drama in my life," she said.

"We're home!" Sebastian called out as they walked through the front door. Abby stepped into the large living room and immediately took in the view. It didn't matter how long she'd been living here with her uncles, she never grew tired of looking out at the Seattle skyline over Puget Sound.

She sank down into one of the large overstuffed chairs, facing the large bay windows and placed her violin case next to her. This home wasn't what Abby once had with her own parents, but Sebastian and Rodger tried really hard to make her feel welcome. It was as close to normal as anything could be.

"Dear God!" Rodger rushed in from the kitchen, holding an infant at arm's length. He thrust their baby in his husband's direction. "Here."

"Whew! He smells!" Abby noticed the foul odor emanating from Evan's diaper. She waved her hand in front of her as she watched Sebastian hold his nose cautiously. Baby Evan was smiling brightly.

"Why me?" Sebastian asked, realizing Rodger had retreated to the couch next to Abby's chair.

"You're the only one who can change a diaper that bad without gagging," Rodger explained covering his nose with his hand.

"That's true," Abby added with an amused smile.

"The two of you are diabolical," Sebastian commented and took his son upstairs.

"Are the two of you still thinking about getting a nanny?" Abby asked.

Rodger sighed. "We go back and forth. We're still learning so much. Margot helps a bit with advice, but it's a lot more work than either of us imagined. He's worth it though."

"Yes, he is," Abby agreed brightly.

"So?" Rodger asked eagerly.

"They asked me to play at the Holiday Invitational," Abby told him. Her grin was wider than the picture window.

"I knew you would! You practiced so hard. You've spent the last six months pouring yourself into that instrument. I was so worried when you got back after..." He trailed off, unsure if he should continue.

"After Benjamin." Abby smiled reassuringly. "It's okay. You can say his name. It's hard, but I don't regret moving home."

"I'm glad you're here, Abby. And I'm so proud of you for sticking with the violin."

"Thanks." Abby blushed slightly.

"We have dinner in a bit. Go get washed up. Our surprise guest will arrive on the next ferry," he said, glancing down at his watch.

"Any hints about who's coming?" she asked eagerly. She pulled out her phone, checking for any text messages. "Is it Nina? Sarah? Warren? Tell me!"

"Not a single clue," Rodger said with a wicked smile before retreating into the kitchen.

Abby collected her violin case and traipsed upstairs in a mock huff.

In her bedroom, Abby placed her violin case in its spot next to her music stand and kicked off her shoes. She opened the window and breathed in the fall air. The view was not dissimilar to the one in the living room. She listened to the water lapping lazily at the rocky shore below, littered with pieces of driftwood and seashells.

In the distance, spires of glass and steel rose from the Earth, like engineered stalagmites. Behind the city, Mt. Rainier dominated the skyline; Seattle's silent guardian.

Abby turned back inside and began undressing. She rummaged through her closet and found a pair of comfortable jeans and a t-shirt.

Her phone vibrated. It was a text from Nina. A smile spread across her face when she thought of her friends back in England. They had been the best part of her schooling there. She opened a picture of Nina, Warren, and Sarah standing in front of the Sphinx in Egypt.

"They're having fun," she said out loud. "I guess they aren't my mystery guests, then."

She tapped in a quick reply and then told them about the concert. She put her phone down on the dresser, then picked it up again. "I should tell Madison, too."

She texted her cousin the news and put her phone into her pocket.

She sat on the edge of the bed, chewing her bottom lip. For weeks she had been focused only on this audition, and now she didn't have anything to do. She glanced around the room, bored. *I could always practice more,* she thought. Her violin rested in its case below the window, and she eyed it with consideration. Evan would be going down for a nap soon. She wouldn't risk waking him up.

Abby got up and went back downstairs. She wandered into the kitchen where Rodger was chopping vegetables. "Do you need any help?" Abby asked, hopefully.

"Not really," he said cheerfully. He looked at her face and added, "But I'm certain I can find something for you to do." He handed Abby a knife and a sweet potato, gesturing her toward the counter.

"What are we having?" she asked, contemplating the ingredients on the counter.

"Steak, grilled asparagus, mashed sweet potatoes, and salad."

"What about everyone's favorite? Dessert?" Abby asked.

Rodger looked panicked for a moment. "Oh, I hadn't thought of that," he said.

"I think we figured something out that I can do." Abby smiled.

"What are you thinking about?" Rodger asked.

She looked at her uncle. "I really like that gelato thing you did with the olive oil and lemon zest."

"I think we have everything we need for that." Rodger opened the freezer door and gestured toward the gelato. "Excellent idea."

Abby had a momentary flash of familiarity. She wore a bitter smile, remembering the countless times she had helped her mother prepare meals just like this.

"What's wrong?" Rodger asked, noticing the shift in Abby's mood.

She shook her head and smiled. "Sorry. I drifted off for a moment. I was just thinking about…"

"Your parents?" Rodger's expression shifted to one of understanding. He leaned over and kissed Abby on the forehead and resumed his meal preparations. "It's always the most mundane little things that catch us by surprise," he commented.

Abby nodded, doing her best to not dwell on her loss. *It is a day to be happy,* she reminded herself. *I shouldn't have to fake it.*

"All right, this little guy is in much better shape," Sebastian said, as he entered the room with Little Evan, who was clapping his hands together and cooing. Abby brightened, seeing her little cousin so happy. Somehow, even at less than a year old, the small child made life seem much less complicated.

"I'll take him," Abby said, eagerly holding out her arms for her little cousin.

"Oh sure, now that all the hard work is done," Sebastian teased before handing Evan to Abby.

She pulled the baby close and gave him a big hug before taking a seat and setting him on her lap. He looked up and gave her a bashful smile. "Oh! He's so cute," she squealed. "I completely understand every old person's desire to pinch the little cheeks!"

"How is dinner coming along?" Sebastian asked, glancing over at his husband's efforts.

"I'm close to done. I won't grill anything until we're all here," Rodger said, as he cleaned the countertops.

"Abby, would you mind watching Evan for a bit while we go pick our guest up at the ferry?" Sebastian asked.

"Of course I don't mind," she said. Looking down at Evan, she feigned a surprised look. "The parents are out! We can get ourselves into some trouble."

"Do you have the keys to the liquor cabinet?" Sebastian asked Rodger playfully.

"Yep," Rodger confirmed with a smile.

"Well then, I don't think the two of them can get into too much trouble," Sebastian teased.

"Adults are no fun, Evan. Remember that," Abby said playfully explaining the reality of life to her little cousin who smiled and waved his arms in excitement.

"We'll be back in about thirty minutes," Sebastian called out as he and Rodger fled through the front door.

"See you later," Abby said playfully. She bounced Evan in her arms. She looked down at the little boy as he let out a big yawn. "It's nap time, isn't it?" She glanced at the time on her phone. "I think I could use one myself," she added. All the excitement from the audition was starting to settle in.

She cradled Evan in her arms, rising. She bounced him gently while she walked back and forth around the room. In almost no time, his eyes were growing heavy.

He produced another big, infectious yawn. Abby caught herself yawning along with him and walked back over to sit on the couch. She leaned back, cradling her cousin against her chest as he drifted off. Abby closed her eyes and joined him.

CHAPTER TWO

It felt like only a few minutes before Abby heard the front door open. She wasn't even aware that she had fallen asleep. She batted her eyes open and glanced down at Evan, who was sleeping peacefully in her arms.

She sat up, blinking the nap from her eyes as a lean woman with long red hair stepped into the foyer. *Mom?!* Abby tried to shake off her soporific haze. Her heart leaped in her chest, and tears fell onto her cheeks. The fair features… the freckles… the beautiful face… *How?* She gasped, trying to get a breath, but it felt as though all the air in the room had suddenly disappeared.

Abby opened her mouth to cry out for her mother and stopped. Did her mother always have tattoos on her arms? *That isn't right…* Abby stood, careful not to disturb the baby. She cautiously walked over to the group in the entryway. There was a long pause as everyone in the room stared at one another. No one knew what to say.

"Hey kiddo," the woman said shyly.

Recognition settled in at the sound of the woman's voice, so like her mother's yet distinctly different. "Aunt Wendy?" Abby choked on a moment of disappointment, feeling guilty that she hadn't given her aunt a warmer welcome.

"Well, don't just stand there. Come, give your aunt a hug!" Wendy said brightly.

Abby pulled herself together. She handed Little Evan off to Rodger before giving her aunt a big long hug. It had been such a long time, at least since the funeral. She had forgotten how much they looked alike.

"You okay kid?" Wendy whispered into Abby's ear as they embraced.

Abby nodded silently against her aunt's shoulder. "I was asleep when you came in. I think I was a little startled," she said. "I'm really happy you're here!" She consciously pushed her excitement to the front of her emotions, drowning the pangs of grief.

Abby stepped back and gave the other woman a thorough look. Wendy was only a little more than a decade or so older than Abby, in her late twenties. She bore the Whitlock family genes well, just as Abby's mother had. From up close, Abby could easily see her genetic ties to Sebastian as well. Her red hair only just brushed the edge of her shoulders with a slight curl at the end. It was her deep green eyes that made Abby feel like she was staring into the eyes of her own mother.

"You look good, and we have some catching up to do," Wendy said warmly looking to her brother. "I may be staying for more than a visit," she added.

Rodger interjected before Abby could ask. "We've invited Wendy to stay with us for as long as she likes."

"You're moving in?" Abby asked, with more excitement.

"Let's not jump the gun." Wendy laughed. "But I think I will stay for a while." She smiled and turned her attention to the tiny child sleeping in Rodger's arms. "Besides there's a new family member I want to get to know. He's absolutely adorable." She looked down at her nephew with a big smile.

"Do you want to hold him?" Rodger offered the baby to Wendy, adding, "I have to go cook anyway."

"Can I?" Wendy looked excited.

Sebastian smiled as he collected Wendy's luggage. "Come on, I'll show you to your room," he said before heading up the stairs. "Bring him with you. He's particularly adorable when he's sleeping."

"I'll get settled in, and we'll all catch up," Wendy said with a warm smile. She turned and followed her brother up the stairs, taking the sleeping infant with her.

There was a brief pause before Rodger approached his niece. "Are you sure you're okay? You looked like a ghost when we walked in," he said.

Abby bit her lower lip and took a deep breath. "I was a little disoriented from my nap," she explained. "When I saw Aunt Wendy, I... I forgot how much she looks like Mom."

Rodger's eyes went wide for a moment, and then he nodded. He wrapped his arms around Abby and gave her a squeeze. "Come on, let's see to dinner while they get settled in."

Abby followed Rodger into the kitchen. She propped herself up on a stool next to the granite counter and watched silently as her uncle begin pulling things from the refrigerator.

"I hope you aren't disappointed that Wendy's here," Rodger said.

"Not at all," Abby said. "I'm just surprised. I always thought her life was consumed with her horses in Telluride."

Rodger nodded. "She never got along with Vivian." He shrugged as if that was all there was to it and began tossing the salad.

"Grandmother?" Abby questioned. "What did they ever have to do with one another?" she asked. "I mean, I know Wendy is part of the coven, but she has never shown much of an interest in Kane affairs before, right?"

"That's true, and that is probably best," Rodger muttered, finishing with the salad and setting it aside.

"Why?" Abby asked, her curiosity peaked. "Did something happen between them?"

Rodger gave Abby a sly smile. "There is a history."

"Stop keeping me in suspense," Abby protested playfully as Rodger pulled several plates from the cupboard.

"I really shouldn't say," Rodger told her seriously. "Get to know your Aunt Wendy a little better, and I'm sure she'll tell you all about it." There was a hint of a smile on his face. "Could you set the table?" he asked, handing her the small stack of plates.

"Of course," she said, stepping into the formal dining room and setting the table for four but realized there were two extra plates. "Uncle Rodger, why are there six plates?"

"Margot and Madison will be coming shortly," Rodger explained.

"More surprises?" Abby asked playfully.

"Something like that," Rodger said from the kitchen.

Abby caught herself grinning. Even though Margot was her father's cousin, she had always been more like a second mother to Abby. She was excited to see them. Still smiling, she finished setting the table.

"Don't worry I'll be on my best behavior around her," Wendy said, as she descended the stairs with Sebastian. "She's an adult now. It will be fine."

"That's beside the point," Sebastian said, a note of disapproval in his tone. He lowered his voice so as not to wake the child in his arms.

"You set a lovely table," Wendy said as she approached through the living room. She paused briefly to glance out at the breathtaking view of the water through the bay windows.

"We'll finish this conversation later," Sebastian warned, not fooled by Wendy's attempts to change the subject.

"Now that's a view," she commented.

"As Dad would have said, 'we paid a pretty penny for it,'" Sebastian commented.

Abby saw a momentary flash of sadness break its way through her aunt's cheery façade. It was a look she was too familiar with. Wendy quickly recovered and took a deep breath.

"I wish I had met Grandma and Grandpa Whitlock," Abby said remorsefully.

"I was only fifteen when they died," Wendy said, looking to her brother. Sebastian put his hand on her shoulder. "If it hadn't been for you and Jessica…"

Abby flinched internally at the mention of her mother's name.

Sebastian pulled Wendy close and kissed her forehead. "That was a tough time for all of us," he added reverently.

Abby saw the faint threat of tears welling in her aunt's eyes. For a moment, it looked as though Wendy might actually cry, but then her aunt stiffened and took a deep breath, composing herself. She grabbed Abby's hand and dragged her to the couch where they could sit.

Wendy smiled and looked Abby in the eye. "You look a lot like my sister," Wendy said her smile melting to a weak grin. "I didn't realize coming home, would be so hard." An uncertain quality lingered in her tone. "I'm glad I'm here," Wendy said with more resolve. "I plan to get to know you a lot better."

"Margot and Madison should be here in fifteen minutes," Rodger called out from the kitchen.

"Margot?" Wendy raised an eyebrow. "It will be nice to see her again. She's one of the only Kanes who doesn't despise me," she said slightly under her breath.

"That's why we invited her," Sebastian commented coyly as he stepped into the kitchen.

Abby chuckled nervously. "Who is taking care of your house and the horses while you're here?" she asked, uncertain what else to say.

"I took on a business partner a little over a year ago. He will see to things for now," Wendy said. "I plan to stay for a while. I've been hiding long enough. It's time for our family to come together."

A chime from the doorbell cut off any reply Abby had. "I'll get it," she called out. Moving to the front door, she swung it open to a young woman Abby's age. "Madison!" she squealed. Her face brightened with excitement at seeing her cousin.

Madison hurled herself at at her cousin, pulling her into a bone-crushing hug. "Abby!"

Abby took a brief moment to admire Madison's beautiful, long blonde hair and crystal-blue eyes. From the faintest hint of freckles on her nose and cheeks to her sharply defined lips, her classic, empirical beauty was something Abby had always envied. And of course, Madison, flaunting her looks in a cute summer dress with a light sweater, knew it.

Abby looked past her cousin to see a tall, lean woman, moving up the steps with regal elegance. Her perfectly maintained blond hair brushed shoulders in a classic flip. She was every bit as beautiful as her daughter.

"Hello, Abby." Margot smiled and gave her a gentle hug and a peck on the cheek. "You look lovely as always." Her voice was melodic and soothing, coaxing Abby into an easy smile. As a child, it was the voice that had told them bedtime stories. This woman was as much a mother to Abby as her own had been. She hadn't realized how much that voice meant to her.

I wonder how much different this last year would have been if I hid with Margot and Madison during the conflict with the Thanos, Abby wondered briefly before returning the hug. She held on longer than she meant to, soaking in the comfort Margot offered.

"Is something wrong?" Margot asked.

"Nothing at all," Abby reassured, still holding onto her aunt. "It's just good to see you."

Margot looked at Abby, a weighted stare playing across her face. "I saw you two days ago." She smiled and gently patted Abby's arm.

Abby stepped back, releasing the older woman, and pulled herself together while Margot and Madison greeted Wendy. *My mind is all over the place today,* she chided herself.

"Who's ready for dinner?" Rodger called out jubilantly from the dining room. "Hello Margot, Madison," he said, greeting them each with a warm hug.

"I've always admired this view," Margot commented as she passed through the living room into the formal dining room.

Madison took Abby's arm and virtually dragged her through the living room. "I'm so excited for you!" she said. "The Holiday Invitational is a big deal!"

Abby smiled brightly. "Yes, I still can't quite believe it."

"Can't believe what?" Margot asked, joining them at the table.

Abby waited a moment for everyone to take their seats. "I was selected to be a guest artist for the Holiday Invitational. I will be a solo guest artist at the symphony."

"Abby, that is fantastic news," Wendy exclaimed.

Margot beamed at her proudly. "I've been going to your concerts since you were five years old, believe me when I say it has been an amazing journey to watch you grow as a musician."

"Thank you," Abby said bashfully.

She looked around the people sitting at the table. Rodger was a gracious host, making certain everyone at the table was taken care of. Sebastian sat holding his son, looking down at him with eyes that sparkled with pure love.

Margot engaged in idle chat with Wendy while primly sipping her wine. Madison bantered playfully with Rodger, attempting to coax him into letting her drink. Her mother's disapproving stare that put a stop to that joke before it had begun.

This is it, Abby thought, her heartwarming with an intense emotion she was unable to name. *This is my family, the people that are closest to me. I love all of them so much, but...* She couldn't help but notice the two places that were not set at the table. She looked at the space between Wendy and Margot. *That's probably where Mom would have sat.* Her eyes were drawn to the space between Madison and Rodger... *Dad.* There would always be people missing from the table.

An eerie chuckle, strange and dry, drifted through the room. It was a thin sound, so faint Abby wasn't sure what she was hearing at first. The cackle floated through the air, leaving a sick feeling in Abby's stomach.

She glanced around the room. Everyone was engaged in conversation, pleasantly enjoying their dinner. *I'm the only one who heard it?* Abby thought, looking around the table. *Great, now I'm hallucinating. Grief really does play tricks on you.*

Wendy raised her wine glass in front of her, gathering everyone's attention. She turned to Sebastian and then Rodger, looking at them warmly. "Thank you for having me. It's been too long since I've been with family." She then turned to Margot, "And thank you for making me feel so welcome. It's good to know I still have allies among the Kanes."

"You were always welcome here," Margot said sincerely.

"Our doors, at least, are always open to you," Rodger said.

"A toast to welcome you home, and to family," Sebastian said raising his glass.

Abby held up her glass with the rest of them. "To family!" everyone said in unison.

"Abby," Jessica called up the stairs. "Come down! It's time for breakfast!"

The morning sun left a bright beam across the floor as Abby glanced at herself in the mirror. She was wearing her favorite jeans and a lavender blouse which she had been saving just for the first day of spring. It was too lovely a day, not to celebrate. She grinned at her reflection. "I'll be down in a minute," she called out as she straightened her collar.

She shoved her textbooks into her book bag and removed her phone from the charger next to her bed. She looked for her purse for a moment and found it, out of place on top of her dresser. "How did that get there?"

"You know they say only geniuses talk to themselves," Evan said, standing at Abby's bedroom door.

"I guess I should do it more often." Abby laughed, giving her father a smile.

"Of course, a couple hundred years ago they probably would have burned you at the stake," he jested.

"That's a lovely thought, Dad. Thank you for that one," Abby said sarcastically. "What did Mom make for breakfast?"

"I don't know, but it smells like there's bacon involved," Evan said brightly. "Shall we?"

"She'll yell again if we don't get down there in a minute," Abby warned as she stepped through the doorway and headed down the hallway. As predicted, her mother was standing at the bottom, getting ready to call up again. When she saw Abby and Evan, she laughed.

"Hurry up, you two!" Abby watched her mom's long red hair swing over her shoulder in playful irritation as she quickly disappeared back into the kitchen.

Jessica Kane had milky-white skin with dark freckles. She had green eyes and a smile that could melt the coldest heart, yet somehow her mother could manage to turn her friendly face into some of the fiercest expressions imaginable. Just then, her expression was one of joy; Abby couldn't get enough of it.

"We almost got in trouble," Abby's father said, as he followed her down the stairs.

"We're both always in trouble," Abby teased.

"Yes, you are," Jessica agreed as they entered the kitchen and sat at the dinette table. Abby anxiously waited for her mother to place a plate in front of her. Bacon, eggs, toast, and homemade strawberry jam.

"Your mother called earlier," Jessica said, as she placed a carton of orange juice on the table.

"What did she want?" Evan asked, disinterested.

"She didn't say," Jessica replied. "You know your mother doesn't speak to me any more than she has to."

"And I don't speak to my mother any more than I must," Evan said playfully before shoving a piece of bacon into his mouth.

"Be nice to your mother," Abby said sternly, addressing her father with a playful smile. "She's the only mother you've got."

"Did you hear that?" Evan said, sitting back in his chair, folding his arms. "She's repeating my own words back at me."

"Well, it is what you say to me when I'm mad at Mom," Abby jested.

"Your mother isn't Vivian Kane," Evan said, taking a sip of his coffee.

"Thank you for that," Jessica said, letting out a sigh. "Don't forget the Putnams want us to come over for dinner Friday evening."

"Really?" Evan sounded disappointed.

"Yes," Jessica said. "Do you want me to get us out of it?"

Abby smiled and took a bite of her eggs. Something moved across the entrance to the kitchen, catching her eye. She glanced up, but nothing was there. She shook her head and turned back to her breakfast. Her eyes were playing tricks on her again. She hoped it wasn't a sign that she needed glasses.

"What is the date of your next concert?" Evan asked his phone in his hands. "I want to make sure it's on my calendar."

"It's…" Abby started but trailed off. She squinted her eyes in the direction of the kitchen door, trying to be sure of what she was seeing. A little girl in pigtails and a gray dress was running back and forth across the entrance to the kitchen.

"What's wrong?" Evan asked.

Abby shook her head. "I… I'm sorry. Who is that?" She stood and walked back into the hall. She looked in both directions, but the girl was gone. She turned back to see both her parents looking at her worriedly.

"What is it, Abby?"

Abby shook her head at her mother. "It was nothing."

Her parents shared a look. "Abby, what is it you think you saw just now?" her mother asked.

"Just a little girl," Abby said. "I don't know, maybe I'm just overly tired from finals."

Her parents paused, both looking at her strangely.

"Do you think she… has it?" Evan asked, looking to his wife.

"Has what?" Abby asked, somewhat concerned.

Jessica shook her head, reassuringly, "Nothing," she said with a warm smile. "It's just... our family, my side of the family, sometimes... sees things."

"I'm going crazy?" Abby asked even more concerned.

"No, no, nothing like that," Jessica's tone would have been laughter if it wasn't so tight and controlled.

"Sometimes we, witches I mean, can develop special gifts. We think you might have one," Evan explained.

"A special gift? So that little girl was real?" Abby asked.

"It's difficult to say," Jessica said. "She obviously isn't here now, or we would see her."

"I hope this stuff doesn't get weird on me," Abby said, as she finished off her toast.

"Try not to worry about it," Evan said. "If something develops, we'll help you figure it out."

A chill, as if someone had left a door open to the winter wind, blew through the house. Abby looked around. There were no open doors or windows. The hairs on her neck rose, and something other than the cold sent a chill down her spine.

She looked at her parents. There were still talking as though nothing was wrong. Abby glanced over at the entrance to the kitchen again. There was no little girl.

Well, that's a relief, she thought.

Something fell on her hand. She looked closely and saw what looked like a flake of ash. Looking up at the ceiling, Abby could see nothing out of the ordinary.

Then she noticed a faint puff of steam as she let out a breath. The cold feeling was getting stronger, and she began to shiver.

She looked around the room. Everything was fine. Her parents were happily chatting, the sunlight filtered in through the window, even the stainless-steel refrigerator sparkled as always.

Something was wrong.

She heard a faint sound. It was difficult to discern at first but, soon, Abby could clearly make out an evil sort of cackling. It was an old woman's menacing laughter, supported by the sounds of dozens of people pleading and crying out for mercy.

The horrific laughter grew louder and louder. Abby covered her ears, but it did nothing to block out the sinister laughter closing in on her. Abby let out a deafening scream, and the sound stopped.

There was darkness. Abby's chest was heaving. Her lungs craved fresh air.

A rumbling sound came from somewhere, followed by the sounds of footsteps. The door burst open in a flood of light as her uncle rushed to the side of her bed.

"It's all right," Sebastian said, pulling her into his arms. "Abby, I'm here. It's okay."

Abby began to sob. He rocked gently back and forth as he held her tight. "I'm here. I'm not going to leave you," he said in soft, comforting tones.

Too much emotional poison tainted her soul with a malady she could no longer bear. Uncontrolled tears pour from her, expelling her fear and pain.

It wasn't more than a couple minutes before the tears dried up and Abby began to feel numb. It washed through her, mercifully extinguishing the turmoil. It was cold, solid comfort, one she had come to know very well since her parents' death.

"You're safe here," Sebastian reassured. "What was it this time?" Sebastian asked. He sat beside her and rubbed her back comfortingly.

"Mom and Dad," Abby whispered. Her response was followed by silence. There wasn't much Sebastian could say anyway, so Abby just leaned forward into his chest and did her best to relax, grateful for the human contact.

"You don't usually wake up screaming from those," Sebastian observed gently.

Abby nodded. "I know. I think all the family being around today put me in a weird headspace around Mom and Dad," she confessed. "I could feel their absence at dinner." A pang of grief stabbed through her numbness, and a fresh tear ran down her cheek. She wiped it away.

"Yes, I felt it too," Sebastian said.

Abby looked up at her uncle, curiously. "How do you handle it so well?"

In all this time I don't think I've seen him cry once, she realized.

Sebastian looked at her thoughtfully. "I haven't handled it as well as I try to make you think I have," he confessed. "In the first couple months after they died, I poured all my attention into keeping you safe, but I promise you I had more than a couple good breakdowns. After you went to England, I was a mess for a long time. Rodger helped me, and now we have Evan to focus on. I still miss her, but it gets better." He held her close as he lapsed into silence.

I don't have a Rodger, I don't have the people I rely on the most in the world anymore. There's just me now... I'm alone... Abby thought. They have so many things to focus on. *They don't need me here, dragging them down.* Abby knew her constant nightmares were waking up the house.

I shouldn't be intruding on their lives like this, she thought. *They would probably be happier if I wasn't around.*

"Abby?" Sebastian said hesitantly after a long pause. "Do you think maybe your nightmares are getting worse?"

"Worse?" she said, surprised by his question. "I don't know..." *Are they?* she thought. *They're the same grief and guilt and pain they've always been.* The ghost of an echo floated into her mind as she remembered the evil laughter in her dreams.

"Have you ever thought about talking to someone?"

"I'm talking to you, aren't I?" she said. *I knew it, he doesn't want to hear about my problems.*

He patted her shoulder. "A professional, I mean. You've been through so much more than most people ever have to deal with, and all within the last two years," he explained. "I know grief comes and goes in waves, but... I'm worried you're not making any progress. Maybe talking to someone would help."

Abby sat up, "Someone? You mean a therapist?" She looked at him incredulously. "I can't do that."

"Why not?" Sebastian asked. Both curisity and concern colored his voice.

"Can you imagine Grandmother's response if she ever found out?" Abby asked horrified.

Sebastian grimaced. "This isn't about her Abby. Besides, Vivian Kane is not the best role model for emotional health, wouldn't you agree?"

"Oh," Abby said, recalling her grandmother's more infamous drinking binges. *That is true...*

"I don't want to see that happen to you, Abby. Keeping your emotions bottled up like that can be so messy. This shouldn't be about what Vivian thinks, or Margot, or Madison, or even what I think. At some point, you need to make these decisions for yourself. Consider it, please? Or if not therapy, at least try to find something that helps you process what you're feeling."

Abby took in a deep breath and let it out slowly. "I know I need to come up with some way to deal with all of this. I have the violin... playing helps, so do my morning runs, but you're right, they aren't enough. I can't really go to a therapist, though. How do I explain to them my parents were murdered by a crazed death witch? They would lock me up after the first session." She tried to find a point of humor in the idea. "That is unless you know of someone Awakened I could see."

"None that I'm aware of," Sebastian admitted. "You could try leaving out certain parts."

"Doesn't that defeat the purpose?" Abby asked. "I would have to be careful and guarded the whole time. I don't think I would ever feel comfortable with that."

"That's true," Sebastian conceded. "The risk of letting something slip to someone who has not been Awakened would be an enormous barrier." A deep silence fell over the room again, it's weight pressing down on Abby's thoughts.

"You are right, though," Abby said at last. "I do need to figure out more ways to cope with all of this."

Sebastian wrapped his arms around her again, holding her head to his shoulder. "You're not alone, Abby," he said. "We'll get through this together."

CHAPTER THREE

Abby drove her car up Roy Street, scanning the house numbers for the right address. Charming bungalows and family houses with perfectly landscaped front yards lined both sides of the road. It similar to her old neighborhood, and Abby could imagine what it would look like in the spring when everything was in bloom.

I'm not too far from the old house, actually, she thought as images of her mother's rose bushes drifted in her mind.

She pulled over to the side of the road and parked. Tiny raindrops began to coat her windshield, and Abby reached for her umbrella in the back seat. She pulled her violin case from the trunk and quickly made her way up to the house. She carefully navigated the wet slippery steps and knocked politely on the front door.

After a few moments, a middle-aged woman answered the door. Abby was impressed immediately. Her hair was cropped so close it looked nearly bald, and her dark brown eyes sparkled in the misty gray light. She wore a simple black dress that just brushed the tops of her feet, and her bright beaded jewelry contrasted beautifully with her dark skin. Her whole appearance was understated yet playful. Abby found herself immediately returning the woman's gentle smile.

"Irene Templeton?" Abby asked.

"You must be Abigail Kane," the woman said, extending her hand.

"You found the right place. Come in." Her warm fingers wrapped around Abby's. "Oh good, you brought your violin.

You would be surprised how many people don't even bother to bring their instruments with them to meet their accompanist the first time."

Abby looked shocked then smiled. "I can't imagine wasting your time that way."

Irene smiled again in reply and ushered Abby inside.

As she followed the pianist inside, she gaped in amazement. The main room was like a museum dedicated to the creation of sound. Pictures of famous classical and jazz musicians covered the walls in framed portraits. Instruments from every culture and era were displayed. She saw everything from ancient Middle-Eastern ouds and dutars, to African talking drums, and so many others that Abby didn't recognize. They were all lovingly displayed around the room.

"Your home is stunning, Ms. Templeton," Abby said, her awe evident on her face.

"Irene. Please, call me Irene," she said.

"Only if you call me Abby. Is that a kalimba?" Abby asked, her voice filled with wonder.

Irene glanced over her shoulder to where Abby pointed, a proud smile on her face. "You have a good eye, and you seem to know your instruments."

"It's different than the one I've seen in books. Is it quite old?" Abby asked, then blushed. "I'm sorry, I'm being nosy."

Irene smiled. "It's quite all right. I love to show off my collection. It took me a long time to find one with the traditional bamboo keys. I am quite proud of it," she said, guiding Abby where a grand piano sat, taking up nearly half the room.

Irene took a seat on the piano bench. "The director sent over your resume. Very impressive. I'm looking forward to practicing with you."

"Thank you, Ms. … Irene," Abby corrected herself. "I've been told you're a music history professor at the university?"

"That's correct," Irene confirmed. "I also perform with the symphony from time to time. I play the harpsichord for them on occasion."

"I love the harpsichord and the clavichord, it's so much better than the tempered piano most symphonies use," Abby commented.

Irene laughed, "Oh Abby, you and I are going to get along famously," she said, catching her breath. Abby smiled along with the older woman. "So, let's tune up your instrument and give it a run-through. We'll see if there are any rough spots we need to start focusing on."

"Great," Abby said. She carefully removed her instrument and began tuning. When she was satisfied that her chords matched the tune from the piano, Abby nodded.

"All right, let's see. *Concerto Grosso in D Minor, opus 3 number 11*," Irene said, spreading the sheet music on the piano. "God, I love Vivaldi," she added.

Abby grinned and spread music out on her own stand.

"One...Two...Three...Four," Irene counted out the beat before striking the first note.

Abby let her fingers fly through their positions as she listened to Irene play the piano accompaniment. It was a challenging piece but managed to come effortlessly as her heart and mind rode the melody.

Abby watched Irene's fingers dance across the piano keys, and felt the vibrations from the bow in her own hand as it created each accompanying note. She let herself go, feeling the nerves that had been building in her stomach over the last few days settle. She didn't need spells, curses, and ritual incantations; this was real magic.

As she played the last note, she breathed in deeply. A hint of regret lurked on the edges of her emotional awareness. She didn't want to stop.

"That was lovely Abby," Irene said after the last note faded. "Nearly flawless. Have you played this piece before?"

Abby nodded, lowering her violin and bow. "Once a couple of years ago. I've been practicing since Mr. Schreiner sent me the piece a couple days ago, and," she added with a sly smile, "Vivaldi is one of my favorites, too."

Irene nodded, sitting back from the piano. She contemplated Abby for a moment. "You have a mournful quality to your style. I'm not sure how else to describe it. An emotional core of sadness that comes out in your music. It's a quality I don't typically hear from musicians your age."

Abby's gaze dropped to the floor.

"You are very talented," Irene added. "I have an ear for this sort of thing." She smiled as if to reassure Abby that her observation was, in fact, a compliment.

Abby nodded awkwardly. *Jesus, Abby! You still don't know how to take a compliment.* "Thank you, Irene, I guess... I know a little something about sadness."

"I had planned to schedule us for practice five times a week, but I think we would do just fine with two a week up until the end of November. Then we should consider going to five times a week just to keep everything fresh. The week of the performance you'll be practicing with the symphony," Irene explained. "Did you study the Suzuki discipline?"

"Yes," Abby said.

"I thought I could hear it in your technique, which is nearly perfect by the way," Irene commented. "Let's run through it a couple of times and then practice again on Thursday," she said, returning her attention to the sheet music.

The street denizens of the city were out in full force. The cold autumn air wasn't yet enough to drive people away.

College students loitered near the streetcorner coffee shops, while evening commuters waited patiently in their suits and uniforms for transit to arrive. Harried parents rushed their children along, keeping them out of traffic. Buskers and musicians occupied every block. Above it all, glass towers loomed overhead, casting the downtown area in permanent shade.

"The Ginger House," Abby muttered under her breath as she read the discrete signage hanging over the busy street. *My favorite restaurant,* she thought as she approached the restaurant. *Madison must be trying to cheer me up.*

The restaurant had a large dining room filled with booths and large tables in the center. A second-floor open gallery contained smaller, more intimate seating. Bamboo shoots sporadically adorned the dining area. Hardwood and dark colors offered a modern aesthetic, and the dim lighting made it feel even more private.

Abby approached the host counter. "Abigail Kane," she said, uncertain what the name on the reservation would be.

A young woman scanned the computer screen. "Of course, Miss Kane, right this way." The hostess collected a set of menus and motioned for Abby to follow.

They weaved through the large dining room toward a set of stairs. The young woman guided her up the stairs and down a long walkway lined with small bistro tables and chairs until they reached the end where a small booth was situated with a commanding view of the entire restaurant.

As Abby approached the table, a pair of striking blue eyes set against cream-colored skin looked back at her. "Hailey," Abby said, unable to contain a smile to convey her excitement.

"Abby!" The girl jumped to her feet, her long black hair swinging over her shoulder as she stood. "I've really missed you," she said, pulling Abby into a friendly hug.

"It's been too long," Abby replied. There was a lump in her throat, and her voice cracked with emotion. She was surprised by the depth of her emotion at seeing her old friend. This was someone she had known since she was in the first grade, and one of the few witches she knew who was not also part of her family's coven. In many ways, she felt like family, but that was no reason to get watery-eyed from just a hug.

Hailey grabbed Abby's arm and pulled her into the booth next to her. "Madison texted me a few minutes ago. She is running late."

"As expected." Abby laughed.

Hailey grinned. "It gives us a few minutes to catch up. "I'm glad you're finally up for a visit."

"I know, I feel bad," Abby admitted. "I've been back for a while. We should have done this months ago."

"Don't worry about it," Hailey said, waving her hand as if it were no big deal. "Madison has been keeping me up to date. I know you've been through a lot lately. How are you holding up?"

Abby took in a deep breath. "I have good days and bad days. "There isn't much to say really. At this point, it's about trying to piece my life together and figure out what my future might look like" Abby looked at her friend. "I'm sure you know all about that."

"I certainly do," Hailey said, taking a sip of her water.

Abby looked at the mournful expression on her friend's face. "How long has it been since Michael…?"

"He's been missing for nearly two months now," Hailey said, looking down at the table.

Her voice was so quiet Abby could barely hear her.

"I miss my brother every day. The family hasn't exactly been taking it very well either," she said. "Everything is kind of a mess."

"I know how that is. I can't say my family is coping with everything, either." Abby shook her head. "But then again, coping isn't really a skill of the Kane family."

Hailey let out an awkward chuckle. "We may be the only two sound-minded people in our families," she added with a touch of sarcasm.

Abby let out a laugh of her own. "Sometimes it feels that way," she agreed. "At least I have a few people in my family I can count on." She cleared her throat and adopted a more serious tone. "You can always talk to me, you know."

Hailey visibly swallowed and offered a brave smile. "I know," she said reassuringly. "Enough about me. Did I hear you have some good news?"

"Madison told you? She just couldn't help herself."

"She didn't say what, but she did mention it was really good news." Hailey giggled. "I think it was her playful way to torment me. So, what is it?"

"I auditioned to be a guest artist for the Holiday Invitational with the symphony," Abby said, putting on a cool demeanor.

Hailey's face brightened. "Abby! That's great news!" Ignoring Abby's attempts to downplay her excitement, Hailey almost squealed with excitement. "When did this happen?"

"A few days ago," Abby explained. "I've already started practicing with an accompanist. I hope you'll come to the performance."

"Of course! I wouldn't miss it for the world. Text me the date, and I'll put it on my calendar," Hailey said. "I'm so proud of you. I wish I had kept up with playing like you did."

"You were always quite good," Abby said.

Hailey laughed. "Thanks, but you were the one with the real talent. It was just a hobby for me. I did enjoy spending all those years in orchestra with you, though. We had some good times in there," she said wistfully, her thoughts drifting to the past.

"Remember when we went to that competition in Walla Walla, and we all sneaked out of the hotel at two in the morning and played capture the flag in the vineyards?"

"That was a blast!" Hailey laughed. "Remember how Tammy Black was certain she had been bitten by a rattlesnake and we took her to the ER?"

"I do. I also remember it was only a scratch from one of the vines," Abby said, laughing along.

"Mary Price had shaken some coins in her pocket, and Tammy didn't know the difference," Hailey said wiping away a tear of laughter.

"Oh, she was such a drama queen, wasn't she? All those cello players were always so dramatic," Abby jested.

"Those were good times," Hailey said, finally catching her breath.

"Thank you for that," Abby said, as she regained her composure. "I haven't had a good laugh in a long time. I needed it... a lot."

"Any time," Hailey reassured with a friendly smile. "Oh, there's Madison," she added.

"Sorry I'm running late," Madison said, as she slid into the booth. "Mom asked me to look in on Grandma Fiona on my way."

"Is Aunt Fiona all right?" Abby asked.

"She's fine," Madison waved it off. "She just had a difficult day with her dialysis. Tired mostly." It was obvious Madison was doing her best to shake off her own worries.

Now isn't the time to press, Abby thought.

"How are things with Tom?" Hailey asked as they began looking over the menu.

"Tom?" Madison questioned innocently. Her ruse was poorly played. "Oh him," she said as an afterthought before returning her attention to the menu. "I lost interest in him weeks ago."

Hailey shared a knowing look with Abby. "That didn't take long."

"He wasn't very smart," Madison said. "Besides it wasn't going to get very serious anyway," she added a hint of remorse in her voice.

"Why do you say that?" Abby asked.

"He isn't a witch, and I wasn't about to awaken him." There was a moment of shared silence weighted with uncertainty.

"There really isn't a deep pool of options for us, at least not around here," Hailey said, observing the crowded restaurant as if it contained the whole of Seattle. "What about you, Abby? When you sent me an email last Christmas, you were really into some guy... Brandon?"

"Benjamin," Abby corrected as a lump suddenly appeared in her throat. She swallowed the emotions swelling under the surface at the unexpected turn in the conversation. "It didn't work out." Her voice was somewhat faint as she spoke. She glanced up to see Hailey looking at her with uncertainty. *Please don't go there*, Abby repeated over and over in her head. It was as if her friend could read her mind.

"Well the two of you are doing better than I have," Hailey said mercifully taking the heat off Abby. "I haven't so much as looked at a guy in the last two years. Besides I'm not like the two of you. I wasn't born into a big powerful coven."

"Oh please, come on," Madison said. "If I were a guy, I'd rather deal with your coven any day," she added.

"I haven't met everyone in your coven, but your Aunt Vera seems really nice," Abby said encouragingly.

Hailey nodded. "I suppose there are some advantages of being a member of a coven that is in decline."

"Don't say that," Abby said, giving her friend a hopeful nudge. "I know it's been hard times for you and your family, but it doesn't mean they are on the cusp of dying out."

Hailey's smile carried an unspoken thank you. "Maybe you're right," she conceded without much hope.

"You two are depressing as hell," Madison said abruptly, soliciting a healthy laugh. "We need to pull ourselves out of this funk. So, I've decided we're going to have a girl's night."

"Isn't that what we're doing right now?" Abby asked.

"Nope. This is a catch-up session," Madison explained. "We need to go out and have some real fun. Just the three of us. No boys, no coven politics, just FUN."

"Did you have something in mind?" Hailey asked, just as amused as Abby was.

"Yes, as a matter of fact," Madison said slyly.

"Well out with it," Abby pressed, leaning forward in her chair excitedly.

"In a couple days they're doing a haunted tour of Seattle's underground city," Madison said mysteriously. "Doesn't it sound like fun?"

"I've always wanted to do that," Hailey said, excited.

A haunted tour? That sounds horrible.... Images of ghosts and tendrils of blond hair floating in the water flashed through Abby's thoughts. Her last experience with ghosts did not go well. She quickly shook the memory from her thoughts.

"Are you all right?" Madison asked. "You went quiet all of a sudden."

"I'm fine." Abby forced a smile. "I'd love to spend more time with the two of you," she said.

"Then it's settled." Madison clapped her hands together for emphasis. "The haunted tour it is!"

Abby wrapped herself in a heavy robe against the chill of the evening and hurried into the bedroom. *Why is it so cold?* She scowled at the thermostat and adjusted it. Happier hearing the heater kick on, she finished drying her freshly washed hair and began brushing her teeth.

The haunted tour... how did I get roped into going on that? she wondered, as she swished the mouthwash in her mouth and spit it out. All day, she had been thinking of a way to get out of it. *I really do want to spend more time with them, though.*

Abby plugged her phone into the charger by her bed and noticed her earrings sitting on the nightstand. They were the small button pearls that her mother had given her; she would be heartbroken if they get lost. She carefully opened the ornately carved lid of her jewelry box and placed the earrings inside.

Her eyes lingered for a moment on a flash of color. A blue stone with purple flecks winked in the dim light. She hadn't look at it in almost a year. The hand-crafted platinum ring sat at the back end of the jewelry box on a velvet pillow. It was one of the nicest pieces in Abby's small collection, but one she couldn't bring herself to ever wear again.

A swelling of emotions began filling Abby's thoughts as she gazed down at the ring Benjamin had given her. Every emotion she had ever felt for him washed through her. Abby fought to keep from being overwhelmed. Fear, anger, sorrow, regret, betrayal… and so many other things. A tear formed in the corner of her eye, and she quickly shut the box, closing out that part of her past.

I've shed enough tears over Benjamin Hodge.

Abby crawled into bed and collected the book sitting on her nightstand. She found her place and began reading. She hadn't even made it through the first paragraph when she caught her thoughts wandering off, remembering Benjamin sitting on the couch in the small house they had briefly shared.

"This is ridiculous," Abby muttered under her breath. She closed the book and tossed it on the nightstand before turning off the light. She rolled over and pulled the blanket up to her chin and snuggled in for the night.

She closed her eyes and waited for sleep to take her. Abby tossed and turned, trying to find the most comfortable position possible, yet sleep did not come. It was maddening, and so Abby laid on her back and crossed her arm over her breasts. She began taken in deep breaths and concentrated on clearing her thoughts as she would if she were preparing to enter the Sight.

Nearly everything she about it either came from books or personal experience. She had no teacher with the Sight; even among witches, her gift was rare. There was still so much for her to learn, but this was her favorite use. During her time studying under Ms. Grace in England, she quickly learned that the basics of the Sight were very like the basics of simple meditation. And it often put her to sleep.

She slowed her breathing and reached into a quiet place within herself, slowing pushing away all other thoughts until her awareness settled on a single point. If she were calling the Sight, she would be tapping into her magic, but tonight she simply let her thoughts drift in the stillness.

Abby opened her eyes and saw tall blades of grass all around her. The moon and stars glimmered the open, cloudless sky above. She sat up abruptly, startled to find herself somewhere other than in her bedroom. *This isn't right,* she thought. *I was only meditating. What I am doing here?* She came to her feet and looked around. A long line of trees positioned just beneath the moon. A light fog drifted in the night, glowing in the moonlight.

She turned. Her breath froze in her chest. She was standing next to a large shed-like structure resting just over the water of a large pond. The dark green paint was beginning to chip away, and the roof was missing several shingles. Abby could hear the water lapping at the grassy shore.

No… this can't be.

A light shone through the single window on the back end of the structure. Benjamin's black SUV was parked a few feet away. Then the sounds of shouting came from the floating structure.

Abby rushed toward the front of the boathouse and encountered the large double doors. She took a deep breath and flung the doors open.

She stopped, frozen in her memories from last spring.

"Stop!" Abby yelled, but Benjamin and Josephine ignored her. Wood splinters swirled chaotically, enveloping everyone inside in a magical tempest.

Abby ran to the dock and began to cast a spell to create a massive wave. It was the only thing she could think of to do.

As she began speaking the words and making the gestures she could feel a large hand cover her mouth and a strong arm wrap around her binding her arms and lifting her from the ground.

"Not this time," a voice whispered into her ear.

Abby pushed with all her might and fell backward onto the hard wooden planks. Pain shot through her hip. Her hand landed in something warm and sticky. She looked down. Her hand was drenched in blood. Abby gasped and looked to her left. A pair of dark eyes stared back at her. Sarah! Seeing her friend's lifeless face, she tried to cry out, but no sound emerged.

Abby looked around, realizing she was surrounded by bodies. Edgar Kincaid stared forward, his face contorted in pain. Warren's face and body were covered in deep cuts. There was blood everywhere. One by one, Abby looked into the dead faces of the people she'd come to care for. Nina, Madison, Fiona…

Abby screamed and scrambled to crawl past the horror she was seeing. She slipped, her hand sliding through a pool of blood. She landed face down on something soft. Pulling herself upright, she came face to face with the pair of green eyes she missed the most.

Mom…

Tears ran down Abby's face. She couldn't move. All she could do way sit there, weeping.

Cold, menacing laughter filled the room.

"Abby!" A familiar voice cried out. She could feel two hands shaking her. "Abby! Wake up!"

She opened her eyes. Rodger was sitting next to her on the bed, watching as Abby woke from her dream. *Another nightmare… one of many.* She hear Little Evan crying in the other room, awoken by her screams. A pang of guilt stabbed her chest.

"It was a dream, Abby. You're all right now." Rodger pulled Abby into his arms and held her. She stayed the comfort of his affection, holding on to the peace it offered. Rodger held her and stroked her hair.

A dream... it was only a dream.

CHAPTER FOUR

Abby drove up to the large iron gates of her grand-mother's estate. She pulled up to the security box and waved at the camera pointed directly at her from atop the high brick wall. She waited only for a moment before the gates slowly began to swing inward.

Every type of classic shrub graced the driveway of Vivian Kane's estate. Thick prickly rose bushes and tall evergreen edges lined the drive, while apple and cherry trees stood behind. Everything was faded now, muted by autumn.

The road took a sharp corner, and the home of Vivian Kane came into full view. Abby was never quite as impressed as she should be. Even from the top of Queen Anne Hill, the grand manor sat like a monument bearing down on the city. It stood like the Colossus of Rhodes, flaunting its excess and extravagance.

White marble pillars and statuary juxtaposed the modern style of the home with its large open windows accented by old rococo fixtures. The whole thing was a strange blend that did not theoretically seem possible, let alone in good taste. Yet somehow Vivian managed to create a modern home accented with old-world charm and elegance. Abby still preferred the colonial house she grew up in, but she had to admit that this bit of pretentiousness was just Vivian's style.

It was a lovely evening. The crisp air was not too cold, and it was clear. Strings of white Japanese lanterns hung above the driveway between the house and a large fountain.

They glistened softly, offering a festive touch to the night. Abby passed under them, pulling up to a long string of parked cars. She turned off the engine and glanced at her phone.

She was only a few minutes late. *Grandmother probably hasn't joined the party yet,* she thought. She stepped out of the car, careful to keep her heel from catching the delicate silk fabric of her deep-blue evening gown.

"Good evening, Mr. Greenly." Abby greeted her grandmother's butler warmly as she climbed the front steps. The older gentleman was one Abby knew well from her years in and out of this house. He stood stiffly in the doorway.

"Good evening Ms. Kane." His studied expression grew into a genuine smile at seeing Abby. "The other guests are in the formal living room," Mr. Greenly stated officiously after recovering from the brief moment of informality.

"Has the birthday girl made her grand entrance yet?" Abby asked.

"Mrs. Kane is still seeing to a few final preparations." Mr. Greely replied carefully.

Abby tried not to laugh while she nodded. "I'll just show myself in then," she said, as she stepped into the grand entry.

It was a cold room; nearly everything was white. The refined elegance that was inherent in Vivian's style touched every part of the entryway. Barely another color to distract from the frosty feel. It always reminded Abby of a sterile hospital ward.

Abby moved through the enormous chamber into a grandiose hallway. White stucco walls lined with old portraits guided her down toward the living room, where she could already hear the chatter of guests.

She paused at a large mirror in the hall, giving herself a brief check before entering the party.

The living room was an enormous open space crowded with people she barely knew. It was a small group by her grandmother's standards, but Abby wasn't sure where to begin making small talk with the roughly two-dozen family acquaintances. Couches and chairs were arranged in various conversation nooks. Abby quickly scanned them, looking for a friendly face.

Abby spotted Margot loitering near the grand piano, wearing a powder-blue floor-length dress, and an expression that matched her own.

Abby weaved her way over to the piano and summoned a smile. As she approached Margot, Madison joined them from the other side of the room. "Good evening," she greeted her aunt and cousin.

"Hello, Abby!" Madison said with excitement, pulling Abby into a bone-crushing hug. "You look incredible."

"Thank you," Abby replied. "I love your dress." She turned to her aunt. "Margot, you look positively elegant as always," she added.

"Thank you, Abby, I don't think I've ever seen you look so lovely. You are becoming a remarkable woman," Margot said with sincerity. "I can't believe how fast you girls have grown. I feel so old."

"You're not old," Abby reassured.

"She acts like she is," Madison said sarcastically glancing at her phone.

"Well if I do, it's because I have to deal with that mouth of yours," Margot jested. Madison sighed in a huff.

"Is Aunt Fiona here?" Abby asked. "I haven't seen her."

"She's here, but I think she went upstairs to see Aunt Vivian," Margot said. She was about to say something else but paused. Abby followed her gaze across the room.

An older gentleman wearing a black tuxedo was escorting a tall, bird-like woman with bleach-blonde hair. He carried a carved wooden cane as if it were his last bit of protection from the other party-goers, while she wore no expression at all.

"Who are they?" Abby asked curiously.

"Lawrence and Syble Kane," Margot explained. "I'm not sure you girls would remember them. They rarely visit."

"They are Kanes?" Madison asked, looking at the couple making small talk. "They look weird enough to be Kanes," she added.

Her mother shot her a glare. "They may have very little to do with the day to day functions of the family, but they are still members of this family. And members of the Coven."

"I think I remember hearing Grandma talk about them," Madison said. "Isn't Lawrence Grandma and Aunt Vivian's cousin?"

"Yes," Margot responded dryly.

"Why would they make a point to come to Vivian's birthday party?" Abby asked. "I don't think I remember seeing them around before."

"I haven't seen them in at least three years," Margot commented and shrugged.

"What do they do exactly?" Abby asked.

"They're jet setters, living off their share of the Kane fortune, squandering it on parties and lavish trips." Margot frowned. "They contribute very little to the family. I wouldn't trust them if I were either of you."

"Why is that?" Abby asked curiously.

"There are few lines in the sand those two haven't crossed," Margot explained. "They're just good at not getting caught, that's why they haven't embarrassed the Coven. My mother has cleaned up a few of their messes."

"I hadn't realized we had such black sheep," Abby commented as she watched Lawrence and Syble interact with several guests.

"Lawrence supposedly has a particularly vicious repertoire of curses, several of which he specifically constructed to reenact the biblical plagues. As for Syble, she's perhaps one of the vainest women I know. She would do almost anything to stay looking young... and probably has." Margot shook her head.

After Margot's description, Abby thought about moving to avoid them but found herself trapped as they approached.

"Margot," Lawrence and Syble said in virtual unison. Abby refrained from cringing at Syble's shrill voice.

"This isn't little Abigail all grown up, is it?" Lawrence questioned, looking Abby over. She didn't particularly care for how long his eyes lingered in certain places.

"Well, I dare say it is!" Syble screeched. The woman leaned in, giving Abby a polite hug without really touching her. Lawrence moved in and gave her a hug as well, lingering just too long for Abby's comfort.

"It's nice to see you both again," Abby lied politely.

"Hello, Darlings!" a melodic voice rang out jubilantly. The conversation around the room stilled, as all eyes moved to the top of the stairs where Vivian stood. Abby was more than grateful for the interruption.

The woman of the hour rested against the upper banister of a sweeping staircase. Her stark white evening gown sparkled like a chandelier in the lighting of the hall. Everything about her, from the thick fur wrap around her shoulders to the way her hair was styled up, displaying her enormous diamond earrings, was carefully calculated for this moment. She was breathtakingly flawless–just as she had planned.

Everyone clapped and raised their glasses as she descended the staircase with well-practiced elegance. Vivian paused halfway down and gazed beneficently upon her gathered family and friends. "It touches me deeply to see so many people I love and cherish here this evening. You have all come so far just to celebrate my birthday," Vivian announced. "I am honored that you all made it out for this occasion. Especially now, as this is a special year."

"Is it because there's a zero in this birthday?" someone yelled from the crowd soliciting polite laughter.

Vivian paused. "Who invited the comedian?" she snickered. "This year will mark a crowning achievement and define not only my life but the course of this Coven for generations to come. I have great things in store for all of you."

Vivian paused and glanced around the room. "Abigail?" She smiled at her granddaughter before calling out again. "My darling Abigail Kane, please come up here and join me for a moment."

Every eye in the room turned toward Abby. She froze, mortified, even as she was unsure what was happening. She slowly moved forward as the crowd parted before her. She could feel her face turning a bright shade of red. She climbed the stairs wearing the best smile she could conjure and stood next to her grandmother. The smell of liquor was evident as Vivian reached out warmly and gave her a kiss on each cheek.

"Look at my beautiful granddaughter!" Vivian said soliciting applause from the crowd. "She is the future. One day she will take my place as leader of the Kane Coven and carry on the legacy and traditions of this proud family. I know that I leave everything in capable hands. I am so very proud of my beautiful and talented granddaughter."

She paused, looking at Abby as sincerely as her wine-glazed eyes could manage. "I have been truly blessed these many years," she added sincerely. She gave Abby a genuine smile before turning back to her audience.

"Tonight, I celebrate another year with you all, an important year. With many new beginnings." Her guests clapped politely.

Abby stood, shocked into stillness as her thoughts raced.

The next leader of the Coven? She stared at her grandmother. *What is she thinking? I'm eighteen! I can't lead anything!*

"Let us descend upon the dining room where I have been assured a magnificent feast has been prepared," Vivian proclaimed, pulling Abby from her internal panic.

Two members of the house staff opened the double doors into the dining room, and the guests began to funnel toward the enormous banquet table.

"This way, Darling," Vivian said escorting Abby toward the feast.

Abby took several deep breaths and pulled herself together. As she entered the room, she saw that an absurdly large table, set for thirty people. There was a name tag in front of each napkin, written in ornate calligraphy. Abby searched for her name, and her eyes flew wide when she found it. She glanced up at her grandmother for any sign of what the woman was thinking. She was seated at the opposite end of the table from Vivian, at the head of the table. Abby knew enough about formal place settings to know that it was a spot typically reserved for the co-host.

What is that woman doing? Abby thought.

Abby took her seat as she watched her grandmother make her way down the table, speaking to each of her guests. *She is a skilled entertainer,* Abby thought, watching Vivian navigate the social complexities of her guests.

She took a deep breath and tried her best to not be irritated with her grandmother. *How could she have put me on display like that? Why would she make an announcement like that and not speak to me first? This is insane...* Abby closed her eyes for a moment and rallied her resolve. *We'll have a conversation about this later,* she thought and set her mind to enjoying the evening.

Each course was a masterpiece of fusion cuisine consisting of all of Vivian's favorite foods. Abby was grateful when she found herself sitting next to Aunt Fiona. Her grandmother's sister was sunken and frail, looking every bit her age. Aunt Fiona is more quiet than usual, Abby observed. Abby did her best not to worry and decided to spare her any small talk.

On Abby's other side was an elderly gentleman named Harold Parkinson. Their very brusk conversation was over practically before it began, though Abby managed to ascertain that he was a witch from Minneapolis. From the way he kept ignoring her to stare at the woman in white at the far end of the room, Abby got the impression had a long-standing crush on her grandmother and had no interest in small talk.

On the far side of Fiona was a round woman with cropped, frizzy brown hair. Gisela Kane was a pear-shaped woman with short, stilt-like legs that barely brushed the floor as she sat in her dining chair. How she managed to walk with such a strange figure seemed to defy Abby's understanding of physics, but the woman still managed to show up at every family gathering.

Her round face and pug-nose were a source of hilarity for Abby and Madison when they were very small, but now Abby at least had the grace not to laugh at the odd woman.

"How are you, Gisela?" Abby asked, hoping to spark conversation.

A pair of dark eyes turned sharply toward her and Abby noted a suspicious glint in them. Gisela's gaze danced nervously around the room, as though she were on constant watch for someone doing something they shouldn't.

Gisela placed her fork down and finished chewing on the last remnants of her arugula salad. She looked offended that Abby would even speak to her. "What did you ask me?" she questioned as though she hadn't heard.

Abby immediately regretted her foolish attempt at small talk. "I'm sorry, I didn't mean to bother you. I was just wondering how you are doing."

Gisela regarded her with suspicion.

Abby looked at her cousin's beady eyes and ill-fitting green satin dress. She thought of a large toad sitting at the table.

"Fine," Gisela said shortly, disdain etched in every line of her body.

"Gisela, there is no reason to be rude," Fiona interjected, giving the woman next to her a look of warning.

The round woman shrugged. She turned her attention back to the plate in front of her, ignoring everyone else at the table.

Well, that went well, Abby thought sarcastically. She resigned herself to spending the meal quietly and focused on her salad.

"Vivian tells me you plan to attend Oxford next fall," Fiona stated, breaking a long stretch of silence.

"It's true," Abby responded, surprised that her grandaunt had decided to start a conversation. "I plan to pursue my musical studies there."

"What a fine choice of schools," Fiona stated. The older woman spoke almost as if she were restraining herself. "I have also learned you will be performing near the holiday," she added as an afterthought.

"Yes," Abby said, excitedly. "The Seattle Symphony has asked me to play at the Holiday Invitational."

"You're still playing?" Gisela asked, abruptly joining their conversation. "I figured you would have given up on that by now."

"No, I still play," Abby said refraining from letting Gisela have a piece of her mind.

"You have always been quite good," Fiona said in Abby's defense. She waved her half-finished salad away when the staff came around.

"Hopefully she learns how to be 'quite good' at some other things," Gisela said bluntly.

"What do you mean by that?" Abby couldn't help but be offended, though she hoped she kept it from her voice.

"Vivian just declared you her heir to the Coven," Gisela spat out. "What do you know about being the matriarch of a family? Especially one as powerful as we are. The only thing you know is how to play that silly instrument. Hardly an appreciable skill when it comes to dealing with the intricacies of our society."

For a split second, Abby warred between anger and guilt. She felt a lump form in her throat as the guilt won out. *She isn't wrong*, Abby thought. *I don't know anything about running a coven, I barely know how to be a witch...*

"Do I detect sour grapes, Gisela?" Fiona said, looking down her nose at her cousin before taking a sip of her wine.

"You're not wrong Gisela," Abby said, soliciting surprised looks from both her cousin and grandaunt. "I actually agree with you. I don't know anything about running a coven."

Gisela raised an eyebrow and snorted. "At least you know that much."

Abby felt inadequate. *Of course, I don't know how to run a coven,* she thought, *I barely know where I fit into things here. I can't lead anyone.* Gisela had bluntly articulated every whirling thought she'd had since her grandmother's announcement. She looked around the room, focusing on the conversations happening around her, hoping it would hold back the flood of insecurities she trying to keep at bay.

"Really, Gisela," Fiona said. "My dear sister Vivian isn't going anywhere anytime soon. There will be plenty of time for Abigail to learn and prepare herself for the responsibilities that will not fall to her yet for many, many years."

Abby batted her eyes and stared at Fiona for a few seconds. *For a woman who has barely spoken to me in the last eighteen years, why is she suddenly coming to my defense?* "Thank you, Aunt Fiona," Abby managed to say, her voice tight. "I hope you're right."

The staff placed a bowl of watercress soup in front of her, and she quickly began eating, hoping it would distract her from her unsettling thoughts.

Dinner passed, and Abby made her way to the couch. The rich, fatty foods swirled in her stomach like a storm, threatening her with illness. She sat quietly, hoping a lack of movement would help the large meal settle.

"I had to sit next to cousin Syble," Madison said, plopping down on the couch next to Abby. She shuddered theatrically. "If I have to listen to her talk for another minute about her moisturizing routine, I'm going to scream."

"I had a lovely chat with cousin Gisela," Abby said, trying not to sound as bitter as she felt.

"Oh, no. Does she still smell like cat piss?" Madison asked making a face.

"Ask your grandmother. She sat next to her," Abby responded with amusement.

"Come along Madison," Margot said, as she approached. "You have school tomorrow."

"Seriously? I'm a straight-A student. Surely, I can skip out on a day?"

"Not with the tuition I pay for that school," Margot said, with a stern motherly glare. "It's your last year, and you'll be eighteen in a couple months. My job is nearly finished, don't make these last few moments any harder than they have already been."

Madison rolled her eyes. "Fine," she said and gave Abby a hug. "I'll see you in a couple days."

Abby nodded, "Right, the infamous Kane Coven Samhain party, how can I forget?" It was one of the biggest events of the year. Allies and friends of the Kanes from all over the world would be here, making this party seem like a small, intimate gathering.

Madison playfully hit Abby on the shoulder. "What? We have plans with Hailey, remember!"

How could I forget, Abby shuddered internally. "Oh, right. See you then…" Her voice trailed off as she stood, waving goodbye to both of them.

Abby sat and watched the guests depart one by one. *I better get out of here,* she thought. *I don't want to be caught alone with Grandmother.* She stood and threw her purse over her shoulder, making her way toward the exit.

"Darling!" Vivian called out.

Abby paused, she closed her eyes for a moment. *Damn.* She sighed and resigned herself to the confrontation that was coming. She put on a smile and turned to face her grandmother.

"Goodbye, Sonya, I'll see you at the Samhain Ball," Vivian said, escorting a particularly well-dressed woman to the door.

As soon as her guest had stepped out the door, Vivian turned to Abby. "Darling, I'm so glad I caught you before you left." She glided smoothly toward Abby and pulled her into a close hug. The scent of scotch layered over wine permeated Vivian's breath, burning Abby's nostrils.

"I should really go," Abby said. *I don't want to get into it with her when she's drunk,* she thought.

"Darling, what is the rush, I happen to know the ferry back to Bainbridge Island left five minutes ago. There isn't another one for over an hour. Besides, I was so busy attending to my guests we barely had a chance to speak." Vivian easily dismissed the very notion of Abby's departure, guiding Abby to a small couch.

Abby took a deep breath and surrendered to her grandmother's insistence. "All right," she said. "Since when did you take an interest in the ferry schedule?" she asked, barely disguising her sarcasm.

"Ever since you moved onto that remote little island."

"It's hardly remote," Abby said her irritation beginning to show.

She looked at her grandmother and paused. "Is there something wrong?" She asked as her irritation built.

"I heard about your little concert, dear," Vivian said, sitting next to Abby on the couch. Around them, several members of the household staff began clearing cocktail glasses from the room. "What a nice distraction for you."

"Distraction?" Abby said incredulously. "You know this isn't some hobby, right? I have wanted to play the violin professionally all my life."

Vivian smiled at her, piteously, "Oh, Darling, I thought you had grown out of that ages ago."

"Grown out of it?" Abby shouted. "This is what I want to do with my life. I happen to have people who are telling me I might be able to make a name for myself with this. Professional musicians who think I have talent. I'm not going to turn my back on the violin just because you refuse to take me seriously!" She wasn't sure where the words were coming from, but she knew they were true.

"Oh, Abigail, please." Vivian looked away, pained. "You have duties and obligations. Playing the violin is a lovely hobby, but surely you understand, you don't have time to commit to anything more."

And there it is... Abby looked at her grandmother, icy anger settling over her. *Duties and obligations.* "Does this have anything to do with the ambush you laid on me earlier this evening?"

"What on earth do you mean?" Vivian asked, her tone somehow both accusing and defensive. She reached up and clutched the diamond necklace fastened around her neck. "What ambush?" The professed innocence in her expression was laughable.

Abby stood and headed toward the door. "I'm not going to do this while you're drunk," she said pointedly.

"I'm not drunk, Darling," Vivian insisted as she stood. "I assume you mean the announcement I made, declaring you my predecessor as Matriarch of the Coven."

Abby paused. "Why do you do that? Why do you pretend to not know what I'm talking about when you obviously do?" She turned to face her grandmother.

"Darling, please," Vivian pleaded. "Let's not be cross. This is something to be celebrated. I thought you would be delighted."

Abby was not impressed. She stared at her grandmother, a stony expression in her eyes.

Vivian knew her feeble attempt had failed, and the old woman's expression melted into a stern glare. "Surely it could not have been much of a surprise, Darling. You knew I intended to have my son–your father–take over when the time comes, and I must step down."

"We aren't royalty, there isn't a line of succession," Abby said doing her best to rein in her temper. "You can name anyone as your heir. There are plenty of people in our coven who are far more prepared and, frankly, better suited than I am."

"Darling, don't say that," Vivian insisted closing her eyes, pained at hearing Abby suggest anyone else. "You are perfectly suited to accept the mantel. Besides, it's not as if I'll be stepping down any time soon. I'm still quite young after all," she added surreptitiously.

"In the meantime, you're going to take the wheel of my life and steer it in any direction you see fit, all in the name of preparing me to be the next matriarch." Abby's voice rose as she gave voice to the one thing that had been festering in the back of her mind ever since the announcement was made.

Vivian stared at her with a blank stare.

Abby was uncertain if her grandmother was surprised to have her motivations revealed or if she was masking something else. There was a crushing silence.

"You know that isn't what I want, Darling," Vivian said cautiously.

"It isn't?" Abby questioned. "Is that why the violin should be nothing more than a mere hobby of mine?"

"Darling, there are so many important things in our world that need our attention." Vivian sighed. "We are not some normal family who can wantonly follow every flight of fancy that comes along."

Abby stared at her grandmother. "The violin is not a flight of fancy," she said evenly. "My music is important to me. Is there really no room in your world for things that are important to me?"

"Of course, there is, Darling," Vivian said reassuringly. "But… sometimes, sacrifices have to be made."

"And you'll decide what sacrifices I should make?" Abby said defiantly.

"You're obviously upset," Vivian said. She waved her hands in defeat and stood. "Perhaps we should save this discussion for another time." She walked over to the liquor cabinet and pulled out a crystal decanter full of a golden-brown liquor.

"What sacrifices did you make?" Abby asked quietly as Vivian took a large gulp from her glass.

"I made plenty of sacrifices." Vivian's icy tone left a chill in the air. Bitterness hung on every syllable she didn't say.

She finished off the last of her drink in one gulp and stared at the crystal decanter sitting on top of the cabinet.

"So I see," Abby said, doing little to temper her own words. The silence was stifling as Abby stared at her grandmother. Vivian stood frozen in some strange hypnotic state, locked into a staring contest with the bottle.

As she watched her grandmother struggle with herself, Abby's irritation gave way to concern. It was unlike Vivian to abandon theatrics and drama for such a strange aloofness. "Are you all right?" she asked, taking a step forward.

Vivian batted her eyes as if she had been jarred back into the room abruptly. She took in a deep breath and looked at Abby with renewed poise.

"Of course, Darling," Vivian said, as she discarded her glass on the cabinet and turned to face Abby. "I certainly didn't mean to ambush you this evening. I thought you would be pleased." It was the closest Abby had ever heard her grandmother come to an apology.

"It was a surprise. I'm not a particularly big fan of surprises," Abby said simply.

"You will be great, possibly even better than I have been at leading this Coven," Vivian said, her hand reaching out for the glass. She stopped short and pulled away. "You're a smart girl. A bit naïve, but that's beginning to change... this last year has changed you so much, my Darling." Vivian's words were accompanied by a contemplative look.

Abby didn't know what to say. There was an unsettled nervousness growing in her stomach. Her grandmother's mercurial mood shift was too jarring.

"I think it's hit us all hard," Abby said. "I can't do this without them... I still feel the loss of Mom and Dad every day, every hour... every minute." She wiped away a tear as it escaped down her cheek.

Vivian shook her head, looking away from Abby. "You probably should head toward the ferry terminal," she suggested, a tight pain rattling in her voice. "You don't want to take any chances that it might be too full. You would not want to have to wait for the next one."

It's late at night, the ferry will be at half capacity at best, Abby thought, but knew better than to argue at the weak excuse.

"You're right," Abby agreed. "I'll be going then. Goodnight, Grandmother."

"Goodnight, Darling," Vivian said, almost desperately.

Abby headed toward the hallway. Just before stepping out, she glanced back.

Vivian stood leaning against the cabinet, still starring at the full bottle of bourbon.

"Happy birthday," Abby said, as she closed the door behind her.

CHAPTER FIVE

A crash from behind the counter gave Abby a jolt. "You're jumpy tonight," Madison observed.

Abby appreciated the reassurance, however ineffective it was. "Sorry," She collected her coffee from the bar as a barista quickly began cleaning up a broken mug.

Madison took Abby's arm. "We're going to have fun!" she insisted. They made their way to a table next to the window, with a clear view of the door.

Abby still wasn't sure how exploring the Seattle Underground could be considered "fun," but Madison and Hailey both seemed so excited, so she couldn't let them down.

Whatever. It will be fine, Abby thought, taking a deep breath. She looked at her cousin. "You're right. We'll have fun."

Madison glanced down at the time on her phone. "Hailey should be here any minute," she said.

Abby watched out the window to see if their friend was among the crowd. Dozens of pedestrians passed by, illuminated by the pale street light above. Tiny specks of rain coated the window from the light sprinkle misting the city.

In the distance, Abby saw the historical buildings lining the streets of Pioneer Square. She loved Old Town. The old brick buildings built at the turn of the twentieth century, with Romanesque facades and Victorian spires were all so beautiful. Down the street slightly was the historic iron pergola, with a glass roof providing a covered walkway around the triangular intersection.

Abby sighed. Seattle. It was almost six months since she came back, and she was still amazed by how glad she was to be home. A familiar face pulled Abby's attention away from the night outside. Hailey's face, half-hidden beneath a black hoodie, came into view. The streetlight reflected off her cobalt-blue eyes like fireworks in the night.

"There she is," Madison said, shoving her phone back into her purse. "I was about to text her."

Abby stood as Hailey entered the coffee shop. After a quick hug, she quickly surrendered her friend to Madison, who did the same.

"Are we ready for a fright?" Hailey teased, wiggling her fingers in the air to emphasize the spookiness.

"I can hardly wait," Madison responded gleefully as she took another sip of coffee.

Abby hesitated. "I've been looking forward to spending time with you," she responded honestly.

"Do you want something to drink?" Madison offered, pointing to the counter.

Hailey smiled. "Nah, I'm okay. We only have a few minutes, though. We should head over to the gathering point."

"I've heard it's pretty fantastic." Madison beamed with excitement. "I had a friend who did the history tour of the old buildings downtown, and she loved it. They didn't go into the Underground, though."

Abby took a sip of her coffee.

"I'm ready to go when you are," Hailey said cheerfully.

Madison's smile grew wider. "Let's do it!"

The three of them gathered their things and made their way to the door. Abby tossed the remainder of her drink in the garbage as they left. As they stepped out onto the street, Abby could hear the thumping sound of music coming from a nearby nightclub. She glanced over to see a long line of young adults wearing club clothes and sporting trendy styles.

"Too bad we aren't old enough to get in there," Hailey commented as they made their way in the opposite direction.

"Speak for yourself," Madison said.

"You're a year younger than both of us," Abby said, laughing.

Madison looked at her with a devilish grin. "Not according to the ID I procured a few months ago," she said, patting her purse.

"Madison Kane! Does your mother know?" Abby scolded, imagining the look on Margot's face.

"Of course not!" Madison laughed.

"I bought fake ID a couple years ago, but it was so bad I never worked up the nerve to try using it," Hailey said, chuckling.

The three of them made their way past the pergola and through a small triangular park that was situated among the old historic buildings. Clothing boutiques, small restaurants, and cafés occupied the first floor of the brick structures; many of them already closed for the evening.

A small, well-lit storefront broke a line of darkened windows. Bright fluorescent lights cut through the darkness, illuminating a sign on the door that read "Seattle Underground Tours."

"Here we are," Madison said, opening the door to a narrow gift shop.

The brightly lit room was filled with assorted tourist merchandise. Hailey browsed through lighters shaped like the Space Needle, snow globes with miniature skylines, and stacks of t-shirts while Madison approached a young man standing behind the counter. Abby absentmindedly flipped through rotating racks filled with picturesque postcards.

"You all right?" Hailey asked.

Abby conjured a smile. "Yes, of course," she said, doing her best to quell the nerves rumbling in her stomach.

She never shared all the details about what happened last spring with either Hailey or Madison, so Abby couldn't fault her for not realizing how hard this was. *It's just... ghosts,* she thought, trying not to shudder.

"You're a terrible liar," Hailey said gently. She took Abby's arm and smiled. "Let's have some fun. It's Halloween! Or at least it will be in a few days." Hailey said encouragingly, "We're all due for a good fright."

Abby shook the growing anxiety from her head. "Why did I let you talk me into this?" she growled playfully.

Madison rejoined them. "This way," she said, ushering them to the back end of the shop.

"Have either of you been down in the Underground City before?" Hailey asked.

"Never," Abby responded as they queued up at the back of the shop. They found a set of stairs leading down into a brick-lined basement.

"My mother warned me away from it. Apparently, there are all kinds of 'terrible things' in the Underground," Madison said, emphasizing her mother's words in a mocking tone.

"I came down here once when I was about eight with Mom and Michael," Hailey said. Her voice caught on her brother's name, and her expression grew dark.

Abby patted her friend's arm, offering her a smile. Hailey nodded, and the three of them descended the staircase into a dimly lit room where six other people stood milling about. The basement was larger than Abby expected. It had an open feel, despite being underground.

The room had brick walls with wood paneling on the upper half, and the floor was old, unfinished concrete riddled with cracks. A wooden bar lined one wall, which Abby was sure must have been a speakeasy from the prohibition era–or at least someone's interpretation of one.

The walls were lined with old black-and-white photos. Many appeared to be of the earliest settlers. Old buildings and grim people stared back at her like phantoms captured forever in a wooden frame. Abby looked at one photograph showing a row of old houses near the waterfront. The forest, only a few blocks away, was encroaching on the small settlement. Nothing in the photograph bore any resemblance to the city above them.

"That's a picture from the oldest settlement on Alki Point," a younger woman said, as she approached. "All of the founding families originally homesteaded across the bay, in what is now West Seattle," she added with a smile.

Abby looked at the woman. She appeared to be in her mid-thirties, and Abby guessed she was the tour guide. "I think I remember reading about that."

"Libby," the woman said, offering her hand. Her hair was pulled back in a loose bun, and she had an easy, studious smile.

She doesn't look too scary, Abby thought as she shook the woman's hand politely.

"You must have done your research before visiting our little city," Libby commented.

Abby chuckled. "I'm actually from here."

"Oh! Sorry," Libby said. "I just assumed. Most people we see are tourists."

"Well, I'm a tourist this evening," Abby quipped.

"I hope you enjoy the tour. Don't hesitate to ask questions if you have any," Libby said, before moving on to welcome the next group.

"Thanks," Abby said absently, her attention already on the next photograph.

"It's already a little creepy down here," Madison joked, holding her purse to her chest.

"I don't think any of these old buildings are still around," Hailey said.

"Some of them are," Libby replied as she walked past them and approached the counter. "But they're down here now," she added with a sly smile. "Gather around folks, and we will get the tour started."

Abby and the others gathered near the counter, turning their attention to the tour guide.

"After the Great Seattle Fire of 1889, the city was rebuilt in stone above the remnants of the previous settlement. This is how the Underground City came to be," Libby said, starting their tour with a brief history lesson.

"For nearly a decade, business continued in the Underground. They were accessed through basements and cellars of the very buildings that currently stand in Pioneer Square today." Libby waived at the old photos on the walls before continuing. "However, as the city grew above ground, the Underground City started taking a dark turn. By 1910, it was overrun with opium dens, brothels, and gambling parlors."

A cool breeze tickled the back of Abby's neck. She glanced over and saw a doorway with a black velvet curtain. The fabric rustled slightly. *That must be the entrance to the Underground City,* she realized.

"By late 1910, local authorities all but abandoned policing the Underground, and it had become a hive of lawlessness," Libby continued. "Over time the buildings became structurally unsound, and general health and cleanliness fell. It wasn't until the 1920s, after several outbreaks of plague and several collapsed buildings, that the Underground City was officially condemned. Of course, we will only be venturing into areas that have been designated as safe. But make no mistake, what you will see this evening is only a small portion of an elaborate network that extends for miles."

"This is a lot more interesting than I thought," Hailey whispered.

Abby nodded and did her best to concentrate on what the guide was saying. A cold feeling settled in her shoulders as she felt a chill down her spine.

"Alright, let's get started," Libby said.

"This is so exciting," Madison said.

Abby's breath quickened as their tour guide rounded the counter and approached the velvet curtain. She inhaled deeply through her nose and breathed it out slowly.

Libby stood at the entryway as Abby and the others gathered around. "What you are about to see is the very real remains of Seattle's earliest history." Libby paused for a dramatic moment and then pulled the curtain back to reveal a long passageway that disappeared into darkness.

Abby let out a sigh of relief. She was embarrassed. A small part of her had expected something to jump out at them. Instead, there was a perfectly ordinary brick hallway with an unfinished concrete floor.

Libby reached around the corner. Lights lining the ceiling flickered awake. "This way. Please stick together. No wandering off. Some parts of the Underground are very unstable, so it is important that you stay with the group."

Madison led the way, excitedly chatting with their fellow tour-goers. Hailey held back with Abby, seeing the uncertain look on her friend's face. Abby gave her a reassuring smile and stepped into the hallway after her cousin.

"At the turn of the last century, Seattle was the first point of entry from the Alaskan Gold Rush," Libby said, turning to face the small group. "Buildings like these catered to some of the more unsavory needs of miners, loggers, and hunters," she said, continuing her history lesson.

The further along they traveled, the wider the corridor became. The old chipped bricks and crumbling mortar in the walls still held with the occasional wooden beam. Most looked newer as if to support new construction from time to time.

The Underground smelled musty and dank. A strange humidity that lingered in the air in contrast to the cool temperature. "Flooding was a constant concern for the Underground settlers," Libby continued." When the tide came in, toilets would turn into geysers." She gestured into what Abby thought was an apartment, or perhaps a small home, it was difficult to tell for certain. The room cluttered with debris and loose bricks, and an ancient-looking toilet sat in one corner.

Abby looked around in fascination as they walked along the passageway. Occasionally the wall would be interrupted with a doorway or window. A dilapidated sign hung from one rusty old hinge, its words long faded. An old window revealed a chair and counter with unfamiliar tools and antiquated devices used by dentists during the early settlement.

"Gambling houses and opium dens were the preferred form of entertainment in the middle of the nineteenth century, until 1852, when one enterprising settler moved from Pennsylvania to Seattle..."

Abby's attention wandered as the corridor opened into a large space. New wooden beams had been constructed to reinforce the ceiling and walls. She could see where old beams had rotted away over time and been replaced, most likely by the tour company. The floor was uneven and somewhat treacherous. There were several hallways that departed the room, each disappearing into the dark.

As the tour group moved through the large chamber, Abby was transfixed on a corridor to her left. It was a long hallway, not unlike the one they passed through before. No fluorescent lights dangled from the ceiling. Instead, the light crawled down the hall from where they stood, disappearing after a few yards into utter darkness. Only a thin velvet rope, the type you would see at a movie premier barred entry into the unstable passage.

The hairs on Abby's neck stood, and an eerie chill passed through her. Her heart began to race, and her mouth went dry. What? She peered into the darkness, searching for the source of her unease. Her instinct was to open the Sight only slightly, but Abby resisted. *Not here, not now,* she repeated over and over until the urge passed.

"… the first brothel in Seattle." A hand on Abby's shoulder caught her attention. She spun to look at the guide. "Miss, please stick with the rest of the group."

Abby blinked and turned to realize she had fallen behind.

"Oh sorry," she said. She shook off the strange allure of the dark hallway and hurried to catch up. Both Madison and Hailey gave her a curious look.

The tour group moved forward to the far end of the large chamber. Abby found herself at the tail end of the line as they began making their way down another brick hallway. Abby followed the group quietly, but she couldn't help glancing back the way they came.

In the darkness behind them, stood a gray figure, barely visible to the naked eye. It was watching them.

Abby gasped, unsure at first if she saw anything. She peered closer. A sickly gray glow, muted by the shadows, began radiating from the shadowed form.

Not again. Memories flooded her mind: spirits swarming and choking her in a hotel room: the blood-stained ghost of a blond-haired girl standing on the edge of a lake: dark magic: dark curses… It was here again. The unmistakable sensation of decay and corruption. Death.

Abby leaned against the wall to catch her balance. There was no telling what horrors she would See if the Sight opened now. *Breathe,* she told herself over and over as her heart pounded uncontrollably. *Breathe…* She turned her attention inward for a brief moment, willing the Sight to close.

Nothing happened. Abby bore down on the feeling, closing herself off to Fate.... *but I'm not using the Sight,* she realized.

Her eyes snapped open in shock. *What is this?*

The ghost continued to stand just as he was. He tilted his head curiously. His hand reached down and pulled on a chain, revealing an old-fashioned pocket watch. He looked down at the time and then back up at Abby.

Struggling to breathe, she stood paralyzed against the old brick wall. *No! I can't be seeing you without the Sight. You can't be real!* she silently screamed at the ghost.

A wicked cackle traveled through the air, faint and crazed. It echoed faintly down the crumbling brick corridors from somewhere far beyond the apparition in front of her.

She glanced again at the figure in the hallway and watched as the darkness consumed him. The maniacal laughter faded into silence. The only sound was the ramblings of the tour guide down the hallway.

A droplet of water dripped on her hand, snapping her back to her surroundings. She was shaking. Her whole body was covered in a cold sweat. She wiped it away with the sleeve of her jacket and pushed away from the wall, trying to regain her breath.

"What the hell happened to you?" Madison said, approaching. Alarm was written on her face.

"I... I'm not feeling well," Abby said, not wanting to explain what she had just seen. Not here. Not where others might overhear.

Madison looked uncertain but said nothing.

"You don't look well," Hailey said, as she came up beside Madison. "You look like you saw a ghost," she added with a touch of humor.

Abby's eyes widened. *Did she know?* Hailey blanched. She didn't say anything else, the look on her face and her silence were more than an answer.

Madison and Hailey flanked Abby, each taking an arm as if she were incapable of walking.

Though her knees felt unsteady, Abby could walk, and she shook them off. The three of them caught up with the tour guide, who merely gave them a curious look without stopping her speech. Abby was grateful Libby didn't skip a beat as she continued to drone on about Seattle's early history.

Abby followed through the tour, not seeing anything. She felt more stable as part of the group, just blending in. She listened with half an ear to the dull tones of the stories and history being shared as they weaved their way through a maze of hallways and corridors. The tour guide articulated every word with practiced precision, but nothing sank in. The context was lost in the sounds of language.

Abby's thoughts were consumed with the ghostly image emerging from the darkness. Thoughts of blood rituals and ghostly spirits intruded on every conscious moment. The crazed laughter lingered in her ears, echoing through her mind. Her mind was drowning in images of death that could not be unseen.

They passed through another large chamber, and the group paused as Libby began another story.

"I think it's almost over." Madison gave Abby's arm a gentle squeeze.

Abby looked around and realized she was getting several strange and sympathetic looks from the other tourists. She straightened up and did her best to try and look normal. Like someone who hadn't seen a ghost and was so terrified that she would run into another one around every corner. Abby wasn't entirely sure she was all that convincing, but she did her best to show them that she wasn't the girl who got scared of the dark.

Libby led the group onto the far side of the large chamber. The tour guide came to a doorway and opened it, revealing a flight of stairs leading up.

Abby silenced the sigh she nearly unleashed. *Oh, thank God. It's over,* she thought, allowing herself to breathe again.

"Thanks for joining us," Libby said cheerfully. "I hope you enjoyed your time in the Underground."

Abby climbed the stairs, happy to put the forgotten city behind her. Madison and Hailey brought up the rear, watching over her as though she would crumble to the ground at any moment.

At the top of the stairs, Abby moved along a hallway that emptied back into the small gift shop. Without stopping, she headed for the door leading out into the fresh night air.

She pushed the glass door open and stepped out into the darkened streets. The street lights offered a soft glow, keeping the night at bay. A tiny drizzle fell from the sky, misting her face as she took a deep breath of fresh air.

"What the hell happened?" Madison asked as she approached from the door. Hailey was right behind her with the same concerned look on her face.

Abby shook her head. "I–I just want to get out of here." She managed to speak, her voice little more than a hollow moan.

"Alright, let's go to the car," Madison said.

"You saw something, didn't you?" Hailey asked gently as they started walking.

Abby nodded.

"I thought it was nothing more than a tourist gimmick," Madison commented. "I never imagined there would be actual ghosts."

"I'll tell you about it when we're in the car," she said, as they weaved around a small group of pedestrians. "I don't want to do this here."

They made their way up the street back toward the car, letting the silence drape around them.

"If you don't mind, I think I'd like to pick the next outing we go on together," Abby joked bitterly.

CHAPTER SIX

Abby looked up at the gargantuan home of Vivian Kane. "I feel like I've been here a lot lately," she muttered under her breath.

"Hey kiddo," Wendy said, coming up alongside Abby as she stepped out of her uncle's BMW. "It looks like your grandmother really outdid herself this time." She pointed to the Chinese lanterns hanging from the trees lining the main drive. Tiny white fairy lights and silver streamers added an otherworldly aesthetic, while dozens of white roses peaked out of the bushes.

"How did she get white roses to bloom in October?" Abby asked.

"She probably had them planted just for tonight," Wendy replied, sharing a mischievous smile with her niece.

"I really wish she wouldn't make such a big deal of everything," Abby said, preparing herself for the festivities, already in full swing inside. "How many people did she invite to this? It looks huge." Dozens of people in formal wear were making their way into the house, and there was a steady line of limos moving up the driveway.

"I think she invited at least twenty covens," Sebastian said, as he rounded the car. Abby rolled her eyes.

He handed his keys over to a valet and turned to his niece. "This is no small affair, Abby. I know that you and your grandmother don't always see eye-to-eye, but the Samhain Ball is an important event in the occult world. The Kane Coven has been building relationships and alliances with these covens for generations. It would be terrible form to snub them now."

Abby sighed, properly chastised. "I understand."

"Not to mention the 'relationships and alliances' it forms for Kane Industries, right?" Wendy added dryly.

"That too." Sebastian nodded.

Wendy turned and faced Abby, an earnest look on her cheery face. "Can I give you some advice?" she asked.

Abby nodded, curious.

"Everyone here is likely a witch, but I wouldn't advertise your special gift."

"My Sight? I hadn't planned to, but why?"

"It's just the Sight is really rare. Some people are scared of it, especially people who have something to hide. Conversely, there are those who would wish to control and manipulate people with the Sight for their own purposes. All I'm saying is be careful. People are going to want to use you, don't let them take advantage." Wendy looked at her lovingly. "Not just for your magic, but for your position in the Coven, too. Just... be wary, okay?"

"It's true, Abby, now that you're going to be more active in the Coven, you're going to meet more people like us. Not all of them will have honorable motives," Sebastian said.

"Please, enough with the gloom and doom. Let her have some fun!" Rodger interjected. He presented Little Evan for the required cooing over his baby tuxedo. Abby was happy to oblige her adorable little cousin.

Abby laughed. "Thanks, Uncle Rodger," she said. "And thank you for looking out for me," she added to Wendy and Sebastian. "I plan to be very careful. While I'm not sure about the role Grandmother wants me to take, I am sure about wanting to know more about our coven and our magic."

"Miss Kane," a familiar voice said officiously. Abby looked to see Mr. Greenly, her grandmother's butler, gesturing her over. "This way, please."

They passed through the grand entry and were guided up the stairwell onto the second-floor mezzanine. They entered an enormous room with white marble floors and ceilings twenty feet high. Abby gasped in spite of herself. *I thought I was done being impressed by Vivian's ostentatiousness.*

A half-dozen marble pillars lined the room on either side, creating a visual break between sections of the room. The entire far wall was floor to ceiling glass windows that looked East, over Lake Washington. The lights from the city skyline twinkled in the water, adding to festivities as if Vivian herself had illuminated the city just for tonight.

A small orchestra played at the far end of the ballroom, filling the room with an unobtrusive symphony. Several guests waltzed in the center of the room, while others rested at small tables around the edges of the hall.

More white roses filled vases everywhere there was room to put one. White Chinese lanterns, like those outside, dangled from the ceiling, casting the whole room in a soft glow. Despite its size, there was a cozy, warm atmosphere to the party.

"This is pretty amazing," Rodger commented.

"Darlings!" Vivian called out as they entered. Her voice carried easily over the party noise, drawing curious gazes first to her, then to the newcomers.

Looking at Vivian, Abby suddenly felt underdressed. Her grandmother shimmered head to toe; from her lavish diamond jewelry to the tiny crystal beads sewn into her floor-length white dress. Vivian looked like an old-Hollywood starlet at a premier.

Abby tugged at her cocktail dress self-consciously. Even the Grimaldi Diamond was nothing compared to the opulence draped around Vivian. She sighed and fiddled with her necklace. The last time she wore it, she wasn't exactly praised for its elegance. She wished Vivian hadn't insisted she wear it tonight.

"You look wonderful, Darling," Vivian said, holding Abby around the shoulders.

"Thank you, Grandmother," Abby said politely, trying not to wrinkle her nose at the acrid undertone of alcohol. "You look magnificent."

Vivian glanced at Wendy. Her warm smile melted to one of wary vigilance. Even as she turned back to Abby, she regarded the other woman as one would an unwelcome snake.

Wendy pretended not to notice and headed into the party.

"Come with me, Darling," Vivian said, pulling Abby away. "Let me introduce you to some very important people."

For nearly twenty minutes, Abby was introduced to witches from all over the West Coast. Names and faces flashed by so quickly, she couldn't have hoped to remember them all. *Let's see,* she thought. *The Preston and Wakefield Covens are from Los Angeles, the Lang and Prusad Covens are from... San Francisco? And someone from Portland... Ughh. I hope Grandmother doesn't test me on this.*

They all seemed to be having a great time. She watched the covens interact with each other as Vivian moved between them like a butterfly in a diverse garden. She knew Vivian loved being the center of attention, but she hadn't realized the integral role her grandmother had established as the social hub of the occult. Her coven was the nexus of magical and political power for all of the west coast covens, and they adored Vivian Kane.

More guests arrived, and Abby was spun around the room. More names and more faces came and went before Abby found a familiar one.

"Is that Cassandra Marsh?" Abby asked quietly.

"Why yes, dear, who else would it be?"

What is the head of the Council of Overseers doing here? Abby thought. She watched the other woman enter the room as if she was sliding on glass. Her deep purple gown looked far more glamorous than the stark gray robe she had been wearing on the day Abby first met her, several months ago, on the night she dispensed justice on the man who murdered her parents.

A young man not much older than Abby accompanied Cassandra. He was a nice-looking fellow, with short brown hair and fair skin. Abby noticed his eyes were large and blue. There was something off about his eyes, they were strange, but she couldn't put her finger on it. The two approached with welcoming smiles.

"Vivian Dear," Cassandra said, approaching and giving Vivian a polite hug and a peck on each cheek.

"Cassandra, it is wonderful as always to see you," Vivian said, a chilly quality to her tone. "I'm deeply honored you flew in to be here this evening, and all the way from Boston, too."

"Nonsense, there isn't a thing I wouldn't do for such a dear friend." Cassandra smiled.

Abby suppressed a shiver. There was clearly a history between them, but she doubted it was as nice as they were pretending. *It's probably better that I don't know.*

"It's nice to see you again, Mrs. Marsh," Abby said, playing her prescribed part in the pleasantries.

"Let me introduce you to my grandson, Patrick Marsh. Patrick, this is Abigail Kane," Cassandra said with a sly smile.

"Nice to meet you, Miss Kane," Patrick said stiffly, shaking her hand.

"Please, call me Abby," she said politely. "It's nice to meet you, Patrick."

"Cassandra, I wanted to introduce you to Amelia Preston," Vivian said, taking Cassandra's arm and pulling her away.

Abandoned by their grandmothers, the two stood awkwardly, gazing around the room. Abby turned to Patrick, who looked somewhat lost. "I think we're being set up," Abby said to cut through the awkward moment.

"I suspect you're right," Patrick said, cracking a smile. "Sorry, I didn't realize what was going on until just now."

"It's all right, I didn't either," Abby said. "So, is your grandmother as headstrong and stubborn as mine?"

"I haven't the slightest doubt," Patrick said.

"I'm a little embarrassed. I recently broke up with someone, everything is rather complicated right now," Abby said, hoping her confession would relieve him of any sense of obligation. "I suspect this is Grandmother's attempt to push me out there again. I'm very sorry she did this to you."

Patrick smiled, revealing a perfect set of teeth. "It's not a problem. It was only a six-hour flight," he said.

Abby's eyes flew open. "Oh no! I'm so sor... you're teasing me, aren't you?" She asked, noting the mischievous twinkle in his eye.

"Guilty." He laughed.

"Hmph. Just for that..." Abby took his arm and pointed to her cousin Madison sitting at a table with her mother, looking bored. "See that pretty girl at the table over there?"

"Yes," Patrick answered with a nod.

"That's my cousin Madison, she's funny, sweet, single, and comes with much less baggage than I have right now."

"A promising start," he said thoughtfully.

"Would you like to meet her?"

"I'd like that," Patrick said with a smile.

Abby escorted him over and introduced him to Madison, who quickly flashed a flirtatious smile. Clearly no longer needed, Abby excused herself, hoping he wasn't a complete creep.

She wove her way through the crowd looking for familiar faces. In a quiet corner, she found Sebastian and Rodger sharing a drink.

"You won't believe what Grandmother tried to do," Abby said, letting her irritation show.

"Oh, God, what now?" Rodger asked. Sebastian rolled his eyes.

"She just tried to pawn me off on Cassandra Marsh's grandson," Abby said.

Both her uncles chuckled.

"What?" Abby questioned, trying not to laugh. "It isn't funny." She slugged Rodger playfully in the arm and started laughing with them.

"Where is he now?" Sebastian asked.

"I paid it forward," Abby said, pointing toward Madison's table.

"Poor guy, I almost feel sorry for him," Sebastian quipped, earning a wicked smile from Abby.

"I really shouldn't be surprised by any of this," she added, glancing around the ballroom.

"No, I suspect this is the first of many attempts to set you up," Sebastian said.

"It's not a bad thing to think about, though," Rodger said unexpectedly. "I just mean maybe it isn't a bad idea to think about dating again, putting yourself out there."

"I agree. Though it might be too soon right now, it's something to keep in mind," Sebastian suggested. "Maybe, after everything is a little more settled, you can consider it."

Abby shook her head, looking around the room for a change of subject.

Sebastian reached out and placed a hand on her shoulder. "They aren't all going to be like the last one," he said sincerely.

Abby sighed. "I know. I just... I'm not ready."

Rodger reached over and gave Abby a hug. "It takes time, and you have a lot going on right now. Don't let what happened shut you down. You can spend your whole life waiting for everything to pass. Don't do that to yourself. You deserve to move on and live your life the way you want to. Don't let anyone or anything hold you back from that."

She looked at her uncle, suspiciously. "You're not just talking about relationships anymore, are you?"

A pair of genuine smiles met her sharp gaze. "Well, no," Rodger said.

"You've been through so much, Abby," Sebastian added. "We just want you to be happy."

She hugged them both deeply, grateful for everything they are always doing for her.

After a moment, Sebastian took a sip of his drink and said, "You really should think about putting yourself out there, though. It will drive your grandmother crazy, and you might even have some fun."

"Oh? Abby asked skeptically. "You're encouraging me to go out and 'have fun'?"

He winked at his husband. "Romance has its perks."

She laughed and gave her uncles a chastising look. "Why couldn't you have had this conversation with me twenty minutes ago? The only guy at this party who's remotely attractive, and I pawned off on Madison!" she said jokingly.

Sebastian and Rodger both chuckled.

"What's so funny?" Vivian asked as she approached with a glass of red wine in hand. She glanced around. "Darling, where is Patrick? He is such a charming young man."

"He's over there talking to Madison," Abby said, gesturing to the table where they were sitting, engaged in a lively conversation.

"Well, Darling, that was a missed opportunity," Vivian said. "He is very handsome and from a good family." She gave Abby a disapproving look. "No matter, there are a number of other fine young men from good families to meet. I was thinking of taking you with me to the Beltane Festival in Cardiff this spring. Perhaps you can meet someone appropriate there."

"I don't want you to go to any trouble, Grandmother," Abby said. "I'm not certain you, and I have the same taste in men." There was an undertone of relief in her voice she neglected to hide.

Vivian narrowed her eyes slightly and pointed her finger at her granddaughter. "Don't get lippy with me, young lady," she said playfully. "I happen to care about your future. The right match will not only secure your happiness but also improve your standing among the other covens."

"Ah! Johanssons!" Abby threw up a hand in emphasis and smiled triumphantly.

"You want to marry a Johansson?" Rodger asked.

"Oh, Darling, no. The Johanssons aren't nearly good enough for you," Vivian said.

"No." Abby laughed. "The Johannsons are the coven from Portland. I couldn't remember," she explained.

Vivian smiled and patted her shoulder. "It's quite all right, Darling. You will have plenty of time to learn all of this."

Before I take over the Coven, you mean... Abby thought, biting her tongue. She didn't want to start a fight.

"Be careful, Abby," Sebastian said, warning her with a smile. "If you're not careful, your grandmother will have you married off to one of the London Seven before the end of the party."

"And what would I do as part of the London Seven?" Abby asked. "They basically run London, and I can't even manage my own schedule most of the time."

"Now, now, Darling," Vivian chided her. "They rule much more than just London. The London Seven oversee the day-to-day functioning of all the covens in Great Britain."

"Yes, thank you. That makes me feel much better," Abby said dryly.

"Be thankful it's just Great Britain. When the Empire was at its height, there were few other witch families anywhere in the world with more prestige."

Abby went quiet for a moment. "The Hodge family… they were once one of the London Seven, right?"

"Yes, before their scandal a century ago," Sebastian said evenly. "They were replaced by the Fox Coven if I'm not mistaken."

"None of the London Seven is worthy of my precious Abigail," Vivian stated with contempt, pulling Abby close as if to protect her. "The Kanes may have lost their standing in England five-hundred years ago, but no one in Europe can compare to us now."

"Oh wait, I remember reading about that," Abby realized. "The London Seven were the ones who drove our coven from Yorkshire in the sixteenth century, right?"

Rodger nodded. "That's right. The Coven fled to France before eventually settling in America."

"And how would you know all this, Pennington?" Vivian asked, a playful hint in her voice.

Rodger looked at her evenly. "I read a lot."

"Didn't one of our ancestors put a curse on them or something?" Abby asked, changing the subject back.

"Yes, and if you ask me, they had it coming," Vivian said.

Gisela stood abruptly from a nearby table, interrupting their conversation. "Vivian, can we please get on with this?" As she waddled over, her green satin ball gown made her look even more like a toad. Annoyance was etched into every step, and she seemed impatient. "We need to do this ritual before midnight."

Abby tried not to make a face at her cousin's manners and conceded that perhaps formal galas were not Gisela's forte.

Vivian turned an imperious gaze on her younger cousin. "You think I am not aware of the limitations of this ritual? It was my curse that suppressed the Thanos in the first place."

Gisela shrank under Vivian's stare. "Of course, Matriarch. I just thought that you might not know how late it was getting…"

Vivian waved her away. "Fine, gather the family downstairs. We'll start the ritual in ten minutes."

"How long will it take?" Abby asked. "I've never done a ritual this involved before." It was difficult to imagine Vivian abandoning her guests for long.

"Don't worry, Darling. It will only be a few minutes. The hard work was done when I cast the infertility curse initially. This is just upkeep. We won't be away from the party for long," Vivian said. "Go get ready. I'll meet you down there." She patted Abby on the cheek affectionately before disappearing into the crowd.

"I don't think I've ever been in the private ritual chamber before," Rodger said. They moved across the grand entry on the first floor and to a door leading to the east wing.

Sebastian quickly stepped forward and opened the door for them.

"Will Uncle Bernard be joining us?" Abby asked after her reclusive uncle. She knew he rarely came to these things, but he was still considered an elder of the Kane Coven.

"I don't think so. He rarely leaves the house anymore," Sebastian said.

"He hardly ever left," Gisela commented. "Even when we were children," she added. He's always up at the old family estate."

Abby had never been to the Kane family estate on Vashon Island, but her mother had shown her pictures of the old Victorian manor once. Abby couldn't imagine anyone wanting to live all alone in an old, rundown house that was practically abandoned. But then again, she'd only ever seen the man himself a few times in her life.

Now isn't the time to dwell on it, Abby thought as she followed her uncles down the long hallway. Old photographs of the family from early settlement days lined the walls in an even pattern, broken only by closed doors leading off into unknown rooms. They were in a portion of her grandmother's house she had never entered before, and Abby stuck close to Sebastian, not wanting to get lost. Wandering the halls had been expressly forbidden since she was a little girl. Though she knew she was in no danger now, nervousness still gnawed at her.

"This way, my Darlings." Vivian stood in front of a large set of double doors, waiting for them. Abby exchanged a quick hello with her aunt Margot, and glanced around, looking to see if anyone else had arrived. It was a much smaller group than Abby had expected. Only Margot and Madison were waiting with Vivian when Abby, Gisela, Sebastian, Rodger, and Wendy walked up."Is this it? I thought the Coven was a lot bigger than this."

"It is," Sebastian explained. "There are only a few of us need for this ritual, though. Your grandmother didn't think it was worth gathering the whole Coven."

"And it isn't," Vivian said definitely. She reached out and tapped the knob of each door and muttered something under her breath. Abby tried to catch the words, but they were in a different language. *Is that Latin?* she thought.

The doors swung open into a large room lined with books. It was cozily lit, but every corner was still bright enough to read by. "This is amazing," Abby said, catching her breath. The bookshelves lining the wall were enclosed behind climate-controlled glass casings to preserve the arcane treasures within. Some of the books looked quite ancient, and Abby couldn't imagine how they had come to be in her grandmother's possession. She saw several scrolls of parchment resting on soft velvet stands; they looked as if they would crumble if touched. Toward the back of the room was a separate glass case that held stone tablets surrounded by a strange mist that funneled down from a pipe above them. Abby had never seen anything like it.

Vivian turned and placed a hand on Abby's shoulder, offering a kind smile. "Now that you're old enough, you can use my library whenever you please, my Darling," Vivian said, proudly showing off her collection.

"Has anyone seen Mother?" Margot asked, stepping in. She looked worried. "I can't find her."

"She's fine," Vivian said. "Fiona went down into the ritual chamber several minutes ago to start preparing."

A sense of relief quickly washed over Margot's beautiful face.

"I told you she was fine," Madison said, giving her mother an exacerbated look.

"Don't give your mother a hard time," Margot said. The look she gave her daughter was piercing, but her tone was resigned.

Madison quickly approached Abby and took her arm. "Patrick is a dream," she said conspiratorially.

"Sounds like you're hitting it off." Abby smiled.

"We exchanged phone numbers," Madison said. "He's already sent a text," she added, showing Abby her phone making certain her mother couldn't see.

"Shall we continue?" Vivian cleared her throat.

"Sorry," Abby said, pulling Madison with her.

Vivian walked over to a break between the bookshelves. Reaching out, she placed her hand on the white surface of the wall. The moment the tip of her finger touched the empty space, a purple glow radiated from the panel. She traced a glyph with her finger, which lingered even after she had removed her hand. As they watched, it slowly began to turn red.

The wall receded, opening into a corridor with a stairwell leading down. Abby felt a wave of energy radiating from the stairs, reaching for her. For a moment, it felt as if the energy was probing her, questioning her presence. She felt dizzy. *It's power,* she thought. *Pure magical energy.*

As soon as the feeling came, it went again, opening the way for her. *I've never felt wards like these before.*

"This way, Darlings," Vivian said, motioning for the others to follow.

Abby watched as her grandmother took the rail with her hand before descending the stairs. She looked to her uncle, who motioned for her to follow.

Small luminescent runes were inscribed on the wall lining the stairwell. As she descended, Abby tried to get a good look at them. Some looked familiar; protective runes and symbols of arcane power, but others were unlike anything she'd encountered before.

When Abby reached the bottom, she found herself in a vast underground chamber with a domed ceiling. The floor was smooth marble, polished to the point it almost looked like liquid. Abby could see her own reflection below her feet.

There was a marble altar in the center of the room, surrounded by several purple, glowing rings on the floor. As Abby approached, she could see more etchings on the rings.

Curious, Abby watched Fiona arrange candles and incense burners on the raised platform. The older woman wore a long, black evening gown, and had her ash-gray hair pulled back into a tight bun. *She looks the most like a witch out of everyone here,* Abby thought, amused. She was glad to see her grandaunt looking so active and well, though.

"Is this everyone?" Fiona asked, turning and counting everyone in the room.

"Me, you, Abby, Margot, Madison, Gisela, Sebastian, Rodger, Wendy," Vivian listed everyone in turn, "and of course our precious Little Evan. That makes nine of us who can participate."

"Eight," Margot corrected.

"Mother," Madison said. "I'm old enough to help."

"You aren't technically a member of the Coven until you're eighteen."

"But, I'll be eighteen in a couple months!"

"Tonight, you will care for Evan so Rodger can be a part of this," Margot said flatly.

Madison retreated to a corner, quietly fuming. "Fine," she said. "I would rather be keeping Evan company, anyway. The rest of you can have your bizarre ritual." She took Evan into her arms and kissed his forehead. "Can we at least stay and watch?"

"Yes," Margot agreed. "I don't know where you got that mouth of yours," she added under her breath.

"I do," Fiona said, raising an eyebrow in her daughter's direction.

"Thanks for the support, Mother," Margot said dryly.

"Can we get on with this, already?" Gisela complained. She looked at Vivian and dropped her gaze.

"Of course, Darling," Vivian said with a saccharine smile. She gave the altar a cursory glance and then regarded the purple rings circling the altar one larger than the next. "Form the circle around the second ring," she instructed.

Abby and the others formed a circle as instructed, while Vivian prepared to facilitate the ritual at its center.

"Link hands," Vivian said. She pulled a vial of dark, red liquid from a small ivory box ornately carved with skulls. Abby grasped hands with Sebastian on her right, and Margot on her left.

"I don't know the ritual," Abby whispered to her uncle.

Sebastian smiled kindly. "It's all right. I don't either," he confessed. "We're here to lend our power to the ritual. Your grandmother will do all the heavy lifting, so to speak."

Abby nodded, somewhat relieved she wasn't about to ruin it for everyone. She was still uncertain what her role would be, but she was grateful to be between these two. She took several deep breaths, focusing on what was happening before her.

Vivian measured several drops of red liquid into a small copper bowl. Green smoke began to grow and billow from the dish, spilling over the edges and onto the floor. After a few moments, the smoke started creeping across the floor until it reached the second circle where Abby and the others stood. An invisible barrier stopped the smoke from advancing as it lapped at the tip of her toes.

"It's time to begin," Vivian commanded. She reached out and lit each candle on the altar with the tip of her finger. The glowing purple ring began pulsating, matching its rhythm to the flicker of the candles.

Abby looked down to see the symbols etched into the marble below were glowing brighter than before. The green mist hovered only a foot above the floor. As she watched, it began swirling around the altar. Tiny bolts of arcane energy crackled and sparked through the mist like a web, building into a small tempest at their feet.

A pungent smell wafted from the strange incense burning on the altar, filling the room. Vivian grasped the copper bowl in her hands and raised it above her head and yelled, "Invoco Vim Negabis!"

Crackling energy came from inside the bowl. The mist swirled around the altar faster, its tendrils reaching for any escape.

Abby felt something course through her body. A visible energy moved through her. It came like electricity, shooting from Margot's hand into her arm, through her chest, and down her other arm into Sebastian. She gasped. Her breath shortened, and her knees felt weak as the energy engulfed her.

"Et Contrivit Te In Anno Une, Et Una Nocte!" Vivian yelled.

The tempest grew. Everyone around the circle was awash in the same arcane energy.

When the green, spiraling tempest reached waist level, the magical lightning shot forward, striking the copper bowl in Vivian's hands. Energy from each person in the circle converged upon the bowl.

A blinding burst of light filled the room, forcing Abby to look away. When she opened her eyes, the room was silent. The green mist was gone. She could no longer feel the energy flowing through her body. The purple ring beneath her feet was nothing more than a pale glow as it had been when they entered.

Abby looked up to see a satisfied grin on her grandmother's face as she placed the copper bowl back onto the altar.

"That wasn't so bad," Sebastian said, squeezing Abby's hand gently.

"It was your first coven ritual," Margot observed. "I should have realized," she said, giving Abby a polite hug. "We could have better prepared you for this."

"It's all right," Abby said, she felt a bit light-headed from the strange sensations she felt during the ritual. "I still feel kind of strange."

"Well, you did just have a rather impressive amount of magical energy flow through your body," Rodger said, as he retrieved baby Evan from Madison.

"Don't worry, most rituals we cast don't use as much energy as this one," Margot told her.

"Only the big ones your grandmother likes to use," Sebastian explained. Abby could detect a hint of disapproval in her uncle's tone.

"Not everyone can wield such power," Gisela grunted as she passed on her way to the stairwell. "Our Coven is fortunate to have a witch as powerful as Vivian."

There was a heavy silence after Gisela disappeared up the stairwell.

CHAPTER SEVEN

Abby finished rinsing her mouth, spitting the remaining toothpaste into the sink. She pulled her hair back into a tight ponytail and secured it with a hair tie. Glancing in the mirror, she made a face. Her skin was pale, and the fatigue in her eyes reflected back at her. She could still feel the lightning coursing through her body from the ritual earlier that evening; it rippled along her skin in an echo of the pure magical energy. She was light-headed as she remembered the electric vibrations that danced across her skin.

After taking a deep breath, Abby turned the bathroom light off and made her way into her bedroom. The house was silent. Everyone else had already fallen asleep. She sighed and crawled into bed, knowing it was futile. Sleep would be a distant hope again tonight.

She reached for her phone on the nightstand and made sure it was plugged into the charger before glancing at the clock. *Nearly four already?* Abby thought *I'm going to sleep through half the day at this point. If I fall asleep before the sun comes up, anyway.*

Abby closed her eyes and did her best to find the perfect position of comfort that would help pull her into the depths of sleep.

A distant whimpering sound came from the hallway. *Evan,* Abby thought, sitting up in her bed. *I'll let Rodger and Sebastian sleep.* She stretched and got out of bed. She picked up her thick winter robe from the chair next to her desk and put it on.

She quietly opened her bedroom door and stepped into the hallway. She didn't want to wake the house with her late-night shuffling. Silently, she made her way toward Evan's room. As she neared the end of the hall, the door to the room next to her swung open. Abby jumped and peered into the darkness.

"Wendy?"

"Hey kid," Wendy said, standing in the doorway. "Did you hear Evan?"

"Yes, I'm just going to check on him. Go ahead and go back to bed, I'll take care of him." Abby said.

Wendy let out a long yawn. "You got it," she said, before closing her door again.

Abby paused when she reached Evan's room, placing an ear to the door to listen. There was silence. She cracked open the door and peeked in before walking over to peer into the crib. Evan lay sleeping peacefully. Abby straightened, watching her adorable little cousin with a smile. "I guess you were fussing in your sleep," she whispered and gave him a peck on the forehead.

Stepping back into the hallway, She carefully closed the door behind without making a sound. As the door clicked shut, the whimpering sound came again, this time it was downstairs.

What was that?

She padded down the hallway in her bare feet to the second-floor landing. She stood at the top of the stairs waiting to see if she heard the sound again. Silence.

Listening carefully, she waited for what seemed like several minutes. There was nothing but the distant sound of the waves moving along the rocky beach a few yards from the house.

With a shrug, Abby gave up and headed toward her bedroom. She was just reaching for her doorknob when the mysterious whimpering sound came again.

Someone is downstairs, she realized and carefully navigated the staircase in virtual darkness.

Moonlight filled the living room with a pale glow. There was no one there. Abby turned to the double doors leading to the study to the right of the stairs. She reached for the switch in the darkness and flipped the lights on. No one..."What the hell," Abby whispered under her breath, before turning the lights off and closing the doors behind her.

It came again, muffled by noticeable. It sounded like someone... a woman crying. Abby concentrated on what direction it was coming from. She followed the sound and found herself staring at the front door of the house. Abby approached the front door and looked through the tiny peephole. There was no one there.

"Hello," Abby said just loud enough to project her voice through the door but quietly enough to not wake everyone sleeping upstairs.

There was a sniffing sound, and a voice said, "Abby?"

A cold chill ran through Abby's body. *That voice... That's Mom!* Abby flung the door open and moved out onto the porch. Her heart was pounding as she searched frantically for any sign of her mother. She knew that voice better than her own. There was no way she mistook it.

"Mom," Abby called out into the night. The only response that came was the sound of the water lapping at the shore. The salty air stung her nostrils as she breathed heavily, her body flooding with adrenaline. She rushed down to the private dock jetting out over the water. She frantically looked in every direction, hoping to see her mother.

"Mom!" Abby called out again, desperation in her voice. *Am I just imagining this? Have I fallen asleep?* She reached down and pinched herself.

"Abby, what's going on?" Wendy said.

Abby turned to see her Aunt Wendy standing at the front door, a scowl of concern on her face.

This isn't a dream... Abby shook her head, "Nothing. Sorry, I woke you up," she said, feeling embarrassed. Her heart ached with raw grief. *Why can't this be a dream?*

"Were you calling out for Jessica?" Wendy asked as Abby approached the patio steps.

"I heard... I thought I heard her voice." Abby paused, looking back toward Puget Sound. "It was just someone that sounded like her. The sound must have traveled across the water," she said, trying to reassure her aunt.

Wendy looked out at the tranquil scene. "I've heard sound interacts strangely with water." She looked at Abby. "Are you sure you're okay?"

Abby conjured a weak smile in her best attempt to be convincing and simply said, "What else could it have been?"

A gust of wind carrying a wintry chill hit her back as she climbed the patio steps. Suddenly, the smell of freshly cut lilies filled the air. Abby felt dizzy. Her legs gave out from under her, and she folded over. She grabbed the rail to steady herself as she leaned over, uncertain if her knees would hold.

"Oh, my God!" Wendy said, rushing forward to help.

A blinding flash lit Abby's vision. She gasped. *What is happening?*

Images flashed through her mind. Her parents. Grandmother. Her old house. The dead, black eyes of Atoro Thanos. Blood dripping from a knife, Skulls. A strange symbol drawn in blood in her father's office. Blond hair floating in the water...

Abby screamed.

She fell backward and landed on something soft. Her breath flew out of her lungs, and everything went quiet.

When she opened her eyes, she was looking up at the night sky. The stars and moon glimmered above her. She just lay there, panting, trying to catch her breath.

"I'm fine," she said as she sat up slowly. There was no response. Abby looked around. She was alone."Wendy?" she called out.

She looked into the night, searching for a sign of her aunt, and found herself in the middle of a large lawn. Her uncles' house was gone, and in its place, an old, white Georgian Colonial stood.

Tears burst from her eyes as she recognized her old home; a phantom monument to a life that was no longer hers to live.

What am I doing here? Panic chased her thoughts away. Uncertainty and fear gripped her for a moment, only to be chased away by a spark of curiosity.

"I'm in the Sight," she said to no one. *It's never worked like this before. Dreams, but never… this. Why?*

Abby came to her feet, wiping the green grass off her nightgown and robe as she stared at the oak door a few yards away. It had been well over a year since she passed through the doors, let alone set eyes on them. *I suppose Fate has something to show me.*

She swallowed the pangs of grief that threatened to unsteady her and approached the front door cautiously.

Abby took a step into the house. Everything was the way she remembered it to be. The antique grandfather clock near the foot of the stairs ticked away as the brass pendulum swung back and forth. The same floorboards creaked when she stepped on them, and familiar family pictures hung on the wall. Not a thing was out of place. It looked exactly the same as it did on that day, the day when everything changed, the day she found her parents dead. Even the lilies on the round table sitting at the center of the entryway were freshly cut.

Abby caught herself holding her breath and forced herself to exhale. *What do you need me to See?* she silently questioned Fate.

She walked forward into the hall, toward the stairs to the second floor. As Abby reached the first step, she felt a peculiar tickle in her stomach. *Something is here...* A faint groan came from somewhere ahead. She paused. *Someone is in pain.* The urge to rush forward tugged at her senses.

Abby followed the pull, cautiously moving up the stairs. Every few steps, she paused, hoping to hear something more.

The air on the second floor was cold, with an eerie chill that numbed her to her bones. Something very powerful was pressing against her Sight. Abby paused and concentrated, doing her best to try and interpret what she was sensing.

Abby stood at the head of the long hallway that she used to play in as a child. She stopped, transfixed by the door to her father's office. The last time she had entered that room, her world had shattered. Abby was sure that if she went in there a second time, everything would change again. It didn't make sense, and she couldn't understand how, but...

Something is there. Abby felt an unseen force pressing against her Sight; a powerful presence, unlike anything she'd felt before. The weight of its power pushed against her arcane sense, hindering her steps. *Something in that room...*

Almost without her realizing she was moving, Abby put one foot in front of the other. She inched her way toward the doorway at the end of the hall.

The silence was overbearing. With each step, her nerves grew rawer. Her skin prickled with fear as she passed a doorway to her right. Abby watched carefully, certain someone would lunge out at any moment and attack her.

Another whimper came from beyond the doorway at the end of the hall. "Help!" It called. She moved faster, toward the door and the sound.

She paused, reaching for the doorknob. A creaking sound came from inside the room. She bit her lip and pushed the door open.

There was a sudden burst of air and Abby turned away, raising her arms to protect her face. As the wind faded away, Abby looked into the room. Two overstuffed leather chairs sat in front of an antique desk. On the wall behind it was the strange pentagram with a strange eye-like glyph in the center. She never knew why it was there, but it was the symbol Atoro Thanos had drawn with her parent's blood. She shuddered in revulsion. Everything was exactly as she'd left it.

Abby looked down at the cream-colored carpet beneath her feet. Two large rust-colored stains blemished the pristine fibers. A gasp that was half sob caught in her throat as the grief swelled beyond her emotional dam. Her knees buckled, and she collapsed on the floor next to the spot where her parents had died.

Abby closed her eyes and wept. She was here, again. It was just how she had left it. She still couldn't save them.

I can't keep doing this, she thought as she cradled her face in her hands, sobbing. Soft sounds began to drift through her awareness. So slowly and quietly at first that she wasn't sure what she was hearing. Cries of pain came from all around her, with no discernible source. Calls for help and terrifying moans of agony and suffering swarmed around her. It was as if dozens of voices were sharing her grief and adding their own.

Abby steadied herself against the wall. A new sound, more distinct from the cries, interrupted her thoughts.

It was a strange creaking sound like old boards shifted back and forth. *I need to see what it is I have been brought here to See.* Abby opened her eyes and turned her head to her left.

An old wooden rocking chair sat in the far corner of the room. It was crudely made and was worn and cracked from use. *This was never here before,* Abby thought, staring at the strange piece of furniture. As she watched, it slowly rocked back and forth, empty.

A shadow moved behind it, catching Abby's attention. She slowly approached the chair, peering through the gaps in the wood into the dark corner. An eye stared out at her.

Abby jumped back, startled. "Hello?" she asked it, questioning what she was seeing.

The eye stared at Abby with uncertainty.

Abby could see only a small portion of a child's face staring up at her curiously.

"Why are you here?" a little girl's voice asked from behind the chair.

"I don't know," Abby answered honestly.

"What's your name?" Tiny hands held the slats in the back of the chair as if they were prison bars.

"I'm Abby." She crouched down until her eyes were at the same level as the little girl. "Who are you?"

The little girl looked around, frantically searching for something. Eventually, she leaned forward until her small head was almost resting on the planks in front of her. "Lily," she whispered.

"Are you all right?" Abby asked, trying to seem less threatening.

Instead of an answer, the little girl simply nodded.

"Can you come out of there?" Abby asked, urging the girl forward.

Slowly, a small girl no more than eight years old emerged. She wore an old gray dress, and her hair was in pigtails. Her eyes were sunken deep into her skull as though she were sickly. Her skin looked as though it was stretched thin over her emaciated body. The little girl stood nervously, watching the door into the hall as though she were waiting for someone.

"Where did you come from?" Abby asked.

Lily stared up at her, her head tilted slightly as though she were confused. "I'm from right here," she said, as though it were obvious.

"Have you always been here?" Abby asked.

"I don't know," the little girl said, glancing over Abby's shoulder.

"What's out there?" Abby asked.

The little girl's eyes widened as she looked up at Abby. "You don't want to go there," Lily insisted. "I'm not supposed to talk about it." Lily shook her head.

"Who told you not to talk about it?" Abby questioned with concern.

Lily stood silent for a moment, she then looked in both directions and behind her again. "The bad lady," she said quietly. Another cry came from the far wall. "Are there other people in here with you? I keep hearing people crying..." Abby said. She searched for the source of the sound until she was staring directly at the symbol. It glowed in the darkness like a beacon.

Lily's eyes widened again. "Please don't, Ms. Abby," she pleaded, her big eyes welling with tears.

Abby reached out and placed her hand on the wall.

"No!" Lily shouted and rushed for the door. The little girl fled down the hall, disappearing into the darkness.

A single wail came through the wall. It drifted through the symbol as if it were an open window.

"Hello?" Abby asked, her voice uncertain.

The whimper stopped abruptly.

Abby took a step toward the symbol on the wall.

"Abby? Is that you?" A woman's voice called out.

"Mom!" Abby cried. She leaned forward, peering closer at the symbol on the wall. *It's her voice, I know it is!* Abby pounded and pounded against the wall, tears stained her cheeks. "Mom! Come back!"

There was no answer. Abby crumbled to the floor. Her hands were bruised and bleeding. *Why? She cursed at Fate's cruelty. Is this my torment? Am I going to be stuck in this forever? Why is the Sight making me relive this, over and over again?*

She screamed her frustration. The room all around her grew dark. All color faded into a dull gray. Tiny flakes of ash hovered in the air like a strange mist. Through the ashen fog, Abby saw the soft glow of the strange symbol. She leaned in. "Mom?" she called hopelessly.

There was only silence.

There has to be something. She reached along the wall, desperately looking for any sign of her mother. Abby's eyes rested again on the blood-painted symbol. She leaned in, peering closely. She stood there, staring for several heartbeats before she realized she was looking through a transparent hole in the very center. It was as if she was looking through the eye into another room.

Beyond was a dark room with old brick walls chipped with age and decaying mortar. It was no more than ten feet deep, and perhaps that far across with a crude cement floor. It looked like a cellar or prison chamber.

Two figures dangled from chains on the far wall. They were covered in filth, and their clothing was in tatters. The floor below them was stained with blood.

"I'm here!" Abby shouted desperately.

One of the people dangling from the wall moved slightly. She pounded against the unrelenting wall. Her fists struck the old plaster paneling, leaving a small dent. "Mom!" she cried in near panic. "Dad!"

The figure to the left moved again slightly. It was difficult to tell what color her long hair was under the grime and ash, but Abby was sure it was the same deep red as her own. The woman's head turned up slightly. One of her eyes was swollen completely shut.

"Mom!" she cried, trying to push her way through the wall. The hard surface held fast. "Mom!" she cried again. Abby pressed her hands to the wall, looking for some way to breach through to the other side.

Jessica Kane muttered something unintelligible. Abby stopped, hoping to hear her mother's words.

"Mom, please," Abby cried.

With barely any strength, Jessica looked up. Her face was streaked with fresh tears, and her expression full of pain and fear. "Run!" she cried and went limp, the effort taking all the strength she had.

Abby screamed, trying to break through the wall. With each pound of her fist, the glow flickered and grew brighter until the room was filled with intense light.

The door to the office slammed shut with a loud bang. Abby spun, startled. Around her, the ash fell in large flakes, and she could smell something burning. The room was colder than before, belying the smell of smoke.

She listened in the darkness and reached out with her Sight. There was a presence in the house, something powerful... horrifying. Malice, hatred, and disgust riddled every inch of her former home.

Abby scrambled to her feet, putting her back to the wall. She watched the door carefully, waiting. Any minute, something would burst through and reveal itself. She could hear her heart pounding as she held her breath.

She felt a presence, warm and familiar, standing next to her. Mom…

"Help us, Abby," her mother's voice whispered in her ear. Desperation and pain colored the words.

Abby turned, but her mother was not there. On the far side of the doorway, Abby could hear someone climbing the stairs. She stood frozen with uncertainty, listening to the footsteps in the hallway.

Thump… Thump… Thump… They moved closer, one slow step at a time.

Bambambam!

A loud pounding sound against the door. She watched the wood buckle slightly from the force of the blows.

"Help us, Abby!" her mother's desperate voice called out again.

A menacing cackle came from the other side of the door. Abby had heard that laugh before.

"What are you?" Abby yelled. "What do you want?!"

Her words only incited the laughter into a more frenzied horrific crowing.

All at once, the pounding stopped. In the silence, the door opened.

The light from the occult symbol illuminated a few feet down the hallway, casting shadows all around the figure before her. It stood motionless, staring at her. Dark robes draped over its frail form. It appeared as a statue hidden in the darkness.

Menace radiated off the shade, bombarding Abby's senses. Cries for help and for mercy drifted down the hallway from beyond the figure. The anguished screams grew louder and louder until Abby couldn't shut them out.

Abby took a step back. "Who are you?" Her voice faltered as she spoke.

She stumbled over something and fell backward, catching herself on the wall. She tried to take another step but was stopped by something on her shoulder. Abby looked over.

In a blink, the spirit was behind her. A sickly, gray hand reached out, the knuckles bent and curled. The familiar menacing cackle rang into her ear as she felt a cold sickly breath against the back of her neck. Fingers with nails that were jagged and chipped into sharp points wrapped around Abby's shoulder.

Abby pulled away and turned to face the malevolent spirit. She saw two black wells staring back at her. She could not pull her gaze away from its eyes. The empty pools became larger and larger, growing until they could barely fit in the otherworldly face. Abby was being pulled her into the nothingness.

She tried to look away, but the endless darkness pulled her closer and closer. The eyes grew until the darkness was all around her. In her. Abby fell into the shadowy gaze as if the world around her had disappeared.

There was nothing.

"No!" Abby screamed in defiance.

She closed her eyes, concentrating. *I have to get out of the Sight!* She began to breathe and focus...

The evil laughter surrounded her.

Concentrate...

"Help us!" the words echoed from the wall behind her. "Abby, please save us!"

Concentrate...

Silence.

She opened her eyes. A pair of bright blue eyes stared at her, worriedly. Abby stared up at the face framed by night sky. Colors, sounds, fresh air... *I'm back.* She breathed in, but it only came out as a frightened and strangled gasp.

"Abby? What happened?" Wendy demanded.

"Something is wrong." Abby managed to force the words from her dry throat. "Mom and Dad need help."

CHAPTER EIGHT

"Why don't you lay off a bit," Sebastian said in an angry whisper. Abby began to stir at the voices.

"What do you mean by that?" Vivian questioned. Abby could hear the clink of ice cubes dropping into a crystal glass then the sound of liquid being poured.

"I just mean, something is going on, and the last thing we need is our coven's Matriarch completely sloshed," Sebastian growled.

"Oh, Darling, I know how to handle my liquor," Vivian snapped back. "Frankly, it's the only reason I tolerate half the people in this Coven." The sound of ice clinked in her glass as she took a rather generous gulp.

Abby's eyes began to flutter open. The lights were mercifully dim.

"How long do you think she'll be out?" Sebastian asked in a hushed tone. "It's been almost a day."

"I don't know Darling, but Margot assured us she will be fine," Vivian said.

"Vivian, Margot admitted she was only speculating. She told me she isn't as much of an expert on such things as you like to pretend she is," Sebastian insisted.

"Believe me, Darling, when it comes to my grand-daughter, I don't take any chances that could put her at risk." Vivian leaned down and gave Abby a peck on the forehead before finishing off the last of her drink.

"What do you suppose she saw?" Sebastian asked.

"Why don't we ask her," Vivian said. "She seems to be waking up."

"How..." Sebastian stopped before finishing his question. "Abby?"

Abby attempted to sit up but fell back against the pillows. Her body felt like a useless heap; her strength was completely drained. She tried to move her hand to her stomach, but only grew exhausted from the effort. She let her hand fall and raised her head slightly to look at her grandmother.

"Darling, what happened to you?" Vivian asked, moving to the side of her bed and brushing away the stray hairs in Abby's face. "Did you overexert yourself using your special gift?"

Abby started to shake her head and stopped when the pain hit her. "I wasn't using it. At least, not on purpose. It... came over me. Uncalled."

Vivian sat on the black leather couch in the living room, looking concerned. "Are you certain it wasn't a dream, Darling?"

"I was there, Vivian," Wendy confirmed.

Vivian gave Wendy a blistering look. "Perhaps you didn't realize it, but I was addressing my granddaughter," she snapped.

"Can we please not fight," Abby said, rubbing her forehead. "I'm still so tired."

"Sorry," Wendy said. Vivian glared but said nothing.

"It doesn't sound like a dream," Rodger said, getting back to the original topic.

"No, I was able to consciously pull myself from the Sight," Abby stated.

Sebastian looked worried. "What do you suppose it means? Jessica and Evan are in some kind of trouble?"

Abby shook her head. She tried her best to remember the glowing symbol, her parents' captivity in some kind of ghostly prison, the little girl, and the old twisted hand. A tear escaped the corner of her eye.

"They're trapped," Abby managed to utter. Her voice was so weak both Vivian and Sebastian had to move in closer to hear.

"Trapped?" Sebastian leaned in. "You're parents? But how?"

"I don't know," Abby said. She sobbed, choking on the tears she didn't shed the night before. She steeled herself and told them everything the Sight had shown her.

"I can't get Mom's cry for help out of my thoughts," Abby said quietly. It was taking all her remaining energy to hold herself out of her emotional sinkhole. It would be far too easy for her to slip back into it.

"What is happening?" Wendy questioned in disbelief.

Vivian sat quietly, staring off into the distance, as though she was following a thought that had taken her on a great journey.

Abby shook her head. "I don't know. They're already dead. I don't know what could possibly be wrong." She was uncertain of what to say. She still couldn't believe everything she had Seen and heard. The image of her mother and father dangling from the wall, beaten and suffering...

Her mother's voice rang in the head, over and over, *'Help us, Abby!'*

"Did you hear anything from your father?" Rodger asked.

"No," Abby said.

"You should never forget who your enemies are," Vivian said, breaking her weighted silence.

"What do you mean?" Wendy asked.

Vivian pursed her lips. A displeased look spread across her face. "You know what the Thanos did. What they are," she spat. She pierced Abby with a gaze that looked right into her soul.

"Necromancers... death magic..." Abby muttered as random thoughts began to link together. Slowly, a terrifying picture began to form in her her mind. "The Thanos... They–are they tormenting my parents?"

Abby was barely able to speak as the emotional deluge swept her away with grief.

"Do you think that is what's happening?" Sebastian asked, looking at Vivian. "Could this be a Thanos trap?"

The older woman shifted uneasily in her seat. "They are treacherous and loathsome fiends. The Thanos are capable of far worse," she said, obviously irritated.

"The Thanos!" Sebastian growled. "How is this possible?"

"Do the Thanos have the Sight?" Abby asked.

"No, Darling, of course not," Vivian said with a quizzical look on her face.

"Then unless they have mastered a way to manipulate the Sight, what I saw was not a lure for some trap," Abby explained. "I know what I Saw was real. Fate was trying to show me something." She watched as Vivian's resolve melted away.

The older woman stood abruptly and began pacing. "I should have seen this coming. I was a fool to think they would submit honorably."

"Why, after all this time?" Rodger asked. "Why are they trying to get Abby's attention now? It's been over a year."

"It's November first," Abby said. "All Souls Day."

"Is this because of the ritual we cast last night?" Rodger asked.

"No, it's because today is the day when the veil between the dead and the living is the thinnest," Sebastian said.

"I thought that was a myth," Rodger muttered.

The room fell quiet as everyone explored their own thoughts. Vivian stood and walked to the window, her mind wandering a million miles away. "The Thanos have cursed them into some kind of torment," she said quietly.

Hearing it spoken out loud sapped what little strength Abby left. Her remaining resolve was stolen by the reality she couldn't deny. She reeled, curling into a ball, and began sobbing into her pillow.

Through her unchecked tears, she realized someone had placed a hand on her back. She turned her head slightly. Sebastian sat next to her, gently stroking her neck and shoulders. Her wracking sobs continued until she was gasping for breath.

"There now, Abby. It's okay. Shhh. Everything is all right..." he said soothingly.

"No! It... isn't!" she screamed between gasps.

"You're right, it isn't. But you need to calm down."

"Here. Darling, take this," Vivian approached with a glass of water and two blue pills in the palm of her hand.

"Vivian, really?" Sebastian questioned angrily.

"Darling, it's just Diazepam. Can't you see she's having an anxiety attack?" Vivian shoved the pills in Abby's mouth before she could object, and put the glass of water to her lips.

"You keep Diazepam in your purse?" Sebastian asked.

"Oh, please," Vivian said, rolling her eyes at the man's pointless question. "Come on, Darling, this will make it feel all better. You need to rest. You have been through a great deal."

Abby swallowed. If the pills will end this horror, I'll take them, she decided. She could feel them sliding down her throat.

Abby looked at her grandmother, standing as still as a statue. Her hands were laced together with her chin resting on the points of her two index fingers. She looked like she was in some kind of trance, or deep in concentration.

Slowly, Abby's heart and mind calmed enough that she could think again. "Grandmother?" she asked softly.

Vivian blinked, snapping back to herself. She looked down at Abby with concern in her eyes.

"Is there something wrong, Vivian?" Sebastian asked as he walked over to the older woman.

"No, I'm fine," she said, convincing no one. "Are you certain that is everything? Is there anything else you haven't told us?"

"I'm sure there's more, but I can't remem..." Abby let out an enormous yawn. Already she felt the pull of fatigue. The emotions drained whatever she had left, and the pills were already starting to kick in.

"I'm going to the house tonight," Abby blurted out impulsively. Her grandmother stopped abruptly and turned to face her, and the others gave Abby a curious look.

"What do you mean, Darling?" Vivian looked genuinely alarmed.

"I'm going to my old house tonight," Abby repeated. "There is something about that symbol on the wall, I don't know what it means, but that is the source of where I heard my mother calling out for help. I'm going to try and learn what I can." She leaned back, resting her head.

"You will be doing nothing until tomorrow, Darling," Vivian told her as sleep fumbled at the edges of her consciousness.

"Vivian, are you certain that is wise?" Abby heard Sebastian ask. "We have no idea what kind of curses or guardian spirits the Thanos might have placed there. It could be incredibly dangerous."

"She shouldn't go alone," Vivian said. "I will go with her."

"Thank you," Abby smiled, half asleep.

Vivian sighed. "Though I don't know what you hope to gain by doing this."

"Answers," Abby said. "Hopefully...answers." She yawned. "Thank you, Grandma."

A peculiar look passed over Vivian's face, as though she was called something unfamiliar and was uncertain if she should take it as a compliment or an insult. "Rest, Darling. I will see to this. You needn't worry," Vivian reassured.

"But–," Abby said in protest before she was cut off.

"Shush, Darling," Vivian said, pulling the covers up around Abby's shoulders.

Abby closed her eyes, giving herself over to the lull of sleep.

"Vivian, we need to find answers," Sebastian insisted.

"I know," Vivian said, uncertainly. "I'll see you tomorrow," she added, excusing herself and escaping through the front door.

Abby's stomach was in knots as she stood in front of her old home. Though she had visited through the Sight only the night before, it was the first time she physically set foot at this house since the day her parents died.

She glanced behind to see both her grandmother and her uncle Sebastian giving her a reassuring look.

It was a strange feeling entering a place once so familiar. Now it was nothing but a hollow shell full of old memories. The furniture was gone, and a musty smell permeated the entryway. The floor creaked as Abby stepped onto the polished hardwood.

"Do you sense anything yet?" Sebastian asked as he followed her into the house.

"Not yet," Abby responded, taking a deep breath to calm her nerves. "It will be in Dad's office."

They made their way to the second-floor room that Abby had visited in the Sight the night before. Light from the windows shinned down the hall, illuminating the clean wood flooring. Though unlived in, it was neat and tidy.

They paused in front of the door. Abby took a deep breath and readied herself for whatever might be on the other side.

"Darling, are you certain you're up to this?" Vivian asked, a note of uncertainty in her voice. "We could bring in some kind of specialist," she added.

"What specialist?" Sebastian asked. "If we knew of anyone trained in the Sight, wouldn't we have brought them in to teach her how to use it?"

"I don't know," Vivian snapped.

Abby looked at her grandmother. Vivian's gaze was transfixed on the office door. *Does she see something? How could she? She doesn't have the Sight...*

Abby shook her thoughts away and cleared her mind, allowing the Sight to open slowly. There it was again, the pain, the sorrow, the agony... It was just as intense as she remembered. Abby did her best to push through and concentrated on what she was sensing through her supernatural sight.

She opened the Sight slightly more and pushed the door open. Cries for help overwhelmed her. *There are so many of them!* Abby steadied herself against the wall. She tried to push through her fatigue. Abby sifted through the cries of horror and pain coming from her father's office, searching for a familiar voice. *There are too many of them! What is happening here?*

A hand rested on her shoulder, and Abby closed the Sight. She involuntarily dropped to her knees, breathless.

"Let's take a break," Sebastian suggested. "I can tell this is taking a lot out of you," he added, exchanging a concerned look with Vivian.

"What did you See, Darling?" Vivian asked cautiously.

"Cries for help. Screaming, agonizing cries," Abby said. Even though the Sight was closed, the pleas still haunted her. "There are so many of them," she added, shivering. A drop of moisture dripped from her forehead. She wiped her forehead with her sleeve, and suddenly realized she had broken out in a cold sweat.

"Take a break, Abby," Sebastian suggested. "We'll look around a bit without your gift."

He reached out again and pushed the door open, and they followed him in. There was a blinding flash as the lights flickered on. Abby blinked. The room was empty. The furniture was gone, the walls freshly painted, and the blood-stained carpet had been torn up, leaving behind an unfinished floor.

"That is what we're here for," Abby said, pointing to the occult symbol on the wall.

"We looked into it right after your parent's death. I thought it was a warning, some kind of declaration of war," Vivian said. "But, we never found anything."

"Why is it still there?" Abby asked.

"I don't know," Vivian said, stepping into the room. "I told the contractors to sand it away and paint over it. In fact, I'm quite certain they did," she added. Her expressions of concern and curiosity seemed to be in a permanent battle for prominence.

"Well, it's back," Sebastian said.

"I don't like this one bit," Vivian said under her breath. She slowly approached the blood-stained symbol.

"Don't touch it," Abby warned.

Vivian gave her a scathing look. "I wasn't about to touch it, Darling. I'm scared, but I'm not a fool," she said. "It's a good thing we didn't sell this house as we discussed this last summer," she added as she studied the arcane symbol.

"Didn't you notice the symbol came back when you were considering the sale?" Sebastian asked.

"I didn't bother to come back to this room," Vivian said around a lump in her throat. "Frankly, I had never planned to set foot in this house again." She turned away from the others, facing the window.

"This is the epicenter," Abby said. "It isn't a coincidence; this is also where I saw Mom in my vision last night," she explained, pointing at the symbol again. "I met a spirit last night as well. She warned me not to come in here."

"A spirit? Truly?" Vivian asked in disbelief.

"Yes, of a little girl. She seemed very afraid."

"Maybe you shouldn't open the Sight here," Sebastian said, a troubled look on his face.

"I have to," Abby said, working up the nerve to do what she needed to do. "We have to understand what's happening if we're going to help them."

She turned to face the symbol on the wall. Even though it was a dull rusty brown, Abby couldn't forget how it was made, nor who had done it. She stood mesmerized for what felt like an eternity.

"Are you all right?" Sebastian asked, noticing her hesitation.

Abby nodded. She closed her eyes and began to concentrate, allowing the Sight to open slowly, ready to close it again at the first sign of danger. She felt almost weightless as her mind opened. A new awareness began to fill her thoughts.

Screams filled her mind. There were more than before, all calling for help and pleading for mercy. They grew louder and louder until Abby thought she'd never be able to hear anything else. She felt faint. As the cries grew, darkness licked at the edges of her senses. The last thing she remembered before she passed out was the echoing of a vicious cackle.

CHAPTER NINE

Abby rolled over and looked at the old-fashioned clock on the nightstand. *Seven... In the morning or evening? How long have I been sleeping?*

She carefully sat up in bed and gave herself a moment to find her bearings. The haze of sleep still muddled her brain. She stared at the closet door on the far side of the room until her eyes focused. *Oh, it's my room.*

As she sat up, Abby felt light-headed and slowed her movement. She set her feet flat on the floor and lingered for a moment, uncertain if she could bear her own weight. She paused and took several deep breaths.

"You look like someone ran over you with a semi," Madison said from the doorway.

Abby jumped and instantly regretted it, grabbing her throbbing head. "I didn't see you there," she said, clicking on the lamp next to her bed. "Jesus." She winced and shielded her eyes. "How long have I been asleep?"

"Almost two days," Madison said, as she sat next to Abby on the bed. "Everyone has been worried about you."

"Two days?" Abby asked incredulously.

"Almost," Madison answered reassuringly., She wrapped her arm around Abby's shoulder. "Everyone is downstairs talking about... your parents."

"Who is everyone?" Abby asked.

"Aunt Vivian, Sebastian, Rodger, Wendy, my mom, and Grandma," Madison said with a pitiful look in her eyes.

"Grandmother says your mom knows a lot about this stuff," Abby said.

"They seem to think she does." Madison sighed.

"Has she dealt with something like this before?" Abby asked.

"I don't know. I asked her this morning, and she gave me a dirty look," Madison said. "So, I dropped it. She is pretty upset, that's all I know."

"I should go down there," Abby said. She tried to get up and collapsed down onto the bed.

"Yeah, maybe you should take it slow. There really isn't any rush."

"I don't want my parents to..." Abby's words were choked off by a sob. Hot, burning tears began to streak her face as she leaned into her cousin, who just held her.

"Sorry." She felt silly apologizing for her breakdown, but couldn't stop herself from saying it anyway.

Madison shook her head. "Don't apologize," she whispered, giving Abby a kiss on the forehead. "You were there for me when Dad died. We're family. It's what we do."

Abby nodded. "Thanks," she said, her voice beginning to regain its strength.

"Don't mention it," Madison said, giving her a squeeze.

Abby took in a deep breath and let it out slowly. "I have to pull it together. Mom and Dad need me," she said, trying to refocus.

"Now, there is the Abby I was waiting for." Madison smiled reassuringly. "We have a pretty messed up family, and we fight all the time, but somehow we seem to pull it together when we really need to, right?"

"Right," Abby agreed.

With Madison's help, Abby got out of bed. She wobbled a little, squinting her eyes against the light, but eventually made it to her feet.

"That spirit really put the whammy on you," Madison observed.

"What?" Abby asked. Then she remembered the sickly hand on her shoulder, being turned around, and being pulled into dark eyes that held an endless expanse of nothingness. Abby shivered, repulsed by the memory.

"It's all right. I'm here." Madison gave her a reassuring smile, and together, they made their way into the hall.

Abby took the first step cautiously but was more stable than she expected. The next one came easier, and before long, she found herself on the main floor.

To her left, Abby saw her family sitting in the sunken living room, speaking in hushed tones.

"I'm awake," Abby called out as Madison escorted her into the room.

"Darling," Vivian said, standing and sweeping Abby into a hug. Her gesture was a bit too dramatic to feel authentic, but Abby returned the hug. There was the faint, acrid scent of alcohol on her grandmother's breath, but Abby couldn't do more than notice.

"Come, Darling, have a seat," Vivian said. She took Abby's arm and escorted her to a vacant spot on the couch.

Margot's friendly smile greeted Abby as she sat. "I'm glad you're feeling well enough to get out of bed," she said.

"Abby is a lot tougher than she looks," Sebastian said. He wore a proud and somewhat relieved, grin.

"Hey kid, it's good to see you moving around," Wendy added.

"Do you need anything to drink? Eat?" Rodger asked, standing.

It wasn't until her uncle posed the question that Abby realized how parched and famished she was. She gave a simple nod, and Rodger disappeared into the kitchen.

"Have you been talking about Mom and Dad?" Abby asked, hoping someone might have answers. She quickly modulated her optimism, knowing it wouldn't do to get too excited. *What could they have learned in two days?*

She observed the carefully maintained neutral expressions on each of the faces looking at her and sighed.

"Dear, I can assure you this will be our number one priority, for the entire Coven," Fiona stated. Her words sounded guarded, but her grandmother's sister always tempered the truth with caution. "We have only just begun our investigation."

"Yes, Darling, focus on recovering," Vivian insisted.

At least she seems more sincere, Abby thought, and then shook the thought away. "What did happen to me?" she asked, looking at her cousin Margot.

"Can you describe to us what you Saw in your vision?" Margot asked.

Despite her hesitation, Abby recounted the sickly hand on her shoulder and the eyes that consumed her with darkness before blacking out.

"I can't be certain," Margot said. There was a lack of confidence in her voice.

Abby was nervous but kept listening.

"Sometimes particularly powerful spirits are able to manifest, even affect the world of the living," Margot continued. "I can only imagine the spirit placed you in some kind of miasma."

"Miasma?" Madison asked.

"Some spirits can manipulate the world of the dead. Abby must have entered that spiritual world through the Sight. I suspect it might have overwhelmed you with despair and grief," Margot speculated.

"They can do that?" Wendy asked.

"Yes." Margot nodded as she spoke. "In many ways, spirits and ghosts are manifestations of the most powerful of human emotions. That is why some linger instead of passing on. They are bound close to the veil that separates this world from theirs. Their strongest emotions–regret, fear, even anger–keep them between worlds."

Margot paused. "The more powerful spirits have learned to use this emotional energy to make themselves stronger. They sometimes feed off the emotions of the living. They can sense them. Sometimes they are even drawn to them."

"Considering what you experienced in there, Abby... it makes sense," Sebastian suggested gently.

With a weak nod, Abby agreed. "Is it doing this to my parents? Did the Thanos put whatever that thing is there to torment Mom and Dad?" she asked, barely able to hide the desperation she had for answers.

"I can't say with any certainty," Margot conceded. "But it's possible."

"It would seem unlikely a random spirit would target Evan and Jessica," Vivian said.

There was a coldness in her voice Abby hadn't heard for a long time.

"The Thanos put that spirit there, I'm certain of it."

"That may be so," Fiona stated calmly. "But I do not believe they will provide us with answers or assistance. Starting a war with them again at a time like this would be unwise. Especially since we cannot be certain, they are involved. This family has more than one enemy, Dear Sister."

Vivian gave Fiona a displeased look. She then softened and raised an eyebrow. "Perhaps," she conceded.

I wish she would talk to me about what she's going through. We could help one another, Abby thought as she saw the struggle in her grandmother's eyes. *But she won't.*

"How do you know so much about this?" Abby asked. "I thought you were all about weather magic and astrology."

Margot looked uneasy. "I don't really know all that much really, just a little."

Abby could tell it wasn't something to press, at least not right now. "There is something about that symbol on the wall,' Abby said, her thoughts returning to her parents. "Didn't you say you had it sanded away and painted over when we cleaned out the house?" she asked, turning to her grandmother.

"Yes, Darling," Vivian said, somewhat distracted. "Nearly a year ago," she added as she shifted her focus back into the moment.

"It came back," Abby stated. "It must mean something. My parents. I'm sure I saw them through the center of the pentagram," she added.

The room fell silent as the truth weighed on everyone.

"I wasn't going to mention this," Fiona stated, breaking the silence. "Perhaps we should consider seeing what we have in the vaults. The necromancer's artifacts are still in there."

"What artifacts?" Madison asked.

"Are you talking about the artifacts we took from the Thanos?" Margot asked.

"Yes, of course," Fiona stated. The intense gaze she aimed at her sister, persisted.

"I remember you telling me about them last year when I was at school," Abby said. "When we were talking about what started the war between the Kanes and the Thanos in the first place. You said we refused to return them, and they have been trying to get them back for centuries."

"Those would be the ones. Yes," Fiona confirmed.

"Can we use them somehow to help us?" Abby asked.

The two elder sisters shared another look. Vivian's expression became suspiciously nonchalant. "Well, Darling, we could," she said. "I'm not certain we're quite that desperate, though."

"Desperate?" Abby shouted. "My parents are suffering, trapped in pain so terrible their souls reached out to me through the Sight. They asked for my help! If there is anything–anything these artifacts can do to free them, how could we ever not use them?" She tried to stand, her anger spurring her to her feet, but she fell back into the couch.

"Darling, please," Vivian protested. "You can't possibly understand the realities of death magic. Necromancy is a terrible arcane practice. Those artifacts are connected to powers none of us are suited to wield. By solving one crisis, we could create another one just as horrible, perhaps even worse."

"Nevertheless," Fiona countered before Abby could protest further. "A thorough investigation might be helpful. Such an avenue of research needn't require the actual use of the artifacts. We can look into their effects and purposes and determine if they are suitable. Then, and only then, we will use them if we can do so safely."

Abby had never heard her grandaunt sound more authoritative. The decisions and decrees for the Kane Coven were generally left to Vivian. Abby stared at the woman in surprise, listening to every word.

"Our family has spilled enough blood keeping those items out of the hands of death witches." Fiona continued, "If there is any possibility one might help, I feel it is at the very least an option that should be considered."

All around the room, people were nodding solemnly.

"I would be willing to help," Wendy offered.

"Out of the question," Vivian barked.

"Why?"

Vivian stood irritated. "I cannot possibly express to you how dangerous handling those artifacts can be. Certainly, no rank amateur will lay hands on them."

"I'm not an amateur," Wendy countered. "I've been studying witchcraft since I was eleven, just like the rest of you."

"No," Vivian said, resuming her place as Matriarch. "While Margot is researching whatever spirit is lurking in that house, you will be doing research on that symbol. I don't have the time to do it myself, and you seem to be good with books."

"Was that a compliment?" Wendy asked smugly.

Vivian scoffed and turned away from her.

"I do," Fiona stated into the awkward silence.

"Mother?" Margot questioned.

"I am just as experienced as you, Vivian," Fiona said. "And few people have more respect than I do for the dangers of dabbling in necromancy. I want to do my part for Evan and Jessica."

"I have some pretty good ideas where I can start my research," Margot said. "This will be my primary focus, Abby. Evan and I grew up together. This is important to me, too."

Abby smiled, feeling the warmth of her cousin's words. She knew her parents were important to them, but it was easy to forget. She blinked away the tears and instead just answered, "Thank you."

"We're all going to help," Sebastian reassured her.

"We aren't going to stop until it's resolved," Wendy added.

"But first you need to eat something," Rodger said, returning to the living room with a plate of food and a large glass of juice which he placed it in front of Abby.

"Eat, and rest, Abby. We will figure this all out," Sebastian said.

CHAPTER TEN

My fingering is off… I'm rushing… Abby reminded herself to breathe as she continued playing through the piece.

"Ugh! I'm sorry," she said, pausing and repeating a phrase she had just botched.

I sound terrible! she thought, rushing through the last few measures. She carefully lowered her instrument.

"I'm sorry. I'm really off today," she said, looking at Irene apologetically.

The other woman nodded, a compassionate smile shining in her dark eyes. "It's all right. Every performer that ever was and ever will be has been known to have an off day from time to time," she said, gathering the sheet music from the piano.

"Shouldn't we practice some more?" Abby asked, worried her accompanist was giving up on her.

Irene placed her music on a shelf next to her and smiled, shaking her head. "Your heart isn't in it today. Sometimes it's best to just let it go and start fresh another day. I'm going to go make us some tea, and we can chat for a while." She excused herself and disappeared through the dining room.

I must have been even worse than I thought, Abby thought. *She's right, I guess.* It wasn't a lie that her heart was elsewhere. Thoughts of her family hadn't abated at all in the week since her vision.

"No, not now," she whispered, quickly blinking away her tears.

Abby strolled over to one of the many bookcases that lined the wall next to the piano. She casually glanced at the titles, trying to distract herself. "*The History of Melodic Chant*," she read. She grabbed the book and flipped to a random page. "The simplest chants form from the intoning of…"

Abby! Help us! … her mother's cry pushed out the words in front of her.

Stop it! She fought back. "Gregorian chant originated in the first century…"

Help us, Abby! The memory of her mother chained to the wall blocked out all other images. Try as she might, Abby could not make herself focus on the page. She sighed and put the book back in its place.

Ugh, I can't even read anymore… Maybe I should drop out of this performance, she thought as she looked helplessly around the room. *How can I possibly do this when I need to be helping my parents?*

"Tea," Irene sang out melodically. The older woman entered the room, carrying a silver tea set on a sterling tray. She looked at Abby and pursed her lips. "Do you want to talk about it?" She set the tea service down on the coffee table.

"Talk about what?" Abby asked innocently.

"Whatever it is that's making your eyes red, and your concentration disappear?" Irene answered in the same tone. She carefully poured Abby a cup of tea in a bone china cup and placed it on a saucer before handing it over.

Abby examined the small plate with pink roses painted on the sides and along the edges. "Ah…" she said and took a seat on the couch next to Irene.

"Do you take cream or sugar?" Irene asked politely.

"Neither, thank you," Abby said, accepting the offered cup. She brought the tea to her lips and took the tiniest of sips. The warm, aromatic flavors danced across her palette.

Suddenly the world felt a bit lighter and less grim. "This is very good. Thank you."

"There is nothing like a good cup of tea to soothe the nerves," Irene commented as she prepared her own cup.

"I'm very sorry about today," Abby said apologetically. "I know my playing was a mess."

"You really don't need to apologize, Abby." Irene reassured her. "Like I said before, distraction isn't anything to be ashamed of. Life happens to all of us. Whatever it is that's causing you to be there instead of here when you're playing.... Well, it happens to the very best." Irene said.

"I'mgoingtogohomelaterandpracticehard,"Abbysaid. "I know I can do better."

"I know you can, too," Irene said confidently. "But practice isn't going to help you. You truly have a gift, Abby. Mr. Schreiner saw it, and I've seen it right here in my living room. I've heard you play this piece before. You nail it almost every time. It's the kind of gift people like me wish we had and are only lucky enough to encounter once or twice in our lifetime."

Abby could feel the tears lingering on the edge of her perception, and she did her best to hold them at bay. "I don't know what to say. I don't think anyone has ever paid me a compliment quite like that before," she admitted.

"I mean it," Irene said and took another sip. "I suspect whatever it is that is bothering you, isn't going to go away on its own. So, if you want to tell me, I am here to listen."

The older woman's expression was sincere. Abby wanted to tell her, she wanted to break down and spill every fear and every worry that was racing through her head. Her emotions were stampeding in an endlessly maddening circle of doubt and frustration. She wanted someone to talk to. Someone who would listen to her talk about what she's been through. Her parents, the Thanos, even everything that had happened last spring...

There were no solutions. Talking wouldn't solve any of her problems. *I can't tell the truth to just anyone,* Abby realized. *Not the real truth. I would need a... a witch therapist.*

"I've been thinking about my parents a lot lately," she eventually said. "They died a little over a year ago, and I haven't really been dealing with it well." *At least it's a morsel of truth.*

Irene took a deep breath and nodded. "Grief can be a hard thing to process," she said reverently. "I understand how hard this must be for you. I'm very sorry for your loss."

"Thank you," Abby replied. A single tear broke through her resolve and ran down her cheek. "It's all coming up again. It's like I just lost them and now..."

"You just moved back from overseas, right? I imagine it's hard being back home when they're not around."

Abby nodded lamely.

"Of course," Irene added, sympathy coloring her voice. "The holidays are coming up too. It's always a difficult time when we have lost someone. Their absence can be felt more prominently."

Thank God she made that assumption, Abby thought. Emotions pressed against her defenses with such force she was certain her walls would breach. *Although she's not precisely wrong...* "It doesn't feel like it's getting any easier," she managed to utter.

"I don't know that it really does," Irene said, shaking her head. Her own kind expression had melted away into something far more somber. "Grief isn't something we 'get over.' All we can do is find our focus again and learn how to live without the ones we lost. But the pain... that doesn't ever really leave. Over time it might be less obvious, and maybe the time between melancholia grows longer, but the pain will always be there. It's part of loving."

Abby was afraid to speak. Irene's words felt formulaic, but at the same time, it was as if she spoke directly to Abby's pain.

"It's all right to grieve Abby," Irene said. "It's all right to have your breakdowns and let the tears go."

"Sometimes, I'm afraid if I let go, it's never going to stop," Abby confessed, tears beginning to push through.

"I know that feeling, all too well," Irene confessed, handing Abby a tissue. She leaned back and took another sip of tea. "How is the rest of your family doing?"

Abby took a deep breath, clamping down on her wild emotions. She allowed herself another sip of tea, her agitation settling slightly. "Not particularly well," she said evenly. "My grandmother will barely speak about it, and she drinks almost all the time. She thinks she's hiding it during the day, but I can smell it on her."

"I see," Irene acknowledged. "Alcohol can be a great anesthetizer of unwanted feelings. Drinking, unfortunately, comes with its own set of problems."

"I know," Abby said, doing her best to temper the bitter resentment she wanted to ignore. *I should be focusing on my parents and the Thanos, not Grandmother,* she thought. She was annoyed at the unimportant emotions that kept rising to the surface. She had more important things to worry about, why was she still thinking about it?

"A nice, long, hot shower," Irene said with a grin.

The unexpected comment snapped her back to the conversation. "What about them?" Abby wondered.

"It was the place I felt most comfortable, allowing myself to have a breakdown. The tears disappear down the drain, and no one knows they were ever there. I always imagine the water washing away all the emotions I don't want to feel. It helps… at least for a time," Irene explained.

"That… actually, it isn't the worst idea I've heard." Abby smiled. "Thank you. I might give that a try."

"Please do," Irene said. "It's best not to ignore it, Abby. Whatever it is. Let yourself have the freedom to feel whatever it is that you're feeling. Give yourself at least a moment and move through it. You'll find that the other side of the tunnel really does exist."

"You're right. I know you're right," Abby said. "I don't know why I fight against it so much."

"Because it's uncomfortable to sit in the pain," Irene said. "But it passes, just like everything else. Your pain isn't permanent, either."

"Thanks," Abby said sincerely. "It feels good to have someone to talk to about it. It's hard to talk to my family sometimes."

"I understand," Irene said. "Sometimes it's nice to have someone who isn't connected to any of it to talk to. You can talk to me any time you need."

Abby chuckled, seizing on a hint of humor to lighten the moment. "You might regret making that offer," she said, as she sipped her tea.

Irene's face brightened when she smiled. "I doubt it," she smiled. "I mean it, I don't mind at all. If nothing else, my teapot is always full."

"How are you feeling?" Sebastian asked as they leaned against the deck rail and gazed out over the crystal-blue water of Puget Sound. The deep horns blasted as the ferry launched from the dock.

Abby paused, unsure of how to answer. "Fine," she eventually replied. She wasn't even convinced by her tone.

"Abby, you don't have to be strong for me," her uncle said. His sincerity was heart-warming, but his timing was terrible. There was no way she was going to let herself fall apart on the ferry.

"I'm doing as well as can be expected," she said, hoping her revised response would appease his concern.

Sebastian wrapped his arm around Abby as she stared out across the water. A crisp autumn breeze rustled her hair. She gazed upon the dark evergreen trees that carpeted the hillsides behind them as they departed Bainbridge.

"I know you are, Abby," Sebastian reassured with a squeeze. "but Rodger and I are a little worried."

"Am I that bad?" Abby asked. *Do they see something I don't?* she wondered. *Am I not even doing as well as I think I am?*

"You've lost a little weight, and frankly, you never had much to lose in the first place. Especially after last year. Rodger says you barely touch your food at dinner. You're waking up screaming almost every night again, and I can tell that..." He trailed off, carefully choosing his words. "I know you are having a hard time with this. Hell, all of us are struggling. But it's because of that, that the one thing you can't do is let yourself go. Abby, you need your strength. When the time comes, we will need you to be there when we break whatever curse is holding Evan and Jessica...where they are," he finished half-heartedly.

Abby sighed, mulling over what he was trying to tell her. *He's one of the few people I can actually trust. If I don't listen to him, then...*

"You're right," Abby said, searching for the resolve she needed. "I need to be strong. There is no telling what that horror was I encountered through the Sight. And... wallowing isn't helping."

"Hopefully, we'll have answers, and soon," Sebastian said. "Margot, Fiona, and Vivian have been working tirelessly for the last few days."

"Do you think that's what this meeting is about?" Abby asked. She'd only ever been to the main headquarters of Kane Industries a few times when she was younger.

She was surprised when the call came from Margot to meet everyone there.

"I'm not sure," Sebastian replied. "I hope so. I want answers as badly as you do."

"Do you think it would help if I used my Sight again?" she asked. "If I–"

"Abby, no! You can't risk that." The alarmed look on his face cut her off before she could finish.

"If I practice more," she continued. "I might be able to learn something that can help us and protect myself."

Sebastian looked unsure.

"I need to master the Sight in order to be more useful. Sometimes I feel like it uses me."

He sighed. "I'm no expert, but I have read up on it a bit. My mother had it after all–as did yours. Though I've never seen it as strong as your gift. It runs on our side of the family, but there just isn't a lot of information out there. Everything I've read would indicate the Sight is a powerful force of Fate. It is truly a rare thing for Fate to allow mere mortal insight," he said with a smile. "I believe I read something to the effect that the Sight cannot be controlled, but it can be tamed."

After a slight chuckle, Abby smiled and stared into the water, watching the wake of the ferry curl along the hull. "Well, that's certainly been my experience," she commented. "Hopefully, if I can tame it, I might be of some actual use to my parents."

"Abby," Sebastian scoffed. "We wouldn't even know there was a problem if it wasn't for you. Just because you don't know what to do next doesn't mean you can't be useful. You've already proven that you can control the Sight better than you could last year. There's still time. The beauty of having a coven is that you have many people who can help. We can't all know everything, and we watch out for one another."

"Are all covens family as well?" Abby asked curiously. It seemed to be the case, but she was still learning so much.

"No," Sebastian responded, apparently relieved to change the subject. "There are more than a few covens who are just like-minded people that band together. Most are probably solitary practitioners. Some simply leave their family coven for various reasons, more often than not over disagreements."

"Family isn't always easy to deal with," Abby said. She nodded as her thoughts wandered off.

"No, they are not," Sebastian agreed. "But, at the same time, they can be an incredible thing when you need them. Your grandmother isn't the easiest person in the world to deal with, but I would never doubt she loves you, and you know there isn't anything we wouldn't do for you."

"Don't worry," Abby said reassuringly. "I'm still part of this family. And if Grandmother has her way, I will be replacing her as the Matriarch someday. Whatever that means."

"It's not as terrible as it sounds, Abby," Sebastian said. "Despite Vivian's best efforts to convince everyone otherwise, she does still answer to the Coven. She has a great deal of power and influence among our kind, but that doesn't mean the Coven is hers to do with as she pleases."

"Oh?" Abby asked. "I guess I've never really understood how the hierarchy works."

"It's not so different from any family. Perhaps a bit more... feudal." He chuckled, looking at her fondly. "Well this will be your first official meeting with the Coven, I suspect it won't take you long to figure out how things work. You'll see firsthand how everyone works together."

Abby chewed her lip, thinking. *Works together? Like we're doing now?*

"We've been very lucky to have your Grandaunt Fiona," he said. "She knows how to handle Vivian, and has been instrumental in keeping her from going too far from time to time."

"They have an odd relationship," Abby observed. "They seem close, but there's a lot of tension between them. Sometimes I forget that they're sisters."

"Yes, well, you know your grandmother," Sebastian jested. "You and I have only been dealing with her for a few years. Fiona has been dealing with her for well over a half a century."

"I guess you're right," Abby conceded. "I can't imagine having to deal with Grandmother for that long."

"You'd be surprised how far loyalty will take you," Sebastian said. A worried look flashed across his face.

"Oh, don't worry. I don't have any plans to leave the Kane Coven. Grandmother would have to go completely off the deep end before I would even consider it." She smiled reassuringly.

"Well, I don't think it would ever come to that, but someday…"

She looked at the concern in his eyes and paused. "'Someday' what?"

He took her hand gently and looked her in the eye. Some day you may want to marry, and that's never a simple task."

"What do you mean?"

"Politics, of course. When two witches marry, it isn't as simple as going down to City Hall and signing a few papers. There are negotiations and trades on both sides. Rodger had to leave his coven to marry me. That was a difficult decision for him to make. Some day you might have to make a similar choice."

Abby laughed. "That doesn't seem too likely at the current moment."

"Don't scoff, Abby. Politics are fundamental to the Kane Coven. Even where there's love, negotiations and trades will happen. My marriage to Rodger was little more than an excuse for Vivian to form a political alliance with the Penningtons."

Abby shook her head. "She's been married five times, are you telling me all of those were political marriages?"

Sebastian smiled wryly. "I'm saying that each of those marriages supported the Kane holdings, not just Vivian's love life."

"Sometimes, I try really hard not to hate her." Abby turned to look out over the water, lost in thought. She knew her grandmother was not above anything that would help her reach her goals, but the idea of a political marriage seemed wrong somehow.

"I suspect she truly loved your Grandpa Talbot," Sebastian said absently, staring out at the water along with her.

"Grandfather?" Abby shook her head. "The last I heard from him was when he sent a wreath to Dad and Mom's funeral. How much love could there have been in that marriage? He didn't even attend his own son's wake." A few bitter tears seeped from the corners of her eyes. She blinked them away, letting the wind dry them. "If Grandmother is to be believed, he spends his life sailing between Monte Carlo and Atlantic City, playing cards and chasing skirts. I've only met him in person twice in my entire life. I'm not certain I could pick him out of a crowd if I saw him on the street," she said with a touch of remorse.

"I know Vivian is prone to exaggeration, but... I don't know..." Sebastian said. He was obviously trying to find a way to give it a positive spin, and Abby appreciated his efforts.

"It's all right. I don't want to force someone to be a part of my life if that isn't what they want," Abby said, sounding more cheerful than she felt. "Besides, it couldn't possibly be easy to come around your ex-wife when she happens to be Vivian Kane," she said with a touch of sardonic humor. "Political marriage or not."

Sebastian let out a chuckle. "You, my dear, are correct."

Abby watched the shore growing closer. "They will be announcing our approach any moment," she said. "Shall we head back to the car?"

"We probably should," Sebastian agreed. "We can't keep the Kanes waiting."

CHAPTER ELEVEN

Sebastian drove up the hill onto Fourth Avenue. It came into view as they crested the hill. Unlike its more modern neighbors, Kane Tower was an older building with small windows breaking through the granite facade. The building jutted into the sky, with the highest floors becoming increasingly smaller, like a miniature version of the Chrysler Building in New York.

Though Abby had been here before, she had spent very little time at the corporate headquarters of her family's business. There was never any reason. She remembered going there with her mother as a little girl. The would surprise her dad at work, but she had been too young then. She never paid attention to the business that was happening around her. This was already very different from that time.

The car descended into a dark underground parking garage. Fluorescent lights flickered intermittently, casting deeper shadows than they dispelled. Sebastian drove past several concrete-reinforced walls separating the garage into small bays that each held a dozen or so vehicles. They navigated smoothly to a back corner near an elevator and pulled into a reserved space with a sign that read 'Sebastian Whitlock.'

"Come here often?" Abby quipped.

"Probably not as much as I should," her uncle replied.

A short elevator ride took them to the top floor where they were greeted by a sharply-dressed woman waiting for them behind a solid oak desk. "Mr. Whitlock, Miss Kane," the woman said warmly. Abby had seen her years ago, but she couldn't remember the woman's name. "Everyone is waiting in the boardroom."

The two of them walked along the hallway to the front of the building, heading for the main boardroom. The halls were lined with portraits of her ancestors–former CEOs, Presidents, and past board members of Kane Industries. They made it about halfway down the hall when Abby froze.

A lamp shone on an old calotype photograph of a man in his late sixties, dressed in an old-fashioned business suit. It was the first in the series of portraits to be a photo instead of a painting, and Abby guessed it had to be at least 150 years old. It wasn't the age of the image that had her transfixed though, it was the man in the picture. *I know him... I think... isn't this the ghost I saw at the Underground tour?* Abby wasn't sure if she remembered it wrong.

She searched around the picture for a name. A small brass plaque on the frame read, 'Marcus Kane CEO 1863-1889.' She looked up and stared at his eyes. The way he held himself and the suit he wore was hauntingly similar. *But why would my ancestor be in the underground ruins?* she thought.

"Is something wrong?" Sebastian asked, noticing Abby had fallen behind.

She hesitated for a moment. "No, I don't think so," Abby said. She then picked up her pace and caught up with her uncle, shaking off the unsettling feeling.

Sebastian stood at the double doors at the end of the hallway, waiting for her. When she caught up to him, he knocked twice and walked in. They entered a simple meeting room that would have been unspectacular, except for the near-perfect view of Elliott Bay, forty stories below.

Several members of the Coven were gathered around a large mahogany table, waiting for the others to arrive.

Rodger and Wendy were already seated and engaged in a quiet conversation, while Margot flipped through some papers. Cousin Gisela stood impatiently by the window and turned to glare at them as they entered the room. Vivian's face brightened when she saw Abby.

"Darling, please come in," Vivian said, standing and ushering Abby and Sebastian into the board room. The soft white fur around the cuffs and collar of her suit tickled Abby as she brushed past.

Sebastian quickly took his seat next to Rodger, while Abby sat near the center of the table with her grandmother.

"Hello Abby, I'm glad you're feeling better," Margot said shortly after Abby took her seat.

"Hi Margot," Abby said, trying to steady her nerves. Even though everyone in the room was family, this was a Coven meeting, the first one she had ever been invited to attend.

"You are coming for Thanksgiving dinner at my home, aren't you?" Margot asked.

"Of course, I can't imagine anywhere else I would rather be," Abby said, smiling.

"Must we endure the small talk much longer?" Gisela interjected, coming over to the table.

"It will just be another moment, Darlings, we are still waiting for–" Before Vivian could finish her sentence, a soft knock came at the door, as the last two people entered. "My dear siblings," she finished smoothly. Fiona and Bernard Kane came in and closed the door behind them.

Fiona stood straighter than Abby had seen in some time, though she still appeared worn out. Her wardrobe was still various layers of black, causing Abby to wonder if the older woman was in eternal mourning. She appeared elegant but frail.

Next, to her, Bernard looked like a bear escaped from the forest. He was a grizzled old hermit who Abby had only seen a handful of times in her life. He had an unkempt beard, and wild hair that looked like a bristle brush, and his whole demeanor was gruff and uncompromising. His cruel, beady eyes still scared her.

Vivian cleared her throat as they took their seats. Her demeanor instantly turned officious, and she placed her hands on the table.

"We gathered here in this official capacity as a Coven to discuss important matters regarding two of our own. As matriarch, I have made it our primary objective to free Evan and Jessica Kane from whatever ghostly torment they are currently enduring. I have assigned Margot to take the lead on this investigation." Vivian poured a glass of water for herself while continuing. "Abby, could you please recount for us the events you saw through the use of your special gift."

Abby shifted in her chair as all eyes turned in her direction. She had spent the last couple of days revisiting her experience and searching for every detail. Even the smallest thing could be important. By now, she could recite the events of that night by rote. She repeated everything she remembered in a calm tone, distancing herself from the emotions that surfaced. When Abby finished, there was a long pause as everyone reflected on her story. She could sense the uncertainty in the air.

"How do we know this wasn't just a bad dream?" Gisela asked doubtfully, just as Vivian first had.

"There is a difference between having a dream and using the Sight," Abby replied. "I can tell the difference. Using the Sight comes at a price, dreams do not." Gisela narrowed her eyes, and Abby could tell she wanted to say something more but was holding back.

"Margot, you were brought in on this after it happened. You have the most experience of anyone in this Coven dealing with the dead. Have you been able to discern anything from your research so far?" Vivian asked.

Margot looked uneasy. "Well it would be a mistake to consider me an expert," Margot said, soliciting a snort from Gisela. Margot turned her attention to Abby. "It sounds to me like a specter."

"Isn't that the same thing as a ghost?" Abby asked.

"Not exactly," Margot said. "A specter is far more powerful than your typical ghost. They have the ability to affect the world of the living in ways that can be very dangerous. They are anchored here by some of the most terrible of emotions. Hate, anger betrayal. They believe they are righteous in what they do. Unlike many ghosts, they understand they are dead, and as a result, they have learned how to gain a great deal of power over other ghosts and the spirit world."

"So what you're saying is, this is some kind of super ghost?" Wendy asked.

"Essentially." Margot nodded.

"Dreadful Darling, just dreadful," Vivian said, absently playing with the glass in her hand. Her go-to method for dealing with any foe was to curse into oblivion, and she was clearly uncomfortable at the thought that she couldn't. "How do we get rid of it?' She asked bluntly.

"It's probably too powerful to simply banish," Margot explained. "At least by anyone in this Coven. The way I see it, we have two options. We can continue our investigation with the resources we have at our disposal, or we consider finding outside help."

"Sebastian, don't you have a friend who's a Haitian voodoo priest?" Wendy asked, soliciting an eye roll from Vivian who could barely look at the young woman.

"Yes," Sebastian responded. "I could give him a ring."

"I'm hesitant to call in outsiders," Vivian interjected. "Especially a lowly hedge magician."

"Are you objecting because you're afraid we'll look weak by consulting outsiders for help?" Sebastian asked, barely hiding his sarcasm.

A cold glare crept across Vivian's face. "Among other things, yes," she responded simply.

"We just ended a conflict with another coven. All eyes are on us, at the moment," Gisela said. "If we seek outside help, the other families will see it as a sign of weakness."

"Do we even have the research material we would need to pursue this?" Wendy asked. "It's been a while since I've read the coven histories, but I don't recall any of the Kane ancestors dabbling in necromancy."

"I have been researching some of the necromantic artifacts we keep hidden in the vaults," Fiona stated. "While I have not completed my research, there are several books among the collection I intend to focus on."

"I can try using the Sight again," Abby offered quickly before she lost her nerve. The thought of encountering that spirit again made her sick, but she was willing to do whatever it took.

A heavy silence settled over the boardroom. "I would recommend extreme caution," Bernard said, his face almost entirely obscured by shadow. When he leaned forward, his weathered and wrinkly face came into the light. "We have no way of telling what this specter is capable of."

"What about your research, Vivian?" Rodger asked. "Have you learned anything about the symbol on the wall?"

"Not yet, Darling. I have been in contact with an old friend of mine who is a rare book vendor," Vivian explained, giving Abby a wink. "It is hard to gain any real information, as the topic is considered distasteful at best."

"Because of the stigma against necromancy, you mean?" Wendy asked.

Sebastian shook his head. "Most covens will hardly part with a book on the topic due to their rarity, let alone the fear that a text might fall into the wrong hands. There is a lot of power out there that people don't want known. Or shared."

Vivian nodded along as if what he had said was her words. "Still, my contact has assured me she will have something on the symbol within the week."

Abby sighed, and Vivian reached over to pat her hand.

"We will find answers, Darling," Vivian reassured. "Let us do a little more research before you take any further risks. Clearly, this spirit is powerful. I couldn't bear to have anything happen to you."

Abby simply responded with a nod.

"What about Syble and Lawrence?" Margot asked cautiously.

"What about them, Darling?" Vivian asked.

"They are members of this Coven, and it's a poorly-kept secret that they have dabbled in a few things we'd rather not discuss. But is it possible they might have connections or resources that might be helpful in this investigation?" Margot asked.

Vivian pursed her lips and turned her gaze upon her brother.

Bernard leaned forward slightly, his face covered in deep crevices across his leathery skin. "Syble's particular arcane predilections are unlikely to be relevant to any of this. Lawrence... It seems unlikely, but perhaps it would be worth discussing with him. I will do so," he said.

"Thank you, Bernard," Vivian gave her brother a warm smile. "It means a great deal to me that you ventured out to join us today."

He leaned back in his chair, his face once again obscured by shadow. Abby thought she heard Bernard grumble under his breath, but couldn't make out what he said.

"Have David and Cordelia been notified of what is going on?" Rodger asked.

"Yes," Vivian reassured. "They are flying in from Maui. I believe they will be here by Thanksgiving. We will discuss more specific strategies at that time."

Gisela slammed her hand down on the table, causing everyone to jump. "Why isn't anyone talking about the real issue?" she demanded.

Everyone turned to look at her. Vivian's steely glare pushed the other woman back into her chair.

"What real issue are you referring to?" Sebastian asked calmly.

"Where this is all coming from," Gisela shot back as though it were obvious. "The Thanos have started the war again! This is nothing less than a full-blown attack on our family."

"This might not be a new offensive," Margot suggested. "While I have no doubt that the Thanos Coven is involved in this, we must remember that whatever this spell is, the glyph was made when Evan and Jessica were murdered eighteen months ago," she explained cautiously. "This entrapment could have been going on all along without us knowing it."

"If we all agree that the Thanos are responsible, then we should act against them at once!" Gisela shouted again, more loudly.

"Are we certain it is the Thanos?" All eyes turned to Fiona as she quietly spoke.

"What are you saying, Dear Sister?" Vivian asked, cautiously.

Fiona placed her hands flat on the table and cleared her throat. "I do not wish for the words I am about to speak to be misinterpreted. I am not in any way exonerating the Thanos for what they have done, but this Coven has many enemies. Wars have begun through subterfuge and intrigue. Our enemies know we are fresh out of our war with the Thanos, and it would be easy for a smart enemy to stir up those old tensions.

"While there is no question about the origins of the symbol, we know almost nothing about the spirit attached to it on the other side. I do not feel it is in our best interest to assume at this point that it could only come from the Thanos. We would be wise to learn more before we act."

Fiona's words rang in the stillness of the room. It was a possibility no one had wanted to consider. If they did have other enemies, it would mean a much larger scale problem than they had anticipated. The idea of a Witches' World War sent a chill down Abby's spine.

"Do you have any candidates in mind, Mother?" Margot asked.

Fiona raised an eyebrow. "The Pentacost Coven in Atlanta for one."

"Pentacost? Why do I know that name?" Abby asked.

"Your grandmother's third husband was a Pentacost," Fiona said.

Vivian gave her sister an inscrutable look. "I divorced Mordaci over thirty years ago. How could they possibly be still upset about that?"

"I don't think it was the divorce that bothered them, my Dear Sister. I think it had something more to do with the curse you placed on their family afterward. But I'm certain we know nothing of holding a decades-long grudge," Fiona said plainly.

Abby noticed Vivian clenching her fists. *Fiona really does know how to get under Grandmother's skin.* She reached under the table and placed a gentle hand on Vivian's. Her grandmother gave a start, then flashed her a grateful smile as she regained her composure.

"My sister is right," Vivian said eventually. "The Thanos, and the Pentacosts, aren't our only enemies. We should proceed with precaution. We do not want to be played as fools by some upstart coven. Whoever they are."

There was a brief pause met with silence. "If there aren't any other questions, I will move on to the next order of business," Vivian said officiously, glancing down at a piece of paper on the table in front of her. "We have the matter of mineral rights inside the Mount Rainier Wilderness Area, and those wretched environmentalists getting in the way of our extraction efforts."

Abby let her mind wander, only vaguely listening to her grandmother complain about business. Images of her old home still clung to her. What horrors were her parents enduring while they sat around arguing about possible enemies? Aside from the Thanos, who was even strong enough to make a deal with a specter? *It makes the most sense,* she thought. *It has to be the necromancers. Right...?*

Fiona was right, they needed more information.

The city lights across the water sparkled in the night sky as Abby passed the large bay windows and crawled into bed. *I haven't slept well since...* Abby quickly shut down her line of thought. She was tired of the nightmares. Like an infestation, the thoughts haunted Abby nearly every moment. Sleep was perhaps the only reprieve, but even then, her dreams betrayed her.

What is that symbol! she internally screamed her frustration. Why couldn't they find any answers? The entirety of the Kane Coven researching tirelessly for a solid week and nothing. They kept running into dead ends. How were they ever going to break this spell?

Abby furiously closed her eyes. *I'm not dwelling. I. Am. Sleeping,* she told herself firmly. She lay in the silence, counting her heartbeats until sleep began to creep up on her.

Something light and soft landed on the tip of her nose. Abby reached up and brushed it away.

Another. This time on her upper left cheek. Abby sat up and switched on the lamp. She wiped her face and looked at her hand. There was a small smear of gray ash on her finger. "What?"

She looked up. Her ceiling was perfectly fine. She got out of bed and opened her door. *There is nothing burning?*

Outside her window, the city lights were pale and muted as though someone had turned down a dimmer switch. She approached the window and gazed out into a world shrouded in oppressive darkness. Even the trees only a few yards away from the house seemed sickly, gnarled and warped.

What is this? She pinched her arm to make certain she had not slipped into a shallow dream state. *I'm awake...*

Her own reflection on the glass came into focus and stared back at her. Inside her room, it was snowing. Abby glanced over her shoulder away from the window. Nothing. When she turned and looked at the reflection, small flakes were drifting down gently from above her.

"What is happening?"

Abby walked over to the edge of her bed and sat. She closed her eyes and cleared her thoughts, opening the Sight. Like water swirling down the drain, her awareness was pulled into a different place.

When she opened her eyes, Abby was sitting on the edge of her bed, but the room was different. The ceiling appeared warped and discolored from years of water damage. Small flakes of ash fell from the ceiling, coating the floor in a thin layer of soft flakes of ash. All the colors of her room–from the blue blankets on her bed to her green rain boots by the door–everything had faded and was now a pale reflection of how she remembered it.

There was nothing on the other side of the large bay windows but ash, as though the entire house had been buried. Abby stood and opened the bedroom door into the second-floor hallway. Ash fell there too. The ceiling was rotting away and looked like it was on the verge of collapsing.

A cold wind blew against Abby's bare neck. She turned and saw a little girl standing near the window.

"Lily?" Abby called out.

The little girl stared at her blankly with large, sad eyes. She looked like she was about to cry.

"Are you okay? Can I help you?" Abby asked, inching closer.

The little girl shook her head and turned. She looked behind her expectantly, as though she was waiting for someone to come up behind her.

Abby followed her gaze but only saw the window and the ash falling beyond.

"What's wrong?" Abby asked more cautiously.

The little girl stared at her, struggling to speak. "Sh... sh... sh... she's coming," the little girl stuttered.

"Who's coming?" Abby asked, uncertain what the little girl could mean.

"Th... th... the old wo...wo...woman," the little girl said. Her voice was barely more than a whisper. Her eyes were wide, and her hands were trembling. "Y...y... you shouldn't... b... b... be h...here."

Her small body convulsed in a tremor, and Lily let out a whimper. Before Abby could speak, the little girl bolted across the room and into the hallway.

"Lily!" Abby called out, racing toward the door. The little girl had vanished as if she had never been there. "Lily!"

A low, dry cackle began somewhere behind Abby. A foul stench, like rotting meat, filled her nostrils. She clutched her stomach, trying not to retch.

She did not want to turn around. She knew what was there. If she didn't turn to face the horror standing behind her, she would be safe from the dark, endless eyes that had pulled her into the miasma of death.

Abby slowly turned, terror making her feet move of their own accord. A withered old woman stood in front of the window, no more than five feet tall and slightly bent over. She looked frail and weak, but her body emanated a sight blue-gray glow. Her flesh looked like granite covered in flakes of ash. She wore a brown Victorian dress and blouse with a gray apron and bonnet. Her face was wrinkled with deep valleys and spotted with pockmarks, and her fingers were bent and gnarled with nails that looked like broken talons. The old woman's small eyes narrowed on Abby, looking down at her over a hooked nose.

Abby instinctively took a step backward.

A wicked smile crept across the crone's lips, revealing a mouth full of decayed teeth. Her oppressive gaze made Abby tremble.

Abby couldn't breathe, she couldn't move. She was too afraid. Any moment those eyes would consume her once again.

"So young and pretty," the old crone said with a gravelly voice. "You were almost mine, you know." She laughed evilly.

Abby took another step back. "Who are you?" she asked, her voice trembling.

"You will know me soon enough." The woman let out another wicked cackle. "You were supposed to be mine, but he failed." The devilish grin on the malignant spirit's face caused Abby to gag again.

"Atoro Thanos?" Abby asked. "Did he send you after us?"

The spirit laughed, menace in every sound she made. "You have many questions... is it because they keep the truth from you? Or are you truly a fool?"

"Truth? They?" Abby questioned, backing herself up against the wall. She glanced over to see the doorway only a few feet away. She could make a run for it if she had to.

Close the Sight. I have to close the Sight.

"There are many truths you do not know young one," the old hag whispered softly, a mischievous grin on her face. Her teeth were jagged and covered in rot. Green saliva oozed from the corner of her mouth. She took a step forward, and Abby summoned every ounce of her resolve to not flinch.

"I will learn the truth, and then we will destroy you!" Abby's voice trembled, adding a lie to her defiance. She concentrated as hard as she could, shutting down her awareness. The ash stopped raining down on them.

The spirit looked around, surprised.

Abby kept concentrating. The lights grew from a dull glow to a gleaming radiance. The colors began to grow brighter back to what they were. The rot and decay began to fade, and Abby's bedroom started returning to normal.

The spirit looked at her curiously. "Oh my. You are strong. Just like your parents," the hag cooed spitefully. "Too bad." She reached into her apron pocket and out a large, rusty knife.

Abby gasped and inched her way toward the door, trying to escape. The specter remained by the window. Abby paused when she realized she wasn't being followed. She turned back to look at the spirit.

With a sickening grin, the old woman thrust the knife into her own stomach. She yanked up, pulling the blade up to her sternum.

Abby shrieked in horror, then stopped, shocked. There was no blood. No ichor or ooze seeped from the wound. It wasn't the gory scene she expected. As Abby watched, her horror turned to confusion.

A buzzing sound came from somewhere near the old ghost. As Abby watched, a big black fly crawled its way from the gaping bloodless wound. Then another, and another. Suddenly a swarm burst from the old woman's belly, filling the room.

Abby raised her hands to protect her face from the bugs. They swarmed over her. She felt a sharp pain on her arm and then her shoulder. She lunged over her bed toward the bathroom, trying to escape the stinging insects.

Abby flung the shower door open and turned on the water as she swatted and ducked, trying to get away. She threw herself under the flow of water. The pain stopped.

There was silence. The only sound was the water raining down on her from the showerhead. She opened her eyes. The flies were gone. She looked near the drain to see if the water was washing them away. There was nothing. Abby's breathed heavily and looked on her arms. There were no marks. *Was I imagining things? What did she do to me?*

She turned off the water and stepped out of the shower. Her pajamas were soaked, but there were no other signs of what had just happened. She watched the bathroom door closely, waiting for the ghostly woman to appear, but there was no one. She leaned over to see further into her bedroom. The ash was falling again. The lights were muted; the colors, faded. The old spirit stood by the window, staring at her with a menacing smile.

"What do you want from me?" Abby whimpered.

"I want you to start asking questions," the spirit said. Her words seemed to carry a warning.

"Ask questions? Of who?" Abby asked, completely confused.

The old woman smiled as if she had been waiting for that very question. "Why don't you start with your grandmother," she suggested with a smirk. "There is much she is not telling you."

"What do you mean?" Abby asked. "What isn't she telling me?"

"That is for you to find out," the hag responded, giving her a knowing smile. "You should hurry. Not knowing the truth has cost your parents everything. What will it cost you, I wonder?" She raised a hand and snapped her finger. Suddenly the sound of moans and pleas for mercy broke out.

In the window's reflection, Abby could see dozens of people clutching at the old spirit's feet. They tugged and pulled at her dress, begging for mercy. Their bodies were covered in open sores and bleeding wounds, starved, and emaciated.

"Soon you will join my chorus!" the old woman said gleefully. "Listen to them sing!"

"You're insane," Abby said under her breath.

The apparition snapped her finger again, and the wailing spirits disappeared. The old woman's head tilted slightly.

Abby blinked, and suddenly the creature was standing right in front of her. She shrieked in surprise.

The old woman's mouth opened, her gaping maw was inches away. A foul stench erupted from her throat, causing Abby to wretch. She pressed herself against the wall, trying to get away.

Abby closed her eyes. *Close. Close. Close... close.* she repeated over and over as she concentrated on closing the Sight.

When Abby opened her eyes, she was standing in the bathroom, and the world was just as she remembered.

Is she gone? Abby stood against the wall, panting. She quickly turned on all the lights. She looked around the bathroom and through the door into her bedroom. *No sign of her,* she realized and began to breathe normally again.

After several deep breaths Abby could feel her heart returning to normal. "What the hell was that about?" she whispered. She glanced at her bed. There was no possible way she was going to fall asleep now.

She paced around the room, trying to shake off the last of her agitation. She glanced at her phone. *The Coven will want to know about this.* She thought of calling her grandmother but stopped. *It's the middle of the night, what can she do right now?*

A shadow passed by her window, making her jump. She paused for a moment, taking a deep breath. *Jesus Abby, you're freaking yourself out!* She stood, carefully staring at the reflections in the window, willing herself to calm down.

The darkness of the night condensed into an image. A form, a face, rotten teeth, black eyes... Suddenly a wicked cackle filled the room.

Abby opened her mouth to scream. The specter rushed forward. Abby stumbled backward, trying to get away. She heard the sound of her heading hitting the hardwood floor but didn't have time to register the pain before darkness took her. Just as her last shred of consciousness began to fade, she looked up and saw the old spirit standing over her, laughing.

CHAPTER TWELVE

"Are you sure you're up to going out today?" Wendy asked as she put the milk back into the refrigerator.

"Yes," Abby insisted.

"Even minor concussions need to be monitored, Abby. Don't push yourself," Wendy said gently as she took her seat at the table next to Evan, who was sitting in his high chair playing with his cereal.

"It's been five days," Abby said. "Besides, I don't even have a headache anymore."

"You know concussions can take up to two weeks to heal, but far be it for me to tell you what to do. You're a grown-up now," Wendy said, taking a sip from her coffee mug.

"You sound just like Mom," Abby said. Her own joke hit her like a lead pipe to the stomach the moment she realized what she had said.

It was obvious from Wendy's face she picked up on Abby's abrupt mood shift. "It's all right," she said with a smile. "My sister was a very wise woman, I don't mind the comparison at all."

Abby quickly finished off her coffee and took another bite of toast. "I'm going to head out," she said, collecting her purse from the counter.

"Do you really think Vivian is going to let you help?" Wendy asked as she poured herself another cup of coffee. "She's been pretty reluctant to involve you, thus far."

"That's why I'm not going to go see her," Abby said. "I think it's time to pay Aunt Fiona a visit."

Wendy tilted her head, considering the possibility and then nodded. "Good luck," she commented.

"Thanks," Abby said, heading for the front door.

Mercer Island was a quiet bedroom community only a few minutes outside the downtown Seattle business district. It was a densely populated island, with six-figure price tags for even the smallest parcels of land. Old-money Seattleites shared their neighborhoods with ultra-wealthy tech billionaires and dotcom entrepreneurs. Enormous mansions lined the waterfront with private piers housing every kind of yacht.

The further Abby drove, the more claustrophobic she felt. She never understood the appeal of this island. The freeway rested on a floating bridge surrounded by choppy water. It churned angrily, like a living moat keeping outsiders away.

Abby pulled off the freeway onto a street that quickly took her onto a tree-lined avenue. She turned onto a residential street that headed down toward the water. Farther from the center of the island, the houses were large, and more spread out like she was used to on Capitol Hill. Walls and gates provided private access to the most sprawling acreages.

She drove along a tall brick wall lined with thick, green bushes until she came to a large wrought iron gate. A large, stylized letter 'K' worked in wrought iron decorated the top of the gate. *This is definitely it,* Abby realized and looked for a place to park.

She walked over to the security box at the left of the gate and tapped in a seven-digit code. The tiny light on the security box flashed green, and Abby saw the iron gate slowly swing open. She offered a grateful prayer to her father for making her memorize it. Although she'd never used it before, she had never forgotten the numbers.

She passed through and found herself walking down a freshly paved driveway that cut through a thick grove of evergreen trees. The root system made the concrete uneven in some places. Abby watched her footing as she picked her way down a slight hill. She rounded a corner, and a large old brick house came into view.

Abby's jaw dropped. It was much more impressive than she expected. The century-old home had an old-Seattle, gilded-age feel to it. Ivy crawled along the face of the solid brick walls. The house was surrounded by a perfectly maintained lawn, and a marble birdbath stood in front of the main walk, empty. All the birds, save for the scavengers, had departed for the winter already.

Abby approached the house and rang the bell. The whole aesthetic reminded her a bit of her boarding school in England. *This is quite a bit smaller than Armitage Hall though,* she conceded.

There was a long pause, and no one answered. Abby reached out to ring again when the door abruptly opened.

An austere woman stood in the entryway, giving her a look that would have been a glare on someone more amiable. "Ah, hello, Mrs. Pugmire. I'm here to see Aunt Fiona," Abby said politely. She tried to layer a bit of an apology into her tone, knowing she wasn't expected. She was undoubtedly interrupting something important. *I should have called first.* She could feel her guilt seeping into her cheeks, turning them a faint pinkish color.

"I... needed to speak with her about something," she added quietly.

Mrs. Pugmire's expression didn't change, but she nodded slightly. "Come with me then."

As she entered the house, the heavenly scent of freshly-baked bread wafted from the direction of the kitchen. Her empty stomach rumbled, and she inhaled deeply, enjoying the aroma.

Abby followed Mrs. Pugmire across the grand entry to a large door just beneath the staircase. The older woman pulled a large ring filled with keys from her pocket and searched for a moment, eventually settling on an old key shaped like a skull. She slipped the key into the lock and held it for a moment, without turning it. A slight green glow pulsed around the edges of the doorway, before fading away. Then the door simply opened.

Mrs. Pugmire guided Abby down a flight of stairs. At the bottom, was a large hallway that led to the left and to the right. Finely polished hardwood peeked out from under a dark-blue runner. Mrs. Pugmire took a right turn, and Abby followed. *It's a good thing she's here,* Abby thought. *I would have gotten lost for sure.*

The dark hallway smelled musty, and she noticed that unlike the foyer above, the walls were barren of any photos or paintings. There was only the occasional wall sconce, offering a faint light. As they moved down the hallway, Abby noticed there were not many doors, and that were there seemed mostly unused. The carpet that ran along the center of the hall had occult symbols worked into the threading. Abby looked closer, examining the tiny spiral designs with pentagrams and elemental symbols in the center.

When they reached the end off the hall, Mrs. Pugmire stopped and turned back to Abby. "Wait a moment. I will let Mrs. Kane know you are here to see her."

Abby nodded, and the older woman turned to knock on the door. Mrs. Pugmire paused for a moment before entering. More symbols, like those in the carpet, were carved into the wood paneling around the door. *This must be Aunt Fiona's sanctum,* she thought.

Abby waited only a few seconds before the door opened, and Mrs. Pugmire said, "You may come in now, Miss Kane."

Abby stepped through the doorway and found herself in a large room. The floor was a shiny white linoleum, a bright contrast to the rest of the house. Stainless steel counters and cabinets lined the walls. A sink stood on the far wall next to a large medicine cabinet. *It's not a sanctum, it's a sick room,* she realized.

A large machine about the size of a refrigerator stood in the center of the room. Small digital screens were attached by long cords to a central port. They periodically beeped, in no pattern Abby could discern. Though a round window in the center, she could see something inside going around and around, making a slight swishing sound. Several tubes ran from the machine toward a large overstuffed chair, which held the fatigued and frail form of Fiona Kane.

"I didn't realize this was one of your dialysis days," Abby said apologetically. "I shouldn't have bothered you."

"Thank you, Mrs. Pugmire, that will be all," Fiona said, and the other woman quickly departed, closing the door behind her. Fiona gave Abby a faint smile. "It's quite all right, dear. I have all the time in the world when I'm attached to this wretched contraption. Speaking with you may pass the time."

Abby stood awkwardly, unsure of what to say or how to act. Her timing was terrible. She didn't want to bother her grandaunt, but leaving now would be weird. And she still needed to talk to her.

"Normally, either Madison or Margot sits with me while I have my treatments, but they're both busy today."

"You don't mind if I sit with you for a while, do you?" Abby asked as she pulled up a chair.

"Of course not," the old woman said, adjusting the tubes dangling from her arm. "Though you should know, your grandmother will be arriving shortly. If you were hoping to ask me something privately, I would get about it. We don't have much time to waste."

Abby smiled. "I'm not really trying to hide anything from Grandmother," she explained. "I just figure you're more likely to let me help in a meaningful way than she will."

"I understand. Vivian can be overly protective at times." Fiona sighed, pursing her lips. "And surprisingly careless at others," she added under her breath.

"Can you help me?" Abby Asked.

Fiona raised an eyebrow. "Did you have something in particular in mind?" Fiona asked curiously.

"The best tool I have at my disposal is the Sight. I would like to use it if I can," Abby suggested.

"Are you sure? After what happened to you the other night? How is your concussion?" Fiona asked her stern expression turning softer.

"The headache is gone," Abby said, rubbing the lump still sticking out slightly on the back of her head. "The doctors said to take it easy for a couple weeks, but I'm all right."

Fiona looked at her as if she was trying to read Abby's thoughts. "You're very brave to offer the use of your special gift. But I wouldn't advise the use of the Sight, not at this point. It's far too dangerous. This spirit is far too powerful. You weren't even intentionally using your Sight, and she was able to manifest in the physical world to attack you. Using the Sight would only put you in more danger," she said cautiously.

Abby felt like there was more that her grandaunt wasn't telling her. "What is it? There's something else to this isn't there?"

"In truth, we still have no idea what we're up against. She has proven herself worse than we had previously imagined. I worry about what this could mean for you. And for the family. Fiona looked at her with a discerning eye. "I…"

"Hello, Darling!" Vivian said, bursting through the door. Vivian stopped abruptly upon seeing Abby sitting next to Fiona. The gaze of the Coven Matriarch turned to her sister.

"Hello Vivian," Fiona said. There was an inexpiable expression of guilt in her eyes.

Why would Fiona feel guilty about anything? Abby wondered. "Hello, Grandmother," Abby said, standing and giving Vivan a proper greeting with a brief hug. Vivian stiffened slightly when Abby wrapped her arms around her.

"Darling, I didn't expect to see you here this morning," Vivian said with an empty smile.

"I came to pay Aunt Fiona a visit. It was a surprise," Abby explained.

Vivian's weighted glare softened slightly. "I see," she said, moving into the room and placing her purse on a counter near the dialysis machine. "Well, it is nice to see both of you." She leaned over and gave her sister a kiss on the forehead. "How are you feeling this morning?" A hint of sincerity lingered in her words.

"Tired," Fiona admitted.

Abby offered her grandmother the chair she had been sitting in. "Thank you, Darling," Vivian said, taking a seat as Abby collected another chair. The swishing of the machine rumbled in the awkward silence.

"I was asking Abigail how she is recovering from the attack last week," Fiona said.

"Such a terrible thing," Vivian said, almost in a trance. She was staring at the doorway.

Abby looked at the door to see if there was something holding her gaze.

"You haven't seen her again, have you, Darling?" Vivian asked, turning to Abby. Her eyes looked glassy.

"No," Abby reassured. "Not since that night," she added, doing her best to keep the memories of the attack from her mind.

"Sebastian says you're still having trouble sleeping at night," Vivian said, obviously assessing Abby from head to toe.

"Being attacked by a deranged spirit isn't exactly sleep-inducing," Abby said, trying not to sound too sarcastic. "But, it's getting better," she added. "Last night was a lot better."

"I'm glad to hear it, Darling," Vivian nodded.

"Besides, it isn't the attack that is disturbing my sleep right now," Abby said. "I can't stop thinking about Mom and Dad."

There was a momentary break in Vivian's carefully maintained composure. Her lips pursed, and her hand came to her neckline, fidgeting with a strand of black pearls. "Well Darling, we are doing our best," Vivian said, but her words lacked the self-confidence Abby was used to hearing from her grandmother.

"I want to help. It's already been two weeks since Mom called to me for help, and we're not making any progress! Please, I need to do something before I go crazy," Abby begged. "I can't sit around and rest all the time. I need to be a part of the investigation."

"Vivian, we really should let her help," Fiona said.

"Was that what the two of you were discussing when I arrived? Were you conspiring to gang up on me?" Vivian halfheartedly accused.

"I'm going to help," Abby insisted. "One way or another. I can't keep letting them suffer."

"She was asking my advice on trying to use the Sight again. I advised her to wait until we learn more," Fiona explained simply.

"No, My Darling, it's far too dangerous," Vivian said, waving away the idea as she would a fly buzzing around her. "This specter seems focused enough on you. We don't need to provoke her more than necessary. At least not until we know how to deal with her."

"Then what can I do?" Abby asked, unwilling to let her grandmother off the hook. She watched as Vivian and Fiona exchanged glances.

"We really should find her something to do, Vivian," Fiona said. "They're her parents, after all."

Vivian gave her sister a glare and then looked back to Abby. "I suppose I can have you help me with the Soul Web."

"The what?" Abby questioned. "Soul Web? What is that?"

"It's the marking on the wall; it's keeping your parents' souls bound," Fiona said, looking to her sister. "Vivian, you haven't told her yet?"

"I hadn't the time until now," Vivian explained. "I certainly wasn't going to bother her with it while she was convalescing."

"You found something? You should have told everyone! What else have you been keeping from me?" Abby demanded. "How long have you known?"

"Not long, Darling," Vivian said dismissively.

"Well?" Abby asked.

"Well, what, Darling?" Vivian deflected innocently.

"What did you learn? What is the Soul Web?"

"A clever annoyance," Vivian stated.

"It seems to be a pocket dimension in the spirit world," Fiona explained. "We don't yet know much about it. We're still researching how it works, but we think that's where, and how, your parents are being imprisoned.

"Now that you're well enough, I can have you help me with deciphering the ritual that will destroy the Soul Web," Vivian added.

"So, you already have a ritual to free them?" Abby asked cautiously. It seemed too good to be true.

"Yes," Vivian said simply, relief in her voice.

"It doesn't solve all our problems," Fiona said, giving Vivian a look of warning. "The spirit... I don't think she's going to let your parents go, even if we can break the Soul Web."

"No, it seems unlikely," Vivian conceded.

"Isn't Margot working on that?" Abby asked.

"Yes, she should be," Vivian replied.

"She is working very hard, Abigail, I can assure you," Fiona stated, but there was reservation in her voice.

"But what?" Abby asked, sensing the lack of confidence she was hoping for.

"This line of research isn't quite going as we had hoped," Fiona said.

"The power of the spirit exceeds anything we have found in the books we have available to us," Vivian admitted begrudgingly. "I've spoken to Ms. Grace, she's working on finding more... explicit books on necromancy with some hope we might find something. It's taking time. Such books are not merely laying around, nor are people who own them eager to sell or loan them out."

"Surely, there is someone who can help us," Abby insisted.

"We have family that could help," Fiona said quietly.

"Not now," Vivian uttered under her breath.

"Please, no more secrets," Abby insisted, rubbing her forehead. "Who are you talking about? What family?"

"Distant cousins," Vivian said, giving her sister a displeased glare. "But, there isn't any cause to contact them just yet."

"What do you mean?" Abby demanded. Her neck and jaw tensed with the anger she felt rising inside. "Every minute we wait, my parents are suffering in this Soul Web!

Why would you even hesitate to reach out to anyone who can help? Especially family!"

"You don't understand Darling," Vivian protested. "The Archibald Sisters might be family, but they aren't members of the Coven. Their mother was our aunt, and she married into a different coven. We barely know them."

"The Archibald Sisters?" Abby questioned. There was something familiar about the name. "Their name... It sounds familiar."

"It should," Fiona said, adjusting the hem of her skirt. "They're quite famous. I would be surprised if you haven't read one of their books, probably a bestiary."

"Bestiary... Was that the book on mystical creatures, the one that explained which ones are real, and which ones are extinct?" Abby asked, searching the recesses of her memory.

"That was one of their more famous books, yes. *The Practical Bestiary.* It's standard reading for most novice witches," Vivian said dryly. "I think I gave it to you on your twelfth birthday."

"Fourteenth," Abby corrected. "So, they're experts on all things mystical and unknown?"

"In a manner of speaking," Fiona stated. "They have experience dealing with powerful spirits."

"So, why haven't you contacted them!" Abby insisted. "They sound exactly like the kind of people we need helping us."

"It isn't that easy, Darling," Vivian said, putting her hand up. "The Archibald Sisters aren't... easy to approach."

"They're very reclusive. One has to find them first," Fiona explained. "We are making efforts to locate them. But, we can't count on them being willing to help us. Plus, there's no telling how long it might take to locate them," she added, sitting back in her chair and placing her hand over her heart.

"We're exhausting you," Vivian said. She then turned and gave Abby a stern look. "Darling, we should go. This talk is distressing Fiona."

Abby looked to her grandaunt, noting the fatigue in her eyes. "You're right," Abby conceded. "I didn't mean to mean to bother you. I'm very sorry."

"It isn't you, my dear," Fiona groaned, gesturing at the machine next to her. "My treatments always take it out of me."

Abby nodded and stood. She hesitated by the door.

"Go along, Darling. My sister and I have business to discuss," Vivian said.

"Shouldn't you do that another time?" Abby insisted. "You and I have business to discuss as well, and Fiona needs her rest. You just said so. We shouldn't keep her from it any longer."

Vivian looked to Fiona who avoided making eye contact. "Very well, you're right," Vivian conceded. She stood and gave Fiona another peck on the forehead before gathering her purse from the counter. "I'll come by tomorrow when you're feeling better," Vivian said.

Abby held the door open for her grandmother to pass through first. For some reason, she felt like her grandmother would bolt back into the room. "She doesn't look like she's doing very well," Abby observed as they made their way down the all toward the stairs.

"She's been doing dialysis for nearly ten years now," Vivian said absently. "It takes its toll on the body."

"Isn't there something that can be done for her?" Abby asked. "Some kind of potion or spell?"

"Oh yes," Vivian said, as they began climbing the stairs to the main floor. "Your uncle Rodger comes from the Pennington Coven. They are renowned healers. He makes an elixir for Fiona. She drinks it every night."

"But she's still sick," Abby said. "Why doesn't it make her better?"

"Darling, magic doesn't cure everything," Vivian said, opening the door to the main floor. "If it weren't for the elixir, my beloved sister would have passed many years ago. We are most fortunate to have someone like Rodger Pennington in our coven."

Abby had never heard her grandmother speak of her uncle with such respect. She sounded almost proud to be associated with him. "I didn't realize," Abby said in wonder.

"I don't think Fiona is fond of speaking about her health," Vivian said. "And I'm not surprised he didn't tell you. Rodger isn't a braggart. He's done a great many things to help members of our coven in their time of need."

"Is everything all right," Mrs. Pugmire asked as she approached from the living room.

"My sister is very tired. Would you mind checking on her in a few minutes, Mrs. Pugmire?" Vivian requested politely.

"Of course, ma'am," the older woman stated officiously. "I'll take her some tea."

"Thank you," Vivian said, as she and Abby made their way to the front door.

"You're going to search for the Archibald Sisters, aren't you?" Abby asked, almost pleading with her grandmother to consider it.

"We have so many things on our plate right now, Darling. We simply can't spare anyone to embark on such a complicated task," Vivian said. "There is someone who has offered to help, but, she's done so much already."

"Ms. Grace?" Abby asked, remembering Vivian's oblique reference to her at the board meeting. *She's nearly the only friend of Grandmother's who is altruistic enough to do something like that,* she thought. *Or capable.*

"Yes, Darling," Vivian said, opening the front door and stepping out into the chilled air.

"What can I do in the meantime?" Abby asked.

"Come by my place tomorrow morning, and I'll put you to work."

"Thank you," Abby said, relieved. "What are you going to have me do?"

"I don't know for certain, but it will give me some time to figure something out," Vivian said.

"You're not just putting me off, are you?" Abby asked suspiciously.

"Darling, really! Am I truly that dismissive of you?" Vivian protested.

"You really don't want me to answer that," Abby stated, doing her best to keep the sarcasm to a minimum.

Vivian smiled and wrapped her arms around Abby. "Be careful on your way home. I can smell snow on the air."

CHAPTER THIRTEEN

"When is our next practice scheduled?" Abby asked as she finished putting away her instrument.

"Thursday at 1:00 p.m." Irene reminded, pulling Abby's coat from the closet and holding it up for her as she put it on.

"I felt better about today's practice," Abby said, hoping her improved focused would be noticed.

"Indeed," Irene said politely. "Much cleaner today. I take it things are settling at home?"

"A little," Abby said. "At least enough. I'm holding it together a lot better," she added with a smile. She wasn't entirely lying. Sleep was elusive, but she was feeling better now that she had gotten Vivian and Fiona to agree to let her help.

"I'm glad to hear it," Irene said, as they made their way to the door. "Be careful on your way home. They're predicting snow."

"That's what my grandmother said earlier this morning," Abby said. "Thank you again," she added as she stepped out onto the front steps. As she walked onto the cobblestone walkway toward the street, she noticed a snowflake falling slowly to the ground. Low, white clouds began to sprinkle tiny little specks of snow.

"Drive carefully!" Irene warned. "It looks like the weather has arrived after all. You know how the hills get around here in the snow."

A ball of nervousness settled in Abby's stomach as she contemplated the steep hills that she would have to navigate on her way home. "I'll be careful. Thanks again," she said.

By the time Abby reached her car, the snow had already picked up. Larger flakes were falling, and the world around her was beginning to accumulate a light dusting.

She descended Capitol Hill at a slow speed into downtown Seattle. The traffic was dense, and pedestrians lined the streets. Abby turned on her windshield wipers to keep the snow from accumulating on the window.

She cautiously followed the car in front of her until she turned to pull into the ferry terminal. Abby flashed her pass and pulled into the vehicle bay to park. She turned off the engine, but let the heater run for a few more minutes.

As the ferry began to slowly depart from the docks, Abby leaned back in her seat and closed her eyes. She gently dozed until they reached the terminal on Bainbridge Island. It didn't feel like a real nap, but at least she was warm.

Too quickly, they arrived, and Abby pulled back onto the road. An inch of snow coated the island. The trees were covered in white, leaving almost no hint of the lush green hidden beneath. The streets were starting to ice over, and everything was quiet. It was as if the entire island had fallen into winter in the time it had taken her to get home.

Abby proceeded with great caution. The roads were treacherous, and her car shifted on the ice a few times, but she maintained control. Her shoulders grew more and more tense the longer she stayed on the road. *Almost home,* she told herself. *Just a little farther.* She slowed down until she was inching along the roadways.

She finally came to her driveway and slowly turned, starting down the angled pavement. The car began to slip. Within seconds the anti-lock brakes kicked in. Panicked, she pumped the breaks a few times, to no avail.

The car slipped sideways down the slope. Abby's mind raced through every terrible scenario. *I'm going to hit the house!* She pictured the car spinning off into the lake. Her breath caught, and she started to hyperventilate. She couldn't scream. *Am I going to die? Like this?*

The car slid to a gentle halt at the bottom of the driveway, a few feet from the garage doors.

Abby rested her forehead on the steering wheel as she took deep breaths, crying over her useless panic attack. "Home," she whispered as she tried to calm herself down. "I'm home." She gave herself a few moments to steady herself and stepped out of the car.

As she approached the front porch, Abby noticed a set of footprints in the snow. They were large footprints with deep, heavy treads. Abby traced the path of the prints with her eyes and realized they went around the side of the house.

As far as she knew, no one was home, and there weren't any other cars around. Abby placed her violin case and purse down on the patio, and cautiously followed the footprints to the edge of the large house. The snow fell all around her, muffling any sight or sound. Only the subtle lapping of the water a few yards away broke through the quiet.

Abby peered around the corner. There was no one in sight. The tracks continued to the back of the house, stopping in front of each window before continuing on. Whoever it was, they were looking inside. This wasn't one of her uncles making sure the house was weatherized.

Gulping back her erratic breathing, she approached the back of the house. *This is stupid, Abby,* she scolded herself. *If it is some prowler, you should call the cops. What are you doing?*

Abby removed her gloves and shoved them in her pocket. The snowflakes were getting bigger and falling quickly. It was becoming increasingly difficult to see more than a few feet in front of her.

Her intuition was screaming at her to get into the house and call someone. *It's not like I can get back in the car and leave, not in this weather,* she thought. *Maybe it's nothing.*

Abby paused at the back of the house. I need to get inside. Her survival instincts overruled her curiosity. Turning back, she headed for the front door.

An unseen force hit her. She flew backward through the air, slamming into the snowy ground. Abby quickly scrambled to her knees, looking frantically for the source of the attack.

A man dressed in black stood a few feet away. The snow was beginning to cover his shoulders and head, but it took only a moment for Abby to realize she was staring at death itself.

His long black hair and beard had grown scraggly and unkempt. He was barely recognizable from his formerly tidy self, but Abby recognized him all too well. His black eyes were still wells into the world of death.

"Atoro Thanos," Abby muttered as she stood. "You are breaking the treaty by being here."

"I care nothing for treaties," Atoro growled in broken English. An evil smile crawled across his face. "You have met an old friend of mine, yes?"

Abby swallowed her fear and held her resolve. "The specter? You brought her here?" she whispered.

Atoro met her question with laughter. "I? I brought no one. You know nothing of Mother Damnable," he growled. He looked to his right as if there were someone there. He seemed to be listening to something, but Abby didn't see anything.

"Very well," he said, responding to something Abby didn't hear. He turned and looked at her, his expression predatory. He was hungering for her destruction, and it showed in every line of his face. "It is time and past to finish this, little witch."

Abby dived back into the snow as a wave of black crackling energy shot from his hands. It flew past her, slamming into the snow a few inches away. A sizzling sound erupted where it hit.

"Rego Glacies!" Abby yelled, pointing her finger at the roof. All the snow that had accumulated on the roof began sliding down. It cascaded onto Atoro, knocking him to the ground.

Abby jumped to her feet and began running. Her parents had both been experienced witches, and Atoro had killed them with little trouble. She didn't want to wait and see what he could do to her.

She ran to the front porch, grabbing her things as she flew through the door. She slammed it closed, locking it behind her. She knew it would only buy her seconds, but every second gave her a chance to think of a way to escape.

Abby saw the large man through the living room window. He was lumbering toward the front door, slowly but inevitably. She rushed to the back wall where she would have a clear line of sight when he burst through the door and began gathering her energy for a spell.

A few seconds went by, and there was nothing. Abby watched the doorknob closely, waiting to see if he would try to unlock the deadbolt or just burst through.

Nothing happened. A few seconds passed. Still nothing. The only sound Abby heard was the panting of her breath and the slow ticking of the clock in the hall.

Where is he? No movement. No sound. *Maybe he took off,* she thought, though she was wary of letting in any hope.

Abby slowly crept to the window. She peered outside, but there was nothing. It was as if he had disappeared entirely.

Cold filled the room. Within a few seconds, the steam of her breath was in the air. The sound of footsteps came from upstairs.

She ran to the other side of the room, looking over at the stairs. No one there, but she was sure he heard something. Abby began backing away from the window, keeping her back to the solid wall as she moved carefully toward the kitchen.

Glancing to her left, she caught sight of her reflection in the glass of Rodger's china hutch.

Something was behind her.

A ghostly visage began to manifest. As the spirit took form, Abby could hear heavy footsteps descending the stairs. She looked over just as Atoro Thanos reached the bottom landing.

Abby ran into the kitchen, looking for a weapon or an escape. As she entered, she saw a ghostly presence standing near the sink. The apparition looked like an old man, gaunt and sickly with gaunt cheeks and grease-stained hands. He wore overalls with a filthy t-shirt and has murder in his beady eyes.

"Kill her," an old woman's disembodied voice urged. It was the spirit...Abby was certain of it. Her voice came from everywhere and nowhere, all around them. At Mother Damnable's command, the thralled spirit lurched forward, moving toward Abby.

Her mind stalled. Racing thoughts refused to form into a coherent plan of action. She didn't have the spells or training to fight ghosts like this. She looked back into the living room for an escape route.

Atoro Thanos drew a vicious looking knife from his belt as he came down the hall toward the kitchen.

The ghostly man lunged forward. The kitchenette table flew across the room, knocking her to the floor. Abby felt a sharp pain in her right hip but seemed to be unhurt.

She made a motion with her right hand and yelled, "Salius Cytrificus!" The table flung toward Atoro. He skillfully dodged it and continued toward her. The wooden furniture flew past him, shattering the living room window.

Abby scrambled to her feet and ran through the kitchen toward the back hallway. The spirit moved to intercept, but Abby pushed past him. She desperately flung open the door to the basement and flew down the stairs.

Her uncles' wards pushed against her for a moment before allowing her to pass. She ran into the sanctum and ducked behind one of the counters. She waited, doing her best to catch her breath while listening for the sound of the door opening. The magical protections her uncles had placed here were strong, but she was keenly aware that she had cornered herself. All she could do was pray that they would shield her from Atoro's apparitions.

Only a moment passed before the doorknob rattled. The door burst from its hinges and tumbled down the stairs, crashing against the concrete floor. Abby stifled a shriek.

"You cannot hide from me!" Atoro growled as he descended into the basement sanctuary. "Will you scream like your mother did when I gutted her?"

The memory of her mother lying in a pool of blood, her face contorted in pain, hit Abby like a train. Her parents had suffered–were still suffering–because of this man. *No more,* she thought.

Rage propelled her to her feet. She stood and turned to face Atoro Thanos, extending her hand. She bent her wrist and crooked her fingers, making the hex gesture Vivian had taught her. "Androvia Brrakathos!" She spit the curse with every bit of vile fury inside her.

The concrete steps beneath Atoro's feet exploded, tossing him into the air. He slammed into the ceiling, before crashing down to the floor. Rubble rained down, covering him in chunks of concrete and dust. Atoro let out a moan, stirring under the debris.

Abby rounded the counter and grabbed a jar of lavender-colored liquid from a cabinet. She carefully removed the lid and peered inside at the faintly glowing fluid. As Atoro began to stand, Abby stepped forward and splashed it in his face.

Atoro screamed in pain and clawed at his face.

Abby grabbed the knife from where the necromancer had dropped it. For a sickening moment, she realized she was holding the knife that had killed her parents.

Swallowing back the bile rising in her throat, Abby raised the knife in both hands. "This is for my mother, you sick bastard!" She slid the blade into his stomach. He screamed a second time.

Before Abby could pull the knife out and stab him again, Atoro Thanos made a fist and punched her, knocking her back. She fell backward, her head slamming against the concrete floor.

Abby lay stunned for a moment, blurry and unsure what was happening. The man bent over her, reaching for something. She blinked several times, trying to regain her wits. As the world came back into focus, she saw her enemy nursing his wounds.

Abby tried to stand.

Atoro kicked her in the side.

She rolled over on the concrete, trying to push herself away from him.

"You put up a better fight than the other Kanes I've killed," Atoro said. "But no matter. Now I pay my debts." The lumbering hulk of a man crossed his middle and ring fingers and extended his index and little fingers at Abby. It was a familiar curse, Abby had seen before. It was meant to kill.

"Nivion Shreddicus!" Atoro yelled.

"Sucidderhs Noivin!" Abby yelled in unison as she crossed her arms. Tiny tears appeared in the flesh of her arms, like claw marks rending her skin. She winced in pain, but her counter curse held.

Atoro picked up his knife, still dripping with his own blood, and licked the blade with the tip of his tongue. "Then it will be a slow death," he growled. The blood staining his lips made him look like a wild beast.

Abby nearly retched, barely managing to hold back. She tried to scramble to her feet as Atoro lunged forward with the knife. He was steps away from her when he stopped abruptly. The sound of a car door slammed shut echoed through the house.

Someone's home! Abby used the distraction to put the counter between Atoro and herself.

"Down here!" she screamed as loudly as she could. Mustering more courage than she felt, Abby faced the necromancer down one more time. "My family is home. You might be able to kill me, but I'm certain they can put up a much better fight than I can."

She saw the uncertainty in the necromancer's eyes. "Another time," Atoro growled menacingly. He slid the knife into his belt. With a chilling salute, his image began to fade. Within seconds he was almost translucent. As Abby watched, he walked into the concrete wall, disappearing completely.

Abby collapsed against the counter. She gasped for breath, her legs threatening to give out completely.

"Abby!" Rodger shouted from upstairs.

"I'm down here!" She stared at the place Atoro had disappeared, afraid he would reappear at any second.

"Holy hell!" Rodger exclaimed as he stood at the top of the basement stairs. "Are you all right?"

"A little bruised up, but I'm fine," she gasped. She slowly made her way to the foot of the stairs and looked up at her uncle.

"What happened?" Rodger asked, taking a few steps down before stopping at the place where her spell had hit. He offered his hand to help Abby over the section that was missing and pulled her into his arms.

"Atoro Thanos," Abby whispered. Her whole body began to shake as the shock of the last few minutes sank in.

Rodger held her tighter. "Atoro did this?" He asked, checking her for signs of serious damage.

Abby nodded.

"Come on," he said, pulling her into the hall. "We should get you–"

Abby grabbed both his arms, forestalling whatever first aid he was about to offer. "He called her 'Mother Damnable.'"

"Who?"

"We need to call Vivian. Call the Coven. They were here–they summoned a spirit to come after me. He is in league with the specter who's haunting us."

CHAPTER FOURTEEN

A soft knock on the door woke Abby from her sleepy haze. She lazily pulled her gaze from the window and rolled over to see who was at her bedroom door.

"Vivian just called. The ferry arrived, and she'll be here in about ten minutes. I thought I'd wake you and give you a chance to brace yourself," Sebastian said with a warm smile as he approached and sat at the edge of the bed. "Are you feeling okay?"

After a moment of reflection, Abby shook her head. "I don't know," she answered, unable to tap into a single emotion. "Right now, I'm not feeling anything." She sat up and propped her back against her pillows.

"I don't even know how I would have reacted if I saw that monster here," Sebastian said, shaking. Abby leaned over and pulled her uncle into a long comforting hug, just as he had done for her so many times.

She didn't speak, she simply held him until his shaking stopped. "I can't keep thinking about what might have happened if one of us had been home alone with Evan when Atoro showed up. You barely managed to survive, and you didn't have a baby to protect." Sebastian shuddered again and sat up.

"It didn't happen," Abby said. "And now that we know he and this... Mother Damnable are in some way connected. It's all the more reason to work hard to resolve all of this."

"Mother Damnable... what a name," Sebastian muttered.

"Let's hope it's enough of a name to give me something to go on," Abby said. "It's more than I had before."

"I'm really worried, Abby," Sebastian said his voice cracked with emotion. "I'm worried about you. This spirit has taken an unhealthy interest in you. You're the only one she's attacked so far. I don't like it."

"I'm not a fan either," Abby said sarcastically. "I suspect she's targeting me because I can See her."

"Probably," Sebastian said.

The uncertainty in his voice did little to settle Abby's frayed nerves.

"I don't know what I will do if something happens to you, Abby," He continued. "Please, promise me you'll be careful. I know how frustrated you are with our progress, but please, don't take any unnecessary risks."

Abby nodded.

"I don't know much about the Sight. My family was careful only to train those of us that had it. If they felt this gift needed to be kept secret, then it must come with its dangers. It seems like the Sight functions as an open channel of sorts and somehow opens you up to the spirit in some way. If she can reach you this way, then you're more at risk than any of us."

"I haven't really thought of it that way," she said. "I've been working on developing my skills with the Sight for over a year now, but there's still so much I don't know. Even though I'm getting a lot better with it, it's hard to progress without a teacher."

"Despite what your grandmother might say, there is no such thing as mastery when it comes to witchcraft. There is always better understanding to attain and something more to learn."

With a snicker, a smile settled across Abby's lips. "Unlike my grandmother, I don't really have a need to be the best at everything. Thanks for putting a smile on my face. After a day like today, I wasn't certain that was possible."

"We have to remember why we care in the first place. I love you, Abby," Sebastian said. "I've been a part of your life since the day Evan and Jessica brought you home from the hospital. You are really the first person whose life I've been a part of since the beginning. Even though I wasn't your father, I was there for the first of everything. I saw you go from being a diaper-exploding infant to the fine young woman I see in front of me right now. There are few gifts in life more precious than that opportunity."

"Wow, you're making me feel really special," Abby teased as she wiped a stray tear away from the corner of her eye.

"That's because you are," Sebastian reassured.

The doorbell chimed, and they exchanged a sigh. "I guess it's time to deal with the interrogation," Abby jested, not wanting her moment with Sebastian to end end.

The sound of footsteps ascending the stairs filtered in from down the hallway. Sebastian gave Abby a brief side hug and took a deep breath. "Okay, brace yourself."

Abby laughed.

"What's so funny, Darling?" Vivian questioned as she stormed into the room without knocking. "That horrible monster nearly killed you." The look on Vivian's face was that of genuine concern.

Guilt stabbed her gut. *I shouldn't be so critical of her,* she thought. *She's trying her best too.*

"Sebastian was just trying to make me feel better," Abby said, standing and giving her grandmother a hug.

"Darling, tell me everything!" Vivian demanded, taking the chair at Abby's desk. "I knew those fiendish Thanos were involved! As we suspected all along. Now we won't have to worry about linking it to them."

"What's more important is keeping the family safe. Especially Abby and Little Evan," Sebastian interjected.

Vivian's look of glee melted into something more serious. "Tell me everything," she demanded again, turning to Abby.

"There isn't all that much to tell," Abby confessed. "He was here when I came home. He attacked me, and Uncle Rodger came home, so he ran away."

"What about the specter, Darling?" Vivian asked. "How are the two connected?"

"I don't know exactly," Abby said. "I saw them converse. He called her 'Mother Damnable.'"

Vivian sat frozen. Her face turned white as a sheet. Her lips went pale as her eyes widened. She leaned forward slightly. "What did you say?" Her voice riddled with seething anger.

Abby looked Vivian curiously. "Mother Damnable, that is what he called her." She watched her grandmother's expression closely.

Vivian's mouth fell open for a brief second before she quickly recovered, resuming her imperious demeanor. "I see," she growled under her breath. Vivian's eyes shifted away, and then she stood abruptly. "I need to go."

"What do you mean? Do you know who Mother Damnable is?" Sebastian questioned.

"I remembered something very important I have to take care of," Vivian insisted before disappearing down the hallway. Abby could hear her grandmother run down the stairs, slamming the front door on her way out.

"Is it just me, or does 'she knows something' feel like an understatement?" Abby said, furrowing her brow. "Did you see how she reacted when I said the name?"

"I saw," Sebastian said deep in thought.

"What was that all about?" Rodger asked, entering with a mug full of tea he handed off to Abby.

"Vivian is usually a good poker player," Sebastian said.

"We already knew this spirit is powerful, now I'm starting to wonder if there isn't something more personal going on here than we thought," Abby said, speculatively. "I'm going to start researching who the hell this Mother Damnable really is."

There was a light drizzle falling from the overcast sky, a nice relief from the bitter cold and snow. Abby walked up a steep hill surrounded by dozens of other pedestrians. The tall glass towers cast a shadow over the streets, making it almost seem like nighttime beneath the dark clouds and the skyscrapers.

She approached an old wooden door with antique leaded glass windows. Abby opened the heavy doorway and stepped into her favorite café in the city's bustling business district. Several patrons sat at old wooden tables with mismatched chairs. An antique bar had been converted into a coffee house with an elaborately carved counter with cherubs and flowers lining the edge. An enormous mirror hung over the coffee bar making the small café seem even larger than it was.

Abby approached the bar and ordered her drink before finding a vacant table by the wall and claiming her seat. She pulled her laptop out and plugged it into a socket near the floor. She glanced out the window and yawned. These dark winter days were always tiring, no matter how much sleep she got.

She powered up the computer and logged into the internet just as her coffee arrived. "Thank you," she said when the waiter placed the large mug in front of her. She opened a browser and went to a search engine.

It took only seconds for the search to provide a list of results for Mother Damnable. The first result was a Wikipedia page for Seattle's history. She opened the result in another browser tab, quickly scanning the introduction.

> Mary Ann Conklin nee Boyer, a.k.a. Mother Damnable was a brothel owner in the early pioneer days of Seattle, Washington. She was originally from Pennsylvania and migrated to Seattle in 1853 where she opened the Felker House, the first hotel and brothel in the city. She was best known for her foul mouth and her dogs, whom she would set on unwelcome guests. She died in 1873...

Abby pulled out a notebook and began taking notes.

> After her death in 1873, her remains were initially interred in a cemetery in downtown. However, in 1884 the graveyard was closed, and her grave was moved to another part of the city. According to legend, when they exhumed her coffin, it was abnormally heavy. The workers opened the coffin, and her body had turned to stone. She is currently buried at Lake View Cemetery on Capitol Hill, and her year of death is inaccurately engraved on her headstone as 1887...

Abby gasped, causing a few patrons to turn and look at her. She blushed and turned back to her computer. *Lake View Cemetery is only a couple of blocks away from my old house!* Abby thought. *There's no way this is a coincidence.* She sat back in her chair and rubbed her forehead. *Who was she? Is she simply some instrument of the Thanos Coven, or is there something more going on here?*

Abby read page after page. There isn't much here, she realized after spending an hour sifting through search results. *They all pretty much say the same thing.* She reviewed her handwritten notes.

Grandmother knows something, more than she's admitting. Mother Damnable told me she was keeping things;. Maybe she wasn't lying.

A chill ran down Abby's back as she sat in silence in the café, staring at her notes and the computer screen. She sipped her coffee and took a deep breath. *When did my family come to Seattle? They came here from Virginia sometime around the Civil War... Did they know Mother Damnable?*

Abby's thoughts were interrupted when she noticed someone staring at her. She glanced up to see who it was. There was a young man cleaning tables. He had a fresh face and couldn't possibly be much older than she was. He had dark blond hair and a bit of scruff, making him look slightly older. He wore a green flannel shirt, department-store jeans with holes at the knees, and a pair of well-worn sneakers.

She smiled and continued reviewing her notes. *1887... why does that date sound familiar?* She let her mind wander, pulling loose threads together into coherent thought. She had been reading for a couple minutes when she felt a presence behind her. Abby paused and looked up to see the young man standing and looking over her shoulder.

"Cursive? They don't teach that in schools anymore," he said with a smooth voice. Abby looked up into a pair of striking green eyes. His bright smile that lit up his face. "UW or University of Seattle?" he asked with a deep voice.

"Neither," Abby said, returning the smile. "I don't start school until next fall."

"Are you new to the city?" he asked, sounding almost hopeful. "Sorry, I'm Simon," he said, wiping his hands on the apron he was wearing before extending his hand.

"No, I've lived here my entire life, but I can tell you haven't," Abby smiled and shook his hand. "I'm Abby," she added.

"Really? What gave it away?" Simon asked, chuckling.

"It's easy to tell. You're too friendly to be a local," Abby explained.

"Seattle freeze," Simon said. "Yeah, I'm intimately familiar with that phenomenon since I arrived."

"It takes a while, but people will eventually warm up," Abby said.

"You're the nicest person I've met so far. These coffee drinkers around here are really intense," Simon said with a pointed smile.

Is he flirting with me? It had been so long she wasn't sure she knew what it still felt like. Her uncles' words came back to her. *Maybe it is time to move on.* Even though there was a part of her that still cared for Benjamin, the pain of that loss was beginning to fade.

She quickly laughed the awkwardness off. "Most people around here need caffeine coursing through their veins to function in the wintry darkness," Abby explained, gesturing to the weather outside. "I wouldn't take it too personally."

Simon gave her an incredible smile, so genuine and relaxed; it was refreshing. She could tell he was comfortable in his own skin and a person who never learned to be afraid to simply be himself.

Abby glanced at the time on her phone.

"Do you have to go somewhere?" Simon asked.

"I have an appointment in less than an hour," Abby said, smiling. She began putting her computer into her bag and collecting her notes.

"Here, I'll take that and walk you to your car," Simon offered, taking her bag and waited.

"Thank you," she said. "I'm only a couple blocks away."

"In the Sinking Ship parking garage?" Simon asked.

"That would be the one," Abby smiled, she caught herself blushing.

Simon got the door for Abby before the two stepped out onto the sidewalk. "I'll be back in a couple minutes," Simon shouted at the crew working behind the counter. After joining her on the steep decline toward the next block, Simon's expression turned inquisitive. "Now we get to the really good part," Simon said mysteriously. "Will I score a phone number?"

She couldn't help but smile. It was flattering to get this kind of attention, no matter how strange and foreign it felt. "A phone number?" Abby playfully mused aloud for a moment, before pulling her phone out. "Give me your number, and I'll text you."

Simon quickly recited his number and watched his phone. Abby sent a brief message to his phone. "Abigail Kane," Simon said, reading his caller ID aloud.

"I don't think you mentioned your last name," Abby said, entering his contact information.

"Strauss," Simon answered. "So, I've seen you at the coffee shop reading a lot. Do you live in this part of town?"

"I grew up about a mile from here," Abby said. "My grandmother lives in Queen Anne, but I'm living on Bainbridge Island with my family. I love it, but sometimes the island gets a bit small. I'm used to the city."

They strolled down the hill at a leisurely pace, getting to know one another. Abby wanted to like this boy, but a sinking feeling kept edging its way in. It settled in her chest until she could no longer ignore it. She was making a terrible mistake.

She couldn't seriously consider dating this guy. He seemed kind, and in many ways was the kind of guy she always imagined she would want to date. But if things progressed, what would she do? Bring him into her world of the occult and witchcraft? A world where parents are suddenly killed. Where malevolent spirits torment the souls of your loved ones. Where people keep secrets that hurt the ones they love. It was a world where he would be looked down upon by others, simply because he wasn't like them. *It would destroy him,* she thought. *Could I really do that to another person for my own selfishness? He deserves better than me...*

Abby allowed herself to daydream as they continued walking and laughing as they spoke. His sense of humor was charming. There was something romantic about the thought of dating this guy, falling in love, and disappearing somewhere, leaving the world behind and having a simple life. In Abby's heart, she knew it would never happen. She knew she could not bring him into her life or escape into his. Abby realized she needed to stop what she was doing. With one more brief smile, she made up her mind.

As they approached the parking garage, Abby guided him around the corner. There was slightly more privacy. *This is all I need,* she thought, glancing around. Abby turned toward him and looked him in the eye.

Simon seemed confused and then gave a hopeful smile.

Poor guy. He thinks I'm about to kiss him. Abby thought, her heart breaking a little. She focused for a moment, and his eyes locked onto her own.

"Simon Strauss, you will forget you ever met me or spoke with me. There is no Abigail Kane, and when you see the call in your phone, you will erase it as a wrong number.

When I say start, I want you to count to fifteen, at which time you will leave and enjoy your evening." It was a simple charm spell, but she knew it would be effective on the young man. Loneliness buried deep in her soul woke as she spoke the words. She shook her head and gave him a kiss on the cheek. "Start."

As Simon began to count, Abby made her way to her car on the far side of the parking garage. She got in, started the car, and let the engine run for a minute. She glanced over and watched as Simon seemed to snap out of a trance. He looked around briefly and began walking up the sidewalk. Abby watched him until he disappeared.

After several deep breaths, Abby pulled herself together before the seams of her composure buckled. She put the car into gear and left.

"Now that's was the Abby I've been waiting to hear," Irene said, as they played the last note. "I'll admit you had me worried for a couple days."

"I'm sorry," Abby said. "I've been really distracted lately."

"You played beautifully today. It was flawless, and it had a hauntingly sad quality," Irene said, closing her eyes, still consuming the sound. "If you play that piece half as well at the concert as you did just now, you will win over an auditorium of fans," she added as she began putting the sheet music away.

"Really?" Abby said doubtfully.

"Why do you sound so surprised?" Irene asked as Abby began loosening her bow.

"I don't know. I guess I'm feeling a bit off. I didn't really notice."

"On the contrary, I thought you were very focused," Irene said. "Your mood tends to affect your playing, and today, it was for your benefit. You wouldn't be the first artist I've known who used their pain to create something spectacular,""

Abby nodded. "I think you're right," she confessed. It had been an observation she had made herself on several occasions.

"Let me make us some tea before you go. It will give us time to chat for a few minutes before you go back out into the cold," Irene said, excusing herself to go into the kitchen.

Abby sat on the couch and looked at the pictures on the end table. There was a photograph of an old plantation style house surrounded by old dogwood trees. Next to that, was a picture of a distinguished old woman, who Abby assumed must be Irene's mother. There was a faint resemblance shared with the woman in the picture. Several other pictures graced the small table. Some of them looked old; others more recent.

"Here we are," Irene said, returning with a silver tea service. She placed it on the coffee table and took a seat before she poured them a cup of tea. "How are you holding up? It's all right if you don't want to talk about it," she added, taking a sip from her cup.

"It's not that," Abby said. "I met a guy earlier."

"That sounds fantastic!" Irene said effusively. "Why so sad then? Is it your parents?"

"No... Well, yes. Kind of," Abby said. She couldn't really tell Irene why she couldn't pursue a relationship with the young man she met earlier that day.

"Eventually, you're going to have to start living your life," Irene said warmly. "Your parents wouldn't want you shutting down because they aren't here anymore."

"It's not that," Abby said, feeling her emotions swelling. "Sorry," she said, wiping away a tear.

"You're in a lot of pain," Irene observed cautiously. "I'm sorry, I shouldn't have pried."

Abby conjured a brave smile and took a deep breath. "I'm going to be all right," she said, doing her best to reassure herself as much as Irene.

"Abby, can I tell you something in confidence?" Irene's words hung weighted with uncertainty.

"Of course," Abby said cautiously.

"I haven't been completely upfront with you about something. After I explain, I hope you'll understand why," Irene said.

Nervousness swelled in Abby's stomach. *What could she possibly be afraid to tell me of all people?* she thought. "I'm listening," she said.

"Abby, I grew up in a small town a few miles south of Atlanta. My parents were employed by the Willows family. Have you heard of the Willows?"

Abby thought for a moment. "Not that I recall," she said, watching the hesitation in Irene's eyes.

"They are an... exceptional family. Not unlike your own," Irene said with even more caution.

"Exceptional?" Abby questioned nervously. Her eyes opened wide as the realization hit her. "You mean...?"

Irene nodded. "Like your family, the Willows were all witches," Irene said bluntly.

The shock of her words was just like ripping off a bandage. A wave of recognition rolled through Abby. "You... You're Awakened?" she blurted out.

Irene nodded again, visibly relaxing as she spoke. "Yes, for my entire life."

"How long have you known I was a witch?" Abby asked, still trying to absorb the fact Irene was one of the rare non-witches aware of her world.

"I suspected it when I first learned your name, but Kane isn't an unheard-of name. It wasn't until you told me about your parents that I made the connection. Some of the witch families become terribly possessive of the Awakened. I didn't know if you were like that. I hope you will forgive me for not saying something the moment I realized. I had to make certain you wouldn't 'claim' me," Irene explained.

"Claim you?" Abby asked, uncertain of what she meant.

"Yes, some covens virtually enslave people like me, the Awakened. There are precious few of us, and it isn't always easy to awaken new people. It requires a great deal of work, preparing them to see and experience your world. Most families don't want the bother. Instead, they keep people like me beholden to them, sometimes we're little more than slaves. I was lucky. The Willows family were kind, like you. In fact, they paid for my education and gave me all the encouragement in the world that I needed to get me where I am now."

"Of course," Abby said, shaking her head. "I've heard stories like that. I imagined they were from a long time ago. I didn't realize some people still did those things today," Abby confessed.

"It isn't as common as it used to be, but there are still families who are less than scrupulous in many ways. Enthralling Awakened servants is the least of it," Irene said. "Again, I'm very sorry I didn't tell you this before."

"It's all right," Abby said. "I understand. This is your thing to tell. It isn't any of my business, but I'm glad you trusted me enough to tell me."

"I can't tell you how relieved I am, to be honest with you about this. It has been eating me for weeks now. We've become friends, it doesn't feel right when you have to hide something from someone you consider a friend," Irene said with a kind smile.

"I know what you mean," Abby said, shaking her head. "It can be incredibly lonely when you have big terrible secrets to keep."

"Yes, it is," Irene agreed. "Even though I'm not a witch, and neither is my family, it's always made life a bit challenging. Especially relationships," she added gently.

After taking a sip of hot tea, Abby smiled ironically. "Relationships with anyone other than another witch seems too impossible to even consider."

"The guy from earlier?" Irene asked kindly.

Abby nodded. "I couldn't possibly awaken someone simply to date them. It seems... I don't know, cruel."

Irene nodded her agreement. "Most people are not well suited to handle having their life turned upside down like that. I've seen it happen if the relationship doesn't work out your left being responsible for someone you don't want to be with," she explained. "Have you ever been in a relationship?"

Abby nodded. "Not like that, but my boyfriend when I was in England... It didn't end very well," she confessed. "Even though he was a witch, there were a lot of secrets, and he wasn't who I thought he was."

"Oh, Abby," Irene said. "I'm sorry. I hope you don't mind me saying, but..." she picked her words carefully, "Your family is well known for their ability to wield curses. It hasn't brought them the... kindest reputation. The Kanes tend to draw people to them with similar tastes."

"I know," Abby said. "Not everyone in my own family is the nicest of people," she confessed. "There are some very good ones, though."

"That's true of most families, witches or not." Irene smiled. "I wouldn't worry about it too much, Abby. You're eighteen, you have plenty of time. Happiness doesn't come from a relationship or from other people.

They help, sometimes, but real happiness is something you find inside yourself. I find it when I hear something truly great; a Rachmaninoff concerto, or Mendelssohn's Easter Sonata. We find it where we can, and do our best to remain as content as possible in between those moments of happiness."

Abby smiled weakly at the wise words spoken by her newest friend.

"Listen to me," Irene said, scoffing at herself. "I talk about it like it isn't hard. You know, probably better than I do, that it isn't always that easy to find happiness."

Abby nodded, smiling. "I do know."

"Sooner or later, we all lose that innocence we had as children, and the world changes as we begin to realize the world is a harsher place than our parents ever wanted us to know. Find the good people and keep them close Abby, that's the only sound advice I can give you," Irene mused.

"Thank you," Abby said. "I know I'm probably not going to spend the rest of my life alone. Today I just had a reminder of how challenging all this can really be. I think I gave up hope for a couple hours."

"Well, humanity gives us plenty of reasons to give up on it, but if you pay close attention, you'll find the good as well. You have a lot of darkness around you right now, but that isn't the lump sum of your life," Irene reassured.

"I hope you're right," Abby smiled.

"Even the best people are flawed. It's what you look for in them that matters," Irene said. "I live by it. Otherwise, I would go completely mad." Her laugh was light and jovial.

Abby couldn't help but chuckle along with her. She glanced at the time on her phone. "I hate to cut this short, but I have a ferry to catch," she said, sipping the last of her tea.

"Be careful on your way home. We're expecting another cold snap. All this rain today is going to turn to ice soon," Irene warned. She walked Abby to the door and helped her with her coat.

"Another one? It seems to be coming really early this year," Abby said. "The weather knows it's still November, right?" She turned with a chuckle and gave Irene a warm hug. "Thank you again. It's nice to have a friend–they seem preciously rare these days."

"I'm glad to have a new friend, too," Irene smiled. "Now get into that car, it already feels like it's freezing out here."

"Thanks again!" Abby called back as she walked down the steps. Shivering, she pulled her coat tighter around her and walked down the block to her car.

CHAPTER FIFTEEN

After only a couple of hours of drifting in and out of sleep, Abby decided to give up all pretense and rolled over onto her back. She lay in the dark, staring at the ceiling. Her night was plagued with memories of her parents. As each one ended, images of them being tormented within the Soul Web played over and over.

I have to take control of my thoughts, she told herself. She closed her mind and cleared her thoughts, holding the empty space as best she could. There was peace and clarity.

"Alright Abby, pull it together and do something useful," she muttered under her breath. She crawled out of bed and shuffled into the bathroom. She took a long hot shower, letting the water waken her body and mind like a baptism from slumber to awareness.

She threw on some jeans and pulled a t-shirt over her head, then pulled her hair back out of her face and put on a fresh wool sweater, feeling relief from the chill lingering in the air. She glanced at the temperature control panel next to her door, and then looked closer, doing a double-take. *It should be perfectly warm in here, she thought,* rubbing her arms. *There must be something wrong with the heat pump.* She made her way over to her dresser and opened her jewelry box.

She clasped a thin, intricately woven gold chain around her neck. The small heart pendant hung just below the curve of her throat. It had been a gift from her parents; she had worn it nearly every day. Maybe it was a good time to bring it out.

She looked out her window. The sky was clear, and the stars shined bright above. It would be another couple of hours before daylight. The rest of Seattle was still fast asleep. Abby could feel the fatigue in her body, but sleep had betrayed her yet another night. She sat at her desk and closed her eyes for a moment.

Abby could hear the water lapping at the grassy shore. The sun was setting on the horizon, and a cold chill settled over her shoulders. She took a cautious step toward the boathouse. She could hear people inside, speaking. She cautiously inched closer as the sun disappeared over the horizon. Crickets serenaded the approaching moonlight.

"That girl is an idiot. You need to move on!"

The sound of that voice chilled Abby more deeply than the cold fog.

"She isn't an idiot!" A deep voice insisted. Abby gasped when she heard the melodic English accent.

Abby took another cautious step forward. There was a filthy window, not more than a few feet away. She began moving toward the framed glass, emitting a dull light. She leaned over slightly to hide beneath the opening.

"You never got to know her," he protested.

"I didn't have to," the other spat. "She was oblivious even with her precious Sight."

"She was grieving the loss of her parents and worried about her family last year. How can you be so callous?" he questioned angrily.

Abby poked her head over the ledge slightly and looked inside the boathouse. It was exactly as she remembered. Along the walls, were stands where boat shells hung next to oars. They stood in the center of the small structure. His face was contorted in anger, his fists clenched as though he were ready to throw a punch.

"Then you're an idiot as well! She was too stupid to see what was going on right in front of her face," the first one growled dismissively. "I don't think I've ever met someone so pathetic. You had best get over her, Benjamin! She isn't coming back. Not for you."

The wooden floor of the boathouse was covered in blood where they stood. She narrowed her eyes, trying to focus on the dim shapes lying near the racing shells.

They turned abruptly toward the window. Abby contained her gasp and dropped down as quickly as she could. She held her breath, hoping she hadn't made a sound. Only the crickets chirped along the shores of the pond. There was silence inside the boathouse.

Abby looked away from the window, readying herself to run. She watched, barely allowing herself to breathe. She waited. The conversation inside had stopped. *Surely if they saw me, someone would have come outside by now.*

Abby put her back to the wall. She kept watch in both directions, sure someone would creep up and grab her at any moment.

Minutes passed in suspended agony. She crept up slightly to peer through the window. No one was there. Where did they go? she thought nervously. She cautiously watched, waiting to see if they would return. She heard nothing but the crickets.

Abby inched her way to the front of the building, taking each step quietly. She did her best to avoid making a sound. She peered around the corner at the front of the building. The doorway was slightly ajar, but there was no one. Abby quickly glanced behind her, there was no one there either. She couldn't help but feel like someone was watching her. A cold realization came over her, and she looked up.

Nothing. Abby allowed herself to breathe again, trying not to laugh at herself. She glanced once again at the front of the building to be certain the coast was still clear. Satisfied no one was about to leap out at her, Abby rounded the corner and approached the door, walking silently in the grass.

When she reached the door, Abby poked her head through. *They aren't here. Where did they go?* Abby quickly slipped through and closed the door behind her securing the latch. She turned and nearly tripped over something lying on the floor of the boathouse. As she fell, she had a clear view of the bloody body on the ground.

She knelt down next to him and searched for a pulse. The young man lay lifeless in a pool of his own blood. There was a large gash in his head and another horizontally across his stomach. The blood was not warm; he had been dead for a while. A tear streaked down Abby's cheek.

"I'm sorry," Abby whispered. A wave of grief swelled in her heart. Pent up emotions from the last year became liquid running from her eyes. Pain and regret opened the door for other grief–her parents, their suffering, her family–all came flooding over her. It would never end.

The numbness came. That old familiar feeling of nothingness that sustained her after her parents died. The pain was muted and distant–accessible but empty. It felt like the only reprieve she had from the guilt and grief anymore. Abby closed her eyes and concentrated, doing her best to pull herself from the Sight.

When she opened her eyes, her head rested on her pillow. The comforter pulled up to her chin as she stared at the rain-covered window overlooking the Puget Sound. Fat drops rattled the glass, as the sound of water splashing against the roof created a comforting, familiar sound.

Abby could feel the physical tax of her power in her bones. She was breathing heavily, trying to catch her breath. The emotions her vision invoked quickened her heart, and Abby expended what resilience she had to not let the grief and sorrow consume her.

She allowed herself to breathe until her body relaxed. Though her eyes were heavy with fatigue, she knew she would not sleep–at least not for a while.

Abby lay there, letting her thoughts race until she found herself retreating into slumber. She was just on the edge of sleep when a strange sound pulled her back. She tilted her head up. In the distance, she could hear an old, rattling voice. It was singing.

She sat up in bed and listened carefully. The sound was so faint. It was like a strange hymn with an eerie tune. Abby stood and walked into the hallway. A soft, gray glow was coming from beneath the crack of the door to Evan's room.

A sick feeling swelled in Abby's stomach. As she raced down the hall, she started to make out some of the words sung to the haunting melody.

> *"Why fair Maid in ev'ry feature,*
> *Are such Signs of fear expres'd?*
> *Can a wand'ring wretched creature*
> *With such terror fill they breast*
> *Do my brazened looks alarm thee*
> *Such fretting is in vain,*
> *Not for kingdoms would I harm thee,*
> *Alarm not then poor Crazy Jane*
> *Poor Crazy Jane, poor Crazy Jane,*
> *Not for kingdoms would I harm thee,*
> *Shun not then poor Crazy Jane."*

When Abby reached down to turn the knob, a cold chill crawled down her neck. She took a deep breath and pushed the door open.

Evan's bedroom was basked in a sickly gray glow, all the playful colors muted by a shroud of death. Sitting in the rocking chair beside the crib was a spirit of the withered old woman. Her pockmarked face was offset by the jagged decaying teeth revealed by her wicked smile. The old woman's eyes squinted slightly, looking up to Abby as though she had expected her to arrive at any moment. Abby's heart nearly jumped into her throat upon seeing Little Evan sleeping in the old woman's arms.

Abby stepped into the room with uncertainty. She could hear the distant wails of spirits crying out for mercy. "Leave him alone," Abby warned, doing her best to sound menacing. She could tell immediately how unconvincing her threat had been when Mother Damnable began laughing maniacally.

"You have no power over me, you pathetic little Kane!" Mother Damnable spat the name like a curse. The old crone looked down at Evan sleeping in her arms. "This one is special," she said.

"He hasn't done anything to you," Abby said, her words almost pleading.

"He isn't a Kane," Mother Damnable rasped as she ran her jagged finger over his sleeping eyelids.

"Not by blood," Abby admitted cautiously, "but he is certainly our family, and we will protect him."

"He is very special. This one can see me." Mother Damnable stood and returned him to the crib. "We shall be close friends, he and I," she added, cooing over his bed. Abby felt sick at the threat.

"Never!" Abby said, putting herself between Mother Damnable and the crib as the withered spirit stepped away.

"Oh, now that's what I like to see," Mother Damnable said her grin spread across her face revealing her maw of rot. "Protective, motherly instincts. How many Kanes will you be adding to my collection?" The crazed spirit began cackling.

"None," Abby said defiantly. "You're nothing but a parasite, clinging to my family for some perverse revenge."

"Do you really think so?"

"Yes, I do," Abby said.

The certainty in Abby's voice caused Mother Damnable to stop and looked at her. The specter tilted her head slightly.

"I'm already dead," Mother Damnable, said raising an eyebrow. "What can the mighty Kanes do to me now?" She roared with laughter.

Abby felt something crawling up her leg and quickly looked down to see a large tarantula-like spider climbing over her knee. She instinctively swatted it away and stepped back, pushing up against the crib.

"What's the matter?" Mother Damnable asked a wicked smile on her face. "You're in my world now. Just because you're clever enough to see into my world does not mean you have power here, little girl."

"Why did you come here?" Abby asked, looking at the malevolent spirit in the eye. "You didn't come here to toy with me. You have enough spirits trapped for your demented entertainment. You're trying to see what we're up to. You're afraid, aren't you, Mary Ann Conklin."

The crazed spirit gave Abby a terrifying glare. "Where did you hear that name?" the old woman shouted. She growled, low in her chest.

"What's wrong?" Abby questioned defiantly. "There is a lot of power in a name, few know that better than a witch."

Mother Damnable placed Evan in his crib and began to pace, pounding her fists on her head. A strange calm came over the crazed spirit. The old woman looked up and stared into Abby's eyes. "I do not fear the power you invoke with a name. It pales in comparison with the destruction your family will reap upon itself."

"Don't think for one moment I will believe your lies," Abby said.

The old woman examined Abby closely. She could smell the rot and decay all over the unwelcome spirit. "You have many eyes young one, and you continue to see very little," Mother Damnable whispered as she drew closer.

"I'm not scared of you," Abby lied to the old spirit standing face to face with her.

"You should be." Mother Damnable cackled. Without hesitation, the old woman leaned down and bit Abby in the shoulder. Abby screamed in pain as Mother Damnable pulled back a bloody grin on her face. "I bite!" The hag danced around. Her maniacal laughter was punctuated by those two little sing-song words over and over. "I bite!" She sang over and over again.

Abby quickly pulled Evan from his crib and headed toward the door. Before she could make it through, the door slammed shut. Mother Damnable came to a halt as Abby turned to face the old woman.

"I'll be watching," Mother Damnable warned with a menacing glint in her eye.

Abby spun back toward the exit. "Sitltular Bombartus!" she yelled, pointing her finger at the doorway. A powerful force slammed into the door, knocking it from its frame and slamming against the wall across the hallway.

Abby ran out of the room and into the hallway. She turned to look at Evan's room. Mother Damnable emerged from the darkness, her pale gray glow and wicked grin relentlessly edging closer to them. She pressed her back against the wall, holding Evan protectively away from the apparition.

Mother Damnable stood face to face with Abby again.

Abby avoided looking into the spirit's eyes, afraid the dark wells would consume her. The loathsome spirit opened her mouth wide, ready to take another bite.

She winced, but the spirit's jagged teeth did not sink into her flesh. Instead, the spirit unleashed a shrill scream. The sound was horrifying; the intensity was deafening.

Abby instinctively tried to covered her ears, but her hands were full. With her free hand, she reached up and covered her baby cousin's ear instead, cradling the other to her chest.

She felt like her head would shatter from the pressure and the noise. She unleashed her own scream, but she could not hear it through the specter's horrifying shriek. She closed her eyes, trying to close every sense she could. There was subtle popping sound in her ear, then a strange, eerie silence.

Abby opened her eyes, Mother Damnable was gone. Her ears felt plugged like they needed to be popped. She strained her jaw, hoping to find relief from the pressure, but it didn't come. She looked down at Little Evan in her arms. He was crying, but there wasn't any sound.

"It's okay," Abby said. Her lips moved, and she could feel the vibration in her throat, but she couldn't hear herself speak.

Her uncles came rushing out of their bedroom, and Wendy poked her head through her doorway. Sebastian looked at her. Her eyes were wide with terror and confusion. "Uncle Sebastian!" she said. Everything was silent. *Can he hear me? Did she cast some kind of silence spell?*

Sebastian and Rodger both stood in front of her. She could see their lips move, they were speaking, but Abby could not hear anything, nothing at all.

She stood there, tears in her eyes. *It isn't them...* she realized. "I can't hear you. I'm completely deaf."

Sebastian took Evan from Abby's arms as he glanced into the small child's bedroom. Wendy approached as Rodger knelt down to face Abby. He said something.

Abby shook her head and covered her ears. She closed her eyes, willing herself to hear. When she opened them, there was still no sound.

Rodger was already examining the wound on Abby's shoulder. The two crescent-shaped bite marks were already red and swollen and looked like they were on the verge of festering. Rodger looked worried. He spoke to her.

"I can't hear you," Abby said again in frustration. At least that is what she thought she had said. Not being able to hear her own words, she was uncertain if she was articulating herself. Both her uncles and Wendy stopped and looked at her, their faces worried.

Rodger took her arm and motioned for him to follow her. Abby accompanied him as he guided her down the stairs and to the sanctum. The basement staircase was still missing a few steps, and he helped her navigate over the makeshift stairs they had put in after the attack. He quickly pulled out a chair and placed a pen and tablet of paper in front of her. He scribbled something and then set himself to searching for something in the cupboards.

Abby looked down. "What happened? Why can't you hear?" he had written.

Abby steadied herself, and wrote, "Mother Damnable."

Rodger returned with several small jars of ointments and set them on the counter next to Abby. He then paused and read her note. He grimaced slightly and opened one of the jars.

Rodger dabbed a small amount of a dark-green creamy substance onto the tip of his index finger and looked at Abby sorrowfully.

Abby looked at him with curiosity as he applied the green ointment to the bite marks. It felt cold, a nice contrast to the feverish sensation that was beginning to radiate from the injury. Abby couldn't help but wince in pain as she looked down at her shoulder and saw the ointment bubbling.

She turned to see Rodger had written something else on the tablet. "Sorry, it will only sting for a minute or two."

Abby sighed in relief and wore the bravest smile she could conjure. She focused on her breathing, trying to imagine how the strange healing ointment her uncle used was cleaning and purifying the wound.

When she glanced over, she saw that Sebastian and Wendy had joined them. *I didn't hear them come in,* she realized. *When is my hearing going to come back...? What if it doesn't!?* Panic roiled Abby's stomach as her mind began racing.

Rodger nudged Abby with the pad of paper and pen, pulling her back into the moment. Abby batted back several tears threatening to break loose and looked down at the paper. "How did you lose your hearing?"

"The spirit screamed. Loud. Nothing since." She returned the pen and paper. Before Rodger could take it, she snatched it back and added, "When will my hearing come back?"

Rodger stared at her response for a moment and looked at Abby with a pensive expression. He shrugged and shook his head.

Abby took the pen and paper. "Pennington healing. Can you help?" The sense of panic was returning, and Abby fought to keep control of herself.

Rodger read as Sebastian and Wendy came around and read over his shoulders. He then jotted something down, it was long.

Abby was frustrated with the time it was taking to communicate.

Rodger finished and help up the tablet. "I don't know, but I'm going to do everything I can to make sure you get your hearing back. This loss might be temporary. Try not to panic. I'll start researching other approaches if it turns out not to be the case."

Wendy reached down and took the pen and paper. She began writing something as she spoke. She then held up the tablet. "I think it was a Banshee Wail."

Abby shook her head in confusion. Wendy began writing again. "It's a Celtic legend. The spirit of a woman that wails for her lost lover. Her scream is deadly to some and deafening to others."

Abby took the pen and paper. "You think she's a Banshee?"

Wendy shook her head and then started writing again. "Probably not, but she could have similar powers." She held up the tablet so Abby could see, then took it back and added, "If your hearing was taken by arcane forces, it could be restored through the arcane as well."

Abby prayed Wendy was right. If Rodger was as good a healer as Vivian and Fiona claimed he was, she still had hope.

She was on the edge of terror, but Abby did her best to stay from the ledge. There was no reason to give up hope… at least not yet.

She sighed and shook her head to keep the tears at bay. *How am I going to tell Grandmother about this?* she wondered.

CHAPTER SIXTEEN

Sebastian pushed the morning newspaper in front of Abby. *I didn't even realize people still read these anymore,* she thought. She smiled and gladly started looking at the financial section of the New York Times. Though she didn't have the slightest interest in reading about the corporate trends of the week, there was no other way for her to participate in the morning routine.

She looked up from reading and saw Wendy chuckling about something as Rodger began clearing the table. Abby wondered what was so funny. *Would I have found it funny too?*

Her eye fell on the date at the top of the paper. *Oh no!* She leaped to her feet, waving her arms to get someone's attention. Sebastian, Rodger, and Wendy noticed her panicked expression and were looking at her worriedly.

Abby picked up her phone and quickly tapped in a text and sent it to all three of them.

> ABBY: I am supposed to practice
> my piece with Irene today! I can't
> play if I can't hear anything!

She leaned back in her chair, feeling utterly defeated as her family read their phones. Abby covered her eyes with her hands, hoping to keep the tears from coming.

What if I never get my hearing back? I'm never going to be able to play my violin again! She began rubbing temples. Her brief retreat into her own head was interrupted by a tapping on her arm. She opened her eyes when her phone vibrated.

> SEBASTIAN: I'll call and
> let her know you're ill.

Abby took a deep breath and nodded. She then tapped her reply.

> ABBY: I'll follow up with an
> email later this evening.

> WENDY: What are you
> going to do today?

The second message came in while she was typing. Abby looked at her aunt and shrugged.

> RODGER: I will call my
> grandfather about your
> hearing. If anyone in
> my family will know
> what to do it will be him

Abby gave Rodger an appreciative grin.

> ABBY: Thank you.

Abby finished off the last of her coffee and took another bite of toast before shooing Rodger away from the table. She pointed to herself, shaking her head at him. *I'll clean up, it's the least I can do, since I'm completely worthless in every other way,* she thought as she finished clearing the breakfast table.

Sebastian disappeared upstairs to finish getting ready for work. Wendy cleaned up Little Evan and went into the living room to play. Rodger gave Abby a confident smile and made his way toward the sanctum. *I hope he can figure something out,* she thought as she began rinsing the glasses and plates before organizing them in the dishwasher.

Abby filled the dishwasher, feeling hollow inside. The water rushing over the plates should be making a sound, yet there was nothing. The clink of the glasses as she nestled them on the rack went unheard. She knew what sounds they should make, but everything she did was rewarded with silence. It was as if she didn't exist anymore.

Okay, stop it! she scolded herself. *Plenty of people live their entire lives like this, quit feeling sorry for yourself.* She closed her eyes to cement the notion in her mind. It seemed to work, at least for the time being. She closed the door and started the dishwasher.

I just need to figure out ways I can be helpful. I need to stay busy, or I'm going to lose it, she told herself.

She passed through the living room on her way to the stairs and saw Wendy and Little Evan sprawled out on a blanket. Evan was chewing on a teething ring as Wendy changed his diaper. Abby gave them a halfhearted smile and quickly went up the stairs. She went into her room and closed the door. Abby saw her violin case sitting next to her small desk in front of the window. *I can't even practice...* She stared at the case with remorse.

I should give the symphony as much notice as possible. If Rodger doesn't find anything to help with my hearing soon, I won't be able to perform... The realization was a stab through the heart. The emotions she had compartmentalized only moments before began to swell again.

A single tear escaped, and Abby saw her reflection in the window. I look pathetic, she thought as she wiped away the tear. Her hair was a tangled mess. There were dark circles under her eyes from the sleepless night. Her skin seemed blotchy and irritated. Her eyes looked hollow as if life itself no longer lived in her soul.

Pull it together, Mom and Dad need you right now, Abby reminded herself. The pain in her heart quickly turned to grief–a subtle shift, but just as devastating. *I need to do more research.* She desperately tried to think of something she could do.

She moved over to her desk and sat staring down at her computer. Abby moved the mouse, waking the computer from its dormancy. She typed in her password and opened a search engine. *Should I?* She wondered. Abby shrugged. *What do I have to lose?*

With trepidation, Abby typed in the address to a unique website with an esoteric suffix of ARC, short for arcanum. It was a part of the web she had not visited more than a handful of times in her brief time studying witchcraft. The Arcanum was a hidden part of the web maintained by mysterious technomancers. There were more than a few stories about the reclusive witches who specialized in magical technology. She had heard rumors of how technomancers spy on witches who dare to enter their portion of the World Wide Web. This time, it seemed worth the risk.

Abby clicked the enter key, and her browser began flashing. Several arcane symbols flashed across her screen as she waited for her computer to engage with the strange, hidden part of the web. The screen went black. A tiny pinpoint of light appeared in the center and began growing until it filled the screen with a bright light. A few words in Latin appeared across the top of her screen. 'Gratissima Amicum.' *Welcome Friend,* she translated and then smiled. Then a search box appeared in the center of the screen.

She typed the words MOTHER DAMNABLE into the search box and hit enter. Her cursor spun for a moment before the results appeared. There was only one result. Abby clicked on the link.

A website with a gray border came up. There was scarcely anything written, but in the top left-hand corner of the screen was an old black-and-white photo. Abby's mouth went dry. Staring back at her was an image of the old woman–the spirit who had been haunting her for the last couple weeks. Deep crags cut into her withered face as large soulless eyes stared back at her.

That's definitely her then. She shuddered and gazed out her window, unable to look at the picture a moment longer. The old woman's visage was horrifying even when frozen in a digital picture. Abby took a deep, settling breath and returned her attention to the brief article.

Mary Ann Conklin, a.k.a. Mother Damnable. A solitary practitioner from Pennsylvania who was an early settler in Seattle Washington, prior to the Alaskan Gold Rush. She was believed to have traveled to Seattle by ship, along with several other witches who had formed a coven with her. It is unknown what happened to the other witches as Mary Ann Conklin was the only witch in town when the Kane family moved to the fledgling city.

It is believed Mary Ann Conklin had a friendly relationship with the Kane Coven when they arrived and helped them drive several other covens out of the city when they attempted to get a foothold in the area. However, it is believed the relationship soured. When she died, her body turned to stone, an indication of a curse, which led many to believe at some point Mother Damnable ran afoul of the Kane Coven.

"Grandmother definitely knows something..." Abby speculated out loud. *There isn't much to go on, but there must history between Mary Ann Conklin and the Kanes that they don't want to become public knowledge. Is this why she's haunting us?*

Abby stood and started pacing the room, working her thoughts through. *This definitely personal. Whatever happened when the Kanes moved here was obviously bad enough for them to curse her.* Her grandmother had tried to get her to read the family history books several times, but Abby had never found the time to wade through the eight volumes of family lore. Now she was kicking herself for not paying closer attention.

She searched for any links on the page. She sighed, finding none. *I should go to Grandmother's house and look at those history books. If there's anything in there about Mother Damnable, it will be in one of the later books when the family arrives in Seattle.*

She glanced down at her phone. *It's ten in the morning, there isn't another ferry for... What am I thinking! I can't drive! The doctor forbids it, at least until I've learned to adjust... I could take a taxi...*

Her bedroom lights flicked off and on again. Abby turned to see Rodger standing at her doorway. She greeted him with a smile. He pulled out his phone and tapped a message in before looking up at Abby. Within seconds her phone vibrated.

> RODGER: I spoke with my grandfather. He gave me some suggestions on what to research. This will likely take a while. I'm sorry, Abby.

A heavy mood settled over Abby's heart. A part of her had hoped the Penningtons would have some miraculous cure that would return her hearing instantly. *I know magic doesn't work like that,* she thought, *but still...*

Rodger looked at Abby with reassurance. He didn't need to say anything. Abby already knew he wanted nothing more than to take her pain away. But he couldn't. No one could.

He picked up his phone again.

> RODGER: I'm going to get started on that research now

Abby patted his arm and pointed to her computer before replying.

> ABBY: I'm going to Grand-
> mother's library and see
> about getting my hands on
> the family histories.

Rodger looked over her shoulder at the article on her computer, then read her message. He nodded and sent another of his own.

> RODGER: Madison is on her
> way. I think she's planning to
> come over to cheer you up.

There was a pause for thought before offering a shrug. *I guess I'll go tomorrow,* she thought.

> RODGER: Why don't you let
> me see if I can try and get my
> hands on the books for you

> ABBY: Will Grandmother
> will let you borrow them?

> RODGER: I guess it depends
> on how much she has to hide.

> ABBY: Aunt Fiona?

After reading her response, Rodger nodded.

> RODGER: I'll try her first

He waved goodbye and trotted off down the hall.

She turned back to her computer and continued her research. She typed in COVENS SEATTLE WASHINGTON and waited for the results. There were several links, mostly lists of covens in the area, genealogies, and some new articles. She read through a few of them, building a basic timeline of Seattle's occult history.

After a while, she stopped reading as her mind wandered. *My family arrived in the 1860s, and the Westbrooks in the 1870s. If Hailey's family came just after ours... I wonder if her grandmother knows anything?*

Abby closed her laptop and sighed. Looking around the room made her feel lost. She didn't know what she was looking for. Maybe something familiar, something that made her feel connected to the world. There was no sound to remind her she was alive–no music, no sounds of Little Evan playing downstairs, not even the ticking of the grandfather clock in the hall. Even the water outside made no sound when it rushed against the rocky shore.

She looked at her bed. Her pillows and deep down comforter invited her into oblivion, however temporary. Abby crawled under the covers and closed her eyes. Though her sleep had been plagued by many terrible dreams, Abby hoped slumber would be merciful this time.

Abby was startled awake when she felt her bed bouncing abruptly. She cracked her eyes open slightly and saw a face, inches from her own, staring at her with an enormous grin. Abby pulled back slightly and saw her cousin Madison wearing a mischievous expression. Her phone vibrated.

MADISON: Get up LAZY HEAD!

Abby sat up and regarded her cousin with uncertainty. Madison gave an overdramatic sigh and typed in another message.

MADISON: Are you planning
to sleep all day?

Abby flopped back onto her pillows, rolling away from her cousin, and pulled the blankets over her head.

Madison shook her shoulder, trying to get her to move, and gave her a look that clearly said, 'my cousin says the most insane things.' The shaking stopped for a moment before Abby's phone buzzed again.

> MADISON: Do you know
> what time it is???

Abby glanced at the time on her phone: 6:24 pm. She sat up suddenly. I've slept the day away! She glanced up at Madison, who gave her a knowing look.

Madison typed in a new message and hit send.

> MADISON: Come on, let's
> get some food in your
> scrawny self, and then I
> have a surprise for you.

With furrowed brows, Abby regarded Madison's threat of a surprise with uncertainty. Madison sighed again and picked up her phone.

> MADISON: Don't worry,
> It's just for a couple hours.

Madison slid off the bed and motioned Abby to follow.

Abby lethargically dragged herself out of her nice warm den and tapped her phone alive. She paused and typed a message.

> ABBY: I hope you know you
> woke me from the best sleep
> I've had in months.

> MADISON: You won't
> regret it. I promise.

Without waiting for Abby to decide, Madison grabbed her arm and dragged her into the hallway and down the stairs. They passed through the empty living room into the kitchen. There was a plastic bag on the counter that looked like takeout.

Abby looked at her, asking the question with her expression rather than typing it out again. Where is everyone?

Madison smiled and texted a reply.

> MADISON: They went out
> for dinner. Left you in my
> hands. 😈

Madison opened the plastic bag and pulled out several small, white takeout boxes. The smell made Abby's stomach growl. *Massaman curry! And Pad Thai too? Mmmm...* Her mouth was watering in anticipation. From the smell, it was takeout from her favorite restaurant near her old home. The first genuine smile of the day crept across Abby's face.

After setting the contents of the plastic bag on the counter, Madison collected two plates from the cupboard and silverware from a drawer. Abby couldn't help herself, she opened one of the containers and inhaled deeply, letting the smell of the spicy peanut sauce wash over her.

I'm more hungry than I thought, she realized as she began dumping rice onto her plate. Abby spooned huge helpings of everything onto her place and immediately started shoveling the food into her mouth. The sweet, spicy flavors burst in her mouth. Abby closed her eyes to savor it with every bite. She glanced over to see her cousin watching her, amused.

Abby flushed with embarrassment and reasserted her table manners. Sitting upright, she began eating like a normal person. Looking up, she watched Madison type something into her phone. Abby grabbed her own in anticipation.

> MADISON: Have you spoken
> with your grandmother in the
> last couple days?

Abby shook her head and replied.

> ABBY: She hasn't been by in
> a while. And I didn't want to
> try and explain.

Abby waved vaguely in the direction of her ears when her cousin looked up from reading the text. Madison had a knowing expression on her face. After a moment, she hesitantly began typing.

> MADISON: Something is
> going on.

> ABBY: What?

Abby was beginning to feel frustrated with the process of typing everything on her phone. *This is so slow!*

> MADISON: I overheard
> grandma and aunt Vivian
> arguing. Something about
> Mother Damnable, and they
> mentioned Lily.

> ABBY: Lily? The little ghost girl?

Madison shrugged and then nodded. *I think so*, her expression said.

Abby typed, quickly responding.

> ABBY: Waht elsedid you hear?

Abby watched Madison laugh silently over her typos and corrected it.

> ABBY: What else did you hear?

> MADISON: Just that they
> were going to speak with
> Uncle Bernard about it.

Abby sat in contemplation for a few moments. She was sure now, more than ever, that there had to have been some kind of falling out with Mary Ann Conklin. *Why else would she be so hellbent on revenge?* she wondered. *She's been dead for over a century! What kind of grudge holds on that long?*

Abby took several more bites, absently lost in thought, before pushing her plate away. She was getting awfully tired of Vivian's secrets.

Abby's train of thought was broken by the vibration of her phone.

> MADISON: Eat up! We haven't
> gotten to the surprise yet!

> ABBY: This wasn't the surprise?

Madison shook her head, grinning mischievously. She pushed Abby's plate back in front of her, pointedly.

Abby took several more bites to appease her cousin.

Satisfied with Abby's efforts, Madison took her hand and pulled her upstairs. She sat her cousin on the edge of her bed and began rummaging through Abby's closet.

> ABBY: What are you looking for?

Madison glanced down at her phone and gave Abby a wicked smile and a raised eyebrow. She then resumed her search without responding. She had gone through nearly the entire closet before she pulled out a short dress Abby had forgotten she owned.

Madison held the dress out for Abby to take.

> ABBY: And what do you want
> me to do with this?

With a snide glare, Madison pulled out her phone and tapped in her response.

> MADISON: Put it on! Duh. 😕

What are you up to? Abby's suspicious look said.

Madison tapped quickly tapped another response with a serious glare on her face.

MADISON: Put it on!

Abby sent another text, but Madison refused to look at her phone and held out the dress with a warning glare. She exaggerated her words, making it easy to read her lips. "Put it on!"

CHAPTER SEVENTEEN

Abby looked down at the sea-green dress Madison had picked for her. It felt much tighter and much shorter than Abby was used to. What was I thinking when I bought this thing? She looked down at her cleavage and blushed. She pulled out her phone and sent her cousin a text.

ABBY: I'm not sure about this...

MADISON: You're going to love it!

Madison smiled with excitement.

Abby gave her cousin an unconvinced look. She felt so far out of her comfort zone, going to a nightclub in an outfit like this. All she wanted to do was go home and curl up in bed and read a book.

ABBY: What's the point? I can't hear anything?

Madison rolled her eyes dramatically.

MADISON: NO ONE can hear in a nightclub!

Abby sighed in defeat.

ABBY: If you say so

MADISON: I say so!

Madison responded with a playful smile as the taxi rushed through the dark streets toward Pioneer Square.

Abby typed into her phone, feeling utterly ridiculous. She pulled her jacket tight around her in a feeble attempt at modesty.

> ABBY: What's the name of
> the place you're taking me?

> MADISON: Scream

Abby looked at her with uncertainty.

Madison put down her phone and glanced at herself in a compact mirror, touching up her eyeliner. Noticing the look on Abby's face, Madison picked up her phone again and began typing.

> MADISON: Come on Abby! It's
> time to cut loose. Things have
> been too intense lately and you
> need to decompress. 😄😄😄

She isn't wrong, Abby thought as she looked out the window as the glass buildings gave way to older masonry buildings as they entered the older part of the city. She summoned a smile and looked at her cousin. *Alright. I'm going to try my best,* she thought, then nodded.

Madison smiled brightly.

She's so beautiful, Abby observed. She secretly hoped her cousin would get all the attention at the club, so she could hide in some dark corner. It wasn't like she could strike up a conversation anyway. *Wait...* Something occurred to her and began typing in her question.

> ABBY: What kind of club is
> going to let two underage
> girls in?

Madison glanced at the message on her phone and began typing her response with an amused smile.

> MADISON: They don't. They
> let underage YOUNG WOMEN
> like us in.

Abby looked at her cousin, her eyes widened.

ABBY: Madison Kane! What
do you have up your sleeve?
I happen to know you've
been in this place before.
How did you get in?

MADISON: You can just leave
that to me.

ABBY: Your mother warned me
about you.

MADISON: Of that, I have no
doubt.

MADISON: Going out tonight
isn't about following rules and
being a good girl. Tonight is
about letting our hair down
and having fun. I need it, and
if I need it, you sure as hell do!

Abby laughed. The second text was hard to argue with.

ABBY: You've convinced me.

MADISON: I'll believe that
when I see you out on the
dance floor having fun!

ABBY: Ugh, you're relentless!

The car pulled up to an old building that looked like
it was built sometime around the turn of the last century.
A large neon sign was a wide, open mouth with large, red
lips lit up and hovering over the entrance. The whole sign
looked as if someone was screaming. Red lights flashed
the word 'SCREAM' just beneath the open lips.

"We're here," Madison carefully exaggerated the
words, so Abby could read her lips. She quickly paid
the driver and hopped out of the car in her short dress.

She reached out and took Abby's hand, pulling her out onto the sidewalk.

Jesus, she's strong! Abby chuckled internally.

A queue of hopeful patrons dressed in tight, trendy clothing lined up along the front of the building, disappearing around the corner at the end of the block. Three enormous men dressed in all black stood at the door managing the crowd outside. Thumping vibrations blasted from inside the building. The whole thing felt like a living organism, complete with its own heartbeat.

Madison took Abby's arm and approached one of the bouncers with an innocent smile. She spoke to the bouncer. Even though Abby couldn't hear what she had said, it was obvious Madison was working her, figurative, magic.

The man greeted her familiarly and quickly stepped aside to let them pass. As Abby entered the dark entrance, she looked back to see people in the line shaking their fists and protesting. *Well, they seem to know Madison,* she observed.

Madison glanced back and gave Abby a sheepish smile. They passed through a small antechamber that was set up as a coat check. They surrendering their purses and jackets in exchange for a small slip of paper with a number.

The woman behind the counter said something and disappeared into the back room. Without her jacket, Abby wrapped her arms around herself, attempting in futility to feel more modest. Even though she was covered, she still felt out of her element.

> MADISON: You'll get used to it, especially when you see how much attention you'll get in there.

A large red velvet curtain was draped over a door that led past the lobby into the club. Music pounded through the building. Even though she couldn't hear it, the familiar beat vibrated through the floor, pulsing up her legs. It was so clear she could imagine a familiar tune in her head. *I can dance to the vibrations!* she realized. For the first time since her cousin proposed this idea, Abby was excited.

Madison pulled the curtain aside, and Abby stepped through. She stood in a long hallway lined from floor to ceiling with screens playing an endless loop of men and women screaming. Abby didn't like horror movies, but she thought she recognized a few of the clips from some of the slasher films Hailey and Madison had made her watch.

As they reached the end of the hallway, Madison stopped and sent a quick text.

> MADISON: Alright, let's keep
> an eye out for one another.

Abby felt apprehension in every part of her body. This wasn't what she wanted to do, not with everything still lingering in uncertainty and her parents existing in torment, locked away in some spirit prison. *There is nothing you can do right now,* she reminded herself. *Just do this and try to have some fun.*

As they walked along the hallway of screams, the vibrations from the music began to flow toward them like waves of sound. Abby saw another red curtain draped over what she assumed was the entrance to the dance floor. The beat rattled in Abby's chest as they approached.

"Ready?" Madison mouthed. Abby nodded. Her cousin reached out and pulled the velvet drape aside.

Abby was momentarily blinded by a flash of light. She stepped out onto a metal platform overlooking a large dance floor. The music was blasting from every direction. On the opposite side of the room, a raised booth overlooked the entire club. The dance floor was filled with young people bouncing and gyrating to the beats the DJ was laying down. Stage lights flashed from metal scaffolds, mirror balls glittered from the ceiling, and a light mist poured over the floor from a fog machine at the DJ's feet. Andy Warhol-esk neon portraits of people screaming lined the walls. A gigantic bar was settled along one side of the room, where lines of people waited to get drinks.

Abby stood in awe, taking in the scene. Madison nudged Abby and gestured to look at her phone. Abby found a text.

> MADISON: Mother would send me to a convent school if she ever found out I came anywhere near this place.

Abby couldn't help but laugh thinking about Margot's reaction, and nodded her agreement.

Madison motioned for Abby to follow her. She pulled Abby down a few metal steps into a large press of bodies.

As they weaved their way toward the dance floor. Abby felt herself getting swept up in the vibe. She and Madison sauntered into the crowd and began dancing, instinctively moving to the beat. Every fear, inhibition, and concern Abby had been feeling began to melt away like wax under a flame. She allowed her body to move to the vibrations of the music, letting everything else go.

They danced through song after song. *I haven't done anything like this in a long time,* she thought.

She allowed herself to forget about everything in the world except for that moment as she moved and swayed to the vibrations shaking the room. The lights flashed, and the music played. Abby couldn't help laughing as the pure joy of moving her body won her over.

Madison pantomimed holding a cup and drinking, and then pointed to Abby, the question on her face. Abby shook her head, refusing the drink, and kept dancing.

After a few minutes, Abby strolled over to an empty booth and plopped down, letting herself catch her breath. *We must have been dancing for a while,* she thought as she watched the people around her. A hundred bodies danced without a care in the world. The vibrations of the music pounded, and lights flew all over the room. It overwhelmed the senses–mesmerizing and strangely relaxing at the same time.

Abby noticed a small crowd of people standing in front of the booth next to her. In the booth, sat two women wearing matching black tube dresses. Their hair was crimped, and they work dark makeup like new-wave goths. A line of people stood near them, waiting. Abby watched someone slip one of the women a wad of cash, while the other handed back a small baggie filled with something white.

A few moments later, Madison returned with two bottles of water. She looked at Abby's strange expression and mouthed, "What's wrong?"

Abby discretely pointed in the direction of the next booth. Madison glanced over and nodded.

> MADISON: They're doing some
> good business tonight.

Madison shrugged as though it was nothing and twisted the cap off her water bottle before taking a large drink.

Abby felt naïve but had to ask.

ABBY: What are they selling?

MADISON: Probably cocaine
or XTC. Why? Want to try it?

Abby shook her head firmly no. She then typed in another question and hit send.

ABBY: You haven't tried it
have you?

Madison shook her head.

MADISON: I'm curious, but I
haven't worked up the nerve.
What would I do if I liked it?

Abby read the message, and the two of them shared a laugh. Abby nodded her agreement and wrote another question.

ABBY: What are they doing
up there?

She gestured to the balcony on one side of the building when her cousin looked up from reading the text. A staircase was closely watched by a bouncer at the foot of the stairs. It was particularly dark, though Abby could see people sitting in the balcony area.

MADISON: VIP area. You
shouldn't go up there. A lot
of sex and drugs.

Abby's mouth dropped and quickly tapped on her phone screen.

ABBY: Madison! Have you
been up there?

Madison smiled slyly. Abby practically fell out of the booth and playfully slugged her cousin in the arm. Madison typed into her phone.

> MADISON: Only once. I didn't do anything. I'm not into giving it away to complete strangers. Besides, there's something off about some of the people that go up there.

ABBY: What do you mean?

Madison took a deep breath and carefully thought about what she was going to write. She then typed her response.

> MADISON: I don't think everyone here is a normal human. I've seen things. Little subtle things. I think the owner is something different, not like us.

> MADISON: Pretty mysterious, don't you think? 😜

Abby looked around the room, wondering what mysteries roamed the club.

ABBY: And dangerous. What do you think the owner is?

> MADISON: No clue. I'll figure it out, eventually.

Abby stared at her phone for a moment and then looked around the room. She shook her head.

ABBY: Your mother would kill you if she knew you came to a place like this.

Madison nodded her agreement. She looked out to the dance floor and closed her eyes, savoring something. She quirked her head toward the dance floor.

Abby shook her head and let her cousin go. Madison got up and began swaying back into the crowd.

Abby sat back and let herself relax for a couple minutes as she drank more water. Several patrons walked by and gave her suggestive smiles. Abby simply smiled back. It still feels strange to flirt, she thought.

The music pounded. Abby felt it in her chest as it rattled the building. She closed her eyes. The music swirled around her like a tempest. For a brief moment, it was almost as if she could hear it. *Perhaps it was a phantom sound, maybe I could hear it... I don't know...*

She opened her eyes and searched for Madison on the dance floor. Abby watched for a few moments, trying to catch a glimpse of her cousin through the crowd. She didn't see anything out of place, only people dancing to the music. Abby stood and maneuvered her way into the crowd. She didn't exist to the other people who danced all around her. Nothing did.

The strobe lights began to pulse to the beat of the music. The lights continued to flicker off and on, casting the room in frenzied moments of darkness and light. It created a peculiar illusion of movement that felt strange, almost disorienting.

Abby batted her eyes, uncertain. On the staircase leading to the DJ's booth was a little girl with pigtails and a tattered gray dress. "Lily?" Abby muttered, unable to hear her own words.

She pushed her way through the crowd, doing her best to get to the spirit of the young girl. Abby could barely pass through the crowded dance floor. Her lack of height made it difficult to see anything. She continued to dodge waving arms and unexpected side steps.

When she emerged on the far side, Lily was nowhere to be found. She approached the staircase and found nothing. Abby turned to see if Lily was still around.

The strobe lights went dark. For a fraction of a second, Abby saw the slickly gray glow of rot and decay filling a large empty room. A flake of ash fell on Abby's arm.

With each thumping beat of the music, her world flashed back and forth between the world of the dead and the world of the living. She stood, lost in fear as empty, hollow images contrasted with the living dancers losing themselves in hedonistic pleasure.

Faint laughter began blinked in and out in chorus with the world of death. *I can hear!* Abby realized. *In the Sight, I can hear.* Relief flooded through her, making her knees weak. It was an odd sensation, trying to hear with her mind, rather than her ears. As she listened, laughter turned into a sickening cackle.

Abby spun around in a panic, searching for some tangible manifestation of the deranged old woman. Across the empty room, a gnarled and bent figure stood, disappearing for brief moments behind the dancers in the next world.

With each second, the old woman disappeared and reappeared slightly closer. Abby stepped back until she found herself up against the bar. There were people nearby, but they seemed to not notice her. She looked back to where the specter had been. With each blink, she was closer, then closer, and then, standing right in front of her.

The old woman reached out and pointed at Abby. The vibrations from the music disappeared, the flashing between worlds stopped. Abby was completely surrounded by rot and decay.

"You are next!" the old woman growled. The old woman's face was contorted in disgust.

Abby's blood ran cold.

"Why do you torment my family?" she demanded bravely.

The old woman began laughing. "You are a foolish child. You have many eyes, yet you see nothing," she said in her gravelly voice.

"I can see you," Abby said, doing her best to sound threatening. She was certain she was unconvincing.

The old woman gave her an amused smile, blood dripping from her lips. Abby felt something crawl across her feet and looked down. Maggots, worms, and centipedes crawled over her feet, working their way into her shoes. She yelped and attempted to shake them off.

"Death is coming for you," the old woman said. "You'll be maggot food soon. I've sent for them. You will be mine." Mother Damnable's crazed laughter continued. She stepped forward, and Abby stepped back.

Once again, Abby found herself pressed up against a decaying bar crawling with cockroaches and rats.

The old woman reached out with her finger. The nail was crooked like a jagged talon. "You are so sweet and kind," the old spirit said patronizingly. "I cannot wait to break you!"

"Leave us alone!" Abby yelled. Ash began to fall from the ceiling like snow. The old woman's smile widened. She reached out and touched Abby's cheek. Her gnarled hand felt like it was made of stone. "I will see you soon," the spirit insisted. She then raked her talons across Abby's cheek.

There was a sharp pain. Abby yelped as she attempted to move out of reach. The whole right side of her face was on fire.

"Run along now," the specter said with a wicked giggle. "I will treat you better than they treated me," she added, before walking away.

"What is that supposed to mean? What did they do to you?" Abby asked, desperately.

Mother Damnable paused for a moment before continuing, disappearing behind the remnants of the decaying curtains draped across the doorway.

Abby felt the vibrations of the music slowly drift back into the room, as the sounds around her faded away. She blinked several times and found herself sitting in the booth. Her face was on fire. She reached up and felt her cheek. There were four painful scratches, like claw marks down her face. She looked at her hand and saw blood.

Madison rushed over a worried look on her face. She moved closer, taking a closer look at Abby's wounds. She pulled out her phone and tapped in her message.

> MADISON: What the hell
> happened?

ABBY: I saw her again.

> MADISON: Mother Damnable?

Madison looked around as though she expected death itself to jump out at her. She quickly sent another text.

> MADISON: Come on, lets
> get out of here.

She took Abby's hand and hurried to the exit, barely remembering to stop for their coats.

When Abby opened her eyes, she saw a tray of food sitting next to her bed. She spared a moment of gratitude for whichever loving family member had thought to bring her breakfast, before sitting up and reaching for a small glass of orange juice.

Her face stung. She reached up placed a hand against the gauze and medical tape covering her scratches. She felt slightly nauseous, feeling the feverish heat radiating from the claw marks.

Abby reached over to place the glass back onto the tray and missed, spilling all over her pajama bottoms. *Damn it!* Abby thought. She might have said the words but wasn't certain if sound actually came out of her mouth.

She picked up the glass, grateful it hadn't shattered and placed it back on the tray. "Quentifus Desparo," she said, as she waved her hand over the stain. Nothing happened. She stared in disbelief. It was a simple spell, one she'd cast many times to clean up small messes. Was it really so bad that she couldn't even do that much anymore?

I can't even cast a simple spell, she thought. She slouched over, cradling her face in her hands, too tired to even cry. *I can't hear to articulate the words correctly. I can't even do magic anymore...*

Abby rolled over, curling into a ball. *I'm useless. I can't talk, I can't use magic, I can't play my violin... I can't save my parents.* She buried her face in her pillow, trying to chase the dark thoughts away. *Maybe it would have been better it the Thanos had killed me.*

Her thoughts spiraled until sleep claimed her again.

CHAPTER EIGHTEEN

A faint vibration next to her head woke Abby from a fitful sleep. Half-dazed, she fumbled around and grabbed her phone. There was a text from Sebastian.

> SEBASTIAN: I talked to Vivian about those books you wanted to look at. She says they can't leave the house so you'll have to go to her place to read them.

Abby tossed her phone aside without sending a reply. She was too tired. Her face hurt, and she wanted nothing to do with being awake. She rolled over and closed her eyes.

After a few minutes, another buzz came in.

> SEBASTIAN: Rodger thinks he might have found something that will help with your ears.

What's the point? she thought. *Nothing else has worked.* Some part of her knew that she should be excited about the possibility. Rodger and Sebastian were both working so hard to help her, but she just couldn't care. She knew she should, but she didn't. There was no point in hoping they could heal her. Healing magic wasn't a guarantee. *I'll be like this forever...*

> SEBASTIAN: Are you still asleep? We are out running a few errands but will be back this afternoon. Wendy is there if you need anything.

What could I need? she thought, setting her phone aside and pulling the covers up over her head. *I can't do anything anyway.*

Abby rolled onto her side, staring at nothing. Her thoughts drifted through everything she'd seen and heard over the last two weeks, resting on no particular thought. She pushed aside visions of her mother, tortured and chained. She had no tears left for grief. She simply lay there, thinking nothing. Feeling nothing.

Her phone buzzed several more times, but Abby ignored them all, drifting back in and out of sleep.

At some point, she realized that she was staring blankly at the empty wall in front of her. She didn't know how much time had past, but sleep had faded into empty wakefulness, leaving her conscious but unaware.

Her bed shifted next to her. Abby rolled over to see Wendy sitting carefully next to her, holding a pad of paper. Abby turned away again, and Wendy held it in front of her face, where Abby couldn't avoid the words written on it.

"ARE YOU OK?"

Abby sat up, doing her best to put on a stoic face. *Everyone is dealing with so much, the last thing they need is me distracting them from freeing my parents.* "I'm fine," she tried to say.

Wendy gave her a concerned look and shook her head. After a moment, she stood and gestured for Abby to get out of bed.

Abby just sat there, staring at her.

Wendy gestured more impatiently, pointing at the door. *Get out of bed and come downstairs,* she was clearly saying. When Abby still didn't move, she sighed and grabbed a pen from Abby's desk, scribbling a note. When she was done, she tossed it on the bed next to Abby and walked out of the room.

Abby carefully picked up the paper and looked at what her aunt had written.

"Abby, I know you're scared, but you can't give up. We are all working to solve this–the Soul Web, your parents, your hearing–all of it. But it's going to take all of us. You aren't alone, Abby, and you aren't a burden. We're all in this together. We're all here for you. We love you. But please. Just get out of bed and TRY!"

The tears she had been unable to shed since the attack at the club finally spilled from Abby's eyes. She sat, clutching her aunt's note until the wracking sobs faded to soft, gasps.

I can't let everyone down. I need to try... for my family, she told herself over and over until she believed it.

Abby pulled herself together enough to take a long shower. She focused on the routine of it, taking the time to wash her long thick hair, being careful to avoid getting her face wet. She stood in front of the mirror, carefully running the hot blow dryer along her hair. She moved from the roots to the ends, section by section, watching her hair flow in the artificial wind. The small sensations slowly brought her back to herself.

She leaned forward, looking at the gauze covering her cheek. Abby slowly peeled back one corner to reveal the long, oozing gashes. They were slightly raised and red around the edges, appearing only slightly infected. Scabs were beginning to form over their centers, but the edges were still bleeding lightly. She shuddered, remembering Mother Damnable's stony hand raking across her skin. She quickly returned the gauze to her face, doing her best to not think about it again.

As she moved into her room, she saw her Uncle Rodger standing in the doorway. He was holding a small wooden box that was covered in ornately carved occult symbols:

pentagrams, crescent moons, and other elemental markings. A hopeful smile spread across his face.

Abby smiled weakly, in a rough attempt to return his gesture, and motioned for her uncle to enter. He took a seat on the edge of her bed and pulled out his phone.

> RODGER: I have a salve for the
> scratches on your cheeks. And
> something I hope will help with
> your hearing

She gave her uncle a smile and sat next to him. She didn't bother to answer his text. Instead, she simply presented her wounds quietly. Her phone buzzed again.

> RODGER: The salve should take
> care of those scratches in a
> day or two

Abby nodded. She knew there was no one in the whole family better suited to helping her, and she trusted him when he said it would work.

Rodger opened the box and pulled out a round glass jar. He opened the lid to reveal a light-green cream inside. He then reached over and carefully pulled the gauze and medical tape from Abby's cheek to reveal the grotesque wounds. He collected a small amount of the greenish cream onto the tip of his finger and lightly dabbed Abby's cheek. He repeated the process until each open cut was covered with the healing agent. When he was done, he gave Abby a warm smile and picked up his phone again.

> RODGER: Leave it uncovered.
> Open air will help it heal faster.

Abby gave a halfhearted chuckle typed a quick response.

> ABBY: I wasn't planning on
> going out today anyway.

Rodger smiled again and held up a small glass bottle so she could see. It was hard to tell what color the liquid was through the brown-colored glass, but it moved slowly in weird swirls, almost like it defied the physics of the bottle it was in. He set it down and picked up his phone again.

> RODGER: I've been looking into this for two days, with the help of my uncle and grandfather. They are the best Alchemist Healers in the Pennington Coven, Abby. I'm not sure this will work, but I am hopeful.

Before she could reply, she noticed he was still typing, so she waited until her phone buzzed a second time.

> RODGER: I'm going to drop some medicine into each ear. It's a tincture with a spell worked into it. If anything will help, this will. We'll need to do this daily until your hearing comes back.

Abby nodded. Rodger stood and opened the narrow vial of liquid. He leaned over Abby, and she tilted her head as far to one side as she could. She felt a single drop in her ear, and then another. She started to turn her head over for him to do the other ear. Rodger grabbed her head in both hands and held it there for a moment.

> RODGER: You don't want to let it drain out yet. Give it a moment to work.

Oh, of course, Abby thought, feeling foolish.

After a moment, he urged her head over to the other side, and they repeated the process.

There was a part of her that wished it would work instantly. She knew it wouldn't, but it was the only hope she allowed herself to feel. She waited and listened, and there was nothing.

Abby smiled awkwardly and shrugged, not knowing what else to do.

Rodger nodded. "You okay?" He mouthed clearly. She nodded.

> RODGER: Give it some time.
> We will know in a day or two if
> there's any progress.

He stood, getting ready to leave when Abby grabbed at his sleeve. She hurriedly tapped in a text and hit send.

> ABBY: What about the research?
> Have they found anything?

The piteous look he gave her told her everything she needed to know. There was no progress. He patted her shoulder, gathered his things, and left.

Abby sat, waiting, hoping that at any moment her ears would start working. *Why am I even getting worked up over this?* she thought. *I know healing magic never works that fast. If at all...* she pushed away that last thought and crawled back into bed.

Abby made her way into the kitchen and made a sandwich for herself. As she ate, she absently scrolled through her social media, stopping to leave comments now and then between bites.

As Abby finished her simple breakfast, she heard a child's cry from upstairs. *That isn't possible, I saw them leave with Evan,* she realized. A wave of cold washed through her. "No," she whispered. "Not again."

The world shimmered and rippled around her as the ghostly other-world settled over her senses. Abby looked around, searching for any sign of Mother Damnable. Just as she had at the club, she heard through her Sight. Something faint was being spoken, but it was too low to hear. It was a man's voice, familiar but distant.

It came again, clearer this time. "Abby..."

She recognized the voice. "Dad!" Abby bolted to her feet, knocking the tall kitchen chair over backward.

Abby closed her eyes, fighting hard against her own mind and it's racing anxiety. *It's okay, Abby. Listen...* She attempted to still her thoughts. After a few seconds, her mind cleared enough for the Sight to fill her consciousness completely. She opened her eyes, and the world was muted to dull shades of gray.

"Abby!" Evan Kane cried. She looked over to see her father standing at the entry of the kitchen. "Can you hear me?"

"Dad?" Abby's voice shook. He was wearing the same dark business suit as he was the day she had found him. His neatly-trimmed beard and short hair were clean with no trace of the blood that had seeped into the floor as he died. She was uncertain if she was seeing her father's spirit or if it was another of Mother Damnable's tricks.

"It's me, Honey," Evan said reassuringly. He extended his arms.

Abby hesitated. He was here. In front of her. Was it really him? Grief and despair gave way as she rushed to his side. "Dad," she muttered into his shoulder. "I miss you so much."

"I know. I miss you too, Abby," he said in that strong, gentle baritone she would always remember.

"Where's Mom?" she asked, taking a small step back without letting go of him.

Evan shook his head. "I don't know," he said. "The old woman always gets in the way just when I'm about to find her."

"We're going to free you," she said. "I promise. The whole family is working on it." *It really is him...* "We're close to an answer." It was a lie, but she couldn't bring herself to tell him they were nowhere.

He placed his large hand on her head, comforting her as he always did when she was scared. "It will be okay, Abby," he said.

A horrifying cackle echoed from the darkness.

"Abby!" Evan shouted in pain. Her father began to melt away, turning to liquid in her arms.

"Dad!" Abby tried to grab him tighter, but he pooled onto the floor and disappeared. She watched the image fade until she wasn't sure he had been there at all.

The sickening laughter came again. From a dark corner of the room, she watched the grotesque form of Mother Damnable emerge from the shadows.

"Have you had enough yet, young one?" the old woman said, glaring at Abby with a sadistic smile.

"Let him go," Abby said. "Leave my parents alone!"

"Or what?" Mother Damnable laughed, taking a step foraward. Abby took a step back as the malignant spirit moved closer.

"What do you want?" Abby demanded.

Mother Damnable stood in front of a drawer. She opened it slowly, took something out, and turned to face Abby. She then placed a large butcher knife on the counter. "You know what I want," Mother Damnable barked, giving Abby a start.

"I'm going to save my parents," Abby said defiantly, staring down at the sharp blade on the counter but refusing to touch it.

"Perhaps," Mother Damnable said, pacing back and forth. She paused, a mysterious look growing across her face. "Time is on my side though."

"Why did you come out of the shadows now? You could have sat back and waited, and we could have gone another century not knowing what you were doing," Abby observed.

"The world is changing," Mother Damnable said, her grin growing to amusement. "Something is coming. The screams will be beautiful!" she gleefully shouted. The groans of people suffering and crying out for mercy filled the room. Mother Damnable started to dance as if the cries were a beautiful waltz.

"You are insane!" Abby yelled.

Mother Damnable stopped dancing abruptly and looked at Abby strangely. "That is a fair assessment, I think," the deranged spirit agreed. "I do get a bit kooky sometimes." The old hag cackled again. The scent of decay filled the room. "I do have a proposition for you, little girl," she added after a moment. Slowly the specter approached the knife sitting on the counter.

Abby took another step back. "What kind of proposition?" she asked, instantly regretting the question.

A wicked smile crept across the old woman's face. "You could take their place," she said. Her grin turned evil, her rotting teeth made her smile all the more horrifying. The butcher knife slid across the counter toward Abby, moving on its own. "One little slice, and it could be all over. I will set your parents free and take your soul in their stead."

Abby looked at the sharp blade sitting on the cold granite countertop. "You are a liar," she said through gritted teeth. A tear streaked down her cheek. "You would never hold up your end of the bargain."

"I will have you and your parents, one way or the other!" Mother Damnable said, a treacherous glint in the black wells of her eyes. "It is a kindness, you see," she added. "Your torment has already begun. Join me, and your pain will no longer be a burden to your loved ones. They will be free to be happy, and you will be reunited with your parents."

"You are nothing more than a hateful spirit," Abby screamed. "I will not listen to you! Leave this place!"

The old specter glared at Abby. Suddenly the room filled with the sounds of her father crying out in pain.

"Dad?" Abby called out.

Shadows grew from the corners of the room and gathered around Mother Damnable, surrounding her until there was nothing left. Abby rushed forward only to find emptiness. She was gone.

Abby's bravery quickly wilted away as she realized she was alone once more. She drifted out of the Sight and found herself still sitting at the kitchen table.

Tears flowed down her cheeks as Abby stood and took her plate to the sink. Her hands and legs were shaking. She gripped the side of the sink to steady herself and glanced over at the counter next to her. The sharp butcher knife lay, handle first, pointing at her.

She's trying to break me down, Abby thought. *And it's working.*

Abby sat up in bed. She didn't know how long she'd been there. Her sleep patterns in the last three days had been erratic, driven more by a need to escape her reality than physical fatigue.

All weekend, depression had warred with hope. Abby did her best not to anticipate too much. She tried to find ways to be useful, despite her deafness, but was at a loss.

She felt useless–so much of what she used to do, so much of how she used to see herself was about sound. She never realized how much she relied on it before. No matter how hard she tried or how compassionate she was with herself, she hated herself for not being who she used to be.

She knew it was vanity. There were people all over the world who couldn't hear, even ones like her who weren't born deaf still managed to overcome their disability and live great lives. But Abby couldn't forgive herself for what she'd lost, just when her parents needed her most.

She dragged herself from bed and made her way downstairs into the kitchen. Rodger, Sebastian, and Wendy were sitting around the table drinking coffee and reading the newspaper, while Little Evan sat slumped over in his highchair fast asleep.

Abby loved these quiet moments of domesticity. She smiled and poured herself a cup of coffee.

"Maybe we should cancel our trip?" Sebastian asked. "There's been so much going on."

"I know, but if we can–"

Abby spun, nearly spilling her coffee all over the floor. "What did you say?"

Her uncles and aunt looked up at her, startled. Three sets of eyes stared at her, agape. "Abby…?" Sebastian said tentatively.

Her eyes opened wide as a huge grin erupted on her face.

"You can hear us?" Sebastian asked. It was barely audible, a muted sound, like listening through water, but the words were clear.

"I can hear!" Abby cried out. She could hear her own voice, muffled and off pitch, but there.

Rodger stood and walked over to her. He leaned in, examining her ears. "I think it's working."

Little Evan stirred and started fussing. Abby began to cry, too–she could hear him!

Abby nodded. "Yes," she said, her voice seemed distorted and distant, but it was her voice. Abby wiped away a tear. She couldn't stop smiling. She picked up Evan and gave him a big hug, cherishing the sweet sound of his wails.

She turned to see Rodger and Sebastian talking. She could only hear muffled tones when they spoke normally. Abby couldn't make out exactly what they said. *I don't care, it's still something!*

Abby smiled at her family. "Thank you."

Rodger nodded. "I'll glad to be of some use around here," he said. "Come on, let's go down and put your drops in for today. Today is only the fourth day. Let's not stop now.

Abby followed him toward the stairs leading to the basement. Even though Abby was able to follow his words, it required a great deal of concentration. She could tell from the way he was talking he was intentionally being loud, so she could hear.

The cement staircase leading into the sanctum was still a broken mess, but they had managed to place a stepping stool as a makeshift step. Rodger carefully helped Abby navigate the awkward steps.

Abby took the steps cautiously. *It would be just like me to fall and break something now that I'm getting better,* she thought wryly. When she reached the bottom of the stairs, Abby released a sigh of relief and approached the counter where Rodger had the familiar wooden box where he was keeping the ear drops.

"The scratches are almost gone," Abby said.

Rodger looked over and took a closer look. They were little more than four streaks across her cheek. In another day or two, they would be completely gone.

"Barely noticeable," he said. "I'll apply the healing ointment one more time. That should do it, and I think we'll be done with that."

He opened the jar and dabbed a small amount of the light green cream on the four lines embedded on her cheek. "There you go. Now for the ear drops," Rodger said, repeating the process they have been going through for the last few days.

Abby smiled at her uncle, feeling genuinely happy for the first time in days.

She began to cry. Unable to hold back her tears, Abby hid her face in her hands.

"Abby, what's wrong?" Rodger asked, alarmed by her sudden mood shift. These were not happy tears. He had seen enough of both to know the difference. He wrapped his arms around her, letting her lean into him.

"I feel so guilty," she squeaked out.

Rodger pulled back and looked at her face. "Guilty? Sweet girl, why? You should be thrilled that you're healing."

She looked up, started. "I am! I really am. I am so grateful to you, it's just…" she paused, unsure of herself. "Just a little bit ago, I was thinking that there are so many people in the world who are deaf, and they don't have miraculous recoveries like this. I know how lucky I am, but… it shouldn't have worked. I'm so selfish, thinking only of my hearing, but they don't have that chance. I'm so selfish. It shouldn't have worked…"

Rodger held her, stroking her hair. "Magic isn't just something that happens to witches. All those people who are struggling to overcome their disabilities are trying just as hard as you are. Yes, many have accepted their fate and are finding ways to live their lives, and that's wonderful. You should never feel sorry for people who are happy with who they are. And the ones who aren't happy still have options."

She wiped her tears, nodding weakly. "I suppose so…"

"Science is catching up with magic every day," he said. "Even if my ear drops hadn't worked, we would have found a way. Did you know there are cochlear implants so small now that they don't even have to do major surgery? There is always a way Abby. Always."

Abby rested in the comfort of his arms, letting his words work their way into her heart. She knew he was right. After she was done crying, she might even believe in what he told her.

After several minutes she sat up and wiped her face, taking a deep breath. "Thank you," she told her uncle with a smile. "I feel like I've been saying that to you a lot lately."

Rodger smiled a warm, genuine smile, and patted her hand. "You are quite welcome."

He turned to his table and began putting things away. Abby watched him cleaning things, neatly storing them on shelves and in drawers. *Their sanctum is really more of a workshop,* she noted.

She didn't have much experience with sanctums, but they all seem tailored to their owners. Ms. Grace's sanctum back at Armitage Hall had been like a cozy study, with places to brew potions and do research.

On the other hand, her grandmother's was a vast ritual chamber with an elaborate altar for working spells and hexes. Abby looked around the well-lit basement with its wall-to-wall shelving and smiled. *It suits them.*

"Here," Rodger said, handing her the vial of ear drops. "This should be enough to last you until we return."

"Return?" Abby questioned.

Rodger nodded. "Yes, we leave for San Francisco later today."

"I thought that was still a couple days away," Abby said, not realizing how quickly the holiday was approaching.

"Thanksgiving is the day after tomorrow," Rodger said gently. He was clearly trying not to remind her how much time she had lost to her depression.

"I've kind of lost track of time," Abby admitted.

He smiled at her. "You could have come with us, you know."

"I know," Abby said. "I promised Margot I would go to her house this year. It only seems right that I spend the holiday with Grandmother. I'd never hear the end of it if I skipped out on her."

Rodger chuckled. "You're probably right," he said.

"What?" Abby shouted.

"You're probably right!" he said again, more loudly.

She smiled. What a relief to be able to hear something again, It was the first time in nearly a week she had felt connected to the world around her.

Rodger glanced down at his watch. "I need to finish packing," he said, heading toward the stairs. "Don't try putting in more than one drop per day. It won't work, and you'll only run out before I return."

"I won't," she agreed, following him out of the basement.

Sebastian met them in the hallway, bouncing Little Evan in his arms. "Abby, I don't feel good about leaving you here all alone. Not after everything that's happened," he said.

"Oh, can I hold him before you leave?" Abby asked, taking the small child in her arms and giving him a loving hug as she kissed the top of his head. "I'm going to miss him. And the rest of you, too, of course." She smiled playfully at her uncles.

"Abby," Sebastian said in an exasperated tone. "You need to be careful. Just because you can hear a little doesn't mean it's safe yet."

"He's right," Rodger said, standing next to his husband. "Mother Damnable watches us, all of us, but especially you. I have a hard time believing that if she notices that you're here alone, she won't make a move."

Abby cooed at the baby in her arms, then sighed. "It's only for one night," she reassured them. "Tomorrow I'll go to Margot's house. It's at least as well warded as this house. If you're really worried about it, I'll stay with Grandmother over the weekend."

"No need for that. Madison will be over in a bit," Sebastian said. "I think she's bringing Hailey as well."

Abby gave her uncle a scolding look. "Did you call them?" Abby asked. "Aren't you being a little overprotective?"

"Oh, hardly. You haven't seen me at my most cautious!" Sebastian playfully tousled her hair.

"They will probably arrive on the same ferry we'll be leaving on," Rodger said, giving her a mischievous wink.

"Fine, I guess we'll have a fun girls' night," Abby said.

"Good," Sebastian said with a smile. He kissed her cheek and headed upstairs to finish packing.

CHAPTER NINETEEN

Abby gave herself a final glance in the mirror. She tucked away a few stray hairs and adjusted the silk cocktail dress she was wearing for Thanksgiving dinner. As much as she hated these forced family gatherings, she loved dressing for them. Dressed in a dark-blue silk dress that hung to her knees, with blue bead accents worked into the collar, sleeves, and hemline, she felt ready to face the Kanes.

She checked one more time, making sure her hair was secured in its elegant up-do, and then quickly put in her antique studded diamond earrings.

"You look great!" Madison said, as she stepped into the bathroom and stood next to Abby.

"Thanks. I think it's not too bad," Abby said, smiling at her own reflection. Despite the attacks, lack of sleep, and endless days of worry, she felt like she was able to pull herself together nicely. She turned to face her cousin, and her jaw dropped.

Madison was the perfect, fresh-faced girl next door. Her long blond hair cascaded down her back, brushing the light-purple chiffon of the back of her perfectly fitted dress.

"Madison, you are stunning," Abby smiled. "as usual." She turned back to the mirror and touched up her eyeliner, trying not to be disappointed in herself by comparison.

"Come here, let's take a picture together," Madison suggested. Abby stood next to her cousin, who held her phone above them and took a selfie. "I'm going to send it to Patrick."

"Patrick? From the Samhain Ball? That seems to be working out," Abby teased. She put her makeup back in her bag and leaned against the bathroom counter.

"He's coming out for a visit," Madison said.

"What? Really?" Abby asked. "Does your mother know?"

"Of course, silly," Madison teased. "Whose idea do you think it was?" she added coyly.

"I never would have imagined your mother would agree to play host to a guy you had any interest in," Abby jested.

"It was a compromise," Madison confessed. "She wasn't about to let me go spend time with him over the holidays by myself, and Mom didn't seem too keen on traveling with me. So, Patrick and his parents will be coming here between Christmas and New Year's."

"Your mom agreed to that?" Abby asked, somewhat surprised.

"It was that, or I would be as relentless as possible," Madison gave Abby a devilish smile.

"You are a wicked, wicked witch," Abby laughed.

"I guess we should go down," Madison commented as she finished sending the text.

"I just hope I don't have to sit next to cousin Gisela again," Abby said, as they made their way out of the bathroom and down the long hallway.

They descended the grand staircase into the main entrance where the staff was bustling about, readying things for dinner. The front door opened, and Fiona drifted in quietly. She handed her coat over to one of the staff and walked over to join them.

"Good evening, Mother," Margot said, walking over to Fiona.

"You look lovely as always, Margot," Fiona said, greeting her daughter warmly.

Abby looked at Madison's mother. The floor-length pink gown shimmered as she walked, drawing the eye to her long, slender frame. She didn't know how anyone could look good in pink, but on Margot, it was sophisticated and understated. Abby had to agree with her grandaunt.

"I received one of those wretched text message things from Madison earlier today," Fiona said, giving Margot a disapproving look. "She said you are being especially cruel to her of late." There was a hint of rarely displayed humor in her tone.

"No teenager ever had it so good," Margot said dismissively, giving Madison a mock-glare out of the side of her eye.

Abby couldn't help but giggle. It was moments like this when she missed her parents the most. Their fun banter and affectionate teasing were an all-too-familiar pastime in her own family. Abby took a deep breath and put on a smile, determined to keep herself from breaking down before the first course. She knew she would be walking the edges of this pit all day long.

"Have others arrived?" Fiona asked.

"Nearly," Margot said. "I don't believe Aunt Vivian has arrived yet."

Fiona nodded. "Well, the sooner she arrives, the better. I'd like to get this over with."

Abby turned her head, hiding a smirk that crept onto her face. *Is anyone actually looking forward to this dinner?* she wondered.

"Another 'Kane Family Feast.' I wonder if anyone actually looks forward to these?" Madison said, echoing Abby's thought.

"A small dinner would have been nice," Abby agreed.

Margot gently chided them. "Now, now. You know that's not how we do things. Let's try to enjoy this." She looked at them all playfully. "Game faces, Ladies."

They entered the parlor, all sharing a laugh.

Several of the staff stood behind an old, restored antique bar. Margot had gone all-out, stocking the shelves with every bottle imaginable on display. *Grandmother is going to love this,* Abby thought, as she watched the staff preparing drink condiments. She instantly regretted the thought. She silently apologized to no one.

Abby was surprised at how small the party was. She had grown used to the extravagant galas Vivian tended to host. The large sitting room held fewer than a dozen people. And to her delight, Abby knew most of them.

A few people lingered around the bar, awkwardly waiting for the rest of the family to arrive. The four women approached the bar, and Margot offered a warm greeting to the couple waiting there. "David, Cordelia, it's been a long time. I'm so glad you could make it."

"It's great to see you, Margot. Your house is stunning." David said. "Fiona, you are looking well."

The older woman smiled. "That's clearly a lie, but a kind one. Thank you. Do you remember my grandniece, Abigail?" Fiona placed a hand on Abby's shoulder, gently pushing her forward into the conversation.

Abby instantly recognized her distant cousins, though she hadn't seen them in some time. Cordelia and David Kane were a charming pair. They both wore shades of brown, which on them managed to look stylish rather than bland. David's salt-and-pepper hair was slicked back neatly, while Cordelia's black frizzy mane stayed barely contained with strategically placed combs. Their nontraditional look was refreshing.

Abby glanced into Cordelia's aquamarine-colored eyes. They were the thing Abby remembered most about her–always shining like tropical waters glistening in the sun. Ever since she was little, Abby had always found her cousin fascinating.

"Abby," Cordelia greeted with a warm smile. "It's good to see you again."

"It's been quite a while," Abby said, giving her grand-mother's cousin a welcoming hug.

"I'm sorry we couldn't make it to the funeral," David said, moving in and giving Abby a polite hug. "Your father and I were really close. We tried but…"

Abby nodded, biting her lip.

David cleared his throat and said, "Abby, I want you to know that we'll be sticking around to help with the… problem. I would do anything for Evan," he added.

"Thank you," Abby said. She hadn't realized her cousins were even aware of what was happening, but it made sense. Even though they rarely made an appearance, both David and Cordelia were official members of the Coven. They would naturally be included. "It means a great deal."

"You and your parents used to come and visit us every spring. Once things are settled, I hope you will continue with the tradition. We always enjoyed having you visit us, Abby," Cordelia said kindly.

"I would enjoy that," Abby said, imagining herself sunning on the Maui beaches.

"Shall we sit?" Margot gestured to the couches and chairs displayed around the room.

Abby and the others settled in, making polite small talk, and catching up in a way that avoided any serious topic. They hadn't been sitting for more than a couple minutes when the parlor doors opened.

Vivian Kane swept in graciously–the guest of honor receiving applause from an imaginary audience.

"Good evening, Darlings," Vivian said, sweeping an arm out in front of her to encompass the entire room. She held the extended pose for a moment longer than was natural, letting the effect of her long white gown, and perfectly up-styled hair set in.

Only Grandmother would wear white to a feast, Abby thought as she rose to greet the ostentatious woman. "Happy Thanksgiving," Abby said, giving her grandmother a warm embrace.

Vivian took a turn around the room, greeting everyone with extraordinary warmth.

Abby thought maybe she was trying a little too hard to keep the attention on her but reclaimed her seat while her grandmother flounced.

After what felt like several minutes, Vivian sailed back over to where Abby was sitting.

"Darlings! How was your flight from the island?" Vivian asked, greeting David and Cordelia with a polite peck on each cheek.

"It was quite nice, thank you," David said.

Abby thought she noticed a frosty glare between Cordelia and her grandmother but wasn't sure. *Cordelia doesn't like Grandmother any more than Aunt Wendy does,* she realized.

"Cordelia," Vivian said, offering a trite smile.

"Vivian." Cordelia's expression mirrored the same careful control.

"It's so nice the two of you decided to come all this way for the holiday," Vivian said. "Pity you missed my birthday party. It would have been nice to see you. And there's so much more of you to see these days," Vivian smiled wickedly, glancing over Cordelia's sturdy frame.

"Oh?" David said, oblivious.

"It was a shame we missed it," Cordelia said with a coy smile. "I'm always so glad to see you make it through another year."

David's eyes grew wide, and he cleared his throat. "Oh, Darling, look over there," David said, taking Cordelia's arm. "It's Bernard, I haven't seen him in an age." He pulled his wife along in strategic retreat.

Vivian stood fuming, glaring at Cordelia from across the room. She finished off the drink in her hand and handed it off to one of the attentive staff, who promptly brought her another.

Abby blinked. *When did she pick that up?* she wondered.

"Poor David," Vivian said under her breath, shaking her head sadly. "It's really a wonder they're still together. It's always so hard when one marries down."

"This is Margot's party," Abby gently reminded her. "Please try to be on good behavior."

Vivian looked at Abby with feigned innocence. "I am nothing but the epitome of tact and decorum," she said, gesturing at Cordelia, who was fortunately out of earshot. "She's the pitiful one if you ask me. I mean, look at her. She's gained at least ten pounds since the last time I saw her. I would never point that out to her or anyone else for that matter, Darling."

"You… kind of just did, though," Abby said.

"Well, Darling, it had to be said. Now that it's out of my system, I can move on." Vivian took a large sip from her glass and turned to find someone else to greet.

Abby shook her head and walked away. It wasn't a big room, but she managed to escape to a seat next to Madison, who was busily exchanging texts with her boyfriend, ignoring all of them.

Abby looked around, bored. *I wonder how long we have to do this before dinner…*

The door opened. A young man, no more than twenty years-old, came in. He entered quietly, but surely, moving with the confidence of someone who knew he should be there, but also with the desire not to draw anyone's attention. His shimmering blue eyes and neatly-trimmed black hair made him the perfect blend of his parents.

"Gus!" Abby cried and leaped to her feet. She flew into the young man's arms, wrapping him in an enormous hug.

"My goodness, Little Abigail Kane. England was good to you," Gus said with a bright smile.

"No, it really wasn't," Abby bantered, wrinkling her nose and shaking her head. They shared a grin.

"Well, well, well, the great Augustus Kane decided to make an appearance I see," Madison said as she approached.

"I wouldn't miss one or our family's infamous dinners for anything," Gus replied. "It's good to see you, Madison."

Madison smiled and gave him a hug.

"God, look at the two of you!" he said with a brilliant smile. "Such grownups!"

They both playfully hit his shoulders. "Ow!" He laughed. "Did my parents make it? I haven't seen them yet."

"David and Cordelia are right over there," Madison pointed them out, across the large sitting room, where they were trying to appear interested in something Bernard was telling them.

Gus smiled wickedly. "Maybe I'll wait until they're done with their conversation."

"I'm glad you could make it," Abby said, still grinning. "It's been so long. What brings you to town?"

"What? A Kane Family Thanksgiving isn't a good enough reason?" he asked.

"Only if you're a masochist," Madison said dryly.

Abby looked shocked, and Gus chuckled. "So, how long do you think it will be before someone runs crying from the dinner table this year?" Gus asked conspiratorially.

"Your guess is as good as mine," Abby smiled.

"You think we'll make it through the salad?" Madison asked with a laugh.

"Oh, I have faith in our family. I think we'll get to at least the main course," Gus guessed.

"How is school?" Abby asked.

"It's not as bad as I thought it would be. I wanted to take a year off, but now I'm kind of glad I didn't," Gus said.

"Is that because you met someone?" Madison asked coyly.

A sly smirk spread across Gus' face. He reached into his pocket and pulled out a small velvet box. "I suppose you could say that."

"Gus! Is that what I think it is?"

Gus lifted the lid to reveal a beautiful engagement ring with a glimmering diamond.

Abby gasped.

"I'm going to pop the question New Year's Eve," he said.

"Oh my god! It's beautiful," Abby said, looking at the lovely ring.

"More importantly, when are we going to meet her?" Madison said, leaning in for a glance.

Gus chuckled. "I'm not sure yet, probably after the first of the year. It sounds like we have a few things to take care of before then." He gave them both a grim, knowing look.

Abby's mood sobered instantly. "Yes," she said.

"I'm so sorry. You know I loved Uncle Evan and Aunt Jessica. I'm glad to be here and help," Gus said.

"Thank you," Abby said, leaning in and giving her cousin another hug. "It means a lot that you came."

"Nothing could have kept me away. We're going to get things taken care of, then we can all start moving forward with our lives," Gus said, snapping the small velvet box shut and placing it back in his pocket.

"What's the lucky girl's name?" Abby asked, changing the conversation back to happier a topic.

"Rhonda," Gus said. "She's from North Carolina."

"I can't wait to meet her," Abby said.

"She better be really patient and tolerant," Madison said with her sassy voice.

"Madison," Abby scolded. "We haven't even met her yet!"

"I'm just saying." Madison gestured to the Kane family members milling about in the room. "This isn't an easy group to live with."

Both Abby and Gus chuckled softly. "Heh... yeah," Gus said.

Abby followed her family into the dining room. It was very similar to the one at Vivian's mansion, only smaller. The formal room had dark hardwood paneling and a matching floor. An extended table, built for perhaps fourteen, sat in the center of the open space. The table settings were magnificent with fine white china, seven-piece cutlery, four different crystal goblets, and light-brown napkins folded into the shape of a fleur-de-lis. It was elegant, rather than showy, and despite its size, it was somehow very cozy.

"You've outdone yourself again this year," Vivian said, taking her seat near the head of the table, next to Margot.

"Thank you, Aunt Vivian." Margot smiled, accepting one of Vivian's rare compliments.

Abby searched for her spot and found she would be sitting between Madison and Cordelia. She was very pleased to see that this dinner was already shaping up to be different from Vivian's birthday. She took her seat with a smile on her face.

"How is Angelica?" Abby asked Gus, making small talk as the staff prepared to serve the first course.

"You know my sister," he replied. "She wanted to spend the holiday with her friends back home."

"She's starting high school next year. We thought it was time to give her a little taste of freedom," David told her with a wink. "Supervised, of course."

"We thought she was a bit too young to be around for the ritual," Cordelia added quietly.

"What?" Abby asked.

Cordelia looked confused. "Well, she only just turned fourteen. Staying with friends over the holiday is one thing, but…"

Abby blushed. "Oh, no. Sorry, I just didn't hear you. My… hearing hasn't been great lately. I'm glad to hear she is doing well."

While they were talking, a salad had appeared in front of them. Abby looked down at the plate of arugula, cranberries, walnuts, and fresh mozzarella, lightly drizzled in a white vinaigrette. Her mouth began to water. "This looks wonderful."

"Margot has always been an excellent hostess," David commented.

"I simply enjoy getting the family together," Margot said from the head of the table. "Every year, it seems more difficult than the last to get everyone in one place."

Bernard grunted through his bristly white beard as though something was funny and kept eating his salad. Abby looked over and noticed Gisela was picking at her salad, moving the walnuts to the edge of her plate.

"I understand we're close to a solution with our ghostly pest," Bernard said, cutting past the small talk.

"Oh Darling, please, not at the dinner table," Vivian said.

"What difference does it make if it's at the dinner table or the parlor?" Bernard scoffed.

"In the parlor, people may feel free to extradite themselves from the conversation should they choose to do so," Fiona said, in the same tone she would use to scold a child.

"You should consider getting out more, Bernard," Gisela said around a mouthful of cheese. She picked at her salad as if it were some kind of accent to what she had said.

"Just see if I stuff one of those dead cats for you again," Bernard snapped and turned his attention back to the food.

Abby couldn't help but cringe. *Two minutes in and we're already talking about ghosts and stuffed cats? This is going to be a long night after all...*

"I heard you'll be playing as a guest artist with the Seattle Symphony next month," David said, changing the subject.

"Yes," Abby smiled, feeling somewhat embarrassed. "Just before Christmas."

"You must be very good," Gus said. "The last time I heard you play, you hadn't advanced much beyond *Twinkle Twinkle Little Star.*"

"Hey, if it's good enough for Mozart, it's good enough for me," Abby said with a laugh.

"Perhaps she can play something for you while you're in town," Vivian suggested. "A preview, perhaps?"

Abby blushed with embarrassment. "I wouldn't want to make you suffer through it," she said.

"Oh please! David and I love classical music," Cordelia insisted.

"Of course they do," Gisela muttered under her breath.

"What's that supposed to mean?" Madison asked abruptly. The staff began removing the salad course as discretely as possible.

Gisela looked up at Madison and gave her a dirty look. "How impertinent," she sneered.

Madison rolled her eyes.

"I have heard Abigail play. She is an outstanding musician," Margot interjected, trying to shift the focus as the staff began serving the soup course.

"This is a lovely pumpkin soup," Margot said, gesturing to the dishes being laid out in front of them.

"It's delicious," Fiona said after taking a sip. "Is that ginger I taste?"

Margot nodded. "And curry."

"Such a shame Lawrence and Syble couldn't be with us this evening," Gisela commented. "Did they say where they were?"

"In New York," Margot said. "They returning next week."

"I've always enjoyed their company," Gisela commented, sounding disappointed.

"You'd be the only one," Gus said.

"Augustus! Manners, please. They are still your family," Cordelia chided her son.

"I'm certain they enjoy your company as well," Madison said, with an amused smile.

"What is that supposed to mean?" Gisela asked.

"Oh, nothing," Madison said innocently.

"I see you have the same insufferable back-talk your mother had at your age," Gisela growled, shoving a spoonful of soup in her mouth.

"Do I?" Madison asked, amused. "My mother? I always assumed I got it from Dad."

"No," Fiona said abruptly, shaking her head.

"Mother," Margot said, giving Fiona a shocked look. "You aren't helping."

"Sorry dear," Fiona said primly, pretending to zip her mouth closed.

Abby sat quietly and focused on her soup. She was beginning to realize why her parents usually spent Thanksgiving with the Whitlocks.

"Hmph," Bernard added. "I have yet to meet any Kane woman who didn't have a mouth on her."

"Not just the women," Fiona retorted, staring down her brother.

Vivian set her glass down with a heavy thump. Everyone quieted down and turned to look at her. "Darlings, must we have a scene every time this family sits down to have a nice meal together? Just enjoy your dinner," Vivian said, as the staff finished clearing the last of the soup course.

"What's the matter, Vivian?" Cordelia questioned. "Jealous you didn't start it this year?"

"Your imagination is as wild as that hair of yours," Vivian growled.

"Now, now," David said, trying to quell the tension.

"Excuse me for a moment." Gus used the momentary lull to beat a hasty retreat. He smiled quickly at Abby and disappeared out of the door.

Oh sure, he gets to escape... she thought, with a tinge of envy.

The staff began serving the main course. It was a traditional feast of turkey, mashed potatoes, cranberry sauce, and asparagus. The smell was wonderful and earthy, though she wished it didn't come with a side of family bickering. She was quickly losing her appetite.

"I'm not certain I should eat all of this, given how fat I am." Gisela glared at Abby.

"I was six years old when I said that," Abby protested in her defense.

"There's always an excuse, isn't there," Gisela said, shoveling mashed potatoes into her gullet.

Margot rubbed her forehead, and David shrunk in his seat. Abby's face flushed from embarrassment.

"Why are we wasting our time on trivial matters?" Bernard barked. "Don't we have a spirit to exorcise?"

Abby did not want to talk about her parents right now, but it was beginning to seem like a better topic than any other that had come up–at least they all agreed on it.

"Tell me, Cordelia," Vivian said, ignoring Bernard's comment completely. "When did you stop doing those water aerobic exercises?"

"I didn't," Cordelia said. "Why would you think I quit?"

"Hmm." Vivian gave her a look up and down before returning her attention to her Thanksgiving dinner.

"Are you suggesting–"

"Cordelia," David interjected. "Please," he whispered, putting his hand over hers.

"I don't think she is suggesting anything at all," Gisela said. "Everyone here has noticed that you're larger than the last time we saw you," she mumbled.

Cordelia gasped. She batted her eyes, and a tear streaked down her cheek. The first sign of blood. Abby knew it was only going to get worse from here.

Gisela looked over at Cordelia with an incredulous glare. "What is she crying for? She isn't the first person at this table to be called fat," she said, giving Abby another vicious glare.

"Are you really incapable of letting things go? It must have been a lot of work holding on to this all these years," Abby said, shaking her head. "I was a child. I didn't know what I was saying."

"Don't waste your breath," Madison told her. "Miserable people don't let things go."

Gisela turned her glare to Madison. "Why you little…"

"Isn't this turkey delicious?" David said kindly, a little too loudly.

"What shade of lipstick is that you're wearing, dear?" Fiona asked Vivian politely, doing her best to steer the conversation into safe waters. "It's quite fetching on you."

"I really don't recall. I'll have a look when I return home later this evening and let you know," Vivian said.

Abby noticed her grandmother's amusement at the petty banter that had erupted at the table. She felt sick. *Why can't we just have a civil evening for once?*

A heavy silence fell all at once as everyone stopped to catch their breath. The only sounds were of dishes clinking and chairs creaking as people shifted position.

Cordelia sniffled and wiped away a tear. *Big mistake,* Abby thought, trying to stay as invisible as possible.

"She's still crying?" Gisela looked at Cordelia like she was a bizarre zoo animal. She leaned forward and shook her head. "We don't cry in this family, honey," she added sarcastically.

"That is true," Vivian said. "I had my tear ducts removed decades ago," she added, soliciting a chuckle from around the table.

"Was that when you had your second or third facelift," Cordelia retorted.

"Oh Cordelia, I've always admired your wit," Vivian said, taking another sip of wine. "It's rather impressive for someone who's family tree looks like a circle."

"How dare you!" Cordelia yelled. She stood and stormed out.

"I really should look after her," David said, excusing himself.

Margot started to rub her forehead again, and Vivian raised her glass with a satisfied smile before taking another sip.

"Last time we only made it to the soup course before someone stormed out," Fiona observed.

Madison and Abby shared a look and started to laugh. "Looks like Gus was right," Madison said.

"Shall we have dessert?" Margot asked.

"I'm not done with this marvelous turkey," Bernard protested.

Margot looked to one of the staff. "Box it up."

Gus walked back into the room and paused, looking at everyone's grim expressions. "Did I miss something?" he asked.

CHAPTER TWENTY

Abby and Madison retreated back upstairs as soon as etiquette allowed. "Well, that was a disaster," Madison said, closing the door.

Abby smiled at the ridiculousness of it. "I feel bad for your mom. All she wanted to do was have a nice dinner with the family." She unpinned her hair and let it fall around her shoulders.

"She knew who she invited," Madison said unapologetically. "Mom tries too hard. Honestly, does she even know this family?"

"Well, I admire her efforts anyway," Abby said. She reached for the outlet on the desk and plugged in her phone to recharge.

"Did you see how much food was left?" Madison asked, laughing.

"I think your mom let some of the staff take it home," Abby said.

"I think Bernard took half the turkey," Madison called out after disappearing into the bathroom.

Abby sat on the edge of the bed.

"Uncle Bernard sure is an odd one," she said, as much to herself as to her cousin. "What do you suppose his deal is?"

"I don't know," Madison said, popping her head back into the room. Her toothbrush dangled from her mouth. "He's a weird old recluse." She stepped back into the bathroom and spat into the sink before rejoining Abby. "I guess he's into taxidermy. He likes to stuff roadkill or something."

"Gross," Abby said. She recalled seeing trophy heads mounted on the walls of the old Kane estate years ago when she visited with her parents. They had given her nightmares for weeks.

Madison sat next to Abby on the edge of the bed. "Have you had any more encounters with Mother Damnable?" she asked.

In an odd way, Abby was almost relieved to be talking about something real. At least it was a familiar topic. She had spent too much of the last two days making small talk and avoiding the subject. "No, not since last weekend," Abby said. Her thoughts were swirling on the edge of something she couldn't quite put her finger on. "Didn't you think it was strange the topic only came up once, and the moment it did, Grandmother shut it down?"

"I noticed," Madison said. "And my grandmother helped."

"I hate this silence. I feel like they're shutting me out when I specifically asked them not to do that!" She rubbed her face in frustration. "What if this is all more than just a simple plan to reap revenge on the Kanes?" Abby asked, allowing her thoughts to form into words. "How long do you suppose Mother Damnable has been working with the Thanos?"

"I can't even begin to imagine," Madison said. "At least a year and a half... but probably longer."

Abby nodded. Madison was only saying what she already believed.

"It's not a coincidence that Atoro showed up just after she did," Madison said. "I just don't know why."

Abby chewed the inside of her lip. "I could try to find out," she suggested, giving her cousin a conspiratorial look.

Madison looked at her curiously. "What are you thinking?"

"Will you help me with something?" Abby asked, pulling herself from her thoughts.

"Of course," Madison agreed with excitement. "Is it something wicked? Mother isn't letting me help with anything related to the Soul Web, so I'm game for whatever you have in mind."

"Do you have an altar cloth and some white candles?" Abby asked looking around the room.

Madison just looked at her with a huge smile. "What do you think?" she said. "I'll be back in a sec."

Abby cleared an ample space in the center of Madison's room. It wasn't more than a couple minutes when her cousin returned. In her hands, was a folded black sheet and seven large pillar candles. Abby unfolded the large circular cloth, spreading the silk out over the floor. Abby ran a hand appreciatively over the delicately embroidered pentagram on it. "This is lovely," she told her cousin.

"It was my father's," Madison said simply. Her smile was proud but tinged with sadness.

Abby pulled out her phone and turned on the compass app, using it to ensure the top point of the pentagram was pointing true north. She placed candles on four sides of the cloth at the cardinal directional points, then three more in the middle.

"I know the elemental direction candles, but what are those three for?" Madison asked, pointing.

"Focus points," Abby explained. "In addition to Earth, Air, Fire, and Water, these channel the energies Up, Down and Within."

"Huh, I don't think Mom ever used those," Madison pondered.

"You remember that book I was studying from last year with Ms. Grace? I read it there. I think this helps focus the Sight."

"Oh, cool," Madison said. "What am I watching for?"

Abby wished she knew what to tell her cousin. Her past experiences were so varied; it was hard to guess what could happen. "Any sign of distress; wake me up," she said.

"I can do that," Madison agreed. She sat at the top point of the pentagram and crossed her feet under her.

Abby sat in the center of the pentagram, surrounded by the three candles. She crossed her legs and placed her hands on her knees. She took several deep breaths and centered herself, getting ready to call on her magic. *I hope this works*, she thought. *The last time I tried even a simple spell, it didn't work...* Her hearing wasn't fully back, and she hoped against hope that it wasn't still bad enough to disrupt this small ritual.

"Alictus Ignitius," Abby whispered under her breath. The wick on each candle flickered alive with a small flame.

Abby clamped down a thrill of excitement. She closed her eyes and allowed her focus to drift as she attuned herself to the room around her. She could sense Madison a few feet in front of her, watching carefully. Her energy swirled with curiosity and a tinge of worry. Residual energy from dinner pooled in pockets around the main floor of the house. Abby pushed that away, turning her focus inward. She took another deep breath and allowed her mind to still. Abby cleared her thoughts and held the empty space she needed to open the Sight.

Atoro... she directed the Sight. She had never done anything like this before, and she didn't even know if it would work. *Show me Atoro Thanos...*

There was a pinpoint of light in the far distance. It began to grow larger and larger until the bright light encompassed the entirety of Abby's vision. Though the light was bright, it did not hurt Abby's eyes–it was like looking into the sun, but without pain. As the light began to fade, the world became clear around her.

Abby was standing in the entry of her old home. It was quiet. The sun was shining through the windows, filling the room with a warm glow. Fresh cut flowers from the garden filled a vase on the center of a small table in the entryway. There was a pile of unopened mail, and next to it, a small dish for car keys.

There was a creak on the floorboard. Abby stopped and listened. She followed the sound, silently climbing the stairs. Unlike before, she wasn't afraid of what she would find. The old, creaking floorboards and decaying rot were gone, leaving a house that was clean and lived-in, the way she remembered it. This was her home.

For a moment, Abby felt as if she was sixteen again. The terror of the last two years faded away. She was home, back in the life she had lost. She turned the corner and saw the door to her father's office slightly ajar. Someone moved inside, and she caught herself wanting to call out for her parents.

No, she reminded herself. *This isn't real. This is just the Sight trying to show me something.* Abby tried to take a step forward, but her feet would not respond. It's all right. Show me. She directed her Sight again and walked toward the office.

A wicked cackle rang out from beyond the door. Abby swallowed hard and stopped. The room was still well-lit and warm; the cold, decaying world of the dead was nowhere in her Sight. *Maybe she doesn't know I'm here?*

Abby took a cautious step forward, listening at the door. She was uncertain if they could hear or see her, but she needed to hear what they were saying. As she grew closer to the door, she could make out the man's voice. She immediately recognized his thick Greek accent.

"Kill them today," the old crone uttered in her gravelly voice. "This war between your families delays too long."

Are they trying to restart the war? Abby thought, a moment of terror coming over her.

"What about your part of the bargain?" Atoro growled.

"You don't need to worry about me following through with my end," Mother Damnable said. "The arcane nexus grows in your wife's womb. The Messiah of Death is coming!" She shouted gleefully.

She's pregnant again? Wait... no. Is this the past? What is the Sight trying to show me?

"There will be no one with greater power over death than my child," Atoro said with sickening pride. "Nations will fall before him; all covens will bend their knee to us or perish."

"There is a great deal that must be done before your glory is restored. The path has been laid out, but you need to take the first step," Mother Damnable reassured. "Now, send me all the Kanes you can."

"With pleasure," Atoro growled.

Suddenly, the door swung open, and Atoro Thanos walked toward Abby. She was frozen as he came toward her with purpose. She threw up her hands, ready with a counter curse. He strode down the hall and walked right through her, as though she were the ghost. He turned and descended the stairs.

It is the past. Abby gave herself a moment to catch her breath. She glanced into her father's office, Mother Damnable was gone. *But that means...* She followed Atoro downstairs. He was nowhere to be seen, but she knew he wasn't gone.

The front door opened, and Abby heard someone enter. *No!* She spun and raced into the entryway to see her mother set her purse down. She dropped her keys in the dish and picked up the mail. "Evan?" she called, "Are you home?"

"Get out!" Abby shouted, but Jessica didn't move. She could not see or hear Abby at all.

"No!" She began to cry. "No no no…" *Not this day. Why are you showing me this?* she screamed at the Sight.

Atoro Thanos emerged from the shadows, a tall figure slowing taking shape. Abby watched as he pulled a long blade from his belt. She had seen that knife before when he had tried to kill her with it. *Not before,* she realized. *Later, when he tries to kill me a year from now…* The hilt was wrapped in dark leather, and the pommel was shaped like a skull with a diamond in each eye socket. Abby imagined all the people whose blood had been spilled bu that blade.

Abby watched helplessly as Jessica started to climb the stairs.

"Stop! Look behind you!" Abby yelled, waving her hands in front of her mother. Jessica continued to climb the stairs and turned the corner. There was a creak below, and Jessica paused.

"Abby? Is that you?" Jessica called out, looking down the stairs. There was no answer. She stopped in front of Abby's room and knocked on the door. She then opened it and stepped in.

Abby watched as her mother walked across her bedroom to the window.

Jessica unlatched the lock and opened the window. "You need some air in here," she muttered under her breath and headed back toward the bedroom door.

Abby followed her mother, who stopped in the doorway. "Look up. Please look up…" she cried helplessly. She looked over her mother's shoulder. The necromancer was standing at the top of the stairs.

At that moment, Jessica saw him too. She slammed the bedroom door closed, but Atoro threw his bulk into it, pulling it from her hands. Jessica fell back, slamming against the hardwood floor.

"Get out!" She pointed her right hand at Atoro as he loomed over her. "Solticus Maeleus!" she shouted. Atoro buckled over as he flew back, slamming into the rail and falling over onto the staircase below. Abby could hear his body thud against the steps.

Jessica scrambled to her feet and ran into the hallway. Abby followed. Her mother looked over the rail only to see Atoro coming to his feet. Jessica ran down the hallway toward Evan's office. Abby followed her mother, who promptly slammed the door.

"Ontento-Vaildonus!" Jessica shouted, tapping her hand against the doorway. A pale-blue shimmer shrouded the door. Abby watched as her mother searched her pockets only to find nothing. Her cellphone was on the counter downstairs. Jessica rounded the desk and jostled the mouse, awakening the computer.

The sound of heavy footsteps echoed down the hall, coming toward the office. Panic swelled in Abby's heart. Even though she knew what was happening, she couldn't change it. Her helpless tears flowed down her face, disappearing before they could hit the floor.

Jessica maneuvered the mouse and started typing. There was a loud bang at the door, but the mystical shroud fortified it from harm. *He won't be able to get through the wards*, Abby thought. She turned to her mother, who was typing furiously into the computer.

Abby watched the door, praying it would hold. A small spot appeared on the wall between the door and the desk. Abby watched as two hands pushed into the room, tearing through the fabric between this world somewhere else. A familiar cackle erupted from the other side, as Atoro Thanos began to emerge into the room right behind her mother.

"Mom!" Abby screamed. Her mother couldn't hear her.

Atoro emerged from the world of death into the world of the living, standing right behind her mother. His knife was in hand, raised above his head.

I don't want to See this... she thought, trying to will herself from the Sight. Fate held her there, almost as if it was telling her she had to watch.

Abby screamed and turned away. She covered her ears with her hands, and still, she heard the sickening sound of the blade sink into her mother's flesh.

"Abby!" Jessica cried out. She called again more weakly as her strength faded, "Abby..."

"Abby!"

Abby reeled, blinking several times. A pair of hands on her shoulders were shaking her. She shook her head several times while her eyes adjusted to the darkness. Only a few candles offered the faintest warm glow.

"Abby?" Madison said again.

Abby couldn't respond. A drop of sweat dripped from her nose. Her face was wet, and her eyes sore from crying. Fatigue ravaged every joint in her body. She could feel herself tipping over, powerless to stop herself.

Madison reached out and caught her. Madison did her best to pull Abby's dead weight onto the bed. "Just tell me you're okay?" she pleaded.

Abby nodded weakly before passing out.

Madison lay there, holding Abby close in her arms.

"She's slept over twelve hours. I think it took a lot out of her."

Abby could hear talking on the other side of the bedroom door. She opened her eyes and looked around her cousin's room. An enormous pile of stuffed animals was stacked in the far corner from them, near a large window.

Abby stared out the window at the gray cloudy sky as she tried to listen to the conversation outside the door.

"I've read the Sight can take a terrible toll on people," she heard Margot's voice say.

"Did she learn anything?" Vivian said, sounding impatient.

"I don't really know, Aunt Vivian. She has been sleeping since last night," Madison explained.

The door flew open, and Abby sat up. She blinked as her eyes adjusted to the light flooding in from the hallway. A tall, white figure moved around and sat on the side of the bed. Abby looked up and saw her grandmother staring down at her in consternation.

"Grandmother?" Abby questioned her own eyes, still feeling the weight of slumber.

"Yes, Darling," Vivian responded impatiently.

Abby sat up and pulled the comforter up to her chin. Her body was still riddled with aches and fatigue.

"Madison is worried about you. So am I."

"I'll be okay," Abby said, her voice hoarse with disuse.

"Why would you do such a foolish thing?" Vivian scolded. Margot and Madison stood in the bedroom doorway.

"Aunt Vivian, is this really necessary right now?" Margot questioned. "Abby is only doing her best to help," she added.

"Nonsense," Vivian said, waving her hand dismissively. "Darling, you mustn't strain yourself like this. Using the Sight is dangerous with this horrid spirit about."

"She was working with the Thanos," Abby said.

Vivian looked down at her suspiciously. "We already knew that. Why?" Vivian said. "What else did you learn?" There was the faintest hint of a warning in her grandmother's tone.

"Something about an Arcane Nexus," Abby said, doing her best to try and remember details from the night before. "The Thanos made a deal with Mother Damnable. She placed an Arcane Nexus in Atoro's unborn son." Abby looked up at Vivian, worriedly. "If they want Atoro's son, then–"

"Don't worry, Darling. I won't let anything happen," Vivian said, patting Abby's hand gently.

"She said he would be the messiah of death," Abby choked out under her breath.

Vivian sat, looking at Abby with uncertainty.

"Aunt Vivian, do you know what an Arcane Nexus is?" Margot asked.

Vivian shook her head no, without saying a word. She was lost in thought.

"Grandmother," Abby said cautiously.

The old woman pulled herself from her thoughts and gave an ingenuine smile. "What, Darling?"

"Why is Mother Damnable doing this?" Abby asked.

"Well, Darling, I should think it's obvious," Vivian said. "She's working with those horrid Thanos people."

"But why? What does she care about us? She spoke to Atoro as though she was doing them a favor with this Arcane Nexus thing, and he murdered Mom and Dad on her orders. Why? Why would she do this?" Abby's desperation was evident in her voice as she clutched to Vivian's sleeve. Her grandmother knew something.

Vivian's expression went cold. She looked down at Abby imperiously. "I couldn't imagine why."

Abby shook her head. She was tired of being pushed aside. "I don't believe you," she said, looking deep into her grandmother's eyes, unwilling to break her gaze.

"You're obviously very tired, Darling," Vivian said dismissively. She stood and headed toward the door.

"I'm going to find out," Abby said.

Vivian paused and looked at Abby with a stern glare. "I suggest you get your rest," she said. Her voice was frosty. She pushed past Madison and Margot, disappearing down the hallway.

"Things must be getting worse. Aunt Vivian usually has a much better poker face than that," Margot said, moving in and sitting on the edge of the bed. She reached over and placed her hand on Abby's forehead. "You have a little fever. Is that normal?"

"I don't know," Abby said. Her mind was racing a million miles a minute, running wild with all kinds of ideas and explanations for what might have happened between the Kanes, the Thanos, and Mary Anne Conklin.

"Well you can rest in bed for as long as you like," Margot said, giving Abby a kiss on the forehead. "I'll bring you something up to eat." She stood and excused herself.

"She's never that nice to me," Madison said, crawling into bed next to Abby. "What do you suppose Aunt Vivian is hiding?"

Abby shook her head. "I have a million guesses, but I don't know anymore. She says she wants me to be more involved with the Coven, but I feel like they keep pushing me out. I'm just tired of all the secrets. Why aren't they trying harder to break the Soul Web?"

She looked at her cousin. Madison just shook her head, looking concerned.

A determined look came over Abby's face. "I know that there is a history between this family and Mother Damnable," she said. "And I'm going to find out what it is."

CHAPTER TWENTY-ONE

Abby surrendered her keys to the valet before heading into the Hotel Sorrento. It was one of the oldest and most luxurious hotels in the city, only a few blocks east of the downtown business district. *I'm not sure why they wanted to meet here,* Abby thought, *I would have been just as happy to visit them at home.*

She took a sharp right and went down a short hall toward the hotel restaurant. A waitress dressed in all black showed Abby to a table where two people were already seated. Hailey greeted her warmly and motioned for Abby to sit.

Next to Hailey, an impossibly old woman with a kind face sat, slightly bent over from age. Her skin was nearly translucent, and her eyes, once blue, were now faded to a dull gray. She looked as if she was beyond time. In all the years Abby had known her, the woman had never changed.

"Mrs. Westbrook." Abby greeted the older woman respectfully.

Abigail Kane," Patricia said warmly. "You have grown into a beautiful young woman," she complimented.

"Thank you," Abby said, accepting the compliment gracefully. "I really appreciate you taking the time to speak with me today."

"I hope you don't mind," Hailey interjected. "I already told her about some what is happening with your family."

Abby nodded. "Good, that will make this a little easier," she said. "I'm rather tired of secrets, to be honest."

"It sounds like a terrible situation," Patricia said kindly.

"Are you familiar with something called a 'Soul Web'?" Abby asked.

They both shook their heads. "I made a point never to dabble in black magics," the elder Westbrook said, with a note of disdain.

Abby smiled, "That's all right. What I wanted to ask you about today has more to do with Seattle's history than with magic." *I hope,* she added silently.

"We've been learning more and more about the spirit plaguing my family, and I was hoping you could help me answer a few questions."

"Oh?" Hailey said, interested.

"Have either of you ever heard of Mother Damnable?" Abby asked.

Hailey's eyes widened. "That does sound familiar," she said. An uncertain expression came over her. "I don't know from where, though."

Abby sat back, musing over what she'd just heard. So, *my ancestors really were involved with Mary Ann Conklin. But why does she keep tormenting us?* she thought. "Something happened," she said out loud. "Do you know what it was?"

Patricia sat back in her chair, a contemplative look on her face. "Mother Damnable," she said, her voice shaky and weary. "That is a story I haven't thought about for a very long time."

"Can you tell me anything about her?" Abby asked anxiously.

"Mary Ann Conklin was her real name," Patricia stated. "Mother Damnable was a name she earned over the years for many reasons."

Abby nodded. "That's the name I had heard too." She sat forward eagerly, her attention rapt on the older woman. "Please, go on."

"The Westbrooks settled in Seattle only a few years after the Kanes. When we settled here, there was already a solitary practitioner in the city. A woman by the name of Mary Ann Conklin. She had come here a number of years before, with the earliest settlers. She came west by ship, ahead of her coven, who traveled by land. They never arrived."

"What happened to them?" Hailey asked.

"The same thing that happened to many that traveled west; they never made it past the Rocky Mountains. Some claim they abandoned her, but as to which is true...? Your guess is as good as mine." Patricia explained.

"Sounds very sad," Hailey said. "I remember reading about the early pioneers. Many of them sacrificed everything to make their fortunes in the west."

"Indeed," Patricia agreed. "Mary Ann started a small hotel called Felker House. It offered rooms and discrete companionship to sailors coming into port. Back in those days, women rarely made the trek. Those who did typically came with their husbands. If anything happened to their men on the way west and they arrived alone, there was little they could do. Find another husband or learn how to survive on their own. There were few options back in those days. Prostitution was common enough."

"She ran a brothel," Abby said.

"Not to put too fine a point on it, but yes," Patricia said. "Such things were far more common in the lawless west. Police, politicians, and government officials largely ignored such things back in the day. Many of them were likely her best patrons."

"I take it Mary Ann Conklin didn't take it well when two covens arrived on her doorstep in such a short amount of time," Abby said.

"You might be surprised to learn that was not the case. Surprisingly enough, she welcomed both covens when we arrived," Patricia said. "Perhaps she was lonely and longed for some connection to other witches. I can only speculate. But I do know she accepted the presence of both covens better than they tolerated each other."

"Our covens didn't always get along?" Hailey asked, surprised. She spared a glance at Abby and smiled. "But we're so close now." She laughed.

"Hmph." Patricia scoffed at her granddaughter's ridiculous notion. "By and large, the Westbrooks and the Kanes are not as close as you two," she told them.

"Well, Mother Damnable clearly hates us now. What do you think happened?" Abby asked.

"At some point," Patricia said. "Mother Damnable's reputation outgrew her usefulness. By the time our covens arrived, she had already earned her moniker from the local denizens of the city. 'Mother Damnable' was not something we named her. She was feared by everyone, and no one dared double-cross her or harm one of the women in her employ."

"Why?" Hailey asked.

"They say she had a pack of hounds that would chase off unwelcome patrons, and that she was rather fond of throwing rocks at people who displeased her." Patricia grinned playfully at the old gossip, her face stilling again a moment later. "A couple years after we arrived, Mary Ann formed a particularly close friendship with a young witch, much to the detriment of both."

"Who was it?" Abby asked, half afraid of the answer, and already sure she knew.

"Angelica Kane."

"Who was she?" Hailey asked. Her eyes were wide as she got more caught up in the story.

"I believe she was the wife of the coven's patriarch, Marcus Kane."

Abby sat back, thinking. *So, my ancestors really were involved with Mary Ann Conklin. But why does she keep tormenting us?* "Something happened," Abby predicted. "Do you know what it could have been?"

"No," Patricia confessed. "The details of the falling out were never shared with the Westbrooks. Naturally, Mary Ann was no match for an entire coven, despite the fact she was a very powerful witch in her own right. There was something peculiar about the sudden rift between Mary Ann and the Kanes..." she said, drifting off in thought. She attempted to summon old memories she hadn't bothered to conjure in a very long time.

"It's all right. Take your time," Abby encouraged.

"Oh, yes!" Patricia brightened her memory sparked. "Mary Ann and the Kanes quarreled for a brief time. Mary Ann claimed they stole something from her, though I don't know what. It was a bitter and terrible feud. Both Mary Ann and the Kanes attempted to gain Westbrook support, but our ancestors were wise enough to maintain neutrality."

"I know that Grandmother has been hiding the truth of our connection with Mother Damnable. Maybe this is the reason why," Abby said.

She pondered everything Patricia had just told her. *If it is that stone they mentioned, why hide it? What on Earth could be so important that it's worth damning generations of Kane souls to eternal torment?* She was sure that her grandmother couldn't be that cruel. Even at her worst, she would do whatever she needed to protect the Coven.

"I've never been overly fond of Vivian Kane, but I suspect she has her reasons," Patricia said, not unkindly.

"I wonder what they stole," Hailey wondered.

"I did not have the impression Mary Ann had much in the way of artifacts or books," Patricia said. "I suspect perhaps it was research or maybe a grimoire of unique spells."

"Unique spells? Was she gifted in that way? Creating a spell takes a great deal of time and research, not to mention resources and a laboratory," Abby said.

"Yes, but I don't think she conducted... traditional research," Patricia said. "I heard she spent a great deal of time with the local indigenous tribes. They were quite friendly to the settlers when they first came."

"You think Mary Ann learned some arcane secrets from Salish shamans?" Abby asked. "If that's true, there is no telling what secrets she might have learned from them."

"We can only guess. No one knows for certain, except maybe someone in your family," Patricia said. "I do know after Mary Ann made the accusation the feud escalated. Eventually, Felker House was burned to the ground, and Mary Ann went into hiding. But I have no idea what happened after that."

"Did they kill her?" Abby asked.

"She was found dead. If I had to guess, I would imagine one of the Kanes was responsible, but there would never have been any proof," Patricia said. "except..." the ancient woman trailed off, lost in her own thoughts.

"Except what?" Hailey and Abby asked at the same time.

Patricia leveled them both with a look. "I do not believe the vendetta did not end with Mary Ann's death."

"Well, that much is obvious," Hailey said. "Otherwise, why would she be haunting Abby?"

Patricia nodded and continued her story. "There is a mystery around the death of Mary Ann Conklin—it's become an urban legend here in Seattle."

Both girls looked intrigued.

"After she died, she was buried in a cemetery where Denny Park sits today, but little more than a decade later, the cemetery was moved and the bodies exhumed. Every grave was dug up and moved to Lake View Cemetery on Capitol Hill," Patricia explained.

"That's only two blocks from the house where I grew up," Abby commented as a chill ran down her spine. She shivered. *Pull yourself together Abby, this isn't a campfire ghost story–this is important.*

"That's not all," Patricia said.

Abby leaned forward, hanging on every word.

"When Mary Ann Conklin was dug up, her coffin was very heavy. She was never a large woman, and it took ten men to pull her coffin from the grave. When they opened the casket, they found that the body of Mother Damnable had turned to stone," Patricia whispered.

Hailey gasped. Abby shuddered, remembering the stone-like hand resting on her shoulder.

"According to rumor," Patricia went on, "Mary Ann had a special affinity for elemental magic when she was alive. Could some spell of hers have gone wrong? Or was, is some terrible Kane curse? It is all very mysterious."

Abby felt sick. "That sounds like a curse to me," she commented quietly.

"What kind of curse would do that? Do you have any idea what it might be, Abby?" Hailey asked.

Abby shook her head. "I haven't a clue," she replied.

"That's all I remember, I'm afraid," Patricia said. "I hope it was helpful."

"It was. Very helpful, in fact," Abby said. "I can't even tell you how much I appreciate what you've done for me today. You've helped me more than you can imagine, Mrs. Westbrook."

"I do hope you're careful," Patricia said. "This spirit sounds very dangerous."

"Thank you again," Abby said. "I intend to be very careful. Right now, I feel more confident that I'm getting closer to the answers I need."

"I certainly hope so," Patricia said politely.

Abby's mind plunged into a whirlwind of thought. Even though she had learned a few new things, she had even more unanswered questions than before.

"We go away for four days, leaving you to your own devices, and you go and discover all kinds of things," Sebastian said, with a grin.

"I can't wait around anymore," Abby said. "We sit around, going to parties and having lavish dinners while my parents are trapped... I just keep seeing them being tortured. It isn't right."

Her uncle nodded soberly. "No, it isn't," he said quietly.

"Grandmother has been doing her best to keep me out of this, and I don't know why. What is she so afraid of me finding out?" Abby sighed and stared out the window, watching the heavy rainfall silently.

"Vivian is always up to something," Wendy said, under her breath.

Gray clouds blotted out the sun, shrouding the world in gloom. "I'm going to use the Sight again," Abby said. "I hated what I saw, but I did learn more. I want to try and reach out to the spirit of the little girl, Lily. I've seen her several times. I think she might be able to tell me something." She looked over to see her uncle's reaction.

"What do you hope to learn?" Sebastian said with an uncertain stare.

"I'm not sure," Abby replied. "But the more clues I uncover, the better equipped we'll be when it comes time to banish this spirit."

"Banish?" Wendy said, startled. "Do you really think that's possible?"

Abby shrugged. "I have no idea."

"Are you sure it's safe?" Sebastian asked. "So far, Mother Damnable seems adept at turning the Sight against you."

"She has, and I've turned it against her," Abby said. "Once, but it did work. I think I have more control when I'm in the Sight than I realized."

"Yes, but she knows that now," her uncle warned. "Doesn't that mean she'll be more prepared for you as well?"

"I'm worried, Abby," Rodger spoke up. "I don't want to provoke her."

"Neither do I," Abby reassured. "It seems like the more answers I find, the more questions I have. We're not actually any closer to freeing my parents than we were a month ago. I just... can't keep doing nothing." She looked at her uncles and aunt, their worried faces staring back at her. "I need to do this. I need to know Mom and Dad are at peace," she said, her voice catching in her throat.

"We all want the same thing," Wendy said, sincere compassion in her voice. "How can we help?"

"I need to gather a few things. Margot and Madison will be here soon too. Once they arrive, can you all meet me in the dining room?"

"Of course," Sebastian told her. The other's nodded.

Abby smiled at them and headed upstairs to collect a few more things she would need.

Scanning around her room, her gaze fell on a picture sitting on her desk. She looked down at a still image of herself as a little girl with her parents at Magnuson Park. Her short red pigtails were caught mid-bounce as her father threw her in the air. She had always loved that photo of them.

She took the framed picture in her hand and stared down at her parents. For that brief moment in time, they had looked so happy, but now all she could remember of them were their screams of pain, begging her for relief. I need to focus, she reminded herself, wiping away a tear. She set the photo down and turned.

Wait, she thought. *Actually...* She turned back to her desk and picked up the photo again. *Would this work?* Gripping the photo tightly, Abby ran back down the hall. She went into the study and found a yellow legal tablet and collected several pens from the desk drawer and took everything into the dining room.

She was just settling herself close to the center of the table when Margot, Sebastian, and the others filed in, taking seats at the table in relative silence. There was uncertainty among them, Abby could feel it. She couldn't tell if they lacked confidence in her or in her plan, but it didn't matter.

"Thank you for coming," Abby said after clearing her throat. "I'm going to attempt automatic writing. I've been reading about it in one of my books regarding the Sight, and seems like a fairly safe way to contact a spirit without completely opening the Sight," she explained.

"Automatic writing?" Margot questioned. "You are going to summon the little girl and write the answers she speaks to you onto the paper?" she asked, gesturing to the note pad in front of Abby.

"That is my plan," Abby said.

"Why do you need us here?" Madison asked with interest.

"Insurance," Abby said. "You're all here in case I draw the attention of Mother Damnable. I'm hoping that she'll think twice about making a move against me with all of you here," she explained.

"Strength in numbers," Wendy said.

"Yes, exactly," Abby agreed.

"Should we link hands or something?"

"It wouldn't hurt," Margot answered. "Circles restrain energies. They good for keeping things out, or in."

"Alright then," Sebastian said, as everyone around the table linked hands. Sebastian placed one of his hands on Abby's shoulder and Margot, to her right, did the same.

"Okay, I think we're ready," Abby said. She closed her eyes and focused on her breathing, allowing each exhalation to blow away her stress and distractions. When a feeling of peace settled over her thoughts, Abby opened the Sight.

When she opened her eyes, all the color of the room was muted and faded. Ash fell outside the window instead of rain. She was seeing into the realm of the dead.

"Lily," Abby said, her voice barely above a whisper.

"Lily," she repeated, slightly louder. She concentrated on her memory of the little girl she had Seen before, remembering the details of the short pigtails and tattered dress. She thought about how lost, and alone, the child must be feeling in this world of death and decay, and she recalled the way the little girl had called her name when they had met.

"Lily," Abby said, even louder. She waited, hoping she would hear something. There was only silence.

Ash fell from the sky, coating the world in a gray haze. In the bottom corner of the window, Abby saw something. An eye… two eyes… A small face peered in through the window, watching Abby closely.

"Lily," Abby said. "It's okay. Come out."

The little girl seemed uncertain. She stepped out only slightly, one hand and a foot emerging from around the corner.

"It's all right, Lily," Abby encouraged trying to sound as friendly as possible.

The ghostly child looked frightened. She began to take another step out into the open. Lily looked around, eyes wide, clearly afraid someone was watching.

Abby could feel the breath of danger on her neck. "We're all here," Abby said. "It is safe," she added, hoping to bring the girl closer.

"I..." Lily began to speak, but her words were cut short. A gnarled hand with jagged nails and withered gray flesh extended across her mouth. The little girl's eyes widened with panic as the horrific spirit emerged from the ashen world and engulfed Lily in the folds of her dress.

"This one is mine," Mother Damnable said before unleashing a wicked cackle.

Abby closed her eyes again, concentrating. She withdrew from the Sight as quickly as she could. When she opened her eyes, she looked out the window, certain the old woman's spirit would be consuming the little girl. There was nothing but raindrops running down the glass, obscuring the world beyond.

"What happened?" Madison asked, leaning forward.

On the far side of the room, a vase flew off a table, crashing against the wall. Shards of clay littered the floor. A foul stench wafted over them. The room grew cold.

"Something is pressing up against one of the wards I put up," Rodger said.

"Don't break the circle," Margot said. "We share each other's power when our hands are linked."

Abby reached up and grabbed Sebastian and Margot's hands where they rested on her shoulders.

"Malius Primordium, Perdo Spiritum!" Margot called out. She repeated the spell three times before the room fell silent. The cold was gone, and the stench disappeared.

"Do you feel anything against your ward?" Wendy asked.

"No, not anymore," Rodger confirmed. "I told you that you should have put up that ward, Sebastian. It would have been stronger."

"Your ward was more than adequate," Margot said reassuringly.

"What did you do?" Abby asked.

"I used a rebuke spell. It only causes little more than superficial harm to spirits, but it sends the message we are not to be trifled with," Margot explained.

"You scared her away?" Madison asked, hopefully.

"I bought us time," Margot said. "Sadly, I've tipped our hand."

"What do you mean?" Sebastian asked.

"Until today, she and I haven't had an encounter with one another," Margot explained. "Now she knows at least one of us knows something about fighting off spirits. I had hoped to keep that element of surprise a bit longer. At least until we were ready to make a move."

"You did what you had to do," Sebastian said. He regarded the shattered vase on the floor thoughtfully. "It seemed like she was getting ready to attack us."

"Perhaps," Margot said, lost in thought.

A door slammed open. Abby's eyes flew toward the front entry. Margot raised her hand, readying a spell.

"What is the meaning of this!" Vivian shouted, emerging from the living room. "What on Earth do you all think you are doing?" She marched across the room, angrily, moving toward Abby.

"N...Nothing," Abby said, startled. "They all came because I asked them to help me." Fiona peeked out from around her sister's shoulder, her mouth set in a grim line.

"This was your idea? You foolish child!" Vivian's eyes narrowed. "You don't know what you are playing with. You are only making this more difficult!"

"How?" Abby demanded, rising to her feet. "I know you aren't telling us everything. You haven't been very subtle about keeping secrets from us! We can't keep going in the dark. You need to start telling us what's going on!"

"I need do no such thing," Vivian said, her voice haughty. "I am your grandmother. What's more, I am the Matriarch of this Coven. If I keep secrets, it's for the good of the family."

"What are you hiding?" Abby demanded.

"That is none of your concern," Vivian snapped.

"Vivian, please–" Sebastian started before Abby cut him off.

"None of my concern?" Abby shouted, taking a step forward. "You hide things from us, lie to us, and expect us to do nothing while we wait for you to dole out little bits of information here and there. My parents are trapped! They are in pain! I Saw it. They called out to me for help. I don't care what secrets you're keeping, we can't just sit by and do nothing!"

"Nothing?" Vivian cried. "You think we're doing nothing?"

"I don't know what you're doing, you won't tell anybody! We need to be working together to fight back. We need to free them!"

"Of course we do," Vivian said. "And I am working on a spell. You just need to wait for the right timing, Darling."

"I can't wait! It's like you don't even care," Abby cried. "They are my parents!"

"He was my *son*!"

The room went deathly still. Vivian and Abby's eyes were locked, gaze to gaze, neither willing to budge.

Vivian took a deep breath, stepping away from Abby and restablished her composure. "Do you really think I don't care?" she said softly.

"Grandmother, I… "Abby said just as quietly.

Vivian remained silent. No one dared move. After several long moments, she turned to Sebastian. "Darling, do you have any good bourbon?" she asked calmly. "I can see it's time for us all to have a little talk."

"Maybe it would be best if we all retired to the living room," Sebastian suggested.

They all filed quietly into the living room. Tension hung heavily around everyone. They each moved like frightened mice afraid of catching the attention of the python in their midst.

I wonder if she really is going to tell us everything, Abby thought, as she took a seat on the couch next to Madison.

"Oh, thank you, Darling," Vivian said, accepting a crystal glass full of golden-brown liquor. "Stick around, I'll need another shortly."

Sebastian rolled his eyes and set the bottle on the small table next to Vivian's chair. "Here," he said, before taking a seat next to Rodger.

"Please don't get drunk," Abby said, irritated.

"Darling, I never get drunk," Vivian protested.

Everyone exchanged a series of uncomfortable looks around the room.

Vivian nodded and placed her drink down next to the bottle. "Very well," she said defensively. She maintained her sulk for a moment and then sighed. After a moment of silence, she opened her purse and pulled out a small, square piece of paper. She held it out to Abby. "Is this the little girl you saw?"

Abby reached out and took the small picture into her hands. It was an old, faded black-and-white photo. In it was a little girl riding on a tricycle. Abby studied the picture carefully.

The little girl had braided pigtails and a healthy glow about her face. Even though the spirit had looked sickly, there was no doubt this child and the little girl Abby had interacted with through the Sight were one and the same.

"Yes," Abby said, unable to tear her gaze away from the picture.

"Turn it over," Vivian said.

Abby turned the photograph. "Lillian Kane," Abby read it aloud.

"She died of influenza when she was eight," Fiona stated. "She was the oldest. I only barely remember her."

"Why didn't you ever say something?" Margot asked.

"It was far too painful to talk about, Darling," Vivian said, reaching for her glass. "Lily's death had a profound effect on our father. It... it hasn't been easy for any of us to remember her."

A reverence fell over the room, as everyone absorbed what they had learned. The silence was only broken by the clink of ice against crystal as Vivian took another sip of her drink.

"I had no idea you had another sister besides Aunt Madeline," Margot said.

"Don't bring her into all of this," Vivian snapped. "We have enough problems." She took another long drink.

"But..." Abby started.

"What, Darling?" Vivian asked.

"I still don't understand why Mother Damnable is doing all of this. Why does she hate our family so much?" Abby questioned. "Our ancestors did something to her, didn't they?"

Fiona and Vivian shared a look. Vivian shifted nervously. She placed the glass back down and clutched her purse close using it as some kind of shield.

"No doubt she wants revenge for a perceived slight," Vivian said.

"This seems a bit extreme for a mere slight," Sebastian suggested.

"What difference does it make?" Vivian waved the observation away like an irritating insect. "Whatever happened occurred over a century ago. What reparation could we possibly make now? She is a mad, vengeful specter. I doubt our problems will be solved with a polite note telling her we're sorry for whatever our ancestors did to her ages ago."

"Vivian is right," Fiona stated cautiously. "Our focus is better spent on trying to find a solution to the problem. The whys can perhaps be found later when so much is not at stake," she added, giving Abby a glance.

"Fine," Abby stated flatly. "I know there is more to this than you're telling us. But you are right. For now, we need to be focusing on finding a spell to stop her. Keeping the family safe and freeing Mom and Dad is our priority."

Everyone nodded grimly.

CHAPTER TWENTY-TWO

Abby knocked, and they quietly entered the office at Kane Industries Headquarters. "Grandmother?"

"Come in, Abigail," Vivian replied. "I'm glad you could make it."

"I'm surprised you called me," Abby said sheepishly. "I was worried that maybe you were still mad at me for the other day."

Vivian sighed and looked at her with a resigned smile on her face. "I'm not angry with you, Darling. You said some things that I didn't want to hear. And I was worried about you. We really are working on a solution. I need you to trust me."

"I'm trying," Abby admitted. "It's hard when you leave me out of the loop."

"Well, it just so happens, that is why I've invited you here today."

"What?" Abby asked, surprised.

Vivian looked at her, innocently, "Oh, you do still want to be a part of the research we've been doing, don't you?"

"Of course!" Abby exclaimed.

Vivian grinned. "Good. I am expecting a call any moment that you should be here for."

"Who is it?" Abby asked curiously. It felt strange having her grandmother include her. *Don't look a gift horse in the mouth,* Abby. She studied her grandmother's expression. *Take it and run.*

"Do you recall me mentioning distant relatives of ours? The Archibald Sisters?" Vivian asked, placing several papers in a folder and set them aside.

"I remember something about them, yes," Abby said.

"I've tasked an old friend with catching up with them."

Abby looked at Vivian as though she were about to ask for something in return. "Thank you," she said, feeling guilty for doubting her grandmother's motives.

"Is there something wrong, Darling?" Vivian asked.

Abby paused, uncertain of what to say. "No," she unconvincingly muttered. "I'm glad you decided to let me be a part of things."

"Indeed," Vivian said, her expression going neutral. "I admit I am worried about you, Darling. But I…" she hesitated. "I think there is something more going on with the Thanos."

"What do you mean?" Abby asked.

"Motivation, Darling. You have been attacked by the horrid specter many times in this last month, and even Atoro Thanos came after you personally. When he showed up at your house, I assumed he was there for other reasons. But now I'm not so certain." Her expression was one of genuine concern. "He didn't come after any of the rest of us. He came after you."

Abby considered her grandmother's observation. "What are you suggesting? You think this is personal? Some kind of… vendetta for what happened last June?"

"I think it's possible," Vivian said and nodded. "But more, I think that perhaps you are a bigger threat to Mother Damnable than we have estimated."

Abby heard a faint hint of pride in her grandmother's voice when she spoke.

"They came after you. Not any of us. Yes, it may have been personal, based on what happened last spring, but you were attacked four times in as many weeks, Darling. I can't help but wonder why she is trying so hard to get rid of you."

Abby considered what her grandmother was saying. It was true, Mother Damnable was highly focused on her. Because Abby was the only person in the family with the means to interact with her? Or was there another reason? "What if it's true?"

"I should think that keeping you safe and secure should be our priority," Vivian explained. "Darling, I would like for you to consider moving into my house, just for a while. There isn't any place in this city, perhaps the west coast more secure than my home," Vivian explained. Her eyes pleaded for Abby to take her seriously.

"I don't know," Abby said. "I don't want to abandon Sebastian and Rodger. Most of the attacks were at that house. What if they aren't after me, and I was just in the way?"

"Think about it, Darling," Vivian urged. "That's all I ask."

A buzz came from the phone on Vivian's desk. "Mrs. Kane, there's a Valorie Grace on the line for you," her assistant said.

"Thank you, Darling," Vivian said. She pressed a button and switched on the call before hitting the speakerphone. The room filled with a loud whooshing sound, like static or a heavy wind coming through the phone. "Hello! Valorie?" Vivian answered. "Can you hear me, Darling?"

"Vivian," Valorie said through the phone.

"I have Abby here with me," Vivian said.

"Hello, Ms. Grace," Abby added.

"Abigail! It's good to hear your voice," Valorie said. There was a thunderous crashing sound blasting through the speaker. Abby jumped.

"What is going on, Darling?" Vivian asked.

"I'm in the field with the Archibald Sisters. They are hunting down a nest of Lamia in the mountains just outside the city of Thessaloniki," Valorie explained.

"That sounds dreadful, Darling, simply dreadful," Vivian said.

"I have good news," Valorie said, barely distinguishable over the loud noises coming from her end of the call. A scream came through the line, but the sound of the wind made it impossible to tell what was happening. "I have been working with the Sisters on a side project, and it has been keeping me quite busy. However, we were able to find a book that I think will help with your little problem."

"What did you find?" Abby asked, speaking loudly.

"A ritual," Valorie stated. "I hope to be in Seattle by the end of next week. I will bring the ritual with me then. In the meantime, you should start collecting some of the components you will need for the casting."

"Of course, Darling," Vivian said, handing Abby a pen and paper. "Go ahead!"

"You'll need some dirt from her gravesite; three black candles made from the fat of an innocent hanged man; a sprig of Silene Spaldingii, also known as the Spalding Catchfly; a mirror broken in a holy place; a.... stone..." Ms. Grace stated, the connection beginning to break up.

"Valorie, we're having a hard time hearing you," Vivian yelled into the phone.

"This is the worse part..." Valorie said the connection was going in and out. "... There... copper... blood..." A loud crashing sound came through the phone, and the line went dead.

Abby and Vivian stared at one another in silence as the dial tone filtered through the speaker. "Darling, I didn't hear any of that last part. Did you?" Vivian said, breaking the silence.

Abby shook her head.

"I guess we'll have to wait for her to arrive to hear the rest," Vivian said. "What was on the list?"

"The only things I caught were the dirt from her gravesite, black candles made from an innocent man's fat, a sprig of Spalding Catchfly, and a broken mirror. Everything after that was gibberish," Abby said, reading off the list.

"I guess we can get to work on those things for now. The candles will be the hardest part to obtain. You leave those to me. You should work with Margot on getting the dirt from her gravesite and this Spalding Catchfly," Vivian said.

"Okay," Abby said, getting up and heading toward the doorway. She smiled, relieved that her grandmother was finally giving her a task to do. "One thing." She paused and turned with an evil glint in her eye.

"Yes, Darling?" Vivian stood, looking at Abby curiously.

"You're not going to make those candles, are you?" Abby asked.

Vivian looked at her with a disappointed look. "Darling, I would never hang an innocent man just to make such a thing."

"But you would for some other reason?" Abby asked, actually alarmed for a brief moment.

Vivian leveled a stern glare at her. "Don't you have things to do?" she replied dryly.

Abby laughed and turned to go. She paused at the door, hesitating. "Is it really necessary? Such an awful thing..." she said.

"Darling, we're dealing with dark magic. It isn't going to be all dandelions and kitten whiskers," Vivian said. "I'll remind you, you did ask to be a part of things. Are you now regretting that you made that decision?"

"No, I don't regret it," Abby said. She smiled awkwardly before excusing herself. It wasn't entirely a lie, but it wasn't entirely true either.

She quietly closed the door behind her and pulled out her phone to call Madison.

Abby lay on her bed and stretched, releasing as much tension as she could from her body. She had finally had a full night's sleep, but it seemed she was still tired. *Are we really getting close to an answer for all of this?* she thought, staring at the ceiling. *Freeing my parents, banishing Mother Damnable... Is it really that simple?*

The sound of the rain crashing against her bedroom window drew her attention to the cold, gray day outside. Even though it was late afternoon, it was dark enough to be twilight.

Something floated at the edge of her senses, like a wisp of fog trying to get her attention. Abby sat up in her bed and stared at her reflection in the mirror on the closet door. Energy hung thick in the room. It didn't feel oppressive, or malevolent, just... there. *What is it?*

She closed her eyes and began concentrating. With a calm mind, she opened herself to the currents of Fate. Each time she readied her Sight, she became more adept at it. With a moment of pride in her growing skills, she took a breath and let her consciousness submerge into another world.

Abby opened her eyes. She was still sitting on the bed in her room, but the colors were off. The bright-blue comforter looked faded and gray. The walls were ashen and stained. Tiny flecks of ash fell from the ceiling dusting the ground in a strange deathly soot. She knew she was looking with the Sight.

The hinges on her closet door squeaked slightly. Abby watched the door slowly creek open. A small foot emerged from the shadows, then a tiny hand. Eventually, Lily stepped through the clothes hanging in the closet and emerged into the room. The little girl stood in front of Abby.

"She's been watching you," the little girl said cautiously. She glanced around nervously as if she expected her tormentor to jump out at any moment.

"I know," Abby said. "It won't be long, Lily. We're close to having what we need to stop her. It's just a matter of time now."

"How?" Lily asked innocently, looking up at Abby with big weepy eyes. "She's too strong."

"I know it's been a long time, but trust us," Abby said. "We have a ritual that will banish her forever."

Lily looked at her with uncertainty. Abby could tell the little girl wanted to believe her.

"It's all right," Abby reassured. "You will see soon enough," she added and gave the girl a friendly smile.

"I hope so," Lily said. She stared at Abby, searching for something. Then there was a terrifying cackle. Abby looked around the room, frantically searching for Mother Damnable–the source of such a menacing laugh. There was nothing. Abby searched the room, following to the source of the sound. Her gaze rested on the little girl in front of her.

Lily's lips turned into a menacing smile, her teeth rotting right in front of Abby's eyes. The little girl's body began jerking. Abby heard a cracking sound as bones began breaking through skin and protrude from her back. The small body writhed and twisted as it changed. Her skin stretched and tore as her fingers grew longer and gnarled. As she grew in size, her flesh became covered in pocks and turned a sickly gray.

Abby felt a sickening sense of revulsion, but no fear. *Maybe I'm getting used to her tricks,* she thought, surprising herself. "Mary Ann Conklin," she said calmly. "I knew it was only a matter of time before you showed up."

Wicked laughter emerged from the spirit's putrid mouth. "You amuse me, young one," Mother Damnable cackled. "You are so sure of yourself. You think I will be dealt with so easily?"

"Easily? No, but surely, yes. You will be dealt with," Abby said, doing her best to sound as convincing as possible.

"I cannot be removed so easily," Mother Damnable said. Then the room filled with the ghostly sounds of tormented souls, crying and begging for mercy. "Listen to them, sing for me!" She merrily danced to their haunting cries.

"Mary Ann, it isn't too late for you to stop this," Abby said. "Leave. Abandon what you are doing here, and move on before it's too late."

"Ha! Too late?" Mother Damnable yelled. "You are a preposterous one! Child, do you know nothing? It's a hundred years too late!"

"Bargain with me now, and you may be spared," Abby said, hoping the spirit could still see reason through her madness.

"I am no fool!" Mother Damnable yelled, pointing a crooked and bent finger at Abby. "I will never trust the words that come out of the mouth of a Kane. Anyone would be a fool to do so!"

"Please, Mary Ann," Abby pleaded. "Let go of the rage, let go of this insane revenge."

"Insane?" Mother Damnable said. She quit dancing and stared at Abby intently. "I am not insane, foolish little girl. Destroying the Kane Coven is the sanest thing I, or anyone else, could ever do."

"You will be destroyed, not us," Abby said cautiously, but with certainty. "It is inevitable now."

"You have no idea what I am capable of," Mother Damnable said, beginning to pace at the foot of the bed. "You haven't even begun to see what I can do." She gave Abby a cold smirk. "Everything has already been set in motion."

"What do you mean?" Abby asked.

"It's too late, little Kane witch," Mother Damnable sang. "I couldn't stop what is going to happen even if I wanted... and neither can you."

"Stop what? I don't understand," Abby said, a wave of unsettling nervousness moved through her.

"Tick, tock," Mother Damnable said, taking a step backward.

Abby leaned forward. "I don't believe you," she said with conviction.

The old spirit took another step back toward the closet. "You will," she cackled. She stepped into the closet and closed the door.

Abby took a deep breath and began pulling herself from the Sight.

A wave of fatigue washed over her. She slumped down in her bed and allowed herself to rest, paying the toll for communing with Fate.

Abby approached the familiar front door and pressed the doorbell. A loud gong vibrated through the door. Moments later, Mrs. Pugmire answered the door.

The housekeeper looked surprised. "Miss Kane," Mrs. Pugmire said, stepping aside and welcoming Abby into the stately home.

"Is my Aunt Fiona available?" Abby asked.

There was a slight hesitation. "She's having one of her treatments," Mrs. Pugmire stated cautiously.

"Is it all right if I come in anyway?" Abby asked.

"She's been very tired over the last couple of days," Mrs. Pugmire stated. "I'll take you down, but if she turns you out, I won't second-guess her." She motioned for Abby to follow.

The walked down the darkened hallway to the same medical room in the basement Abby had visited before. When they arrived, Mrs. Pugmire stopped at the door and knocked politely.

"Come in," Fiona called out.

The stern woman opened the door and stepped in. "Mrs. Kane, Abigail is here to see you," she said.

"That's fine Mrs. Pugmire," Fiona said, setting aside a magazine she had been reading. "What brings you here to visit your tedious grandaunt?" she said, as Abby came in.

"I wanted to talk to you about a few things."

Fiona tilted her head slightly and smiled knowingly. "You want me to tell you what Vivian has been hiding."

Abby nodded. "You know my grandmother, probably better than anyone else," she explained. "She's done enough things in the last year to give me reason to have doubts."

Fiona reached over and picked up the receiver of an old-fashioned phone sitting next to her on an end table. She waited a moment until someone picked up. "Yes, Mrs. Pugmire. Could you please bring us a pot of tea? … Thank you, dear." She hung up the phone and gave Abby a warm smile. "You might as well settle in."

A sense of relief came over Abby. She wasn't sure how Fiona would respond to the unexpected visit or the questions she brought.

"My sister takes her job as Matriarch of the coven very seriously. I believe her desire to keep us safe is genuine, however, as you have seen for yourself, her methods are at times... questionable." Fiona stated. "She has involved herself very deeply in the politics of our kind. Far more than I would prefer. Vivian has always had something to prove. Though what and to whom, I haven't the slightest clue. Even though she has proven herself time and time again, it's never enough for her."

"You almost sound as though you pity her," Abby observed.

"In my own way, I suppose I do," Fiona agreed sadly.

Abby sat back in her chair, somewhat surprised by the candor of her grandaunt. "She's been drinking a lot more lately," Abby stated.

Fiona gave her a sympathetic look and nodded. "Yes," she said. "I've noticed, too. She is carrying the weight of everything on her shoulders."

"Why doesn't she let us help?" Abby asked.

Fiona took a deep breath. "That is a very simple question with a very complicated answer." She folded her hands primly in her lap. "Do you plan to marry and have a family one day?"

"I don't know, maybe," Abby responded, somewhat confused by the change of subject.

"I think it's difficult sometimes for children–young adults, in your case–to understand a parent or grandparent's desire to protect them," Fiona said. "I would give my life to protect Margot or Madison from the many things in this world that could destroy us. Sometimes we work tirelessly to protect the ones we love from the things we fear might harm them."

"That isn't always good," Abby countered. "I love my parents deeply, and I know they did their best to give me a good life. I wouldn't change anything, but it came at a cost.

I wasn't equipped to deal with everything that happened over the last year. I was naïve and wandered blindly around because I didn't understand the world I came from. I felt supremely stupid."

"You are certainly not stupid," Fiona lovingly scolded. "I do, however, understand what you are saying, and you are not wrong," she added. "How much a child or loved one needs to be sheltered is a question parents and guardians have asked themselves since the dawn of time. It is an imperfect art. In the end, we can only do our best to appreciate what was given us. And hope that the grief does not outweigh the benefit."

"After everything that's happened with my parents, the Thanos, everything that happened last year at school... Being sheltered doesn't help anymore," Abby said.

Fiona gave Abby a world-weary smile. "No, my dear, you are well beyond that now," she agreed. "Promise me you will not look to your grandmother's tastes in dealing with regret and pain."

"How do you deal with it?" she asked cautiously.

Fiona glanced at the large dialysis machine churning only a few feet away. She chuckled bitterly. "This is the price you pay for placing your feelings behind a serene smile. You can pretend everything is all well for sixty years, but eventually..." she sighed bitterly. "Everything takes it's toll eventually. See to it you choose a path that has consequences you can live with."

The door opened, and Mrs. Pugmire entered with a full tea service set. She pulled a small end table from the corner of the room and placed the tea service in front of them. "Is there anything else I can do for you, ma'am?"

Fiona looked at Abby, who shook her head. "That will be all. Thank you, Mrs. Pugmire." Fiona poured Abby a cup of tea before pouring one for herself.

Abby looked down and examined the cup in her hand. It was bone china, with red and pink roses and gold inlay on the rim. It's really pretty, she thought. Inside was a steaming, amber-brown liquid. She took a tiny sip, letting the subtle taste of ginger and jasmine touch her tongue.

Fiona set her cup and saucer down on the arm of her chair. "I know you have many questions," she said, resigning herself to an interrogation. "You must understand I hold many confidences with my sister and other members of our family. Those confidences are important to me. I will answer questions as best as I am able. But there is one thing that I ask of you."

"What?" Abby asked curiously.

"I want you to trust me," Fiona stated. "If there are things that you should know and I am unable to speak of them, I will advocate for your grandmother to tell you, but there are things I cannot speak of."

"I understand," Abby said, nodding her agreement. "I do trust you. More than you know."

Fiona smiled. "Thank you. What questions do you have for me?"

"What is Grandmother hiding?" Abby asked. "She says she's nearly ready to make a move, but she won't share any details of the ritual with me," Abby continued, when Fiona didn't speak up. "Why has she been so secretive about it? We have the ritual already. Ms. Grace brought it to us, so why is she still so reticent?"

Fiona sighed. "I wish there was an easy way to unlock Vivian's psyche for you, Abigail. But I would not, even if I had the power. My sister plays by her own rules. It is possible there are aspects of this ritual she doesn't wish you to know about."

"Why?" Abby demanded. "I've already been attacked, tormented, and emotionally abused by this spirit. What could she possibly be protecting me from now?"

There was a pained look in Fiona's eyes. "That was exactly the question I was hoping you wouldn't ask," Fiona stated. "It's best that you know now, it is something you are going to discover soon enough."

A cold wave rushed through Abby. Her eyes snapped to her grandaunt's face, searching for the reason behind those words. "Wh-what do you mean?" she asked nervously.

"You recall the marking on the wall in your old house, in your father's office?" Fiona asked.

"The Soul Web," Abby responded. "What about it?"

Nodding her head, Fiona continued, "It is made from the blood of your parents. All our research returns to the same thing; It was cast with blood magic."

"So? We know that he used black magic to seal it. That was obvious from the marking itself. What are you trying to say?" Abby was growing impatient.

"Spells cast in blood can only be undone the same way," Fiona explained. "It will take blood magic to undo the spell."

"We're going to have to use blood magic?" Abby asked. Bile rose to the back of her throat as she thought about spilling blood for the sake of magic. She had only encountered a blood mage once before, back in England, and it was something she hoped never to have to face again. Flashes of memories spun in her mind. She was dizzy with images of Benjamin and Josephine, Edgar Kinkaid... the remains of Emily Wright splayed out on the dock.

"I'm sorry, dear," Fiona stated. "I know you have an unsettling history with blood magic. It is a terrible thing to have to know."

"Whose blood are you going to need?" Abby asked. She knew the answer as soon as Fiona winced. "Mine," she said quietly. "You'll need my blood to complete the ritual."

For the first time, every secret that Vivian had been keeping from her made sense. *Of course, she wanted to keep me out of this,* she realized. *I would have done the same.*

"Vivian and Margot are busy trying to come up with alternatives. There is a chance that we can use someone from each bloodline," Fiona said.

"Each bloodline?" Abby asked.

"Your father's bloodline, and your mother's," she explained.

"But I am the only one in the family with blood from both," Abby said quietly.

"Yes, but your grandmother doesn't want to ask it of you," Fiona stated. "She doesn't want you to be the one to make the sacrifice. She's trying to protect you, Abby. You know that, don't you?"

Abby nodded. "Yes." She buried her face in her hands. *Blood magic...*

Fiona reached out and placed a hand on Abby's shoulder. "Try not to fret. They are trying to figure out a way to rework the ritual so that Vivian herself and perhaps your Aunt Wendy or Sebastian could provide the blood needed for your mother's side."

"How much?" Abby asked. "How much blood will they need to cast the ritual? Will it kill me?"

"No, dear," Fiona reassured. "I'm certain it would not. The only reason Atoro resorted to murder was to combine the necromantic energies with those of the blood magic. But, Abby, your grandmother doesn't want you to sully yourself by having to participate in such dark magic. She knows it is not in your nature. We will find another way."

Abby shook her head, violently. "No. I don't want my parents to suffer any longer than they must," she said firmly. "I will do it."

Fiona sighed. "If I were in your shoes, I would do the same," she stated. "But you will need to speak to your grandmother about this. It is not my decision to make." She fell silent while she chose her words carefully. "Please keep in mind, blood magic is very dangerous. Even for an experienced witch. It tends to leave a mark on one's soul."

Abby looked at her grandaunt, a grim expression on her face. "How much worse could it be than knowing what my parents have been going through?"

Fiona shook her head. "That, I do not know."

I really don't want to know how much worse it could get, Abby thought. *But I can't let this go on.* She took a sip of her tea and tried to smile.

CHAPTER TWENTY-THREE

"It sounds like you had a good conversation with Fiona," Sebastian commented quietly, so as not to wake the child sleeping in his arms.

"Fiona has always been a straight-forward woman. I'm inclined to believe everything she said," Wendy added, clearing the table. "You didn't eat much, kid." She regarded Abby's plate with concern.

"I ate all my vegetables," Abby said. "Don't worry, I've been making sure I eat regularly."

Wendy smiled wryly. "If you say so," she said, and left with the dishes.

"Blood magic," Rodger said, accenting it with a shiver. "Terrible stuff." He looked at Abby, concerned.

"Fiona said there is no other way," Abby said. "I really don't want to use blood magic, but I'm not sure we have a choice."

"The intent of the witch is more important than the type of magic. Even necromancy can be used in positive and helpful ways. It's not terribly far removed from healing magic, actually. At least in terms of some of the basic principles." Sebastian said.

"But they are different," Rodger clarified indignantly. "I do understand though, we can't leave Evan and Jessica in the hands of that deranged spirit."

"We won't," Sebastian reassured.

"In a couple days, Ms. Grace will be here with the ritual, and tomorrow morning Madison and I will be making our way to the east side of the mountains to find the herb we need," Abby said.

"Be careful driving through the Gorge," Sebastian said. "The roads get slick by the river this time of year."

"We're covered," Abby explained. "We're going in Madison's car, and Margot had the studded tires put on yesterday. There is also a set of chains in the trunk. We should be covered even in Columbia Gorge, Cascade Mountains, surprise attack snow." She laughed.

"Is Madison driving?" Sebastian asked.

"Yes," Abby said.

"Good," Sebastian stated with an amused smile.

"Why? I'm not a bad driver," Abby protested.

"You're a granny driver," Sebastian said in amusement. He looked to Rodger, who nodded in agreement.

"You fibber! I am not!" Abby protested.

"You totally are," Rodger said. "When I was your age, I probably had about ten speeding tickets... or at least I had been pulled over that many times."

"You've always been good at 'charming' your way out of a speeding ticket," Sebastian said, giving his husband a loving peck.

"You two are so mean," Abby playfully accused. She savored the simplicity of the lighthearted moment. It felt good to just laugh and joke with her uncles, even if it was at her expense.

"I'm glad things are almost over," Wendy said, returning from the kitchen. "With this Valorie Grace coming to town with her ritual, we can finally put all of this to rest." She took a seat and placing a large chocolate cheesecake in the center of the table.

"It isn't over yet, but it will be soon," Rodger agreed.

Abby sat back, withdrawing into her thoughts. There was such anticipation. The ritual was close to happening, and they could finally move on. She just wished there wasn't that tiny, nagging voice inside stopping her from believing it was going to happen.

"What's wrong?" Sebastian asked, placing a small plate with a slice of cheesecake in front of her.

Abby shook herself out of her reverie and put on a brave smile. "Nothing," she said. "I was just thinking about the ritual and freeing Mom and Dad."

"It's pretty much consumed the last couple months of all our lives," Wendy said. "What are you going to do when all this is over?"

Abby shook her head. "I don't know," she admitted. "I've been so caught up in all of this, I haven't stopped to think about an 'after.'"

"Well, we have an idea," Sebastian said. He shared a glance with Rodger, who nodded in the affirmative.

"What are you two up to?" Abby asked suspiciously.

"We just thought it might be a good idea if you had a chance to enjoy some of your gap year," Sebastian said, a mischievous smile playing at the corners of his mouth.

"What did you have in mind," Abby asked.

"We, the three of us, thought maybe after the New Year, you could take a trip over to spend some time with your friends in London," Wendy said.

"You're all in on this? Abby joked.

"You'll be starting school in less than a year," Rodger said sincerely. "It isn't such a bad idea to scout out the Oxford area and see where you want to settle for the next three years."

"I haven't given much thought to anything since we found out what was going on with Mom and Dad," Abby said. "I think I might actually still have a house there."

"Really?" Wendy asked, surprised.

"Well, I don't really know," Abby explained. "I kind of left in a hurry."

"All I know is a gap year is supposed to be fun and full of adventures," Rodger said. "Maybe when all of this is done, you can salvage what's left of your year off."

"I'd like that," Abby smiled. It was a wonderful idea. For the first time in a very long time, she regarded something in her future with hope and excitement. It felt like there was a light at the end of the tunnel.

Abby followed Margot to the third floor of her immense home. Unlike many witches, Margot maintained her sanctum on the top floor rather than hiding it away in the basement. She shared an affinity with air and found she always worked better in the open. Abby found it a refreshing change of pace.

The large room held all the familiar tools of witchcraft carefully organized on tables. The walls and ceiling were nothing but an intricate network of windows. A powerful telescope was perched on a platform at the center of the room, and various star charts were draped on tables and boards. Abby remembered her grandmother mentioning Margot's talent with astrology. It was the first time Abby had seen her sanctum, but somehow it was obvious who it belonged to.

There were several chairs around a table, and Margot motioned for Abby to have a seat.

"The information you found out from Mrs. Westbrook has proven invaluable," Margot said. "Thank you for doing that. I don't think it even would have occurred to me to talk to anyone outside of our Coven."

Abby shrugged. "I was running out of other options."

Margot smiled. "Still, it has been useful. I've been able to identify the location of Mother Damnable's grave."

"That's why I'm here," Abby said. "We need to collect some of the soil from her gravesite."

"Is this for the ritual?"

Abby nodded. "Yes. Grandmother thought you would be the best person to gather it."

Margot sighed. "Aunt Vivian, I fear, has an inflated opinion about my ability to deal with this. My experience with the dead is very limited."

"I didn't even know you had any experience with spirits until this happened," Abby admitted.

"I was much younger. It was before I was married," Margot explained. "It was all rather scandalous as far as the family was concerned."

"How do you mean?" Abby asked. She watched her cousin fall deep into contemplation, and realized she had hit upon a sensitive topic. "I'm sorry, I didn't mean to pry."

"No, it's just... I don't want Madison to ever learn about this, at least not right now. I feel badly enough in retrospect," Margot explained.

"I understand," Abby reassured.

"I was in college and supremely naïve. I was feeling a bit rebellious, and at the time, my mother and I were not on the best of terms. I went through a wild phase and started dabbling in some darker things. I even went so far as to have a brief relationship with a man named Costas Thanos," Margot explained.

Abby's eyes widened.

"I know, I was playing with fire," Margot admitted with a cringe. "But I eventually grew up and got over it. I never really practiced necromancy, and the closest I ever came to it was my relationship with one of them. My mother and your grandmother will never let me live it down."

Abby let Margot's story sink in as she hid her surprise as best she could. "I think we all make mistakes when we're trying to figure out who we are. I've certainly made some... Some really big ones," Abby confessed, thinking of some of her own errors in judgment in the last year.

Margot smiled sweetly. She seemed relieved to make her confession and to have it met with kindness and acceptance–something Abby was beginning to realize was an uncommon response in this family.

"Let's do this now and get it done," Abby said, getting ready for war.

"Excellent idea," Margot said. She collected a leather satchel she had sitting on the table. She opened it briefly and placed some glass vials and hickory stoppers inside. She then put a small leather-bound book in one of the compartments and threw the bag over her shoulder. "I'm ready," she said. Together, they made their way out of the house and to a town car waiting for them.

"Lakeview Cemetery," Margot told the driver as they stepped in.

The car sped across Lake Washington on the floating bridge and onto the backside of Capitol Hill. It was strange returning to her old neighborhood. Familiar old homes passed by as they approached the city's oldest cemetery.

"I can't believe she was buried here this whole time," Abby said. "I used to cut through here on my way to the bus stop. I wonder how many times I passed by her grave and never knew."

"Don't dwell on it, Abby," Margot told her. "There are a lot of graves here." The car pulled into the cemetery and parked near the gate. "Almost all the city founders and Princess Angeline are buried here." They got out of the car and began making their way up the hill.

"She was Chief Seattle's daughter, right?" Abby asked.

"Yes, she was good friends with the founding families," Margot explained. "Including ours."

"Bruce Lee is buried here as well," Abby commented.

Margot laughed. "Yes, his grave is over there where all the flowers are." Margot pointed as they made their way to the back end of the cemetery.

They passed by granite tombstones on their way deep into the oldest part of the cemetery. Many were so old and weather-worn that the names were barely legible. Familiar names, names for which many of the city's prominent streets and buildings were named, flashed by as they passed the markers for the dead. The Dennys, the Bells, and the Yesslers–they approached brick mausoleums and moss-covered grave markers standing in monument to those who had been dead for over a century.

Margot stopped, pointing toward a large tree with roots that were disturbing the headstones around its old gnarled base. "It should be over here somewhere," she said.

Margot and Abby split up and began looking. Before long, Abby called out. "I found it!" She stopped, staring at the small, plain grave marker. It was a simple square stone settled in the earth, etched simply.

MARY ANN CONKLIN
"MOTHER DAMNABLE"
1821-1887

Margot approached and stood next to Abby, who was staring down at the unremarkable grave. "Hmm. I guess I expected something... more," she said.

"Do you think the legends about her turning to stone are true?"

"If the family really did curse her, it's completely plausible," Margot speculated. She opened her bag and pulled out a glass vial.

Abby glanced around to make certain no one was watching. Even though they weren't robbing graves, no doubt someone would find them suspicious. As far as she could tell, the cemetery was all-but empty.

As Margot began collecting soil from around the gravestone, the clear cold sky darkened. A brisk wind from the north came in, stinging Abby's cheeks. Clouds were beginning to gather. "We should hurry before it rains," Abby said, pulling her coat tighter against the wind.

"One moment. I'm nearly finished," Margot answered.

Abby looked down the hill toward the road. The path they had taken was gone. In its place, all she saw was a misty, gray fog. "Margot," Abby said, a note of fear creeping into her voice. "Something's wrong."

Margot looked up.

The clouds were low and very dark. A flash of light exploded inside the clouds, as lightning rumbled within. As the sound of the thunder crackled and rolled toward them, Abby was certain she heard a vicious cackle on the wind.

The clouds hovered over the cemetery and began churning in a counterclockwise direction. Abby started backing away from the tempest.

Margot quickly placed a stopper in a glass vial and carefully placed it in the satchel. As she was standing, a twister touched down twenty feet away. The force of wind knocked them both down.

Lightning shot from the spiraling wind, striking a tree next to the grave. Laughter thundered along the wind as lightning struck the tree a second time. The tree did not catch fire. Instead, it came alive and began swinging and swaying. Its limbs danced in unnatural ways, driven by the force of the specter's power.

A large branch swung down, and Abby rolled out of the way before it struck her. Margot began crawling away and out of reach of the branches. A root sprung from the earth, coiling around Margot's ankle. It pulled her back toward the base of the tree.

Droplets of rain and sleet fell from the clouds as the twister receded back into the sky. Where it had touched down, there was now a glowing gray form.

"You have come to defile my resting place!" Mother Damnable cried.

Abby began concentrating, focusing on the water coating the tree. The dampness began to crystallize. The tree slowed as she forced it into a deep freeze. She hadn't done any serious water magic since she left Armitage Hall, but Ms. Grace had taught her more than enough. Using the force of her spell, she made a crushing motion with her fist. The frozen tree shattered.

Margot hurried to her feet and turned to face Mother Damnable. The apparition laughed. "Your reckoning is coming. The Kane family will pay for their treachery!" the old woman cackled.

Margot concentrated as Abby came to her feet next to her. "Invocitus Pyro Primordium!" Margot called out with her palms extended toward the deranged spirit. A dark-gray flame appeared in her hands.

It was not a natural fire but something different. Abby had never seen anything like it before. "Margot?" she asked nervously.

Mother Damnable's wicked expression quickly changed upon seeing the strange flame burning in Margot's hands. Margot stepped forward, concentrating. She drew back her hand and threw the flame through the air. As it struck, the apparition let out a scream of pain and burst into black flames.

"She's even more powerful than I feared," Margot said, panting. She wiped her hands clean on the front of her shirt.

It was the most unrefined gesture Abby had ever seen her aunt make.

"Now's not the time to worry about appearances," she said dryly in response to the look on Abby's face. "If she can not only manifest in this world but also demonstrate that kind of power... I've never seen or heard of anything like this."

Though she had vanquished Mother Damnable, Abby could tell Margot was even more worried than before.

"What was that?" Abby asked. "That flame?"

"A little something I picked up from my ex," Margot said. "It's called Invocation of the Primordial Flame. It's perfectly harmless to the living. However, it's as dangerous to spirits as real fire is to us. For a normal spirit, that would have been enough to destroy them. I suspect that, for Mother Damnable, it will only put her out of commission for a couple days."

"I hope that's enough time to collect everything else we need," Abby said.

"We had better not waste any time then," Margot said and retrieved her satchel from the ground. "Let's go."

Abby silently followed her down the hill, already planning the next step.

CHAPTER TWENTY-FOUR

The blue waters of Puget Sound reflected the golden sun, creating a bright glistening shine across the surface. It was a cold autumn morning, but today the sky was clear and the sun shined on the water. Winter was in full force and, despite the sunshine, Abby was freezing. She reached over and turned up her seat heater.

"What's wrong?" Madison asked, glancing over at Abby from the driver's seat.

It shouldn't have been a surprise that her cousin could read her. They had known one another their entire lives. Abby shrugged. "Nothing new, I guess," Abby said. "I'm nervous about this ritual, and I have my concert coming up. I haven't practiced as much as I should, but... well, I'm just getting anxious about getting all of this behind me."

"Hmm." Madison made a noise in the back of her throat that made it clear she didn't completely believe her cousin. "What else?"

"Nothing!" Abby said, "I..." she trailed off.

"It's about the ritual, right? I know my mother is careful about saying anything in front of me, but I catch little things, here and there," she said, gripping the steering wheel tightly. "I'm not a kid, Abby. I'm only a year younger than you. I'll be eighteen this spring."

"You'll never be old enough, no matter how old you get," she said, attempting to interject some humor.

Madison pulled onto I-90 East, her sour expression unchanged. She was obviously still irritated with being left out of everything.

"So, are you going to tell me what else is going on?" she questioned. "I know Aunt Vivian is being more secretive than normal, and my grandmother has been an emotional wreck ever since all this stuff started happening."

"There isn't a lot to tell, Madison," Abby confessed. "The ritual is going to require some really dark magic. I don't think anyone is keen on what that's going to be like."

"What kind of dark magic? Necromancy?" Madison asked.

"Blood magic," Abby clarified.

"Ugh, disgusting," Madison said. "Can I help?"

"How about you don't tell your mom some of the things I've been confiding in you, so she doesn't kill me," Abby jested.

Madison snickered and broke a smile. "She's more bark than bite. Besides, Aunt Vivian's secretiveness is hardly a surprise to me or anyone else for that matter. Sorry, but I happen to know Aunt Vivian lies. A lot."

"Do you?" Abby questioned.

Madison nodded. "Don't worry, I can keep what I know under wraps. Besides, it isn't all that much anyway. It's kind of weird what old people think is shocking."

"I'd really appreciate it," Abby said with relief.

Madison mused for a few moments.

Abby enjoyed the quiet. She glanced out the window and watched the mist-covered hills pass by. Large patches of snow lined the busy freeway as they made their way up into the dense Cascade mountain range.

The ski lodges were full and the lifts running, taking skiers up the mountain. Many of the buildings were constructed to look like old-world Bavarian cottages with steep roofs. Abby took everything in, while Madison drove slowly over the icy roads.

"Tell me again, why are we going all this way for some plant?" Madison asked.

"It's rare. According to the research I did, where we're going is one of the only places it grows. At least one of the only places near Seattle," she explained.

"What's it called again?" Madison asked.

"Silene Spaldingii or Spalding Catchfly," Abby said. "I guess it's an endangered plant. The ritual only requires a single sprig, but I figure we'll get a couple just in case."

Abby yawned. The road trip was taking more out of her than she had expected.

"Why don't you take a nap," Madison suggested. "We still have a long way to go."

"I don't want to abandon you to such a long drive without company," Abby protested.

"Don't worry about me," Madison said, reaching down and turning on some music. "I'm more than capable of entertaining myself for a while. As long as the music doesn't bother you."

"Of course not," Abby said. She leaned her seat back and closed her eyes.

She was unconvinced she would sleep at all, but after a few minutes, she felt the pull of slumber on the edges of her thoughts.

As Abby dozed, she saw the snow-covered mountains fall away to the dry, arid east. Rolling hills and vast swaths of land were dotted with enormous wind turbines and covered in ice and snow. They passed large, open fields that would be barren of any crops until spring.

"We're almost there," Madison said, reaching over to turn the radio down.

Abby brought her seat up and groggily looked out the window. In front of them was the mighty Columbia River, cutting through the earth like a major world artery. On either side were steep rocky cliffs, worn deep into the land over the millennia.

"Thanks for waking me," Abby said, yawning away the last of her dazed slumber.

Madison took the last exit before a large bridge that crossed the crystal-blue waters of the river. There was a small community consisting of a gas station, a restaurant, and a motel. She pulled into the gas station. "We should fill up for the ride home," she explained.

Abby pulled out her phone and looked down at the GPS. She glanced out the window at the thin patches of snow. The green patch on her map didn't quite match the white world around them, but she could still get the general sense of where they were going. She zoomed in and looked at the sign on the map. "Ginkgo Petrified Forest State Park," she read aloud.

"That's it," Madison said. "We must be close." She stepped out of the car and began pumping gas.

"Do you want anything?" Abby stepped out of the car and pointed to the convenience store inside the gas station.

"Water would be great," Madison said. "Thanks."

The sun was out when Abby returned, but it was still surprisingly cold. The wind made the sub-freezing temperature seem even worse. Abby was glad she lived on the temperate side of the mountains.

"Let's go," Madison said, taking her water and hopping back into the car.

Abby buckled herself in and pulled a map from the manila folder she had looked at earlier. "I have a map of the park in here," Abby said, showing it to Madison. She pointed to a highlighted portion of the map. "According to my research, we'll have the best luck in this area."

Madison started up the car, but they didn't drive far before they saw a large sign indicating the entrance of the petrified forest. They pulled off onto a gravel road. She looked out the window and frowned at the strange, almost moonscape-like park. "I thought there would be tall petrified trees," she jested. "The name kind of lies, doesn't it?

"No," Abby chuckled. "It's really more of a fossil forest. According to what I read, the forest in this area was covered in volcanic ash millions of years ago. The last ice age apparently eroded the basalt stone that covered everything and exposed the remnants of the forest, which had petrified."

"Huh…. Cool," Madison said. She took in the scenery with new-found interest. "I didn't even realize it was here."

Madison pulled up to a large gravel parking lot adjacent to a wooden building. A sign indicated it was a park museum. There was only one other car in the parking lot, with state government plates.

"Is the museum open?" Madison asked.

"No," Abby responded. "The park is closed for the winter. It won't reopen until late spring."

"I guess we'll have to be careful of the park ranger then," Madison said, pointing to the car parked near the building.

"I wonder what he would think of us picking these endangered plants."

"Don't worry too much. I can be pretty charming when I need to be," Madison said with a wicked smile.

"Which 'charms' are you referring to?" Abby jested. "Your looks, or your spells?" Abby grabbed her satchel, and they stepped out of the car. The wind funneling down the Columbia Gorge was colder than usual, and Abby quickly pulled her coat around her shoulders.

"Both." Madison laughed. She looked around and then pointed. "I think it's this way." Before Abby could respond, Madison was already halfway up the trailhead with the map in her hand. Abby quickly moved to catch up before her cousin disappeared over a hill without her.

The trail was well maintained with gravel and, at times, wooden beams to keep the earth contained. There were markers and information posts along the trail giving detailed accounts of the natural history of the region. Abby was grateful that they only encountered small patches of ice along the path. The last thing she wanted for one of them to slip and break an ankle all the way out here.

The two young women followed the trail up a small hill and into a large rock formation. Huge basalt stones stood all around them. The strange rock formation was carefully carved into geometrical shapes. She saw an information kiosk describing the pictographs of a local indigenous tribe.

"Over here," Madison insisted.

Abby realized she would have to come back. Madison was not about to be slowed down by sightseeing.

When she caught up, Madison was deviating from the trail. They were far into the back half of the park now. Abby's feet were starting to hurt from the hike over the half-frozen ground.

"It should be right over there," Madison pointed. There was a small hill about forty yards away. It appeared to be little more than a rocky mound. Though there was dead grass and the occasional sign of sagebrush, it looked completely barren.

Madison was moving at a fast pace. Abby nearly jogged to keep up. As they approached the rounded hill of ugly brown rock and compact dirt covered in flakes of ice. Abby noticed a small patch of green to the eastern side of the hill. "I think that's it," she said.

Madison moved in closer to take a better look. She pulled her phone out and summoned up a picture of the plant they were looking for. Abby watched as her cousin carefully compared the images in her phone to the hearty green weed-like plants growing in a small patch.

"Are they what we're looking for?" Abby asked.

Madison contemplated for a few more moments. "I think so," she said. "Take a look for yourself."

Abby moved in closer after taking Madison's phone. She observed the picture and then the plant. "I'm certain of it. See here?" She showed Madison the picture on the phone. "The stems and the leaves are the same. Most of these pictures are of the plant when it's in bloom, but these aren't in bloom right now," she explained.

"They look the same to me," Madison agreed. "Is there a special way we need to harvest them?"

"Not really," Abby said. She knelt, pulling a small white-handled knife from the leather satchel she had over her shoulder. She quickly clipped several sprigs from the plants and placed them in a glass jar. She sealed the lid and placed the jar into the satchel. She then pulled out a small vial filled with a slightly-glowing, green liquid.

Madison tilted her head in interest.

"This is a potion Wendy made for me," Abby told her. "It will make sure the plant thrives despite taking several cuttings." She poured the green liquid into the roots. "I don't want to be responsible for wiping out an endangered species."

"Let's get out of here before I turn into a snowman... or snowwoman? Whatever..." Madison said through chattering teeth.

They wasted no time hoofing it back to the car. Abby pushed herself to keep up with her athletic cousin, but together they made it safely back down the hill.

They quickly hopped in the car, and Madison turned on the engine. She fidgeted with several buttons on the control panel to get the heat running. Abby couldn't stop shivering and watched as Madison vigorously rubbed her arms to restore heat and feeling in her limbs.

"I didn't realize how cold it would be over here."

"It isn't that much colder than home," Abby said.

"Tell that to the snow," Madison replied.

"I think it's the wind," Abby said. They both put their hands next to the vents as warm air began funneling into the car.

Madison shifted the car in gear. "Let's go home."

As they were pulling out of the parking lot, Abby noticed a middle-aged man approaching from the building. He was wearing dark-brown pants and a heavy green coat covered in badges. "I think the park ranger found us," she said.

Madison glanced over to see the man approaching and hit the gas. The car spun out and shot down the road. Abby smiled and waved politely as they sped toward the main road. The man had a curious look on his face and turned around, returning to the building.

"At least I didn't have to charm him," Madison said, as she drove back toward I-90.

"What a relief," Abby said, quickly pulling the strap around and latching the seat belt.

"It's still a long way to get back home," Madison said.

"I know. I'm wide awake now," Abby said.

"I know what we should do," Madison said, a wicked smile on her face.

"Oh? What's that?" Abby asked.

"Car jam!" Madison yelled before turning on the radio and blasting it nearly as loud as it would go. As if the Gods of Music were with them, Cyndi Lauper blasted through the speakers.

It's not a girl's day unless Girls Have Fun, right? Abby thought, grinning and singing loudly to the music. The whole car was vibrating as both Abby and Madison sang one song after another. The car thumped down the road as they traveled west toward the Cascade mountains.

It was a nice distraction. Even if it was only a few hours, Abby allowed herself to breathe. She relaxed, pulling herself from the well of grief, fear, and anxiousness that had consumed her for so many months.

Before she knew it, the glass towers of the Seattle skyline emerged over the horizon. "Thank you," Abby said, as they began crossing the bridge over Lake Washington.

"For what?" Madison asked.

"For the road trip. For getting me out of my head," Abby confessed. "I think I needed it."

"Madison looked at her cousin, with a weird look on her face. "You know this was an errand, right? Not a play date."

"I know," Abby said. "Just... thank you."

"Anytime." Madison smiled. She reached over and turned down the radio as they descended onto the floating bridge. Abby watched out the window as they traveled across the water at the beautiful green world surrounding her. The lake was stunning with the reflection of the sun above. The world seemed to bask in a golden haze.

Madison slammed on the breaks. The car lurched suddenly, throwing Abby forward against her seat belt.

Abby spun to look at what was happening. An old woman was standing in the middle of the lane, mere feet in front of them. In one sickening heartbeat, Abby realized there was no way to avoid hitting her.

Time slowed to a halt as the car screeched forward. The old woman looked up. Her withered face cracked into a disgusting grin. Mother Damnable smiled at Abby as the car slammed into her. Her body smashed into the windshield, and her face hit the glass. As the car flew into the air, everything dropped out from under them. There was a crash. Abby looked out the window to her right and saw nothing but murky green water.

CHAPTER TWENTY-FIVE

Dread pulsed through Abby as the car slammed into the deep waters of Lake Washington. She looked over to Madison, who was trying to release her seat belt. Blood trickled down the side of her face. She looked dazed. The sky was clear through the window behind her. The sun, shining down like their last ray of hope, was suddenly cut off, as the water engulfed the window.

"Unbuckle your belt!" Madison yelled as the car began to sink. She grabbed the satchel from the back seat. "Abby! Come on!"

"Abby snapped out of her shock and released her seatbelt.

A horrific cackle echoed through the car, muffled by the water. Abby shuddered from the familiar sound, made eerier from the muted distortion.

Water was seeping into the cab from around the doors and floorboards. The light around them faded as the car sank deeper and deeper.

"Hold on, I'm going to blast the window," Madison said.

Abby braced herself and grabbed the door handle.

Madison pointed her finger at the windshield and concentrated for a moment. "Terram Blitzio!" she yelled. A wave of force shot from her fingertip. The windshield shattered outward, and water poured into the cab.

It was mere seconds before the car was filled with water. Abby pushed herself out into the water. She glanced over to look for Madison and saw no sign of her. The car was sinking into the darkness below. Only a pale light glowed on the surface above.

Abby needed air. She began to kick toward the surface, doing her best not to panic. The cold water stabbed at her flesh, making her body seize up. She called on her power and forced raw magical energy down into her arms and legs, warming herself enough to keep moving. Her feet were numb, and her lungs burned as she resisted the urge to exhale.

As she burst through the surface, Abby gasped for air. Her chest was tight as she panted in the freezing water. She spotted a concrete stanchion a few yards away, attached to the floating bridge. Treading water, she looked frantically around for any sign of her cousin.

"Madison!" Abby called out. A blond head burst from the surface of the way. "Madison!" Abby called again. Abby pointed to the stanchion. Madison didn't move.

Without hesitation, Abby swam over to her cousin and grabbed her arm. Abby was not a strong swimmer. She knew she wouldn't be able to get them both to the bridge. Abby concentrated, calling on her affinity to water. Suddenly the water under them rose up, growing into a giant wave. It washed them both up and over the barrier, depositing them on the cement base below the bridge.

Abby lay on the platform, the concrete solid beneath her. She rolled over to look at her cousin.

Madison was lying next to her. "Thanks," she told Abby weakly before her eyes fluttered shut.

"Madison!" Abby placed her hand over her cousin's bleeding head wound. "Wake up. Madison, stay with me!" She patted Madison's cheeks and shook her gently, trying to keep her from slipping away.

Abby could hear shouting from above. She glanced up to see several people peeking over the edge of the bridge, calling down to them.

"We've called for help," one woman shouted. "Just hang on!"

Abby pulled Madison into an embrace, sharing what little body heat they had. As Abby waited for the sound of sirens, she gazed into the water. Mother Damnable's cackling laughter resonated in her thoughts.

Abby stared into the distance, detaching herself from her body. It was too cold, and she didn't want to be there anymore. She thought about that day she came home from school and found her parents dead on the blood-stained floor. She thought about the markings on the wall that had become their spiritual prison. She wondered at the depravity of the Thanos necromancers, and the vile maliciousness of Mother Damnable. She was done. Done surviving, done trying, done grieving. She was ready for this to be over.

"Abby?"

Abby looked down. "Oh, thank God!" she said, holding Madison close. Sirens drew nearer, and Abby could see several EMTs and firemen, looking over the edge. "Hang on," she whispered. "Just hang on. Help is here."

"We're coming down," someone called out from above.

"It's all right," Abby shouted. "I can make it. Help my cousin!"

"What happened?" Madison asked, her voice was faint.

"Nothing," Abby said. "Just lie still."

Madison gave a faint nod and passed out.

"Help her!" Abby shouted again.

Paramedics dropped an emergency ladder over the concrete barrier. One after another, they swarmed down to them and began tending to Madison. She watched as her cousin was placed on a board and lifted up over the concrete barrier.

Two men came over to Abby, who was trying to stand. "Don't move." One of them placed a firm hand on her shoulder and reaching under her chin to feel her pulse.

"I know you say you're okay, but we are going to put you on a board anyway."

Abby started to protest.

He shook his head. "It's procedure for any accident. We will check you out once we get you away from the water, okay?"

She didn't argue as they laid her back and strapped her to a stretcher. Her limbs were weak, and her body was so cold she was uncertain she would ever regain the feeling in her extremities.

They slowly pulled the stretcher up a bit at a time. Abby watched the sky above her, as the top of the bridge grew closer and closer. When she reached the top, more first responders pulled her over the concrete barrier and carried her to one of the ambulances standing by.

"I can walk," Abby said in protest, but the two officers seemed uninterested. They placed her on a gurney in the back of an ambulance, where two EMTs were waiting to treat her.

They wrapped warm blankets around her and hooked her up to a blood pressure monitor. "I'm fine, really," Abby said.

"What's your name?" One of the EMTs asked.

"Abby," she responded.

"We're taking you to the hospital."

Abby was in no position to argue. *I hate hospitals,* she thought as the siren's blared. "Is my cousin all right?"

"I couldn't say," the EMT said. "We will know more when we get to the hospital. You're lucky. Not very many people survive a plunge into Lake Washington in their car. How did it happen?" she asked.

"I'm not certain," Abby lied. "It happened so fast."

"Were you the driver or the passenger?"

"Passenger. I wasn't really paying attention," she said.

Abby could hear the ambulance siren blaring as the vehicle sped through the busy highways of the city.

"Can we contact someone for you? Your parents or a relative?"

Abby looked at the other woman with uncertainty. "My uncle."

"Do you have his number? We will call him for you when we reached the hospital."

"Thank you," Abby said. She was beginning to feel some warmth returning to her body. It was a relief, but everything happened so quickly she was uncertain.

The EMT turned away from Abby and began speaking into her radio, notifying the hospital that they were en-route.

Within minutes they arrived at the trauma center, and she was carted into the emergency room. Nurses rushed over and immediately took Abby into a room where they began taking vitals.

"Really, this isn't necessary," Abby insisted.

A slender woman in blue scrubs glanced down at Abby and gave her a warm smile. "We'll be the judge of that," she stated kindly.

Abby was having trouble focusing. Everything was a blur as three doctors, and nearly half a dozen nurses introduced themselves and began taking blood, recording vitals and hooking her up to monitors. She lost track of how many tests were run. The doctors and nurses tried to explain it to her, but her mind wouldn't follow what they were saying. She watched it all as though it were happening to someone else.

"You are a very lucky young lady," one of the doctors told her. "You have a couple of minor bruises and a mild case of hypothermia."

"Do you know how long I'll be here?" she asked. "I really need to get home."

"You'll have to forgive our diligence. The kind of accident you had can be very dangerous. Sometimes when people are in a state of shock, they don't realize how badly they are injured. We have to take precautions."

"It's really okay," Abby said. "I'm fine."

The doctor leveled her a skeptical glare.

"Can I see my cousin?"

"Yes," the doctor said. "She's in the next examination room. I'll have the nurse give your uncle the discharge paperwork when he arrives, and then you'll be welcome to go. Just stay bundled up, and if you have any lingering symptoms in the next couple days, follow up with your primary care physician."

"Thank you," Abby said. Abby quickly walked into the next room.

Madison was lying in bed, looking fragile. Margot sat quietly next to the bed, head bowed, holding her daughter's hand. She looked like she was praying.

Abby entered quietly.

"Abby!" Margot called out as she looked up, a look of relief overcame her expression. She stood and pulled Abby into a long hug as if she was holding her own daughter. "Oh, thank God."

"I'm all right," Abby reassured. As soon as she released Margot from their embrace. "How is Madison?" She knew she sounded worried, she couldn't hide it.

Margot batted tears from her eyes. "The doctors say it's hypothermia, and she's in danger of catching pneumonia. The blow to her head wasn't too bad, but they want to keep her here for observation."

She hugged her aunt. The older woman's whole body was shaking; Abby had never seen Margot so worried.

"I've never been so scared in my life," Margot muttered. "I'm so glad you're all right."

Abby hugged her tightly, borrowing her strength and lending a little in return. After a few moments, she walked over to the bed and took Madison's hand.

"We're all right, Madie," she murmured. "We made it."

"You haven't called me that since we were little," Madison said weakly, her eyes fluttering open. "I hate that name."

"Yeah, sorry," Abby said with a smile, wiping her own tears.

"I told Mom what happened," Madison said. "With the ghost."

"We're going to finish her, Abby," Margot said in a firm and reassuring tone. "And this whole nightmare will be over. Soon."

"I know," Abby agreed. "It's time we settled some old scores and close this chapter in our family's history."

"I couldn't agree more," Margot said.

"There you are!" Sebastian said, bursting into the room. Before Abby knew what was happening, she was in the arms of her uncle, then uncle Rodger and then Wendy.

"Are you okay? What happened?" Rodger asked, checking her for signs of injury.

"Let's get out of here," Abby said, looking around the sterile room. "I just want to go home."

"Yes, please!" Madison vehemently agreed.

"Well, it seems I arrived just in time," Vivian said. She strolled through the doorway into the stale hospital room. Contrary to her overly-casual tone, her lips were pursed, and she stood as if she had an iron rod down her spine.

Abby swallowed and offered her a smile. "Grandmother."

"What's the matter, Darling? You weren't expecting me?"

"Aunt Vivian," Margot said. "Whatever it is, can we discuss it outside? Madison needs to rest."

Vivian gave Margot a stern look and then softened slightly. "Yes, of course, Darling." She looked around the room. "My home is by far the most secure. All of you should come and stay with me tonight."

Her invitation was met with surprised faces.

She made a noise in the back of her throat. "Nowhere in the city is there a safer place," she insisted. "Mother Damnable knows we are getting closer. She is more dangerous now than ever." She looked at Abby. "I think she just proved that."

Abby nodded, watching her grandmother closely. Vivian's mercurial nature was far too treacherous to trust, but there was a genuine concern in her steel-blue eyes. Abby could feel it as much as see it.

"You appear to be in once piece, Darling," Vivian said, looking at Abby with genuine concern.

"I'm alright. We both are," she said, motioning to Madison. "Though…"

"I will be staying here with Madison," Margot stated.

"Mom, I'm fine," Madison told her. "You need to focus on the ritual. I'll be all right here."

Abby was keenly aware of the tension in the room. There was so much to discuss, and nothing more to say. If the Coven all moved into Vivian's home, they would be safest, but also a bigger target.

"Do you really think it's necessary?" Sebastian asked, uncertain if he wanted to reside in Vivian's lair.

"I believe it to be the wisest choice, and my sister agrees," Vivian stated. "Fiona has already moved in for the remainder of this crisis."

"I know mother was considering it," Margot said, surprised.

"I believe she had an experience earlier today that settled the matter for her," Vivian said.

"Experience? What do you mean? Is Mother all right?" Margot asked, nearly in a panic.

"She's fine, I assure you," Vivian said, waving her hand. "I think it would be best to discuss such things behind the wards I've placed around my home."

"Are you sure about this?" Abby asked.

"Darling, why do you think I've maintained such a large home? I have spent years fortifying its mystical defenses. I assure you, it wasn't simply for practice."

"You made your home into a... a Kane safe house?" Abby asked.

"Of course, Darling. A need always arises at one time or another. When a threat such as this presents itself, we will always have a safe place to come together," Vivian reassured.

"But... why?" Abby asked.

Vivian looked at her, and her expression softened. "My primary duty as Matriarch is to protect this Coven," she said simply. "And I will do whatever I must to that end."

Abby felt comforted and also chilled by her grandmother's words. *I really think she would...* Abby thought.

Abby set her bags down at the foot of her bed. It was her own bedroom, though the place her grandmother kept ready for her wasn't exactly to Abby's taste. The white carpets, the white walls, and the draperies over the window felt sterile and lifeless. The whole room smelled slightly of disinfectant.

There was a polite knock on the door. Abby looked over to see her grandmother's butler standing in the doorway.

"Yes, Mr. Greenly?" Abby greeted him.

"Mrs. Kane would like to see you in the library," Mr. Greenly said stiffly.

"I'll be along in a couple minutes," Abby said.

"Very well, Miss Kane," the older man said before disappearing down the hallway.

Abby took in a deep breath and glanced at herself in the mirror. *I look like hell.* Her hair was stringy, and her face was devoid of even the slightest hint of makeup. *Oh well,* she thought. *What would I expect after plunging into Lake Washington and barely surviving?*

She zipped up her jacket. Even though her grandmother kept the house at a perfectly serviceable temperature, the chill still hadn't left Abby's bones. She could still feel the stabbing cold throughout her body.

Abby walked down the long white hallway to the second-floor landing. She carefully traversed the grand staircase. She was still weak from the whole ordeal and leaned heavily on the railing. After crossing the grand entry, she entered the north hallway and made her way to the double doors at the end of the hall.

Abby stepped in and scanned the large room for any sign of her grandmother. She found her sitting on a white leather couch near the fireplace.

"Grandmother? Mr. Greenly said you wanted to see me," Abby said, as she approached.

"Hello, Darling," Vivian said, placing a marker in a hefty leather tome and setting it aside. "Thank you for coming down to speak with me."

"Of course," Abby said, sitting on the couch opposite her grandmother. She could still see a strange expression on her grandmother's face. She had been wearing it since the hospital.

Vivian looked at Abby for a moment, studying her. "Why?" she said suddenly.

"'Why' what?" Abby asked.

"Why, after you barely survived another attack, did I have to hear of this from my sister?" Vivian questioned more pointedly.

Abby shrugged and shook her head. "I guess she got ahold of you first."

"You had to be taken by ambulance to the hospital, and the first person you think to call is someone else?" Vivian questioned, raising her eyebrow.

As the flush of understanding ran through Abby, she swallowed. Her guilt immediately gave way to anger, burning in her throat. "I live with Uncle Sebastian," Abby snapped. "He was the first person I thought of because he is always there."

"And not your grandmother is not?" Vivian asked pointedly.

"What exactly is it that you want from me?" Abby asked. She rose to her feet, anger rising from the pit of her stomach. "You want me to go back in time and call you first?"

Vivian glared at Abby, her eyes were wild. The old woman leaned forward and lift the lid off a porcelain jar on the coffee table. She pulled out a cigarette and blew on the tip, causing it to ignite briefly and turned into a smolder. Vivian took a drag and blew the smoke to her side. She sat back and crossed her legs before taking another drag.

"Since when did you start smoking?" Abby asked judgmentally.

"I've always smoked, I simply haven't allowed you to see it," Vivian said. "We all have our secrets, don't we?" she added as she took another drag.

"I'm tired, and I want to go to bed," Abby said.

"In just a minute. You and I have unfinished business," Vivian growled. There were more words lingering on the old woman's lips, but she was holding back.

Abby noted the predatory glint in her eye. "Fine," she said. She sat on the edge of the couch, doing little to hide her irritation. "What do you want to say, Grandmother?"

"I have a lot to say." Vivian uncrossed her legs and leaned forward. "You are pulling away from me," she said. "Why is it that I am always the last to know when anything important happens in your life?"

"I'm sorry your name wasn't the first one that popped into my head while I was in shock from hypothermia," Abby snapped, as her own anger got the best of her. "Is that what you're waiting for? Is that what you need? I'm sorry."

"If I had ever spoken to my grandmother with such disrespect, I would have been buried alive in the family plot," Vivian said coldly. She extinguished her cigarette in an empty crystal glass. She waved her hand, and the scent disappeared instantly. "Your generation is so spoiled and ungrateful," she said under her breath. "You have no idea the sacrifices I've made for you. Everything I have always done for you, and in exchange, I am left in the dark."

"I know how that feels," Abby said pointedly. "What's wrong, you don't like secrets being kept from you? Well, at least we have that in common." Abby stood again and started for the door.

"We're not finished," Vivian said.

Abby kept walking. As she approached the doors, they slammed shut, cutting off her exit.

"Like I said, we are not finished." Vivian stood.

"What's the plan here, Grandmother?" Abby asked, turning and throwing her hands up. "Are you going to keep me prisoner in this room with you until you get whatever it is your looking for?"

"Yes," Vivian said, moving closer. "Until I get some answers out of you!"

"Are you drunk?" Abby said. "How much have you had tonight?"

"Answer the damn question, Abigail!" Vivian shouted.

Abby took a step back, startled. She had never heard Vivian swear at her before.

"Why am I an afterthought?" she said through gritted teeth. "Why are you living in that house with your uncle, when you could be living here with me? Why can't you love me as much as I love you, Darling?" her words deescalated from anger to a plea.

Abby was taken aback by her grandmother's response. She searched the old woman's eyes. "What do you want me to say?" she asked, suddenly uncertain.

"Every day I wake up and try to make this world a better place, for you!" Vivian said. "All I want is to be important to my granddaughter and not some afterthought in your life!"

Abby looked at her grandmother with angry tears in her eyes. The question that had been burning a hole in her heart for the last year escaped from her lips. "I'm so important to you, that instead of keeping me near you when I needed you the most, you shipped me off to England? If I'm so dear to you, why do you have to be half sloshed to have a conversation with me? You don't want me around any more than I want to be here!"

Vivian's eyes filled with rage. The fireplace roared, echoing the embers in her eyes. "I sent you away because every time I look at you, I see your father staring back at me!" She turned away and leaned against the couch.

It was the second time Abby had seen grief in her grandmother's eyes. All the anger and frustration melted away instantly.

"Grandma?" Abby said.

"Just go to bed," Vivian said, her voice thick with emotion.

"I…"

"Just go," Vivian said. She flicked her wrist, and the library doors opened again. Without looking at Abby, she walked over to a panel on the wall and placed her hand against an empty white panel. The door to her sanctum opened, and Vivian disappeared through the door, closing behind her.

Abby stood for a few moments, staring uncertainty after her grandmother. *I don't know how to fix this,* she thought, wiping away a tear. Unexpressed emotions clogged her throat. *She's in a great deal of pain, and I don't know how to help her. I doubt she would let me even if I tried…*

After taking a deep breath, Abby composed herself and opened the library doors and stepped into the hallway. As she made her way down the hall, she saw Fiona approaching.

"Is my sister in the library?" Fiona asked politely.

"She was," Abby said. "She's gone down to her sanctum."

"Are you all right?" Fiona asked, looking at Abby. She saw the puffiness around her eyes.

"I'll be fine. We had a fight," Abby explained.

Fiona hesitated, looking concerned. "Do you have a few minutes? You look like you need to talk."

Abby looked up, surprised. She couldn't ever remember a time when her grandaunt had reached out to her this way. She nodded, "Yes. I think so."

"Come with me." Fiona led her down the hallway and into her own room. It was a small suite, with a sitting room attached to the bedroom. Fiona took a seat on a comfortable-looking sofa and motioned for Abby to join her.

Fiona looked sympathetic. "I'm sorry for everything, dear. Everyone is under a great deal of stress."

Abby nodded. "I know that Grandmother means well. I think she's upset that she wasn't the first person I had the hospital call. But is this really the time to be fighting?"

"No," Fiona said. "And yes. You know that isn't what she is truly upset about, don't you?"

"What do you mean?" Abby asked.

Fiona reached out and gently brushed a few stray hairs from Abby's face, tucking them away. "Things aren't working out as well as she hoped. My sister wanted to spare you from all this. To protect you from having to participate in that horrible ritual. Whenever my sister is determined to do something, she will move the heavens and the earth to make it happen. This time she can't. She can't protect you, and she sees it as a failing on her part. She loves you, dearly, Abigail. I know she doesn't know how to show it, but I know. I hope you do too." She gave Abby a warm smile.

"Yes." Abby sighed and looked at the floor. "I do know. She's never been good at expressing herself, but her timing is terrible. The ritual is only a few days away. Shouldn't we be focusing on Mother Damnable right now? She didn't even ask about the ingredients I've collected."

"She was worried about you," Fiona said. "You are the most important thing to her." She fell silent, watching Abby process everything. "You still have doubts?"

"Not about Grandmother, no," Abby said.

"About the ritual?"

Abby nodded.

Fiona patted her hand. "You are not alone in that. We all have our doubts."

Abby looked up at her grandaunt. "It will work, right?"

Fiona smiled weakly. "We will know more when Valorie Grace arrives."

CHAPTER TWENTY-SIX

Abby glanced at her phone while she stood in the waiting area outside the baggage claim. A lone woman in her late fifties came around the corner, pulling a small travel bag. She was as matronly as ever, wearing a tweed jacket over a brown dress and plain, brown flats. Her shoulder-length hair and harsh bangs were neatly trimmed and precise. Ms. Grace had always been a study in practicality and function. Abby had missed her dearly.

Seeing her mentor again put a broad smile on Abby's face. She smiled excitedly, waiting for her friend to navigate her way through the crowd.

"Abigail," Ms. Grace greeted warmly. The two embraced, and for the first time, her friend didn't stiffen with the simple show of affection.

"It's nice to see you, Ms. Grace," Abby said, with a giant smile. Her greeting was so genuine she caught herself getting emotional. "It means so much that you were willing to come this far to see me and help my family with our problem."

"I must say, I was quite alarmed when Vivian confided in me the details of your family's troubles," Ms. Grace stated. Abby quickly took her bag.

"I'm parked over here." Abby guided her mentor through the crowded corridors of SeaTac airport. "Was your trip comfortable?" she asked, making small talk until they reached the car where they could speak more privately.

"It was fine enough," Ms. Grace stated. "Nine-hour flights can be challenging. Fortunately, I was able to sleep for several hours."

"I don't recall, have you been here before?" Abby asked.

"Many years ago. Before you were born," she replied.

The two of them made their way into the labyrinthine parking garage. They took a crowded elevator up to the fourth floor, and Abby guided Ms. Grace to her black Audi. "Here we are," she said, opening the trunk. They quickly deposited the luggage and then situated themselves.

Abby pulled out of her spot and started the process of driving down the winding spiral drive that would take her to the ground floor tollbooth. She quickly paid her parking fee and cleared the booth, before merging onto the freeway toward the city.

"Do you miss school?" Abby asked, breaking the silence.

"Sometimes," Ms. Grace stated. "I do like to teach, and though I am not at Armitage anymore, I do get to help people, which seems to be just as satisfying."

"Are you settled into the shop in London?" Abby asked.

"Yes, I have books piled as high as the ceiling, right now. I haven't taken on too many customers yet, and I won't until I can properly catalog the entire collection," Ms. Grace explained. "But I love my work."

"Are you going to digitize your collection?" Abby asked, wearing a playful smile.

"Don't be preposterous," Ms. Grace gasped, alarmed at her former student's suggestion of a literary atrocity. "I will have no such contraptions in my shop."

"It could make some things easier," Abby suggested, trying to hide her amusement.

"Book merchants have spent centuries practicing the trade without technological interference," Ms. Grace stated. "I shall do the same. I cater to a very exclusive and discriminating clientele, and I will suit their needs first. I have no need of digitization."

"I was thinking it could help you with organization."

"Hmm, I don't know about that," Ms. Grace stated, her distaste for computers well noted.

"We haven't spoken much about anything that's happened since I left," Abby said, changing the topic. "I've spoken with Warren, Nina, and Sarah. They seem to be having fun gallivanting across Europe and northern Africa. Have you seen them?"

"Yes," Ms. Grace stated. "Nina and Sarah came to visit me on their way back from a trip to the South of France, this last summer. I spent a week with them on the beach and garnered a sunburn for the effort. As for Mr. Lampton, he and I have grown rather fond of one another over the summer. He was kind enough to assist me in acquiring a flat near my little shop."

"Really? You and Warren are on good terms?" Abby smiled. "Last year, you two didn't exactly get along."

"Mr. Lampton has increased greatly in his maturity and has shown remarkable improvement in his ability to demonstrate responsibility," Ms. Grace stated, grading him as though she were still a teacher. "In truth, I have spent much of the summer with them to help them better adjust to being Awakened. It can be a difficult process for those who are enlightened to our world in such an abrupt manner. They seem to be transitioning well."

"No doubt due to your help," Abby said. "I wish I could have stayed and helped them adjust. I feel responsible for their Awakening."

"The fact they were Awakened was not your fault," Ms. Grace kindly reassured. "One cannot live their life completely withdrawn from normal society. Those who do tend to lose their humanity. We've both seen the negative consequences of witches who have done so."

"Yes," Abby agreed, feeling a pang of remorse. She was afraid to ask, but her curiosity won out. "What kind of rumors have you heard?" she finally asked.

"Isobel Hodge has filed for divorce," Ms. Grace stated. "Apparently, she has returned to her family on the Isle of Jersey. It would seem there is an internal rift in the Hodge Coven. Though I cannot say for certain the exact nature of the rift, I believe we can make an educated guess on the crux of their strife."

Abby nodded, unsure what to say.

"Benjamin seems to have isolated himself," Ms. Grace said carefully. "I haven't heard anything… except…"

"What?" Abby asked her heart racing. She couldn't bring herself to ask about him, but once she heard his name, she wanted to know.

"I did learn from a colleague of mine at Oxford that Benjamin is still scheduled to start school next fall," Ms. Grace stated.

Abby knew Benjamin always planned on Oxford. For some reason, with everything that happened, she had allowed herself to believe perhaps his plans had changed. Abby chastised herself for her foolishness.

"Are you still planning on attending as well?"

Abby nodded. "Yes."

"Then I suspect your first year at school could get… uncomfortable," Ms. Grace stated.

"To say the least," Abby agreed.

They fell into silence as Abby took the freeway exit into downtown, heading toward Queen Anne. Even from a great distance, she could see her grandmother's house looming over the city. "Please don't forget, I haven't told my grandmother all the details of everything that happened last spring," Abby said nervously.

"I can understand your discretion, and you need not worry about me breaking your confidence. I will be discreet," Ms. Grace reassured. "However, I see little reason for the topic to come up during this visit. I have another purpose for being here."

"Yes," Abby said, as she began driving up the steep slope.

"Who will I be working with on this ritual?" Ms. Grace asked.

"Margot, my father's cousin, is planning the ritual," Abby said. "She's a cunning witch with a lot of experience. I'm certain the two of you will work well together."

"That is good to hear," Ms. Grace, stated as she watched the houses go by outside the car window. "I did not suspect that it would be left solely to your grandmother. I am glad to see that the whole Coven is involved."

"We're all staying in my grandmother's house right now. It's the safest place for us, with all the protection she's put up," Abby said. "As you can probably imagine, we're eager to get things taken care of as soon as possible."

"I can certainly understand, given the circumstances," Ms. Grace agreed.

Abby pulled up to the gate and punched in the security code. The large iron gate opened, and she drove down the steep incline to a large circular drive in front of Vivian Kane's home.

She pulled up and helped Ms. Grace with her luggage.

"The place looks much as I remember from the last time I was here," Ms. Grace said. "Though it seems a bit bigger."

"She's added on over the years," Abby said as they approached the front door. Abby barely had time to ring the doorbell before the front door opened. Mr. Greenly stood stiffly to greet them.

"Ms. Grace, Mrs. Kane, is expecting you." Mr. Greenly said, motioning for them to enter. "If you would leave your luggage here, I'll have the household staff see to your things. Please follow me," he added politely.

Abby smiled and gestured for Ms. Grace to go first as Mr. Greenly showed them in.

He guided them through the palatial grand entry, adorned with statues and white marble, then down a cavernous hall toward the back of the house. The hallway came to the formal living room. It was large, with one wall filled with windows that looked down upon the city below.

"Valorie, Darling, how was the flight," Vivian asked jubilantly, as she glided into the room. She gave Ms. Grace a friendly hug and a peck on each cheek. "You certainly look refreshed."

"Thank you, Vivian," Ms. Grace accepted the dubious compliment gracefully. "You are as lovely as ever."

"Thank you, Darling," Vivian smiled. "Please come over and join us." She gestured to the couches near the window where Fiona and Margot sat.

They both stood to welcome their guest.

"It's good to see you again, dear," Fiona said, sharing a polite handshake with Ms. Grace. "I would like to introduce you to my daughter, Margot Kane," she added, gesturing to her right.

"It is a pleasure to meet you, Ms. Grace," Margot said, shaking Valorie's hand.

"And you, Mrs. Kane," Valorie said politely.

"Thank you so much for everything you did for Abby while she was staying in England. She has spoken very highly of you since she returned," Margot said.

"It was my pleasure, of course," Ms. Grace said kindly, giving Abby a warm smile.

Abby was relieved to see her mentor seems less high strung and stoic than she remembered from the last year. *Maybe the change in professions has helped,* she considered. *Then again, she isn't my teacher or guardian, so perhaps everything is simply more relaxed.*

"Is it true you're planning on staying after the ritual to see Abby perform?" Vivian asked. "You are, of course, welcome to remain here as long as you like."

"Thank you, Vivian," Ms. Grace stated, her stoic self returning. "It is my intention to attend the concert."

"You have the ritual?" Margot asked. "I'm sorry for skipping the formalities, but I am a bit anxious to get started."

"Of course," Valorie said. She smiled. "I have it with me, and another copy in my luggage." She reached into her purse and produced a small stack of papers. She handed them to Margot without hesitation.

"I hope the Archibald Sisters didn't put you through too much trouble to get it," Margot said, as she accepted them.

"They were... interesting, to say the least. I did enjoy my time with them," Valorie replied. "They seemed quite certain this ritual would work on this specter of yours."

"Yes," Vivian said. "We know how to destroy the Soul Web, but it will do little good if until we eradicate this loathsome spirit."

"I'm certain we shall," Ms. Grace stated with confidence. "Have you been able to assemble the components I listed for you?"

"We have managed most of what you requested. I can go over the components with you later this evening after you have settled in," Margot said. "We've learned a few things about the spirit thus far," she added cautiously, looking to Abby and then Vivian.

"Oh?" Vivian asked, looking to Abby.

"Yes," Abby said. "I've turned up some information in my own investigation." She wasn't about to reveal her true source. Patricia Westbrook had been kind enough to share what she knew, she wasn't going to repay her by turning her grandmother's ire on the old woman. *It is better for her to think I learned it by using the Sight,* she told herself. "I, too, have a special skill set that allows me to see and learn things that are otherwise difficult to discover," she added, obscuring the truth.

Vivian's eyes narrowed. "And what, pray tell, did you learn?" she questioned suspiciously. Abby could tell her grandmother was on edge. A part of her wanted to play with her, but she resisted the urge.

"A great deal, it would seem our family has a history with Mary Ann Conklin," Abby said, watching her grandmother closely. Fiona crossed her hands in her lap and pursed her lips while Vivian remained as still as a statue. It was her eyes that turned to fire. She wouldn't react here, not now, not with an outsider present, but Abby knew the fire in her grandmother's eyes would manifest in some other way soon enough.

"Mary Ann Conklin?" Ms. Grace questioned.

"Yes. It is the name that the spirit used in life," Margot explained, who seemed just as observant as Abby to the reaction of her aunt.

"She was a business associate of the family," Vivian explained, quickly defending herself.

"Mary Ann Conklin ran a hotel for sailors offering them female companionship as they passed through port," Abby explained. "I didn't realize we dabbled in petty prostitution," she said, attempting to lure more out of her grandmother.

Vivian gave her a preposterous look. "Of course, we didn't," Vivian said, tempering her outrage. "She was a witch, we conducted business of a more… arcane nature, Darling."

"What kind of business, Aunt Vivian?" Margot asked, helping Abby to steer the conversation.

Vivian looked to Fiona, who was avoiding eye contact. "I doubt the details of our family business dealings from over a century ago have any bearing on current matters." Vivian dismissed the idea. "Besides, I don't recall specific details. I haven't reviewed that part of our Coven history in a very long time."

"It might be worth reviewing again. Understanding the spirit's motivation could be helpful. Perhaps we could appease her," Ms. Grace suggested, unwittingly helping Abby and her intrigue.

"Then there is a matter of the curse the family put on her," Abby said.

Vivian looked at her, almost seething. "Curse?" she questioned imperiously. "I have a library full of curses that this Coven has accumulated over the last eight centuries. We have no record of a conflict with Mary Ann Conklin leading to a curse. In my mind, it is pure rumor."

"Vivian, perhaps we should show Valorie Grace to her room. She has only just arrived after a very long flight. Besides, we have a big day tomorrow with casting that ritual," Fiona said, standing.

"Yes, of course, you must forgive my manners," Vivian said, standing next to her sister.

"It's no bother," Ms. Grace stated.

"I'm sorry Ms. Grace, I didn't mean to hold you up with all this talk," Abby said. "You should rest. We have a lot to do tomorrow."

"We sincerely appreciate your help," Margot added.

"Of course," Ms. Grace said. "I will speak with you both later this afternoon to finalize preparations for tomorrow evening," she added, before disappearing down the hall with Vivian and Fiona.

CHAPTER TWENTY-SEVEN

"Are you ready?" David asked, approaching Abby as they made their way to the door.

"As ready as I can be," Abby admitted, accepting her winter coat from Mr. Greenly, who stood at attention near the front door of the grand entry.

"Abby," Cordelia approached, giving Abby a tight hug. "I hope you'll consider paying us a visit when all of this is over. You could use some peace and quiet. We'd love to have you."

"Thank you," Abby said, barely able to hear what her family was saying. The racing thoughts of nervousness nearly drowning out the world around her. "I would really enjoy that."

"We mean it," David said. "It would be nice to have you. You are welcome to stay as long as you like. There is nothing more healing and relaxing than the beaches of Maui."

Abby feigned a smile, hoping to appease her relatives. *This will work. It has to. This is going to work.* She repeated it to herself like a mantra. The rest of the Coven seemed so sure. Abby forced herself to be confident as well. *This will work.*

"You have a lot on your mind," Cordelia said, giving Abby a loving pat on the shoulder. "We'll talk about it later," she added before gesturing toward the front door.

David and Cordelia disappeared beyond the door, and for a brief moment, Abby felt alone in the world. She was in the middle of a vast body of water, grasping for a life preserver just beyond her reach. *This will work.*

She closed her eyes for a moment and took a deep breath. Her nerves only settled slightly. A sick feeling swelled in her stomach.

"It's time," Madison said, walking stiffly into the hall. Gus supported her as she walked, clearly unsure if his cousin should even be on her feet. "Oh, stop." She batted his hand away. "I'm not an invalid."

"Will you be all right?" Abby asked.

"I'm fine," Madison told her. "I will be watching over Little Evan, so the grown-ups can focus on the big magic."

Abby detected a mild bitterness in her voice, but let it go. She smiled and hugged her cousin.

"Let's go." Gus offered her his arm, and Abby accepted.

Unlike Madison, Abby was grateful to have an arm to hang on. Her legs felt like they would give out on her at any moment.

Gus smiled at her warmly. "It will all be over in a matter of a couple hours," he said, in a soothing voice. They moved through the front door and approached the town car, where an unfamiliar driver stood, waiting.

Margot joined them as they crawled into the back seat. Abby sat in the middle with her older cousin on one side and her aunt on the other, feeling relieved. The driver closed the door, and before they knew it, the car was traveling the short distance between Queen Anne and Capitol Hill.

Abby sat, her chest nearly heaving from the anxious breaths she took. Gus cracked the window slightly, letting a stream of fresh air filter into the cabin. Abby looked down and realized Gus and Margot were each holding one of her hands. There was little comfort to give, a fact they both seemed to realize. They offered her merciful silence as they made their way toward Abby's childhood home.

As they approached the end of the street, there was a dark shadow over the old Georgia Colonial. Dusk was settling in, and dark gray clouds loomed in the sky, making it feel as if the darkness had never left that morning. The cold resonated in Abby's bones as she stepped out of the car.

"We're going to finish this tonight," Vivian said, emerging from the shadows, giving Abby a start. Vivian then wrapped her arm around Abby.

With a simple nod, Abby agreed. She didn't have any words. The task before them was so insurmountable she could hardly speak.

"Don't worry, Darling," Vivian reassured. "After tonight, we will be able to put all of this behind us." They slowly made their way up the steps.

Abby paused and looked at her grandmother. "We haven't really spoken privately since our... moment in the library the other night." She managed to speak, though her voice was shaking.

"Darling, it was nothing," Vivian said, waving it away. "I'm an old woman who is left alone with her thoughts far too often. What we must do tonight is far more important than any argument we have. Let us focus our attention there."

"I don't want you to think you aren't important to me," she said.

Vivian looked at her curiously. "Thank you, Darling," she said. There was a guarded quality that quickly came over her grandmother. Abby sighed, knowing full well their brief moment of reconciliation was not going to get mushy if Vivian Kane had anything to say about it.

"Out of the way! You're blocking the path," Bernard said gruffly as he approached. He gave them both a dirty look as he pushed past them. The old, grizzled man quickly made his way up the steps and disappeared inside the house.

"Your brother is quite the charmer, isn't he?" Cordelia commented as she approached from behind with Gus.

"There's a reason we don't see much of him," Vivian said, with a disapproving glare. "Come along, Darling, let's get this wrapped up. It's time for all of this to come to an end once and for all."

Wendy and Sebastian were waiting at the front door for Abby and her grandmother to enter. There both wore cautious but hopeful, smiles on their faces as Abby passed. She was going to her parents' funeral all over again.

Abby passed through the grand entry and hesitated at the foot of the stairs. Candles illuminated each step providing a warm glow in the grand entry. To the right, in what was once the formal living room, several people were gathered. They were just silhouettes in the dim lighting, but their voices were familiar. It was Fiona, Bernard, and Lawrence.

She moved through the main entry and placed her foot on the first step. She looked up the staircase that veered off to the left. Along the banister on the second floor, candles guided the way to the room that had once been her father's office.

Abby pushed herself against apprehension. The promise of being able to put all of this behind her spurred her forward. It was time to have her parents at peace, and Mother Damnable dealt with once and for all.

As Abby stepped onto the landing of the second floor, her eyes passed the doorway to her old room. She longed to open the door and step into her old life where death was unfamiliar and loving parents awaited her. But Abby knew it wasn't on the other side of that door, not anymore.

Her heart thumped heavily in her chest with every step she took. The air in her lungs felt thin like she was standing on a mountaintop.

When she stepped through the door, Abby saw Margot. An altar had been set up in the center of the room facing the Soul Web sigil on the wall.

"Abby." Margot pulled Abby into a hug when she saw her. Wendy moved up from behind and stood next to her.

"She's holding up pretty well, all things considered," Wendy said, examining her niece.

"Yes, she is," Margot said, willing the words to make it true.

Abby wasn't convinced by their optimism but managed to appreciate their efforts.

"Darlings, it's nearly time," Vivian said, flooding into the room with Syble and Lawrence Kane in tow. Syble's wild hair was barely contained with a series of strategically placed combs. Her makeup was overdone, and the polka dots on her dress were so vivid in contrast to the dark green fabric it looked like they were moving around.

"Does everyone remember the chant I sent you?" Margot asked.

Abby felt confused. "What chant?" she asked.

"No, Abby, I don't want you to participate in the chant. I need you to use the Sight so we can be certain we've dealt with Mother Damnable. We don't want to move forward with the other ritual until we can be sure she is gone," Margot explained.

"Alright," Abby said, not having realized her role would be different than the rest of the Coven's. *At least not until...* She swallowed thought, trying not to look at the copper bowl sitting at the center of the altar. Next to it was a very large, very sharp-looking knife. The second ritual would require her blood and a great deal of it. She looked away and pushed the anxiousness from her thoughts. Instead, Abby walked over and stood near the Soul Web.

"Everyone form a circle around the altar," Margot instructed. Ms. Grace stood next to her, sorting through the components. Abby watched as her grandmother, Sebastian, Wendy, and all the family members linked hands. She noticed Gisela giving her a nasty glare before turning her back and standing next to Bernard.

It's finally happening, she thought.

Vivian nodded, and Margot began chanting. "Au-tho Spiritus Nixomay!"

"Au-tho Spiritus Nixomay!" they chanted in unison. Their voices were low and harmonic, combining into a chorus of menacing tones.

Abby pushed their chanting from her consciousness. She began to clear her thoughts away, making room in her mind and concentrated on the Sight. As she fought to stay in control of her mind, a flash of light sparked in her mind's eye. She tried to push it away, but the light strobed into her thoughts, growing brighter with each flash. The searing light illuminated her vision until she was overwhelmed. Suddenly the light dampened, turning a dull gray.

She was no longer sitting on the floor in her father's old office. Instead, she was sitting in an open space. There were no walls or boundaries. It was as if she was standing in an empty night, only there were no stars. There was nothing but the hard, stony ground underneath her.

Abby looked all around for any image–something to tell her where she was. A tempest swirled only a few feet away. It stood like a behemoth on the empty landscape all around her. Swirling like a great storm, the twister remained grounded. Its funnel extended into the air well beyond Abby's ability to perceive.

Abby stood and move slightly closer. There was a sound of chanting riding the winds. She took a few steps closer… *It's them,* she realized. *It's the family chanting!*

She came closer to the tempest. The wind was nearly overwhelming, but no matter how powerful it was, it carried the sound of "Au-tho Spiritus Nixomay!"

Abby stood at the edge of the powerful storm, twisting and turning in front of her. She was watching the ritual from the outside, or from the other side. Her Sight allowed her to see the swirling energies her family called.

She reached out, extending her hand into the center of the storm, keeping it in place as she cut through the air itself. She took a deep breath and stepped into the storm. The wind swirled all around her. There were shadows of people standing in a circle their hands linked.

Abby stood in the eye of the storm. There, sitting on a throne upon a raised dais, she found Mother Damnable.

The old crone lounged lazily on her seat, while dozens of wretched spirits crawled along the gray stone floor. They were chained and bound at the foot of her throne, starved, and emaciated, mewling in agony.

Mother Damnable sat regally on her throne. Her flesh hung from her skeletal body like rotting meat, and her teeth were jagged and broken into sharp peaks. Her eyes were hollowed dark pits. Her clothing reduced to nothing but rags. Dozens, perhaps hundreds of tiny, silver cords flowed behind her. They floated, rising up into the sky and disappearing beyond sight.

The old woman's head turned, her dark wells narrowed in on Abby as she stood at the edge of the storm. A thin smile spread across her lips. "Is this what they devised? Is this the demise I am to fear?" she asked mockingly.

"They've started the ritual," Abby said, motioning to the tempest swirling around them.

"Yes, and as you can see, I'm still here!" Mother Damnable laughed. "The storm cannot vanquish me. Your ritual will fail," she added, through the laughter.

Abby watched the demented spirit with uncertainty. Doubts began festering in her thoughts as she realized Mother Damnable did not seem to be distressed in the least. The spirits at her feet begged to be freed, their pleas, more urgent and desperate than before.

"They will keep chanting until you are destroyed," Abby said, rallying her bravery.

"Then they waste every breath, and every word," Mother Damnable said, as her amused smile turned into something more wicked. "I grow weary of your pathetic games." She stood. Abby instinctively took a step back.

Why isn't it working? Abby wondered. Panic beginning to build in her stomach. "What are you?" she asked, unable to imagine how the spirit could resist such a powerful ritual.

"I am something your family never anticipated," Mother Damnable said, taking a step down on the dais. The shackled spirits cleared a path for her, crawling away and whimpering in fear. The silver cords floating around her followed as she moved. "Now that I have all the Kanes assembled in one place, I will finish you all!" She laughed maniacally.

The old woman turned slightly and took a handful of the cords. She sorted through them until she found one string in particular. Though it appeared no different from the other strings, Mother Damnable held it in her hand and turned to Abby with a wicked smile. She then abruptly pulled the line. A chiming sound radiated from the cord.

Abby stepped back, instinctively recoiling from the sound. She saw a crackling-kind of energy appear beside Mother Damnable. Slowly a crack began to form in the air. A hand emerged and tore through the fabric between two worlds, just as she had Seen when Atoro Thanos killed her mother. The hands pulled, tearing the rift wider and wider until it was the size of a doorway. Finally, a familiar man stepped through.

"Atoro Thanos," Abby said, her voice riddled with fear and disgust.

"Now is the time," Mother Damnable said. Her grin turned into a terrifying maw of jagged teeth as she unleashed her unworldly laughter.

He growled with menacing glee as he held up his knife.

"No!" Abby rushed to stop him.

"Not so fast," Mother Damnable said. She whipped one of the silver threads around. It flew from her hand and wrapped around Abby.

Abby fell, unable to move. She watched, helpless, as Atoro approached the edge of the tempest. His blade moved with precision, piercing the torso of one of the shadows in the circle. Sparks flew from where the blade entered the chest of the shadowy figure on the other side.

"No!" she screamed. Abby couldn't tell who it was, but the form crumbled to the ground. As the figure fell, the tempest grew unstable and began to dissipate.

"The storm is gone! The ritual is over." Mother Damnable began dancing in place.

"What do you want I should do with this one?" Atoro questioned, turning to look at Abby.

Abby kicked off the tie that bound her. She scrambled to her feet and backed away, putting as much distance as she could between herself and Atoro Thanos.

"Look at the girl cower!" Mother Damnable laughed. "Don't waste your time with her. I can finish her off. Kill the others!"

Atoro grinned and pointed his wicked knife at her. "I will see you soon," he said menacingly. He stepped sideways through an invisible barrier, leaving no trace. From the other side of the veil, Abby could hear screaming.

"No!" she screamed again.

Mother Damnable held her hands out. Abby watched as billows of black smoke began to form, coming from every direction. The haze closed in around them, tighter and tighter until it formed a close circle. When Abby thought she would be wholly engulfed, it stopped. Black tendrils of smoke swarmed around them, lapping at an unseen wall, eagerly waiting to strike.

"The time has come for you to join my chorus of souls," Mother Damnable said sweetly. She reached down and picked Abby up by the neck, holding her up just high enough her feet couldn't touch the ground.

Abby closed her eyes and pulled herself from the Sight. As she began to come out of her vision, she heard an otherworldly howl. The Sight dropped back around her suddenly, knocking her off her feet. She sat up, dazed.

Abby tried to get her bearings. She blinked, glancing around her quickly. She could still see Mother Damnable, but she could also see the Coven, running around in chaos. Everything was a mix of gray mist, vivid colors, flickering candlelight, and ash falling from the ceiling. She was stuck between worlds.

She tried to call out to them, but no sound emerged. A heavy form slammed into her, knocking her back to the ground. Mother Damnable crawled on top of her. The crone's jagged claws forced Abby's eyes open.

There were screams and cries. Abby's eyes narrowed in on a body lying on the floor covered in blood. *Rodger!* He lay sprawled out, unconscious.

A second terrible scream caught Abby's attention. Cordelia collapsed, thrown backward by Atoro's sharp blow. Abby watched her grandmother squaring off with Atoro. His face was spattered in blood.

"Dominus Departius!" Vivian yelled, pointing her finger at the necromancer.

He flew back, slamming against the wall. The large man quickly came to his feet, growling. Just as Vivian was about to unleash another spell, Gisela barreled past her toward the door, knocking Vivian down.

Margot stepped forward and unleashed a spell; a crackle of electrical energy blasted from her hand. Atoro dodged and leaped at her, his knife ready to sink into her flesh. Margot flinched and stepped back. Atoro's knife sank into her stomach.

Abby screamed as she watched blood pour from Margot's wound. Panic washed over her aunt's face as Atoro pulled the knife from her stomach and sank it into her flesh once again.

"No!" Abby screamed as she watched her aunt crumble to the floor, unmoving.

"Watch as they all die!" Mother Damnable crowed.

Gus slammed into Atoro, tackling him to the ground. The two men struggled as Sebastian and Vivian readied spells. Fiona rushed to her daughter's side. Cordelia screamed incoherently at David's side, adding to the chaos. David watched, waiting for a line of sight on the man grappling with his son.

Gus crawled on top of Atoro and began punching the necromancer with his bare fists. There was a vengeful rage in his eyes. With gritted teeth, he rained blows down on the murdering necromancer. Abby watched her cousin manifest all their shared hatred onto the degenerate witch. He was going to kill the man who had murdered her parents, and she was relieved. *He won't be able to hurt us anymore*, she thought hopefully.

As Gus continued to unleash his relentless attacks, Vivian, Bernard, and Sebastian began attending the wounded. Abby tried to pull away from Mother Damnable, but the spirit was too strong.

The fighting stopped suddenly. Gus bowed over Atoro's body, resting his weight on the necromancer's shoulders. He let out a low, guttural moan and slipped to the floor. Abby saw a drop of blood drip from her cousin's mouth. He hit the ground with a sickening thud. Laying sprawled on the floor, she saw it–a knife handle, protruding from Gus' chest. The blade was completely buried in his flesh.

Mother Damnable stood, placing her foot on Abby's back, pinning her to the floor. The malevolent spirit stretched out her hand toward the young man who lay lifeless. She began cackling.

"Another one for my collection," Mother Damnable said in her gravelly voice.

Silent tears rained down Abby's face. She watched, helpless as the spiritual form of Gus emerged. It rose from his body until he was standing above the young man he once was. "No! Gus!" Abby screamed in the Sight. No one could hear her.

Chains shot up from the floorboards and wrapped around him, binding him to the world of the dead. They swirled around his arms and legs, tying him down. The confused and disoriented look on his face gave way to one of pain and horror as the chains began pulling him into the floor. With Mother Damnable's magic, the house itself was consuming him.

"One of mine!" the spirit sang gleefully. "Only a matter of minutes before I can claim those other two!"

Abby tried to pull away but had nowhere to go.

Atoro Thanos rose to his feet.

Abby looked over to her family, screaming a warning they couldn't hear. They were all huddled over Margot and Rodger.

"Turn around!" Abby shouted, knowing it would do no good.

Atoro pulled the knife from Gus' chest and wiped the blood on his black jeans. He turned and approached Vivian who hovered over Margot, unaware of further danger.

"Grandmother!" Abby shrieked, still trapped in the Sight. No one could hear her cries. She could only watch them slaughter her family, one by one.

"Kill her! Kill her!" Mother Damnable cried out in glee.

Atoro raised his knife.

A brief flash of recognition lit on Fiona's expression. The old woman threw herself to one side, raising her hands above her head. "Kar-vane Drok Tumek!" she shouted.

Heads snapped up all over the room, as everyone watched Fiona unleash her spell.

Suddenly the knife in Atoro's right hand began glowing bright red. The metal turned to molten liquid, oozing down his arm. It melted over him, consuming the flesh of his hand before dripping to the floor.

Atoro grabbed his wrist, crying out in pain. His right hand was nothing more than bloody bones. Atoro turned and ran down the hall, leaping over the banister, and disappearing down to the first floor.

"Bernard, come with me! We'll finish him off," Vivian barked. The grizzled old man followed his sister through the door to give pursuit.

Abby pulled herself away from Mother Damnable, willing the Sight to close. She sat there crying, screaming at the horror, until she was gasping for breath on the floor of her father's old office.

CHAPTER TWENTY-EIGHT

There was a heavy feeling in the large white living room. Vivian's typically monochromatic styling matched the sentiments of the family perfectly. Everywhere Abby looked, she saw eyes that had been crying.

Madison rested on a white couch, staring forward, her mind a million miles away. Cordelia stood in front of the fireplace, holding herself up against the mantle. She was staring into the flames as though they held the answers she was looking for. Bernard stood next to a window, looking out at the gardens below. Gisela sat in a chair near the door, her arms folded with a scowl on her face.

Abby sat next to Madison and put her arm around her cousin. The gesture was the only thing she could think to do, and it kept her from falling into her own pit of despair. There was a familiar sense of shock resonating through Abby, like an electrical current. There was no way to make it stop. The haze of grief was all-too-familiar.

Sebastian came in, supporting Rodger, who was pale, but standing. The somberness of the room fell upon them as they entered. They quietly sat on a couch across from Abby and Madison.

Little Evan began fussing in Wendy's arms. Sebastian quickly took his son and gave him a bottle.

The sounds of a small child drew Cordelia from her trance. She glanced over at the small child and approached slowly, looking down with watery eyes.

"He's so precious," Cordelia said, desperate grief filling her voice. The pain in Cordelia's eyes stroked the strings of Abby's own grief. It settled over the room like a contagion.

"Tsk," came from the direction of the door. Abby quickly looked to see who would mock Cordelia's grief. Gisela rolled her eyes and turned away.

Abby stood, furious. "What is your problem?" she demanded.

Gisela looked at her with a glint of outrage in her eyes. "Don't you talk to me like that, you little piss spittle!"

"Why do you always have to be such an abominable bitch!" Abby yelled. She was shaking. Rage had swelled and breached the banks of her composure.

"How dare you!" Gisela stood in outrage. "You're such an idiot! Can't you see we're all here because you were in a hurry to save your parents? You as much as killed Gus! Margot too, if she doesn't pull through!"

Abby recoiled as though she'd been slapped across the face. Before she could respond, the double doors opened, and Vivian entered, followed by Fiona.

"What is going on here?" Vivian questioned.

"Your precious granddaughter is acting all holier than thou when she's the reason Gus is dead! She forced us to do the ritual. All she cares about is freeing her parents!" Gisela said.

"No one was forced to do anything," Fiona said coldly. "We were all there of our own free will. We knew what we were up against... at least we thought we did." Her voice trailed off into silence.

"Abigail isn't to blame," Bernard said, breaking his silence. He turned to face the family.

"Of course, she is," Gisela muttered, folding her arms and plopping down in her chair.

"Oh, be quiet, you glutenous grumbletonian!" Bernard barked. "There is only one person to blame for this." He slowly made his way toward the doors, pausing in front of Vivian. The old woman looked at her brother, bracing herself.

"When our father passed over me in favor of you to lead this Coven, I begrudgingly gave you my support. But this is what you have led us to. This is what you have done with his legacy."

Vivian stood still as a statue under the assault of her brother's words.

"Atoro got away...You let the Thanos win! We lost because of your incompetence! You are responsible for all of this!" Bernard threw open the door and disappeared down the hallway.

Vivian stood like stone, even after he had left. The room was silent save for the crackling of the fire.

Vivian took a deep breath and reasserted her presence. Abby could see the effort she was putting into holding herself together. As she glanced around the room, she saw the same look in nearly everyone.

"The Thanos have not won," Vivian stated with conviction. Her words fell on silence. "It's time to call upon our friends." She let out a heavy sigh. "I will reach out to the Archibald Sisters. They are perhaps the best suited of our allies to help us in this situation."

"If we had reached out to them sooner, my son might be alive," Cordelia said weakly. David wrapped his arms around his wife, silently holding her as she wept.

"We had every reason to believe in the rituals would work," Vivian said, defending herself.

Cordelia's sobs were her only response.

Across the room, Fiona stumbled and caught herself on an end table. Abby rushed to her grandaunt's, making sure she was steady.

"Are you all right, Aunt Fiona?" Abby asked, meeting her gaze. There was a meekness she hadn't seen in the old woman's eyes. Somehow, she looked older, as if all the events of the last few weeks had aged her before Abby's eyes.

"Come along, I think you should lay down for a spell," Sebastian said, taking Fiona's arm and escorting her out of the room. Madison stood and followed.

Vivian had a worried look on her face; it was something Abby had rarely seen before. Even Grandmother doesn't know what to do, she realized. Abby reached over and took her grandmother's arm. Vivian looked down at her, confused momentarily by the gesture. She took a deep breath and acknowledged the support with a nod.

"Good morning," Lawrence said, coming into the room with his wife Syble at his side. She lacked all decorum for the mood in the room, choosing to wear a cheap-looking polka-dotted teal dress. Abby closed her eyes for a moment to avoid having to look at the garish fabric.

"Thank you for joining us," Vivian responded distantly, turning her eyes away from Syble.

"Good of you to show yourself. We haven't seen you since last night," Cordelia said, dabbing her eyes dry. "You certainly escaped in a hurry."

"We thought everyone would have the good sense to follow us," Syble squeaked.

"We could have used your help fighting for our lives," Gisela grumbled.

"Oh my, that room was far too small! There was too much risk of friendly fire," Lawrence stated. "We went down to cover the exit so the fiend wouldn't escape."

"He escaped anyway," Wendy said.

"We were covering the back door, we thought certainly someone else would cover the front entrance," Syble said, as though it all made sense. "Surely you're not blaming us?"

"How very convenient for you," Vivian said pointedly.

"It's not our fault no one thought to cover the front door," Syble said, with a simple shrug. The two of them sat on the couch and settled in.

"What are we discussing?" Lawrence asked, tapping his cane on the floor as if to call the room to order.

"Our next steps," Vivian said with a menacing glare in his direction.

"I will contact the Archibald Sisters," Vivian repeated. "We cannot let this failure set us back. We cannot give up. The stakes are too high."

"I don't see how it's worth the risk," Syble stated.

"Yeah," Gisela stated. "Why should we keep risking our lives?"

"Haven't either of you thought this through?" Abby asked, doing her best to restrain her anger. "Mother Damnable didn't just trap my parents as part of some sick Thanos deal. She has generations of Kanes trapped in her web. Do you think she's going to pass on your soul when you cross over? Every soul she collects is like batteries that feed her lust for power and revenge. You aren't safe. None of us are!"

"But I'm only a Kane by marriage!" Syble protested righteously.

"Do you think that matters?" Abby spat, angrily. "She won't stop until she has all of us!"

"I doubt it makes little difference to the kind of loathsome spirit we're dealing with," Sebastian stated. "I'm not a Kane by blood, neither was my sister. Yet Jessica is trapped in the Soul Web all the same."

Abby watched the blood run from Syble's face. Gisela snorted in disgust and sat back in her chair, sulking.

"Do you really think the Archibald Sisters can help?" Lawrence asked.

Vivian sighed. "I don't know. But we have nowhere else to turn at the moment.

"How do we know they can be trusted? They aren't members of the Coven," Wendy said.

"They are family, though," Vivian said. "Distant, but blood ties, nonetheless. Their maternal grandmother was a Kane. We may still be able to suggest that it would be in their best interest to help us."

"I've heard they are ancient," Sebastian said. "Are they in any shape to really be of any help?"

"Old," Vivian said, raising her eyebrow. "They were old when I was a little girl. However, they are as sharp as they have ever been. And as you are aware, the older you are, the more you know and the more experience you have."

"… And if they can't help?" Abby asked, fear lumping in her throat.

"We can't think about that," Vivian said. Even though her words were certain, Abby knew even the mighty Vivian Kane, wasn't so sure.

"Those two old dingbats are as senile as they come. Why their coven hasn't performed the Ending Ritual on them is beside me," Gisela mumbled, under her breath.

"When I spoke with them, they seemed in perfect control of their faculties," Vivian countered.

Even though Abby wanted to be hopeful, the news of these old sisters wasn't offering the hope she was looking for.

Vivian looked at Abby. There was a softness to her gaze, touched with fresh grief. Abby saw all the vulnerabilities her grandmother was trying to hide.

"Why didn't the banishment work?" Abby asked the question everyone was thinking, but no one wanted to voice.

Vivian shook her head, looking lost. "I don't know," she admitted to the silent room. She walked over to the liquor cabinet and pulled out a crystal decanter. She placed it on the counter, unopened, as she stared off into nothing.

Abby wandered down the halls of her grandmother's stately mansion, trying to think of any excuse to avoid joining her family in the library. There was none. She knew they were waiting for her, and her feet took her there in spite of herself.

As she approached the end of the hall, the double doors opened. Abby could hear a heated argument going on just beyond as Fiona stepped out and closed the doors behind her. The old woman quickly moved to a small settee along one side of the hallway and sat rubbing her forehead with her hand.

"Are you okay?" Abby asked as she approached.

Fiona looked up, surprised. She hadn't expected anyone to see her. "I'll be fine in a moment," she reassured her grandniece.

"Are there no treatments or rituals to help?" Abby asked, moving closer and taking a seat in the chair next to the elderly woman.

"There are," Fiona said dismissively. "None that I care to live with."

"I spoke to Rodger about it once. He said there were ways to 'cure' you of your kidney disease. He admires you for not doing any of them."

"Rodger Pennington is a good man," Fiona said, offering a rare compliment. "He has helped me with a tincture that helps ease the discomfort. It helps minimize the impact of my disease on the rest of my body. It has sustained my quality of life much longer than the physicians originally predicted. For that, I will be forever grateful."

"How bad is it?" Abby asked, uncertain if she was being too personal. Her concern pushed caution aside.

Fiona smiled and took a deep breath. "I still have a few good years left in me," she said. "Enough time to see my granddaughter graduate, perhaps a few more years after that. It's all borrowed time, I'm afraid."

"I'm sorry. I knew you had serious health problems, I didn't realize how serious," Abby said somberly.

"As you can imagine, I have more than a few reasons to want this loathsome Mother Damnable dealt with. The probability of my own demise coming sooner than later is simply one of many," Fiona admitted.

"Yes, I can imagine," Abby said. "It sounded like they're arguing."

"You've been a part of this family your entire life," Fiona stated. "When have you ever seen these people in a room together when it didn't erupt into an argument?"

Abby chuckled. "I can't recall."

"We all care about one another in our own way," Fiona said, staring ahead at the wall, exploring her own thoughts. "We love one another very much, we aren't conventional, and it doesn't always look very pretty, but we do care."

Abby grew quiet, rather than contradict her grandaunt. Compassion wasn't something she was used to from this family.

"What are you planning to do when this is all over?" Fiona asked, startling Abby out of her thoughts.

"You aren't the first person to ask me that," Abby answered her. "I want to go back to England for a short trip, spend some time with my friends, but after that, I'm not really sure. I don't even know if there will be an 'after this.' Do we even have a solution to the Soul Web? Without Atoro—"

Fiona held up a hand, forestalling Abby's tirade. "Let's assume, for the sake of argument, that there is and we just haven't found it yet. What will you do once your parents are free?"

Abby chewed her bottom lip, thinking. "I'm not sure. I'm starting to think this gap year idea wasn't the best. I have too much time on my hands. Maybe I should consider taking some course work in the spring."

"How much do you know about Kane Industries?" Fiona asked.

"Not very much," Abby admitted, embarrassed at her lack of knowledge about the family business. "I know we were timber barons in the early pioneer days, and now we're heavily invested in green technology and renewable energy sources."

Fiona nodded. "Kane Industries in an international conglomerate comprised mostly of research companies," she said. "We have made billions developing technologies related to natural resources. Mining, research, power—you name it." She smiled. "Science and magic are not always so different, you know."

"Why has the family worked so hard to build our business up and maintain such enormous cash reserves? I've never really understood. We're witches, I thought we would be more focused on the arcane."

Fiona took a deep breath. "Who says we aren't," she stated cautiously. "My father was convinced there was a great war brewing between the covens—a view my dear sister, shares. We have been preparing for this war for many years now."

"I still don't understand," Abby confessed. "What does the family business have to do with the probability of some war?"

Fiona regarded Abby with a warm smile. "I know you haven't been an adult for long. I certainly don't mean to patronize you in the least. I guess its time to explain a few things to you. I really don't understand why my sister hasn't already spoken to you of these things," Fiona stated, with a slight hint of disapproval.

"Kane Industries is one of the largest corporations in the world. It has amassed more liquid assets than you'll find in any of our financial records. This family has hidden away billions in blind trusts and in bank accounts around the world. One word from a handful of people in this family, and we can collapse stock markets, plummet entire nations into famine, incite civil wars, inflict economic ruin, and many, many other terrible things long before we ever turn to magic. This is how we fight our wars."

Abby sat quietly, taking in everything Fiona was saying. "I never realized," Abby confessed.

"You weren't meant to," Fiona stated. "Not yet. You would have been brought into the company one day. Perhaps when you were a bit older more and settled."

"Do my uncles know?" Abby asked.

"Of course they do," Fiona stated. "If you'll remember, it was Sebastian who reaped economic destruction on the Thanos. He is quite gifted at using the family's resources. His decisions often yield great results."

"For some reason, I feel like there's more," Abby said, looking to her grandaunt with curiosity.

"There is," Fiona admitted, her reserved demeanor returning. "Covens have many secrets. When one, such as yourself, reaches the right age and becomes a ranking member, you begin to learn some of those secrets. More will be revealed to you over time. As hard as it may seem, you will need to be patient."

"More secrets?" A pained look crossed Abby's face. "Patience isn't necessarily my issue," she confessed. "Trust is."

Fiona gave Abby a knowing smile. "Trust is hard to come by. Especially lately." The old woman paused, uncertainty in her gaze. "You need to be particularly careful, Abby. Be careful about what you confront your grandmother with."

"What do you mean?" Abby asked startled.

"I've noticed how Vivian has treated you the last day or two," Fiona said. "I've seen it before. The cautious reservation, the refusal to make direct eye contact. I know my sister very well, perhaps better than anyone else in the world. Have you been fighting a lot lately?"

"It seems like every day," Abby admitted.

"She is struggling, but there is nothing Vivian despises more than vulnerability. For her, it is the same thing as being weak, and weaknesses are there to be exploited. She has only ever broken down a handful of times in her life that I know of," Fiona explained.

"Does this mean she will start avoiding me again?" Abby asked.

"What it really means is that she trusts you." Fiona smiled warmly.

"Why are you telling me all of this?"

"Because, I can see the pain and frustration you are going through," Fiona admitted. "Your grandmother, like this family, is not conventional. Her love isn't going to look like the kind of love most families share. You can accept this or reject it; regardless, it is what she is capable of showing."

"Thank you, Aunt Fiona," Abby said.

"We have an internship program at our corporate headquarters, you know. Perhaps after the New Year, it would be advantageous for you to participate. There are few better ways to learn about the ins and outs of the family business than by starting out as an intern."

"Who would I be interning with?" Abby asked.

Fiona smiled. "Me," she stated plainly.

"I don't imagine Grandmother would be pleased." Abby smiled.

"Not in the least." Fiona raised an eyebrow. "There really isn't anything she can do about it now, is there?"

Abby considered it for a moment. "She could make my life a living hell," she speculated.

"Not if you are working only on business matters for the corporation," Fiona said, a sly smile curling at the edge of her lips.

"I like the sound of that," Abby said. "I've been wanting to become more familiar with the family business. I guess this is an opportunity once everything is settled with my parents."

"Yes, especially considering the sizable percentage of shares you hold. That your grandmother has been voting with, in your name," Fiona said under her breath.

"Grandmother never really gave up anything when she emancipated me, did she? She released my trust last year, but that's all," Abby observed.

"No," Fiona said. "She controls your vote until you turn twenty-one. You should be ready for it. The day when you can vote with your own shares will come sooner than you expect."

"I feel like such an idiot not knowing all of this," Abby said, shaking her head.

"Dear, you really shouldn't," Fiona reassured. "You have been quite preoccupied with other things of late, not to mention your grandmother is not always forthcoming with information when it suits her purpose. I doubt your uncles are aware of the stipulation, having no particular reason to research such matters."

"How do you know about it?" Abby asked.

Fiona gave her a quaint smile. "Details rarely escape my notice. You aren't the only person in this family with a special gift," she stated.

Abby looked at her grandaunt curiously. "What kind of gift do you have?" Abby asked, uncertain if it was rude to do so.

Fiona shifted in her chair. "Eidetic memory. I can remember anything I've read or seen word for word, with perfect clarity."

"That sounds useful," Abby considered aloud.

"It is for me, rarely for others who like to forget certain details when it's convenient for them," Fiona stated with a coy smile.

Abby practiced her violin. It was the only reprieve she had from the frustration, pain, and death surrounding her. *The last few days have felt so lonely*, she thought. She placed her violin back in its case and loosened its bow. After she carefully secured the latches, she put the case at the foot of her bed. It was almost a ritual in itself. Just as she finished, there was a knock on her bedroom door.

"Grandmother," Abby said upon opening her door.

"Darling, please, may I come in? I would like to talk," Vivian said.

"I've already told you everything I can remember from my vision," Abby told her. "I'm sorry, I can't seem to remember more. I keep thinking if I had been more aware, maybe Gus would still be alive, or Margot would be here, or if–"

Vivian held up a hand, forestalling any more. "It's not that. Please, Darling," she said.

Abby stepped aside, "Sorry." She gestured for her grandmother to enter.

"I won't take up much of your time," Vivian said. Abby could tell her grandmother was uncomfortable. "I simply wanted to talk to you... about our argument other night."

"You mean the night we came to stay here?" Abby asked. There was an unsettling feeling growing in her stomach. Her grandmother was infamous for pretending like nothing ever happened. Why would she bring up an old argument now?

"Yes, Darling, that night," Vivian said with trepidation. "I know things have been strained of late. We've all been under an incredible amount of pressure."

"I know," Abby said, nodding. She offered a comforting smile. "It's been... hard since the ritual."

A sad smile flashed across Vivian's face, disappearing as quickly as it came. "I know you have been frustrated with me, and that you have wanted to be more a part of things," she said. Every word she spoke was agony. Her voice was shaking. "But I stand by my actions. Darling, it could just have easily been you that night. I'm very glad it wasn't."

Abby swallowed the tears that threatened to spill. "Don't say that," Abby pleaded. "Margot and Gus–"

"Are just as much a part of this family as you are, Darling, I know. But neither one is my granddaughter." The smile Vivian offered to Abby was both warm and a little shy. "I do not want the air between us to be strained."

"I don't, either," Abby confessed, surprised by her grandmother's smile. From a woman so incredibly filled with pride, this simple gesture was more of an apology than she ever expected. "I never did," she added.

Vivian's eyes looked tired, and her brow was creased with strain. "I know I haven't been the easiest person to be around."

Abby looked at her grandmother in near disbelief and quickly did her best to hide her surprise. "I... I don't know what to say," Abby said.

"Emotions are running high, I know that," Vivian said. "We need to come together more now than ever, not fight among ourselves."

Abby stood and pulled her grandmother into a hug. There was no scent of alcohol on her grandmother as she wrapped her arms around the old woman. At that moment, it was exactly what she needed to hear from the very person she wanted to hear it from. She never imagined her grandmother would reach out to her like this. She hoped this was a sign that things were going to get better between them.

"I love you, Grandma," Abby said, holding Vivian tightly as if letting go would make everything go back to the way it was.

"I love you too, Darling," Vivian said, despite the awkwardness of her words there was no doubting the sincerity. "Though I wish you would stop calling me that. It feels unnatural."

Abby chuckled, "Alright, Grandmother."

Vivian smiled a little easier this time. "We are not giving up. Everything is going to be settled soon. We will find a way." She stroked Abby's hair lovingly, comforting them both.

"It's been unbearable," Abby confessed, as tears stained her cheeks.

"It has been for all of us, Darling" Vivian comforted.

"Grandmother?" Abby said, so quietly she almost wasn't sure she even said it.

"Hmm?" Vivian responded.

"What..." She knew she had to give voice to the fear lingering in her heart, or it would eat her from the inside. She was so unsure of everything she used to consider real. "What if we can't win?"

"Whatever do you mean, Darling?"

Abby sighed, trying not to cry again. "What if we can't find a way to banish Mother Damnable? Or break the Soul Web? What if they stay trapped forever?"

Vivian was quiet. She sat still so long that Abby had to sit up to check that her grandmother was still awake. For a split second, Abby saw a look of despair flash across the Matriarch's face.

"Well," Vivian said, finally. "I suppose we find a way to live on as best we can and get revenge on those that have hurt us." She pulled back and held Abby at arm's length, giving her a confident smile. "But we won't let that happen."

Abby wished it was as easy as putting on a smile and being sure of herself. She couldn't shake the feeling that somehow she would have to find a way to live, knowing her parents were trapped in eternal torment–and that the same fate would be awaiting every Kane in their afterlife.

"That is more than enough of that for me, Darling," Vivian said, reasserting her guarded demeanor. She pulled a handkerchief from her purse and wiped at Abby's tear-stained cheeks. "I have some research to get back to."

"I know," Abby said. A part of her didn't want to let go of the rare moment she shared with her grandmother, but she knew Vivian was already chafing at the show of emotion. "Maybe after the concert and everything is over, we can spend some time together," Abby suggested.

"I would like that," Vivian said, with a reassuring smile.

Abby watched her grandmother turn and walk away.

CHAPTER TWENTY-NINE

Abby turned over and closed her eyes again, shifting into several different positions, searching for the right one that would lull her into slumber. When the first few attempts didn't work, she did the same again, and then again. *Sleep is not my friend...*

It felt like an eternity passed, Abby sat up and turned the light back on. She checked her phone. *11:25? It's only been twenty minutes?* She let out a groan and rolled on to her back.

Abby closed her eyes and cleared her thoughts. She kept pushing them away until she was drifting in an empty consciousness–not quite awake, not quite asleep. There was a clicking sound, it sounded like hooves striking the earth.

Abby slowly opened her eyes and found herself standing in the grass at the edge of a dirt road. Large potholes filled with mud pocked the makeshift avenue. On the far side was a two-story house with a row of tall shrubs obscuring the entrance. Further down the road were several other homes, built in a similar manner, with whitewashed walls and large porches.

This was too vivid to be a dream, but it also was unlike any place the Sight had ever shown her before.

A horse-drawn buggy passed by. A man wearing a black suit and a top hat sat, holding the reins of the horse. Abby looked behind her and saw a storefront. "Anderson's Feed Shop," it read.

She peered through the window. Crates and barrels were arranged in a haphazard pile in the center of the room, and large burlap bags were stacked against one wall. Toward the back, a man in a brown shirt was leaning over a counter, scribbling something on a piece of paper.

"Get the hell out of here! Ya freeloading jackass!" a familiar voice called out. Her shouts were accompanied by the sound of barking.

Abby spun, searching for the specter yet again. She stood, frozen by the image of Mary Ann Conklin; not the bent and twisted being of death and decay, but a human being, flushed with life.

Across the road from where Abby stood, Mary Ann chased a man from a house. Two large hounds nipped at his heels as he fled.

"Don't let me catch you here again, you mongrel!" the old woman shouted. She turned and looked directly at Abby.

Abby froze. *She can't see me. This is a vision… right?*

After a moment, Mother Damnable disappeared back into the house.

Abby waited for a wagon to pass by before rushing across the muddy road. She approached a row of large bushes lining the front of the house and made her way around to the front walk. A stone pathway led to a small porch and a red door. There was a sign next to the door that read, "Felker House."

This is her home, this is where she lived, Abby realized. *The brothel.*

She approached the door, watching her steps carefully as she moved along the uneven stone path. Abby climbed the two steps up to the small porch, each board creaking underfoot. When she reached the door, she saw it was slightly ajar. Abby reached out and pushed the door open to peek inside.

Inside was a large parlor filled with red, velvet-covered couches and carved wooden chairs. Several men, wearing tattered brown pants held up by suspenders and filthy white shirts, sat with bottles of liquor in hand.

"Shut up and get back to work you little trollop, or I'll put you back on the street where I found you!" Mary Ann yelled in the next room.

A young woman wearing a corset and stockings spilled into the parlor through velvet curtains hanging over a doorway. She had long red hair held up with several pins, and she wore bright rouge on her cheeks. The young woman had a vacant look in her eyes as she stumbled toward one of the men sitting on the couch and plopped down on his lap.

Mary Ann emerged from the curtains with a stern look on her wrinkled face. The large hounds followed at her feet. "Upstairs with you! Second door to the left," she barked. The two quickly stood and disappeared through the curtains. "It won't be more than ten minutes before the next one is ready," Mary Ann said to the remaining man sitting on the couch. "Two dollars," she said, putting out her hand.

"Two Dollars?" the man said in outrage. "That's highway robbery!"

"You can go find some other place to find company if you don't want to pay," Mary Ann said. "Now pay or leave, you cheap bastard!"

The man stood and reached into his pocket. He pulled out a handful of coins and counted out two dollars into the old woman's hand. Mary Ann quickly deposited the coins in a leather pouch tied around her waist and nodded back at the couch. "Wait here."

"Aren't you going to say thank you?" the man asked sarcastically as he took his seat. "Don't they have manners in this God-forsaken town?"

"No!" Mary Ann barked, then laughed loudly. "Just shut up and drink."

The old woman headed back through the velvet curtains and paused. She hesitated for a moment and turned slowly until she was looking directly at Abby. "Who are you?" she said.

Abby stood frozen. She swallowed hard, trying to ease the sudden dryness in her mouth. "You can see me?" she asked softly.

Mary Ann took a slight step in Abby's direction. She regarded her carefully. "Of course, I can see you," she said. She began smiling widely.

The grin stretched and grew, contorting her face into a disgusting leer. She began to cackle.

Abby began to back away until she reached the doorway. She turned and ran. She dashed down the steps and slammed directly into a brick wall.

Everything went dark. Abby shook her head and looked around. She wasn't at Felker House anymore. Dim lights hung from the ceiling, offering a faint glow. It was just enough to make out... *bricks? A brick hallway?* The air was musty and humid. "Where am I?" she muttered. She looked behind her. There was no sign of the brothel house or Mary Ann Conklin.

The brick was old and weather-worn. She looked up and saw that all the electrical wiring for the lights was encased in metal pipes and attached to the brick with screws. Abby followed the hallway a few dozen feet before she came to an old photograph on the wall. She looked at it closely; a row of old houses near the waterfront was framed by the forest, growing along the edges of the town. She had seen it before.

"Why am I here?" Abby wondered aloud. She took a step, and the lights above flickered. Abby paused and looked up. The lights flickered again and then went out.

Pure darkness surrounded Abby. The only sound was the drop of water a few yards ahead. Abby reached out and found the wall with her hands.

Fear churned in Abby's stomach, refusing to settle. *I'm in the Sight, I know I must be. But why show me the Underground?* She stopped and looked down the long hall. In the distance, there was a faint glow. Abby narrowed her eyes to try and get a better look. She couldn't make it out, but something was there.

She slowly inched along the wall toward the faint glow. She grew closer and closer until she was only a few yards away. Abby peered at it until she was able to make out what was causing the pale light.

Abby took several steps closer. It was a wooden box little more than a foot long and nearly as wide. It was a simple design with brass hinges and stained wood.

Curious, Abby took another step closer... then another...

There was a blinding flash. Abby shielded her eyes, but it was too late. She blinked, trying to clear her dazzled vision. Just as her sight cleared, a decrepit creature rushed toward her out of the darkness. She stumbled back and fell.

Abby rolled over quickly to face the flash of white that rushed at her. Hovering a few inches above her head, was a pale, thin man dressed in rags. He was gaunt with sunken cheeks and balding patches in his hair.

He tried to speak and only coughed, spraying spittle all over Abby's face. A grotesque croak escaped his throat. He coughed again. "She comes!" he yelled, his voice raspy.

Abby closed her eyes and concentrated, pulling herself from the Sight abruptly. When she opened her eyes, she was back in her bedroom of her grandmother's house, panting and sweating from exertion.

Abby lay on the bed, clutching her pillow tightly to her chest. She concentrated on her breathing until it returned to normal. The aches that ravaged her joints and muscles began to fade slowly.

She half expected sleep to overtake her in the wake of adrenaline. However, long after her heartbeat returned to normal and her breathing had slowed, Abby was still awake.

She glanced over at the clock. It was 11:30.

Abby quickly changed into a pair of jeans and a black sweater. She put on hiking boots and grabbed a warm winter jacket. She pulled a flashlight from a drawer and checked to make sure it worked and shoved it in her coat pocket. Then she carefully opened her bedroom door, making certain she didn't disturb anyone in the hall.

She made it to the top of the stairs when she heard a door open. "Sneaking out?" Ms. Grace asked, standing in the doorway with a cup of tea and a saucer in hand.

Abby turned, trying to look innocent. "I'm just taking a walk."

Valorie Grace took a sip of her tea and looked at Abby with absolutely no expression on her face. "I have spent nearly twenty years as an educator at a boarding school, Abigail. Do you think I am unfamiliar with what 'sneaking out' looks like?"

"I'm not sneaking out," Abby protested. "I just have to take care of something."

Ms. Grace raised an eyebrow and glanced at the watch on her wrist. "Very little business is conducted at this hour. Not any kind of business you should be dabbling in, certainly," she said, looking at Abby over her glasses.

"It's nothing," Abby protested.

"Then it's lucky for you that I am no longer your guardian," Valorie said. Before her former charge could say more, the older woman disappeared into her room. She reappeared almost immediately with her winter coat.

"Ms. Grace, I can't ask you to join me," Abby said.

"I don't recall you asking," she replied, zipping her coat.

"What I'm doing could be very dangerous," Abby protested again.

"More reason for you to take someone along." She approached the stairs, obviously not to be dissuaded. "Though my duties as your instructor came to an end some time ago, my duties as a friend will never cease, Miss Kane," she added with a smile.

"Fine," Abby said begrudgingly, as she led the way down the stairs and to the car parked at the front of the house. Ms. Grace quickly situated herself in the passenger seat as Abby started the car.

"Where are we going?" Ms. Grace asked as Abby started pulling up the driveway.

"The Underground," Abby said. "There's a series of tunnels under the city that were just built over after the Great Seattle Fire. I think Mother Damnable is hiding something down there," she explained.

"What?" Ms. Grace questioned, unsure if she had misheard. "You were planning to do this alone?"

"Yes," Abby admitted. The more she thought about it, the more stupid she felt. *I really didn't think this through.* "I couldn't ask anyone to go along when it's so dangerous."

The drive to downtown was swift. There were relatively few cars, a rare phenomenon even on a weeknight. Abby drove to the Pioneer Square district, just south of the business center where Hailey and Madison had taken her only a few weeks before.

Abby parked the car near the waterfront, next to an old, rundown warehouse. "I'm pretty sure there's an entrance to the Underground near the Curiosity Shop," Abby said, leading the way.

They walked around the side of an old building and came to a steep stairwell leading into the basement. The stairs worked their way down toward the water, stopping a few feet above, at a concrete platform. A large stylized letter 'K' was etched into the heavy steel door; the logo for Kane Industries.

Abby reached out and placed her hand on the door. She carefully teased the lock open with her magic and opened the door. Peering into the darkened interior, she pulled out a flashlight and handed it to Ms. Grace.

"Thank you," Ms. Grace said, flicking it on and shining it around the room.

Abby looked around. They were standing at the entrance of a large cavernous basement. Boxes and crates were stacked haphazardly wherever they would fit around an enormous rusted out boiler in the center. The entire warehouse smelled of fish and saltwater.

"This way," Abby said, as she walked across the room. "I think the entrance to the tunnels is over here."

"How do you know about this place?" Ms. Grace asked as she carefully navigated her way around the debris covering the floor.

"This warehouse used to be run by my family's company. I remember coming here with my dad when I was little," Abby said.

Ms. Grace frowned. "Yes, but why did you think of it now? Do you actually know where we are going?"

"I have no idea," Abby explained, desperately hoping she didn't sound nearly as foolish as she felt. "I just... I had a feeling."

"I was not aware that the Sight allowed you such extra intuitive insight," Valorie said, surprised.

"It doesn't. Not normally," Abby said. She quickly told Valorie about her dream. "I think Mother Damnable is guiding me here."

"That should be all the more reason not to go in," Valorie hissed. Her tone was tight and frightened. "You are clearly being led into a trap."

"But why would she lead me here just to kill me? She has had plenty of time." They came to an old iron door that looked almost like the entrance to a bank vault. "I think this is it," Abby said.

"For the record, I do not fully approve of this plan, but I will help you," Valorie said, supportively. "I trust you, Abigail."

Abby looked at her old mentor and smiled. "Thank you."

They looked at the solid metal door and frowned. Abby tried to lift the latch, but it had rusted shut long ago. It didn't move at all.

"Is it important to preserve this door?" Valorie asked.

"Not particularly. Why?"

Valorie Grace extended her hand and focused intensely on the door. She made a squeezing motion with her hand, and the large iron door began to twist and contort as though a giant was crushing it into a ball. Ms. Grace made another slight gesture, and the broken door crashed to the floor, out of the way of the entrance.

"Hopefully, discretion isn't a part of this excursion," she stated.

"With any luck, we won't run into anything more horrifying than a rat down here," Abby jested nervously.

The doorway opened into a tunnel. Three treacherous steps led down to a brick hallway. Abby jumped over them, then looked back for her companion.

Ms. Grace stood in the doorway with a trepidatious look. "I see now what you mean by dangerous," she stated, regarding the rickety old steps with uncertainty. She held onto the doorway, and cautiously extended her leg to reach over the stairs. Her dress proved too confining, and she hiked it up slightly, much to Abby's amusement.

"Can I help?" Abby asked, hiding her smile.

"No, I'm fine." She managed to clear the steps, and quickly adjusted her dress, composing herself once again. "Which way now?"

Abby looked in both directions, each disappearing into darkness beyond the range of the flashlight. The walls were constructed from old bricks, chipped and slowly crumbling. Ancient, rusted-out pipes lined the ceiling; some of them dripping water and others completely decayed away. The floor was compacted dirt, and from the water lines near the floor, Abby was sure these tunnels flooded from time to time.

"I'm not sure which way to go," Abby confessed, as she stared into the darkness.

"Can you use the Sight to guide you? If you can master the use of it as an internal map, it could prove most advantageous in any number of circumstances," Valorie mused, her inner scholar escaping in curiosity.

"I'm... not sure," Abby said. She paused a moment and relaxed, opening herself just slightly to the currents of Fate, hoping for any sign of which direction to go. When nothing happened, she blushed, feeling silly. "I don't think it works that way, after all."

"Very well. Shall we explore a little?" Valorie asked.

There was a slight hint of excitement in Valorie's tone, and Abby wondered if her friend wasn't enjoying this adventure a bit. "I don't know why not, as long as we're careful," Abby said. "This passageway seems fairly stable."

"Do you know what you're looking for?" Valorie asked as they cautiously moved along the corridor.

"I'm not sure, but I think it's an old wooden box," she responded.

They made their way down the dark tunnel. No matter how far they went, there always seemed to be darkness beyond the flashlight. After walking for a few minutes, the tunnel emptied into a large room with a low ceiling. There were several collapsed wooden beams scattered around, and the ground was covered in dark water. It was difficult to tell how deep the water was. Abby suspected it wasn't more than a few inches. She paused at the edge of the pool, not eager to test her theory.

Valorie pointed to the edge of the room. "The water doesn't quite reach the wall over there," she observed.

Abby led the way, walking along the wall to make sure it was safe. They stepped over a stagnant pool of water, heading for another tunnel on the far side of the room. A strange gurgling sound came from behind them.

Abby turned and gazed into the black pool. The center bubbled as it slowly began to boil. Valorie stepped forward and stood next to Abby. The water continued to burble and churn. A ghostly figure began to rise from the boiling murk, cackling as it appeared.

Valorie stared at the apparition with uncertainty. "So, she can manifest physically," she muttered under her breath, almost with admiration.

"I thought we told you that," Abby whispered, as Mother Damnable revealed a wicked smile.

"It is not that I don't believe you, I simply have never seen it happen before," Valorie stated in equal parts curiosity and caution.

"You finally made it this far," the apparition said, her pockmarked face twisted into a gleeful expression.

"Yes," Abby responded.

Mother Damnable tilted her head slightly, curious. "You brought another witch..." she sniffed the air. "This one isn't a Kane!"

"What are you hiding down here?" Abby questioned.

Mother Damnable smiled, revealing her rotting teeth. "I thought you would never come. I thought you would never find this place," she said gleefully, as she spun around in a strange, nonsensical dance. "I will show you! I will take you!"

"Abby, are you certain you trust this... creature?" Valorie asked.

"I don't trust her at all," Abby whispered back. "But we didn't come all this way to have a chat."

"Come along, child, come along... You must see for yourself," she cackled and walked past them down the hall. Abby and Valorie followed her, watching their step and hopping over piles of debris accumulated on the ground.

Mother Damnable guided them down a maze of tunnels and rooms. They occasionally happened upon old shop signs; a tailor, a general store, and some Abby couldn't read. The smell was musty and dank.

Before long, they came upon a large room with concrete steps. It took them down nearly three levels into a room so large it felt like an underground arena. "This way," the apparition said, guiding them deeper into the darkness. They came to one of many small doors on the far side of the enormous hall. Mother Damnable walked through the door and disappeared on the other side.

Abby pulled on the doorknob only to have the door break away from the hinges and fall on her. Valorie stepped forward, and the two of them discarded the old wooden door to the side. They made their way forward. Mother Damnable was waiting for them.

"We're almost there," the deranged spirit said in a playful sing-song voice, as though she were speaking to little children.

Eventually, they came to another large room with a ceiling that was maybe twenty feet high. Mother Damnable went to the center of the room and turned, motioning for them to come closer.

"Here we are," Mother Damnable said. Abby came closer and looked around the room. Rubble and debris lay scattered all about, covering the floor.

"What is this place?" Abby asked.

"Take a guess!" Mother Damnable said playfully.

Abby examined the debris. Very little of anything remained. She found rotted boards that might have been part of a table, a few shards of pottery jars, and charcoal stubs. On the wall near the doorway, about a handspan above the floor, was a small glyph carved into the stone.

"This was your sanctum?" Abby said, surprised. "I was told you were a solitary practitioner.," Abby stated.

"Eventually," Mother Damnable said. "I had a coven once, but they never came here." She said with a wild look in her eye.

"What do you want me to see?" Abby asked.

Mother Damnable moved a few feet to a pile of rubble and pointed down. "It's a pile of rocks," Abby said.

The spirit stomped an old, crooked foot angrily. "Look again, girl."

Abby knelt and sorted through the rubble. She removed a fragile-looking wooden box. An old rusted-out clasp dangled from the side, no longer functioning. Abby stood with the box and carefully stepped back, keeping her eyes on the apparition.

"What's inside?" Abby asked.

"Nothing!" Mother Damnable shouted. Her voice echoed through the room. "Nothing! Nothing! Nothing!" She laughed madly, shaking her head around. She stopped suddenly and pointed at Abby. "Look inside, and I shall tell you what nothing used to be!"

Abby opened the box, the hinges squeaked. Inside there were the tattered remnants of the velvet lining. Resting in the box was a leather-bound journal.

"This box holds my legacy!" Mother Damnable stated through gritted teeth. The anger and fury radiating from the spirit set Abby ill at ease. She snapped her fingers, and the book disappeared.

"I don't understand," Abby said, regarding the empty box curiously.

"What is the most powerful force on the planet?" Mother Damnable asked playfully.

Abby thought for a moment. "Love?" she answered, uncertain if it was the answer the crazed spirit was looking for.

"Nature," Valorie stated.

Mother Damnable looked pleased. "You are a bright girl, too. I may just add you to my collection, after all!" Mother Damnable squealed as she danced maniacally, twirling in circles.

She stopped abruptly and gave Abby a treacherous glare. "Nature is an endless source of magical energy when one knows how to tap into such power."

"Was that your life's work?" Abby asked eagerly. "Learning how to harness the power of nature?"

Mother Damnable laughed. She began twirling again, arms wide, as though she were dancing under the moon. "It worked, it worked!" she repeated. The subtle sound of tormented souls began to fill the room as Mother Damnable danced to the macabre melody.

Abby felt a sudden dread move through her like a tidal wave.

Valorie looked at her, alarmed. "Abby, what's wrong?" she asked.

Abby couldn't speak, she sank, unceremoniously, to the ground, she couldn't focus enough to stand. Her head was swimming.

"Leave her alone!" Mother Damnable shouted. "She's about to see! See with the eye in her mind!" she began cackling.

Strange images began flooding into Abby's mind, unwelcome and intrusive. Her head began to pound as the Sight overwhelmed her consciousness. There was a flurry of chaos and uncertainty as Abby fought to focus her mind to See clearly what Fate was trying to show her. She struggled for a few moments. Images came so furiously into her mind; she felt as though someone was trying to fill a teacup with a fire hose. Suddenly, there was peace.

Abby stood in the corner of a square room. The whitewashed walls were newly painted, and the old floorboards were swept clean. A sturdy wooden table sat in the middle of the room, with several bookshelves along the wall filled with old texts.

On the far side of the room was a large, glass window. Outside, Abby watched see a horse carriage slowly moving by. She noticed an oil lamp hanging from a hook on the wall.

A door bust open. Two men dragged a woman into the room and dropped her into one of the chairs around the table. The woman seemed lethargic. She sat hunched over, her white bonnet hiding her face. A droplet of blood dangled on the tip of her nose before dripping onto the wood table.

"It's time to give it up, Mary Ann," one of the men growled. He stood nearly six feet tall, wearing a pin-striped gray suit with a gold pocket watch. Abby recognized him from his portrait at Kane Industries. Marcus Kane, she realized. He looked to be in his forties, with graying brown hair and an elegant top hat. He had mutton chops and had a spiteful look about him.

"We're done with your games. We aren't afraid of you anymore," the other man said, he was no more than twenty years of age, a bit scrawny with a patchy beard. He had beady eyes and a pointed chin. Abby didn't recognize him.

"You are fools," Mary Ann muttered under her breath. "I will get my revenge upon you! Death is no obstacle for me!" She looked up at the two men defiantly.

Abby's heart jumped into her throat. Mary Ann was bruised and bleeding from several cuts on her cheek and forehead.

"Where is it?" the older man demanded.

"Marcus," a woman's melodic voice said at the doorway. Abby looked to see a beautiful woman, no more than thirty years of age, standing in the doorway. She wore a beautiful purple dress with lace and satin folds. Her long, black curls were styled up under a black hat with a large purple feather. An amethyst necklace with a golden medallion shaped like a spider was draped around her neck.

Abby gasped. She looked like a younger version of Vivian.

The beautiful woman sauntered into the room and placed a gentle hand on the tall man's shoulder. "You shouldn't be so rough with her," she said coldly.

"Angelica," Mary Ann said, her voice dripping with disgust. Mother Damnable spit at the elegant woman's feet. The younger man stepped forward and raised his hand.

"Stop," Angelica ordered. The man held his fist. "She's suffered enough," she added, looking at the old woman. A pleased look came over her face when she saw the other woman's defeated state.

"I'm not surprised. I knew the Kanes would turn on me one day," Mary Ann said. "You're all nothing more than mangy animals!"

Angelica circled the table, a predatory glint in her eye as she stared down at the old woman. "Stand her up," she ordered.

The two men grabbed either arm and dragged Mary Ann to her feet. It was obvious she couldn't stand on her own, and the two men held her while Angelica approached.

She lifted the injured woman's chin. "Where did you put it, Mary Ann?" she asked kindly.

"Why would I tell you?" Mary Ann said defiantly. "You're going to kill me anyway. Why would I give you the satisfaction?"

Angelica Kane smiled sweetly. "It will make all the difference in the world when it comes to the manner in which you die, Mother Damnable… such a silly name they gave you. I'll be certain it's on your gravestone."

"I won't tell," Mary Ann insisted defiantly.

"You really are going to make this difficult," Angelica said a smile on her face. She moved around and stood at Mary Ann's back. She then leaned forward until her mouth was at the old woman's ear. "What if I told you I already have your book, and now I'm simply playing with you because it amuses me?" the raven-haired beauty whispered.

"I would say that would make you the conniving bitch I always believed you to be," Mary Ann replied, spitting a mouth full of blood on the floor.

"Yes, I guess it would, wouldn't it?" Angelica said, taking a step back. She pulled something from a small lace pouch hanging from her wrist. Abby quickly realized it was a small blade. Just as she realized what Angelica held in her hand, the young woman slid the blade into Mary Ann's back.

"Ugh!" Mother Damnable cried out in pain. "You vindictive traitor!" she yelled. The fury in her voice was raw and chilling. "The pain and suffering you will reap from this treachery will follow you and your kin for generations!"

"Don't be silly, Mary Ann," Angelica said, as she pulled the blade from the old woman's back and stabbed her again. "We're the ones who do the cursing around here. Such things were never your forte."

The young woman removed the blade and once again sunk the sharp tip deep into the old woman's flesh. Mother Damnable cried out in pain as Abby stood frozen in the Sight.

Angelica pulled out the blade and wiped the blood off on Mary Ann's dress. She held the small knife up to Mother Damnable's face. "See this? I chose this blade specifically for you, Mary Ann. It won't kill you, but you will bleed. Slowly. I will End you as painfully as you deserve!"

As blood dripped on the floor, darkness played at the edges of Abby's vision, closing in on her until there was nothing.

She fainted.

CHAPTER THIRTY

Abby startled awake and found herself on the dirt floor, gasping for air. Valorie was sitting next to her, holding her head on her lap. She could hear Mother Damnable in the background, laughing.

"She's seen it!" Mother Damnable laughed and danced around the room with an imaginary partner. "The girl with many eyes finally sees!"

"Are you all right?" Valorie questioned.

With the smallest shred of strength, Abby sat up and nodded. She heaved over and threw up the contents of her stomach, coughing. Almost instantly, a feeling relief came over her. Abby pulled a bottle of water from her coat and rinsed her mouth out. "Sorry," she said as she tried to stand.

Valorie offered her a hand and helped her to her feet. "I've seen worse," she said kindly.

Abby was relieved she hadn't thrown up all over her friend. She was embarrassed enough as it was.

"You've seen it. You've Seen?" Mother Damnable faced Abby.

"Yes," Abby said her voice barely above a whisper.

"Now you know the treachery of the Kane family," Mother Damnable said, a pleased grin on her face. "Now it is time for you to join me." Her grin evolved into something more sinister.

"You want me dead because of what they did to you?" Abby asked, shaking her head disapprovingly. "What they did to you was terrible. But they are already yours. What you do to us makes you no better than they were."

"To this day, you defile my legacy!" Mother Damnable screamed. "My thirst for the souls of the Kane family will never be quenched!"

"But why lead me here, show all this to me, only to kill me?" Abby demanded.

Mother Damnable dropped her hands to her side, a bored look on her face. The deranged spirit gazed behind them.

A sudden tremor reverberated down the tunnel. A loud crashing noise echoed through the room as the door where they entered caved in. It was completely covered in large stones and rubble. They were trapped.

"Stop!" Abby yelled.

"There is only one way out now!" Mother Damnable said, pointing at a door on the opposite side of the room. "Have fun with my pet!" she said, playfully, then burst out in laughter again. "Don't worry, Kane Girl, I won't go far. You'll be mine soon—just like your parents."

Abby sat, catching her breath as her strength began to return. Slowly, the aches in her joints drifted away, and the mild headache began to clear.

"What's going on?" Valorie asked, her voice filled with concern.

Abby shook her head, still trying to take everything in. "She showed me something," Abby said breathlessly. Another rumble came from somewhere beyond the wall.

"We cannot stay here," Valorie said. "Perhaps we can discuss it once we find our way out of this place?"

Abby did not want to be trapped in a cave-in any more than her friend did. They approached the door, and Valorie opened it. The hinges squealed. On the other side was another hallway, much like the one they had entered through.

"Stick close," Valorie said, leading the way. They started down the brick corridor, taking each step cautiously.

They had not made it more than a few yards when Abby paused. "Wait," she said. When Valorie stopped, Abby carefully moved forward. She took a few steps and knelt to get a better look at a distinct line carved into the floor across the tunnel. She followed the path up the wall and saw it came to some arcane symbols etched into the ceiling.

"What do you see?" Valorie asked, squinting to get a look. "I'm afraid I didn't bring my reading glasses with me."

"It's a ward," Abby explained. "I think it's designed to prevent something from passing. If we keep going, we'll break the ward, and whatever its holding will be free."

"Hmm," Valorie said, thinking. "What kinds of symbols do you see in the warding glyphs?"

Abby carefully studied the etched runes in the brick. "I'm seeing a lot of earth symbolism in the ward inscription," Abby said, as she studied the markings.

"Earth," Valorie said under her breath, deep in thought.

"I guess we have no choice but to go forward to find out," Abby said.

"I'll cross the ward first," Valorie insisted. The older woman stepped over the markings, and Abby followed. There was no turning back now.

They followed the tunnel, coming to a large flooded room. It was cold, and Abby was certain she could smell fresh salty air coming from the corridor beyond. She studied the water carefully. Whatever was trapped within the ward was no doubt somewhere in this room. The ceiling was nearly twenty feet high with wooden beams that appeared to be in the late stages of decay. The fact they were still standing was surprising. The sound of dripping water echoed through the chamber. Abby followed the sound and noticed a crack in the ceiling that appeared damp.

Several broken-down tables with rusted blobs of metal were scattered about the floor indicating the water was very shallow. Abby looked closely at the rusted metal. "Old sewing machines?" she said, surprised.

A large pile of rubble lay against the wall. Abby thought it strange there was no evidence of a cave in or collapsed wall. She motioned Valorie to flash the light on the pile of stones. It moved suddenly, startling Abby. She stepped back and nearly fall.

"Is there something wrong?" Valorie asked, trying to look over Abby's shoulder.

The pile of stones began to shift. They swirled, caught in some kind of twister. Before Abby could tell what was happening, they began clinking together, taking on a humanoid shape.

In the darkness, the rocks formed together into a man, forged of stone and clay. It stood seven feet tall. Its body and face were featureless, and its expressionless gaze was disconcerting. The only marking on its face was the Roman numeral XIII etched into its forehead.

"A golem!" Valorie gasped.

The man of stone and clay stood still for a moment. It slowly became aware of the world, as if waking from a long sleep. The creature suddenly began stomping forward, each step rattling the ground around them.

"Get back," Valorie said, stepping in front of Abby. She raised her hand with her palm facing the creature and then dropped her hand at the wrist. The stone man fell backward into the water.

Abby concentrated on the waters, slowing its energy until it stilled. The water surrounding the golem dropped into a deep freeze, immobilizing it. "I don't think that's going to hold it for long," Abby said, as Valorie began moving toward the doorway. "How do we destroy it?"

"I'm not certain," Valorie stated.

Abby could tell her mentor's thoughts were racing, reviewing every detail she could remember about such creatures.

"It's been a long time since I've read about them. There's something about the number 13 etched on its head. It means something," Valorie added in frustration.

Just as Valorie finished her sentence, the creature began straining. Suddenly the ice around its body shattered. Shards of crystalline water flew through the air, pummeling both women. Valorie was knocked to the ground.

Abby stumbled back against the wall, a stinging sensation in her left arm. She looked down. A small thin icicle had lodged itself in her arm, cutting her deeply. She grabbed at her arm, the ice blade already melting away. She looked for her companion. Valorie was doing her best to pull herself up off the ground when the lumbering golem moved forward.

It brought up its boulder fists ready to strike.

"Ms. Grace!" Abby screamed.

Valorie saw the fists coming down toward her. She tumbled to the ground and rolled to her left. The golem's fists crashed into the ground. The earth rattled, sending shards of ice in every direction.

Abby put some distance between herself and their enemy. "Hey!" she yelled, trying to draw its attention to her. The creature turned and faced Abby as Valorie scurried away against the wall.

Abby pointed to one of the old rusted-out sewing machines and directed her thoughts toward the golem. The heavy scrap metal flew at the stone creature, smashing into its right shoulder. A large chunk of rock chipped from its body and flew across the room. It paused for only a moment and resumed its charge. The creature raised its boulder fists, and Abby leaped out of the way just as they came crashing down.

She landed on the edge of the water. Filth splashed over her face, blinding her temporarily. Abby pushed herself away with her feet and wiped the water from her face quickly.

The golem loomed over her, ready to strike again.

Abby tried to roll away. She hit a large rock, blocking her escape. She looked up and gasped as she realized the creature was about to crush her.

Death was about to claim her. *I guess Mary Ann wins after all...* she thought, oddly calm.

A large metal grate crashed into the creature, knocking it to the ground. Abby didn't waste a moment and quickly came to her feet. She ran to the other side of the room and rejoined Valorie.

"Thanks," Abby panted. She noticed small stones had filled the gaps where they had chipped away at the golem. "That thing is healing itself!"

Valorie blinked several times before a startled look of recognition came over her face. "The head!" she shouted as the golem stood. "All the power is in the headstone. We have to figure out a way to remove the head!"

"That sounds easier said than done." Abby prepared to run as the creature turned toward them.

"Leave that to me," Valorie stated. "Keep him occupied."

Abby ran to her right and climbed a small pile of rubble, putting her back to the wall. The golem's featureless face followed her movement. When she stopped, it turned and lunged.

She placed her palms flat upon the wall behind her, concentrating. "Liquidious Susterram," she muttered under her breath. Abby dropped flat to the ground, and the creature slammed into the wall. Instead of a crashing sound, there was a strange squish. The golem's fists had submerged into the wall as if it were liquid.

Abby quickly rolled out from under the golem and came to her feet. By the time she was back on her feet, the wall had solidified, cementing the creature's fists in place. The golem attempted to pull itself free, but the wall didn't budge.

She glanced over to see Valorie standing against the wall, mumbling something under her breath. Abby couldn't hear what she was saying.

The room began to shake. The golem was straining with all it's might to pull its fists from the wall. The creature fell as something gave way. It stood and turned to them. The boulders where its hands should be were still embedded in the wall.

The creature didn't seem to notice that its fists were gone. As Abby watched, small stones and pieces of rubble flew toward the heavy creature. They gathered at the ends of its arms, forming a new set of fists.

The golem faced them. "Perdosium Terauns!" Abby yelled. As the creature's fist came down on her, it crumbled away, covering Abby in sand and dust.

It stood frozen for a moment, and Abby ran through the center of the room, jumping over ice and splashing through the dirty water. She turned and prepared herself for the next attack.

Just as before, dirt and stones were drawn to the creature and formed a new fist from rubble about the room.

A thunderous sound rattled the chamber.

Abby looked over to see Valorie floating three feet off the ground. Her entire body was enveloped in a web of lightning.

The golem turned and faced the older woman. Before Abby could respond, it charged.

An intense wave of lightning crawled through the air toward the construct. It slammed into the massive creature, breaking its charge. The golem stumbled. Valorie continued to hurl a continuous wave of lightning at the stone man.

The golem began trembling. Suddenly the stone parts crumbled, tumbling into the water as they disassembled. Valorie dropped to her knees, exhausted.

Abby ran toward her friend.

"No!" Valorie shouted. "Isolate the head!"

Abby paused while the words sank in. She dashed into the shallow pool of water at the center of the room. She looked through the rubble until she found the stone with the number XIII etched into its face. She placed her hand over the rock and concentrated.

Water ran over the headstone and froze there, encasing the creature's head in ice.

Valorie approached, breathless. "Good," she gasped out.

"The ice will eventually melt," Abby commented.

"We'll take it with us. It won't be able to reassemble if it is stored properly," Valorie explained. The older woman pulled a rolled-up burlap sack out of her large purse and opened it wide, fitting it over the ice engulfed headstone.

"It's much too heavy," Abby said skeptically.

"Not at all," Valorie said, fitting the bag around the stone and lifting the bag effortlessly. Abby stared in amazement.

"How did you do that?" Abby asked.

"It's a special bag I created for when I go to the farmers' market. It makes everything inside weightless," she explained.

"I could have used one of those in school," Abby joked dryly.

Valorie chuckled. "Let's get out of here, Abigail. I've seen enough of this Underground City of yours. Besides, we should leave before Mother Damnable returns."

They made their way through a cramped tunnel and encountered a ward very much like the one before. With the golem defeated the ward meant nothing anymore.

They didn't have to go far before they came to a metal grate. With little effort, Abby uttered a spell. The metal bars became pliable, and she bent them apart. As Valorie stepped through, she reached back to help Abby.

Soon, they descended into waist-deep, freezing water. "Nowhere to go but forward," Valorie said, looking at the murky water in front of them. "We have what appears to be the Puget Sound in front of us, and a large wall to our backs."

"We should follow the wall until we reach a point where we can get out of the water. It shouldn't be far," Abby said hopefully.

The two of them navigated their way along the wall, shivering in the icy water. Eventually, they came to a set of wooden pilings supporting the boardwalk above. On the far side, Abby found a support beam with a ladder leading up.

Abby trembled. She could barely feel her legs. A cold breeze sent a chill down her back as the wind blew in from the west. Once her friend reached the top, Abby began to heave herself up each rung of the ladder. Her drenched clothing dragged at her, throwing off her balance. She clung to the metal bar with all her strength. One step, then the next in a test of perseverance that she was uncertain she could pass.

"Just a few more steps," Valorie called down.

Abby was still reeling from the use of the Sight, and the tax on her body was draining what little energy she had left.

She pushed herself, uncertain her knees would hold her. When she finally reached the top, she flopped onto the boardwalk like a fish pulled from the sea. She lay there, panting breathlessly.

"We have to keep moving," Valorie insisted.

Abby came to her feet; her knees unsteady. She took Valorie's offered arm to help steady her and looked around to get her bearings. There was no telling how far they were from the warehouse where they entered. She noted several landmarks and considered their position.

"I think we're parked several blocks that way," Abby pointed.

Valorie nodded and headed in that direction, helping Abby to walk.

Step by step, they made their way uphill, closer, and closer to the car. Abby felt like she wasn't going to make it. The journey was agonizing. All she wanted to do was curl up in a ball and sleep. Valorie would not hear of it.

"A little further," Valorie insisted as Abby nearly buckled under the cold. Small ice crystals were beginning to build on the blacktop streets.

"I'm..." Abby couldn't finish her sentence.

"There it is, Abigail!" Valorie exclaimed, pointing at a car parked less than a block away.

Abby willed her legs to keep moving. She put one step in front of the other until they reached the car. She fumbled for the keys in her pocket, dropping them on the ground.

Valorie picked them up and opened the passenger door. She helped Abby buckle in before moving around to the driver's side. "I'll never understand why you Americans insist on driving on the wrong side of the car," Valorie said, attempting a rare display of humor.

"W–wrong side of the road too..." Abby said through chattering teeth as she shivered violently.

Valorie smiled, relieved that Abby was able to joke at such a time. She quickly shoved the keys into the ignition and started the car.

The heat from the vents stabbed at Abby's frozen limbs. Slowly, the numbness melted away, and her nerves reawakened. It was a welcome pain as feeling returned to her body.

Valorie put the car in gear and pulled from the curb. "Do you know how to get back to my grandmother's place?" Abby asked weakly.

"I have a pretty good idea," Valorie stated. "Besides, you can see that behemoth of a house from almost any place in the city," she added.

Abby smiled and allowed herself to slip away into a beckoning slumber.

"What the hell were you thinking?!" Vivian shouted as she burst through the bedroom door.

Abby was startled awake. The harsh lights overhead glared down at her. Her eyes watered. She sat up and leaned against her elbow. "What's going on?"

"It's nearly noon," Vivian said sternly. "I've been waiting for nearly three hours to give you a piece of my mind! Traipsing into the Underground! You were going to go there alone? You are profoundly lucky Valorie went along with you. If she had any clue about the horrors hidden down there, I'm certain she would have talked you out of it. Why would you do such a thing?"

Abby sat up on the side of her bed and rubbed her forehead. Her arm brushed against the covers, and she winced. Her gash was already beginning to scab over, but she was sure it was infected from the putrid ice shard that had caused it. She felt hungover from the night before–battered and bruised everywhere she had skin. "I went to find answers," she said quietly, hoping her grandmother would calm down.

"Answers! What answers were you hoping to find? Your life is far too valuable to take such risks. You're lucky all you encountered was some silly golem! Do you even have a clue what lurks below this city? You're lucky to be alive!" Vivian yelled.

"Can you stop yelling, please," Abby said, pleading for mercy.

"I don't think I've ever been so upset with you in your entire eighteen years of life," Vivian growled. "If I have to worry about you like this, I don't know how I'm going to be able to get anything done to help your parents," she said, only slightly below a yell. Her anger was radiating off her.

"Thank you," Abby said.

"Thank you?" Vivian repeated with uncertainty. "What are you talking about? Did you hit your head?" She sat next to Abby on the bed and began checking for damage.

"No," Abby said. "I'm fine." She took a deep breath, pushing her grandmother's hand away. "Thank you for caring enough to be angry with me," she added. "I know it wasn't the brightest idea I've had. I did learn something, but it wasn't worth putting my life, or anyone else's life in jeopardy."

Vivian looked at her peculiarly. "Darling, why would you ever think I don't care about you?" she said, sounding wounded. "I know I'm not particularly affectionate or doting, but I care Darling. You should never think otherwise, no matter what is happening."

Abby nodded. "I'm sorry, and thank you."

Vivian walked back to the door and paused. It looked as though she wanted to say more, but was biting her tongue. "Get some rest," she said and closed the door behind her.

Abby was staving. Despite her exhaustion, she climbed out of bed and quickly took a shower. There was still a chill lingering in her bones, and the hot water helped thaw her out. She managed to find a wool sweater and pulled it on before heading out the door toward the Dining room.

The servants had taken to leaving food out at all hours for the family to snack on. Abby wondered at how much extra work that must be for them, but right then, she was more grateful than she thought she could be.

She slipped into the large room, grabbed a small plate from the sideboard, and began filling it with fruits and cheese.

"It's good to see you up," Fiona said from the far side of the room.

Abby jumped. She hadn't realized anyone was here. She looked up at her grandaunt.

Fiona sat at the far end of the long table, sipping a cup of tea. She smiled at Abby and gestured to the chair next to her.

Abby took her plate and joined the older woman. They sat in companionable silence for a few minutes while Abby ate. Even with just the light meal, she felt like she was regaining some of her energy.

"You had quite the adventure last night," Fiona said.

Abby nodded, swallowing a mouthful of food.

"Why did you go?" her grandaunt asked simply. "Surely you knew how dangerous it was?"

"I did," Abby nodded, "but after Gus… after everything that happened, I couldn't just sit by anymore. We need to know more about Mother Damnable if we have any chance of ever defeating her."

The old woman nodded sagely and took a sip of her tea. "And what did you learn?"

"Not as much as I had hoped," Abby admitted. "I think I still have more questions than I have answers."

Fiona looked at her, concerned. "Can I help?" she asked quietly.

Abby chewed on her lip, thinking. This woman had always been so cold and distant to her. She hated that it took a family tragedy for them to talk, but Abby was really growing quite fond of her grandmother's sister.

She thought about everything she had seen and heard the night before. The questions Abby had been holding in swelled up. As she looked at Fiona's supportive smile, she made up her mind to trust her.

"Why does Mother Damnable want revenge?" Abby asked. "What did we do to her to warrant this kind of hate?"

Fiona took in a deep breath and held it for a moment and let it out slowly. She considered her words very carefully, before saying, "Every story has its heroes and its villains. We Kanes haven't always been the heroes we want the world to believe."

"Did we do something terrible to Mary Ann Conklin?" Abby asked.

"I believe so," Fiona stated. "The details in our family history books are presented from the Kane point of view."

"I have read the family histories. There's nothing in them. Not really. They were mostly about the rebuilding of Kane Industries after The Great Seattle Fire. The only thing they do say about Mother Damnable is that she went mad from illness and died suddenly."

Fiona nodded, "I have no doubt Mary Ann Conklin has an entirely different version of the story."

"One that includes Angelica Kane?" Abby asked, startling a gasp from Fiona. "I… saw a bit of it, last night, but I'm curious what can you tell me."

Fiona looked nervous but nodded. "From what I have gathered, Mary Ann was the first witch to arrive in the Seattle area. I believe she found some arcane resources and perhaps even a discovery or two from local shamans. When we arrived, she met us as friends. Over time, sickness ravaged her mind even while her powers grew, and eventually, we were forced to have an Ending for her."

"An Ending?" Abby asked. "I've heard that before, but what is it? A spell?"

"A ritual," Fiona answered. "It isn't something we talk about much. It is an uncomfortable topic for many witches. The Ending is a ritual to strip a witch of their power."

Abby gasped. "Is that even possible?"

Fiona nodded. "It is only used as a mercy. If a witch falls to dementia or grows too old to control their own powers, they are Ended to protect the Coven."

"You mean they..." Abby swallowed hard.

"The witch does not survive the ritual."

Abby stifled a gasp.

"I have no proof," Fiona continued, "but I suspect there may have been a dispute. Over resources, artifacts, lovers, who knows? But Mary Ann, a solitary practitioner, was no challenge for the might of an entire coven. If she was Ended, it was for her own good. Or ours."

"You think the Coven killed Mary Ann with this ritual?" Abby asked, horrified at the idea. She remembered the sound of the knife sliding into Mary Ann's back, and shuddered.

"Using the Ending ritual is forbidden except in very limited, and special circumstances. The Council of Overseers would surely have disbanded the Kane Coven if they had done such a thing," Fiona stated firmly.

"But, I wonder," Fiona said. "Our ancestors didn't tell us the details. They wrote nothing down. It was all glossed over. I suspect they weren't interested in the whole truth being handed down to future generations."

"A cover-up," Abby said under her breath.

"I believe so," Fiona agreed. "Ultimately, the details make little difference at this point. She is a demented spirit determined to destroy us."

"If her magic were stripped," Abby speculated, "then everything she's be using to hurt us, all her powers, it comes from the spirits?" Her jaw dropped in astonishment and horror. "They're batteries?"

Fiona nodded grimly. "It could be. We now know she has been pulling the strings of our Thanos enemies like a masterful puppeteer. Getting them to cast the Soul Web, killing a member of our coven... Now we can only defend ourselves until such a time as we can vanquish her."

Abby fell silent, her thoughts swirling uncontrollably. *My parents, the Soul Web, all these attacks... did my ancestors really do that to her? Could they have? And Grandmother...* Abby felt herself growing angrier the more she thought about. She turned to her grandaunt. "Vivian knew all this," she stated suddenly.

Fiona closed her eyes for a moment and sighed heavily. "I believe so," she said, her voice carefully controlled.

Abby rose to her feet. "She knew? She knew why Mother Damnable was doing all this, and she said nothing? While her own son was being tortured beyond death? While I have been spending every night too afraid to sleep, she has been... been keeping their secrets!"

"Abigail, sit down," Fiona said sternly.

Abby obeyed.

"Do not be too hard on your grandmother. Vivian kept their secrets, but so have I. I do not believe that knowing Mother Damnable's motivation would have helped avert any of the things that have happened. These events were set in motion when Atoro killed Evan and Jessica."

Abby stared at Fiona. "Then, this has all been about the war with the Thanos?"

"No, I believe Mother Damnable is the mastermind, though Atoro made a willing pawn."

"How so?" Abby asked.

"The conflict with the Thanos was settled centuries ago. They have little cause to dredge up ancient grudges with a coven halfway across the world from them. Given their penchant for necromancy, it made them easy instruments for her to utilize in her vendetta against us. It was a brilliant strategy."

Abby felt sick. "This... all of this–My parents, Gus, Margot, every attack, every nightmare... it was because of Angelica?"

Fiona shrugged. "I can only speculate."

"Well start speculating!" Abby shouted. "If she succeeds in getting Angelica's soul, what will happen?" The realization of Mother Damnable's plan sunk in like a freight train. Abby reeled, feeling lost. For one brief moment, she could see the end of her family. And she was angry.

"We can't sit in the dark anymore." Abby bit back her fears and turn desperately toward her grandaunt. "If we don't take the fight to her, Mother Damnable will keep killing us off, one by one, until there are no Kanes left. We can't let her win."

Fiona looked grim. "We won't. Of that, I am certain."

CHAPTER THIRTY-ONE

Abby watched out the window as a long black car pulled up to the house and into the carriage house. *They're here*, she thought.

She got up and finished the last of her coffee, slightly burning her tongue. She made her way through the door into the hallway and started heading toward the grand entry to greet her mysterious distant relatives.

Vivian had just descended the stairs in an ivory pantsuit with diamonds draped around her neck and wrist. Mr. Greenly was standing patiently at the door, waiting for the doorbell.

"Darling," Vivian said, looking at Abby. "Are you ready to meet the sisters?"

Abby looked down at her jeans and green wool sweater and then to her grandmother's formal business attire. "I didn't know I should have dressed up," Abby said.

"Who's dressed up, Darling?" she said at the preposterous suggestion.

There was a familiar chime at the door, and without hesitation, Mr. Greenly answered it. "Good afternoon. This way, please," he stated, stepping aside, and motioning their guests to enter.

There was a pause. Abby was beginning to wonder if the sisters had given second thoughts about entering. The two short figures emerged through the door, stopping in the grand entry to gawk at the mansion's interior.

They looked like two halves of the same painting. Their bodies were small and withered with age, and they bowed with matching slumps as they shuffled into the house.

Both wore plain, black dresses with simple black shoes laced up into tight bows. The only differentiation between them was their shawls. One wore a blue shawl, while the other's was purple.

"Welcome, Darlings," Vivian said, moving quickly to intercept the two elderly women. "Thank you so much for coming all this way to help us. I am truly humbled."

"We were surprised," the one with the blue shawl started.

"When you called us," the one with the purple shawl finished. Their voices were as wizened and weary as they looked.

"I am afraid we had no one else to turn to," Vivian said cautiously. Abby could tell it was difficult for her grandmother to be so humble.

"We will assist," the one with the blue shawl said.

"We are quite interested," the sister wearing the purple shawl said.

"Mr. Greenly, will you get our guests settled in? No doubt, you will want to rest after your long journey," Vivian said, motioning for her butler to intervene.

"We shall get settled," the one in purple said.

"Then we shall meet with–" the one in blue started.

"Your granddaughter," the one in purple finished.

"I'm Abby Kane," she said, stepping forward and extending her hand to greet the two sisters.

The two old women examined Abby's hand with great curiosity. The one with the purple shawl leaned forward slightly, almost as if she was about to sniff Abby's hand, while the other began studying her face as though there was something wrong.

"You are the one," the one in blue said.

"The one with the Sight," the sister in the purple said.

Abby looked at her grandmother with uncertainty. "Yes," she answered reluctantly.

"A rarity," the one in blue stated, sounding almost impressed.

"Indeed, Sister, indeed," the one with the purple shawl agreed, sharing a look with her twin.

"I am Inga," the woman with the blue shawl stated with a grim smile.

"I am Bianca," the sister with the purple shawl stated as an afterthought.

"It is nice to meet you," Abby said, withdrawing her hand awkwardly. "I'm happy to answer any questions if you think it would be helpful."

"Very good," Inga said.

"Yes, good," Bianca added.

"This way, please, ladies," Mr. Greenly said, motioning for the two women to follow him.

Abby stood next to her grandmother as they watched the two old women cautiously navigate the stairs to the second floor. After they disappeared down a hallway, Abby looked to her grandmother curiously.

"They are quite a pair," Abby said, slightly amused.

"Yes, they are," Vivian agreed.

"How exactly are we related?" Abby asked curiously.

"They are my great-grandaunt's daughters," Vivian said.

Abby gaped. "They're so old!" She immediate clamped her mouth shut, embarrassed by her tactlessness.

Vivian raised an eyebrow. "Indeed. They certainly learned the secrets of sustaining a long life, but sadly not of youth."

"They are a bit... strange," Abby said cautiously.

"Strange? Darling, you are too kind. They are completely insane, but brilliant, Darling, brilliant. Don't forget that. Sadly, the two are frequently shared traits," Vivian said. "Oh, you needn't worry. They intend to help.

They deserve nothing less than our respect and gratitude," she added, seeing her granddaughter's worried expression. "I would recommend you prepare yourself for a long interrogation. I've been told they are quite thorough."

"I'll do my best," Abby said sincerely. She spent the rest of the afternoon, mentally preparing herself for whatever might be coming.

A drop of sweat ran down Abby's forehead and dropped onto her hand. She quickly wiped it with the sleeve of her sweater. She sat back on the couch, relieved by the lull in the intense questions.

"Tell us again," Inga crowed.

"About the cords," Bianca said, moving closer and studying Abby's expression.

She closed her eyes briefly and took a deep breath. "I told you already, there were about thirty or forty silver cords tethered to the spirit. She pulled on one of them, and it summoned Atoro Thanos," Abby said, wiping away another bead of sweat.

"Did they shimmer?" Inga moved closer, virtually hovering over Abby.

"Did they glisten?" Bianca asked, moving in and hovering just like her sister.

Abby looked toward the door to the library. "Yes," she said, leaning back as far as she could into the couch.

The two women stepped away and began whispering to one another. Abby took a moment to pull herself together. She glanced down at her phone. "We've been doing this for nearly four hours," Abby said. "I don't know what else I can tell you," she added, almost pleading.

"We must know every detail," Inga said.

"Are you certain every cord–" Bianca started.

"Was the same color?" Inga finished.

"I didn't notice any difference in the color," Abby said. "Maybe in size."

"What do you mean?" Inga lunged forward, studying Abby's eyes.

"Yes, tell us!" Bianca hissed, moving next to her sister. She reached out and plucked a single hair from Abby's skull.

"Ouch!" Abby yelped.

Bianca held the hair up to the light studying every millimeter, looking for whatever truth could be found there.

"Some of the cords looked to be... thicker than others," Abby confirmed a detail she hadn't really spent much time thinking about. She never imagined there would be any significance to such details, especially since she had no idea what they were.

"How thick?" Inga questioned.

Bianca discarded the hair and moved in close. Abby felt her breath on her cheek. "How big?" she crowed.

Abby shifted uncomfortably on the couch. "Some were no thicker than a strand of yarn; others looked more like the size of a rope,' she explained.

"Was the cord she pulled–"

"To summon the Thanos, large?"

"Or was it small?"

Abby shook her head, doing her best to try and remember. "I can't be certain, but I think it was one of the larger cords," she responded.

"Was there resistance?"

"When she pulled–"

"On the cord?"

With a big sigh, Abby did her best to try and remember. "I don't think it was very hard; it didn't stand out as being difficult. She pulled on the cord, and he arrived moments later," Abby explained.

"Moments?" Inga questioned.

"Seconds? Minutes?" Bianca persisted.

"Seconds, maybe five seconds," Abby guessed. "He appeared out of nowhere."

"Hmm," the sisters said in unison.

"Do you know what she is?" Do the cords have some significance?" Abby asked, desperate for answers.

"You said Atoro made a bargain–"

"With the wretched spirit–"

"About the child?"

Abby closed her eyes and wiped another bead of sweat from her forehead. "Yes, he made some deal with her to place something called an Arcane Nexus in his unborn son," Abby said. "I didn't hear any details of the bargain. I can only assume he murdered my parents as part of the bargain."

"Blood," Inga nodded, looking to her sister.

"Yes, Sister, blood," Bianca agreed.

"Blood?" Abby questioned.

"Necromancy and blood magic–"

"Are closely related," they said in harmony, as though they were singing a duet.

"Fiona said blood magic was involved in the ritual he used to create the Soul Web," Abby repeated what she recalled from the earlier conversation.

"Yes, yes," the sisters said in unison.

"Blood magic can be used–"

"To empower the dead," they replied.

"Did he empower Mother Damnable somehow?" Abby asked, terrified of the answer.

The Archibald Sisters both smiled, and their yellow teeth emerged from behind their withered lips. They nodded in unison.

"Spirits," they said together.

"All shall be revealed," Inga said joyously.

"In time, Sister, in time," Bianca said with a smile.

There were so many questions, and she couldn't help but hope these strange sisters would have answers. Abby couldn't stop the desperate tone in her voice. "Can we stop her? Can we free my parents?"

"We must confer–"

"Before we answer–"

"You may go now," they dismissed her in unison.

Abby stared at them with uncertainty, then stood and headed to the door. She turned and looked at the Archibald Sisters curiously. The two women had retreated into a corner of the library and pulled a book off the shelf. They were thumbing through pages and whispering.

She opened the door and passed into the hallway, closing the doors behind her. Their questions were more like an interrogation, but she was willing to endure much more if it meant her parents could be freed.

Abby walked to the kitchen, where she found Rodger and Sebastian sitting at a small chef's table. "You were in there just short of an age," Rodger jested as he fed Little Evan from a bottle.

"Those two women are completely wacko," Abby said.

"That doesn't sound good. I was hoping they might be helpful," Sebastian said. The lines of his face settled into a contemplative expression as his mind wandered.

"I think they can help, but they're still off their rockers," Abby said. "I don't even know how to describe their questioning–if you can call it that," she added.

"What do you mean?" Rodger asked.

"They were studying me with almost every question," Abby explained. "Looking into my eyes. Plucking hair from my head and studying it as though it told them something. They wanted to know every detail. I felt like I was being interrogated. I think they were seconds away from asking for a blood test."

Sebastian chuckled. "They sound like quite the duo."

"Oh, you think I'm joking!" Abby playfully slugged Sebastian in the arm. "I'm almost certain their method of examination was a violation of the Geneva Convention."

Their laughter died against the cold metal of the industrial kitchen. In the silence that followed, Abby's smile turned fragile, and she bit her lip to keep from crying. She took a deep breath and tried to put on a brave smile.

"Keep your chin up," Rodger said.

"I'll be all right. Especially if they can actually help," Abby said.

"I doubt they would have kept you for so long if they couldn't," Sebastian told her.

They all sounded more sure than they looked.

The flicker of the candle made the shadows dance across the walls. There was no light, save for the warm yellow glow radiating from the wick of the dark-blue candle sitting at the center of the altar. The black cloth covering the wooden dais was embroidered with an enormous pentagram.

Abby sat at the foot of the altar holding a copper bowl in her crossed legs. Beside her on the floor, was a sharp white-handled knife. She carefully picked up the small blade and pressed it against the palm of her hand.

Abby carefully applied pressure and slid the blade against her soft flesh, leaving a bright pink cut that quickly flooded with blood. She held her hand over the copper bowl and allowed the small stream of blood to run into the copper vessel.

It wasn't long before the blood slowed, and Abby pulled a cloth bandage from her pocket. After wrapping her hand tightly, she set the bowl on the altar and stared into the flickering flame.

"I call upon my ancestors, whose blood I share, whose memories run through my veins. I seek your wisdom, I seek your guidance. Hear my call!" she yelled with conviction. She focused on the flickering candle and concentrated on her spell.

Abby concentrated on the flame. The blood in the bowl began to boil as heat moved from the candle into the blood. She focused intensely. As the crimson liquid burbled to the top of the bowl, a red mist began slowly forming in front of her, above the altar.

Abby continued to maintain her concentration staring into the small flame flickering above the candle. The red mist began swirling and churning in a display of random chaos, contained only by the boundaries of the altar.

As the mist swirled and changed shape, Abby heard something coming from the bloody fog. It was a whimper and then a moan. "Help!" someone shouted through the mist. Abby jumped.

"Who's there?" Abby asked.

Her query was met with moaning and cries of pain.

"Will you speak to me?" she beckoned.

"Please," a woman's voice pleaded through the mist. "Show us mercy..." the voice said, fading out.

"Mom?" Abby said, a tear welling in her eye. "Is that you, Mom?"

"It's so cold," the woman's voice emerged from the mist.

It sounded vaguely like her mother, but Abby wasn't certain.

A horrible scream came through the mist, followed by silence.

Abby maintained her focus, despite the swell of emotions threatening to break her resolve. She pushed her grief aside and did her best to hold the spell.

"I never imagined my granddaughter would become a blood mage," an unfamiliar woman's voice came through the mist.

"Granddaughter?" Abby questioned.

"Abigail Kane, daughter of my daughter. Blood of my blood." The woman's voice recited Abby's lineage. "Did you not call me?"

"Grandmother Whitlock?" Abby asked in surprise.

"Yes," the woman's voice came through the mist. "My daughter was quite young when I died. I never knew you in the mortal coil."

"Did you know me before?" Abby asked curiously.

"I believe it is difficult to hold this powerful spell you've cast. Is this the question for which you summoned your ancestors with your own blood?" Grandmother Whitlock asked.

"No," Abby said. "I need help. I need to save my mother, your daughter, from a powerful spirit," Abby explained.

"I know of my daughter's captivity," the woman said. "She suffers for no crime of her own."

"Can you help me?" Abby asked. "I don't know what to do. Everyone is trying to free my parents, but there is so much uncertainty. I need to know how to end their suffering."

"The one who holds them is powerful. We have tried to intervene, but her power is too great. She threatens to consume us. Already spirits are added to her collection."

"She has Whitlock souls too?" Abby gasped. "How?"

"They are lost, my child," Grandmother Whitlock said, her voice tinged with regret. "There is no hope to end their suffering. Know that I share your grief, dear girl."

"Is there truly no hope?" Abby asked.

"I know your pain, and I have seen the one who holds them captive. I long to see my daughter, but I have been denied. The low spirit who holds her will not bargain with me," Grandmother Whitlock said.

"I can't accept there is nothing that can be done," Abby insisted, clenching back her tears and grief.

"I wish I had answers for you, my dear sweet girl. Hope can be a beautiful thing and other times a cancer," the woman said. "I do wish you luck. Perhaps hope will serve you better than it did me."

"Grandmother Whitlock?" Abby called out. Her plea was met with silence. She concentrated for a few more minutes, and there was nothing.

Abby blew out the candle, and the red mist fell back into the copper bowl. As she got up to turn on the light, hopelessness settled in Abby's heart. *Is there really no hope? Is Mother Damnable simply too powerful?* Abby felt a weight build on her shoulders. Her eyes were dry. The pain no longer summoned tears. Instead, there was heat in her cheeks and a fever of despair.

Abby flipped on the lights. Her blood had turned black, becoming a thick syrup that reeked of the foul odor of death and decay. She took the copper bowl into the bathroom, pouring the contents into the sink. She turned on the water and washed the filth down the drain.

Abby looked at herself in the mirror. There were dark circles under her eyes, her hair looked frazzled and unkempt. Her flesh was colorless, and dark-blue veins webbed across her face. Abby reached up and ran her fingers across her gaunt cheeks.

"I look sick," she muttered.

Abby turned away from her own reflection and returned to her bedroom. The bland white furniture, carpets, and bedspread seemed to make the overhead light even brighter. Abby sat on the edge of her bed and rubbed her eyes. When she looked up, darkness was growing in the corner of her room. A shadow spread across her walls, the ceiling, and the floor. It moved like water, creeping closer as though it were searching for something.

Abby stood, watching the darkness claim everything. It reached for her. Abby fought to free herself, but she was being pulled further and further into the darkness that had flooded the room.

Abby reached for the doorknob, hoping to pull herself free. The living darkness swirled around her arm and climbed up her shoulder. It enveloped her chest and fact until she saw nothing. The darkness consumed her.

 She couldn't breathe. She reached up to her throat, there was nothing choking her. She gasped for air. There was none.

Abby sat up, gasping. There was darkness all around her, but a thin, silver moon poked through the bottom of the shades over the window. Its faint light glowed on her floor. She drew a breath, air filling her lungs. Relief flooded back. She began to breathe again.

A drop of moisture fell on the top of her hand. Abby reached up wiped away the sweat covering her face. *It was only a dream,* she told herself, as reality set in. *It didn't really happen...*

The thought was cold comfort.

CHAPTER THIRTY-TWO

Abby moved her game piece four spaces and took a card. "A get out of jail free card!" she squealed and showed Madison.

Madison stared out the window, watching the rainstorm against the glass.

"It's your turn," Abby said. Her cousin didn't move, an empty stare behind her eyes. Abby reached out and grabbed her hand gently. "Hey, she'll be all right."

Madison shuddered and blinked, finally looking at Abby. "You don't know that," she said.

Abby shrugged and smiled kindly. "No, but I believe it."

"Why?" Madison asked in a shaky voice. She gripped Abby's hand, fear making her tremble. "How can you still believe? After everything that's been happening... I can't lose her, too. I'm only seventeen. I don't want to be an orphan!"

Abby looked down at the game board and bit her lip.

"Oh, Abby! I'm sorry, I didn't mean..."

Abby smiled, weakly, "I know."

Madison fumbled over her words. "I just mean, I don't think I can do this without both my parents. I'm not strong, like you."

Abby wanted to comfort her cousin. She knew Madison was just worried about Margot, but Jessica and Evan's cries for help swirled in Abby's mind until it was all she could do to remain sitting upright. Grandmother Whitlock's words from her dream came back to her, *There is no hope to end their suffering.* "I'm not strong," she whispered.

"Abby..." Madison said, hopelessly.

Abby waved her off. Using every bit of strength she could muster, she put a forgiving smile on her face. "Your mother is strong," she said. "She will pull through this, you'll see."

Madison wiped tears from her face. "I'm so horrible to you, why are you still here?"

Abby picked up the dice and handed them to her cousin.

"I'm here to spend time with you," Abby reassured.

"Well, I'm clobbering you. I hope you're not just letting me win," Madison said.

"I would never." Abby smiled.

Madison looked up and gave Abby a discerning glare. She opened her mouth the argue and was interrupted by a knock at the door.

"Darlings, good. You're both here," Vivian said, smoothly gliding into Madison's room.

"What is it, Grandmother?" Abby looked up from the game, sprawled out at the foot of the bed.

"Rodger called from the hospital a few moments ago. Margot has just woken up." Vivian stated plainly.

"Oh, thank God!" Madison leaped from bed, spilling the game all over the floor with a cacophonous rattling. She hugged Vivian quickly and rushed out the door. "The town car is waiting out front, Darling. Don't forget your coat!" she called after Madison. "That girl," she added, turning to Abby. "She is so very much like my sister."

Abby looked surprised, "Like Fiona?" She had trouble imagining her cold, reserved grandaunt flying from any room in excitement. She glanced curiously at Vivian. Not for the first time, Abby wondered what these two were like as children. "We're gathering in the library," Vivian said. "Our guests have asked to speak with the Coven."

Abby's heart leaped into her throat. "Already?" Abby questioned. "They have a solution?"

"I don't know, Darling, but I find it unlikely they are calling us together to tell us they have nothing," Vivian said. "Come along, dear, we should not keep them waiting. Leave that mess, Darling, I'll have someone come clean it up." She waved a hand vaguely at the game pieces scattered around the floor.

"Oh," Abby said, awkwardly placing the tokens and cards she had picked up onto the bed. "Alright."

Vivian turned on her heels before making her way down the vast hallway toward the grand entry.

Abby nearly jogged to keep up with her grandmother's purposeful pace. Instinctively, Abby reached out and took her grandmother's hand as they walked down the hallway.

Vivian looked surprised at first and then looked down uncertainly at their linked hands, as though she didn't understand the simple gesture. For a split second, her indomitable demeanor slipped. Her face softened.

Vivian took a deep breath and reasserted her carefully maintained outer shell. She stood iron straight, put on a commanding smile, and stepped into the library.

Abby heard the click of heels on the marble behind them, and Vivian quickly pulled her hand away before turning to see who was behind them.

"Good afternoon," Gisela said, with a mean glint in her eye. "It would seem our cousins are more adept than we thought."

"We are lucky to have procured their help," Vivian said coldly, as she resumed her purposeful pace.

Abby followed them into the library, where most of the family was already waiting. Fiona sat next to Sebastian on one of the couches and motioned for Abby to come and sit by them. She quickly crossed the room and took the seat next to her uncle and grandaunt.

"I thought you would be on your way to the hospital," Abby said, surprised to see the woman here.

Fiona smiled, looking old and tired, but more relieved than she had in days. "I am needed here, right now," she said. "I will go after this. Just knowing that she is awake is enough for the moment."

Abby smiled, feeling much the same, and looked around the room. Standing near the fireplace were the two strange sisters dressed in their matching house dresses and blue and purple shawls. They each held a small bundle of smoldering sage, which they waved around in front of the hearth.

The smoke swirled into the cavernous library, spreading a thick herbal scent. Abby noticed several brass braziers dispersed throughout the room with burning coals and sprigs of sage smoldering in the flames. The air was thick with the smell. Abby found it hard to take a deep breath.

"I hope the smoke detectors are turned off," she muttered. Fiona smirked. She does look like Madison, she realized.

"Do you think they have a solution to our problem?" Abby asked her uncle.

"I certainly hope so," Sebastian replied calmly.

"Is all this sage burning necessary?" Gisela questioned loudly as she took a seat next to Syble and Lawrence.

The two wyrd women turned their shared gaze on the middle-aged woman sitting on the couch.

"The sage repels–"

"Odious spirits," Bianca finished.

Gisela rolled her eyes and sat back in her seat.

"Where's Uncle Rodger," Abby asked, not seeing him.

"Putting the baby down," Sebastian answered. "He will be joining us as soon as he can."

Cordelia entered, looking broken. She walked with her head down, only barely holding herself together. David came in after her, looking utterly lost. Sebastian stood and guided them to one of the couches.

Bernard entered without looking at anyone and took a seat in the very back of the room. Abby looked at her granduncle. He looked nothing like her grandmother or grandaunt Fiona. His beard was unkempt, and his white hair was wild and, in some places, appeared matted. The shirt he wore had a food stain on the front.

A part of Abby wondered if he was all right out on Vashon Island, removed from the rest of the family. She understood why he preferred to live alone, holed up in the ancestral estate, but was he really capable of taking care of himself?

Wendy and Rodger slipped in and quickly took seats near the door as Vivian stood, drawing everyone's attention.

"I believe everyone who is planning to attend is present," Vivian said, closing the double doors gently.

"Very well," Inga and Bianca said in their melodic chorus.

"We have discovered what manner of creature–" Inga began.

"Mother Damnable has become," Bianca added.

They paused for what Abby guessed was dramatic effect. Twin eyes darted around the room before the Sisters continued their explanation.

"Phantasm Idolum!" they both said, in unison.

"Also known as–"

"A Skugga–"

"Skugga?" Wendy asked. "I don't think I've ever encountered anything like that in my research."

"Nor would you," Inga stated.

"They are quite rare," Bianca added.

Inga pulled out a strange piece of glass, an inch across and squared, from her pocket. There appeared to be flecks of gold inside the cube. She held the square piece over her left eye and scanned the room through the strange contraption. When she finished, she shared a brief look with her sister and gave her a nod.

"The Skugga is a mere spirit," Inga started.

"Whose strength is forged through–" Bianca continued.

"Necromancy," they said in unison.

There were several gasps in the room, and Abby looked around to see the look of shock on the faces of many of her family members.

"Are you saying the necromancers created her?" Gisela questioned.

"No," Bianca stated abruptly.

"They empowered her," Inga explained.

"How?" Wendy asked. "Is that even possible?"

"Mother Damnable–" Inga said.

"Mary Ann Conklin–" Bianca said.

"Is but a mere spirit–"

"Who bargained for power–"

"With necromancers," they both said in unison.

"She has made bargains–" Bianca said.

"For great power–" Inga added.

"These bonds must be severed–"

"For the wretched spirit to be destroyed."

Abby stared at them, shocked. "She bargained for power with the Thanos? How? Is it even possible to transfer a witch's power?"

Inga and Bianca turned their beady little eyes on Abby. Their gaze felt heavy. Then small matching smiles crept into the corner of their mouths.

"They consort with great spirits," Inga explained.

"She does not, herself, hold such power–"

"In her own right," they said in perfect unison.

"The bonds are her vulnerability," they said.

The looked around the room, clearly waiting for the Kane Coven to see what they were getting at. When it wasn't evident to everyone in the room, they both sighed and continued.

"If we sever these bonds–"

"She becomes a mere spirit–"

"Easily banished–" Bianca clarified.

Abby's eyes went wide. "The threads," she realized.

The Archibald Sisters smiled at her, nodding vigorously.

Vivian's eyes blazed with the fire of vengeance. "How? How do we sever these bonds?" she demanded with hunger in her voice.

"There is a ritual," Inga said.

"That will sever these bonds," Bianca said.

"However," they said in unison.

"It is not easily cast."

"It requires blood."

"The necromancer's blood," they clarified.

Murmurs erupted around the room. "We need Atoro Thanos' blood?" Fiona questioned.

"Indeed," the wyrd sisters said, almost melodically.

"We have to acquire the blood of Atoro Thanos," Vivian said, disappearing into her own thoughts. She slumped against the wall as though her concentration took every resource from her body.

"Yes," Inga stated.

"You must," Bianca added.

"How will we find him?" Rodger asked.

"He proved difficult enough to find during the war with the Thanos," Sebastian added, a tinge of frustration in his voice. "He will be in hiding now, for sure."

"We did search for him extensively," Lawrence agreed. "To no avail, I might add."

Abby listened with half an ear, while hopelessness intruded on her thoughts. Her family seemed more concerned with the futility of trying to track down Atoro Thanos than they were with trying to find him. She turned away, hoping to hide the tears welling in her eyes.

"We must find him," Vivian insisted, pulling herself from her deep thought.

Abby stared at the wall and tried to drown out the voices around her. She couldn't hear their words, they were starting to churn together into an angry chorus of hopelessness. Her eyes narrowed in on something.

An old map of the Washington Territory hung on the wall in a beautiful gilded, gold frame. The geography was slightly distorted, as it was hand-drawn, and likely one hundred years old.

"I know how to find him," Abby said abruptly.

The room fell silent as all eyes fell on Abigail Kane.

"Here you go," Vivian said, placing a large pile of over-sized parchment in front of Abby at the dining room table. "That is everything you asked for."

Abby glanced at Sebastian as he took a seat next to her.

"Are you certain we won't be a distraction?" he asked.

"No, I want you and Grandmother here with me," Abby said. "I read about this in a book, but I've never tried it before. At least not like this."

"Darling, please tell us what you are going to do with all these maps," Vivian pleaded, impatiently. Abby opened a wooden box and pulled out a triangular piece of dark, polished wood. Near the center was a glass circle. A wooden prong tipped in velvet was attached to each point of the rounded triangle. "It's a planchette," Abby explained.

"It looks like that thing you use with a Ouija board," Sebastian said.

"That is exactly what it is," Abby confirmed.

"Yes, Darling, we all know what a planchette is. What are you going to do with it?" Vivian asked.

"I'm going to use it to find Atoro Thanos," Abby explained. "Do you remember, last year when I tried to scry using water? This works on the same theory, but I'm using the map as the focus instead of the dish. If I'm right, I can channel the Sight through the planchette an onto the map."

"It is worth a try indeed," Vivian said, cautiously supportive. "Which map do you want to start with?"

"Do you think he is lingering somewhere in the region? Or do you think we should start with a global map?" Abby asked.

"Let's try the region first. I have a hunch he's sticking close," Sebastian said, leaning over Abby's shoulder.

Vivian began sorting through the stack of maps she had collected. When she found the one she was looking for, she carefully pulled the map from the pile and placed it in front of Abby. It was a map of the Pacific Northwest–Washington, Oregon, Idaho, and the southern part of British Columbia.

"There you go, Darling," Vivian said, taking a seat on the other side of Abby.

"Alright," Abby said nervously and took a deep breath. "Let's see if this works."

She placed the planchette at the center of the map and rested both hands on the bottom. Abby closed her eyes and began clearing her thoughts. *It's all right, this isn't dangerous, you don't need to be so nervous,* she thought, as she struggled to clear her mind.

A few seconds later, everything stilled. In the empty space between this world and the next, Fate filled her mind.

Abby focused on Atoro Thanos. *The necromancer. The man who murdered my parents. The man who tried to murder me...* She concentrated.

Abby's hands began to move. They slowly inched their way across the map on their own accord, pushing the planchette bit by bit. She focused on her hands, letting them show her what she wanted to see.

Abby maintained her concentration until her hands stopped. She held the focus briefly, to be sure there was no more movement. When she opened her eyes, she looked down to see where Fate placed the planchette.

"Its right over the Seattle area," Sebastian observed.

Vivian began sorting through the maps again and pulled out another large chart. "This one, Darling. It's of King County."

"Perfect," Abby agreed. "I need a moment," she added, letting herself catch her breath, paying the tax the Sight extracted each time she used it.

"Here," Sebastian said. He placed his hand on her shoulder and handed her a glass of water. "Take your time. Catch your breath."

Abby took the glass gratefully and took a large sip. The cold water rushed down her throat, helping to calm the swirling energies she had called upon. She let herself fall back against the chair and breathe for just a moment. The ache and fatigue faded.

"I think I'm ready to try again," Abby said.

"Are you sure, Darling?" Vivian asked with a rare sense of warmth in her voice.

Abby nodded. "I'm sure."

She placed the planchette in the center of the map that covered the entirety of King County. Closing her eyes, she gently settled her fingertips on the wooden triangle. She took a deep breath and cleared her thoughts once more. The planchette began to move.

Abby repeated the same process as before. After a moment, Abby withdrew from the Sight and allowed herself to rest. Both her uncle and grandmother leaned in over the map to see the location where the planchette had stopped.

"It looks like somewhere just east of Maple Valley," Sebastian said, as he studied the map.

Vivian pulled back with a displeased look. "The foothills of the Cascades," she muttered.

"Is there some significance to that?" Abby asked.

"None, only that it's remote," Vivian said.

"What's out there?" Abby asked.

"Woods, steep hills, and lakes," Sebastian said. "It's almost an hour's drive out of the city."

"Do we have a map of the area?" Abby asked, hopeful. "I might be able to narrow it down even more."

"I'll look, Darling," Vivian said, as she began sorting through the pile of maps. "Try to relax."

Abby sat back and allowed the aches to wane. She concentrated on her breathing until she was no longer panting.

Vivian pulled out a map and placed it in front of her. "It isn't of Maple Valley specifically, but it covers most of the area between Maple Valley and the southeastern portion of the county," she explained.

"That should be fine," Abby said, taking the map. She placed the wooden triangle in the center of the area and concentrated.

"Are you sure you've rested enough?" Sebastian asked.

Abby answered with a nod. She placed her hands on the planchette and closed her eyes. As the Sight opened again, the pointer began to move. Abby concentrated on Atoro Thanos. She focused on him as intensely as she could until the planchette came to a stop.

She closed the Sight abruptly. Though breathless and fatigued, Abby leaned forward, eager to see the location. Abby stared at the map, confused. The planchette was pointing to a river.

"Is he swimming?" Abby asked, annoyed.

Vivian looked down at the map and gasped. "I should have known," she said, a flash of recognition in her eye.

"What?" Abby asked.

"What is it?" Sebastian asked at the same time.

"Look at the name of the river," Vivian said, pointing at the map.

"The Green River," Abby read aloud. "Why is that familiar?"

"Because it is an infamous river, associated with a prolific serial killer back in the nineteen-eighties."

"He used to dump his victims in the river," Sebastian explained.

"I vaguely remember hearing something about it, a long time ago," Abby confessed. The story tickled old memories of something she had read years before, but she couldn't recall any details.

"That river has seen more than its fair share of death and depravity," Vivian stated, ill at ease. "Where else would a necromancer go to hide?"

"Is there something around here? A building or a safe house where he would go?" Abby asked, pointing to the small portion of the river the planchette had landed on.

"I don't know, but we will certainly find out," Vivian stated with certainty. "I'll take it from here and see what significance there is in this particular portion of the river. You rest, we still have a great deal of work to do."

Abby nodded and trudged back to her room for a nap, leaving Sebastian and Vivian to clean up.

"Your family is in the library," Ms. Grace said, as Abby rushed through the front door into the grand entry. The middle-aged woman stood in a dignified manner with her hands cupped together. "Where have you been?"

"I was practicing with the symphony. What's happened?" Abby asked, worried by the look on her mentor's face.

"Vivian has convened the Coven. It seems your scrying attempt yesterday proved invaluable. You should hurry."

"Aren't you coming?" Abby asked.

"I'm afraid not," Ms. Grace stated. "Your grandmother has called the Coven. Even as good of friends as we are, I am not a Kane. Outsiders are typically not allowed at such meetings."

"But this is important," Abby protested.

"Yes, but it is no offense, I assure you. If there is anything I can do to help, I have no doubt your grandmother will ask," Ms. Grace stated. "Go along now, they're all waiting for you."

Abby set her violin case next to one of the tables and draped her wet raincoat on a chair. She rushed down the long hallway toward the library, opened the door, and quickly stepped in.

The entire Coven was waiting. Fiona and Vivian sat on a couch together, Wendy, Sebastian, and Rodger on another. Bernard stood in the back corner of the library, stroking the whiskers of his beard. Gisela gave Abby a glare upon noticing her. Cordelia sat in a chair near the fire. David stood behind her, resting a gentle hand on her shoulder. Lawrence and Syble sat in leather chairs near a bookshelf. All eyes turned to Abby as she entered.

"Finally, Darling," Vivian said, getting up to pace in front of the fireplace. The flames roared the moment she entered the room.

"I'm sorry. I didn't mean to keep everyone waiting. I was at the dress rehearsal," Abby explained and moved in to take a seat in one of the vacant chairs near the bookshelves.

"Ah yes, your little recital is next week," Vivian said with an uncertain smile. "Well, It's quite all right, Darling. You're here now."

"Come along, Vivian. The girl is here, let's get started." Bernard barked impatiently from the back corner of the room.

"Fine, Darling, fine," Vivian said, straightening the jacket of her white suit. "We have located Atoro Thanos," she began. "Thanks in no small part to Abigail's use of her special gift, we were able to narrow down his location to a relatively small portion of the Green River in the southeastern part of the county. It is a few miles east of Black Diamond, near Ravensdale."

"There isn't a lot out there," Fiona stated.

"No, there isn't," Vivian agreed. "We have a confirmed sighting of him at an old water treatment plant." She held up a map and pointed to the location. "It used to be part of the water treatment facilities for the county and was replaced in the 1970s by a more modern facility approximately two miles downriver. As far as we can tell, it's completely abandoned. That is where he is hiding."

"Who found him?" Abby asked.

"I did," Gisela said gruffly.

"Yes, Cousin Gisela has shown a talent for surveillance during our conflict with the Thanos, and it would seem her skills have proven themselves useful once again. Our thanks, of course," Vivian stated. "It is our belief he hides there at night when he isn't lurking about in the daylight.

We must acquire his blood. Preferably, we capture him alive. In the case that we have to use the ritual more than once, we have the option. Killing him is a completely viable course. However, it should not be our first option."

Vivian leaned forward, somehow managing to loom over every person in the room at once. She leveled a long, even stare on each person in turn. "I do not want even a single member of this family, making the ultimate sacrifice to capture him. Understood? We have already lost too much."

Everyone nodded slowly in agreement. Vivian rested back on her heels, looking determined.

"Who will be going on this mission?" Rodger asked.

"That, Mr. Pennington, is the reason I called this meeting," Vivian said. "I believe a small team would be best. If the entire family gets involved, we present too large of a target for him, as we did at the ritual.

"Perhaps a team of four?" David suggested.

"Precisely my thought," Vivian said, nodding. "I will take—"

"You should stay here," Fiona stated. "I do not think it wise that you be on this team at all."

Abby watched her grandmother's expression turn to outrage, that was quickly contained. "Why on earth not?" Vivian questioned.

"My beloved sister, you have an impressive arsenal of spells, all of which are well suited to utter and complete destruction, not surgical strikes," Fiona explained. "Besides which, you are the leader of this Coven, and your place is to lead us, not to perish in the field. Should anything go wrong, we will need our Matriarch."

Uncertain looks broke out all over the room, and Vivian fumed, searching for the right come back to her sister's sound logic.

"I will go," Abby said, standing. Everyone turned to look at her. "I'm going."

"Darling, this is going to be incredibly dangerous," Vivian said. "You are not an experienced witch."

"I've faced him before," Abby said. "I'm still alive, and I have proven myself."

"Your admirable granddaughter has a point, Vivian," Lawrence said, tapping his cane on the marble floor.

"If the necromancer flees, she's the only one who can track him," Syble agreed in her squeaky voice.

"She's right," Bernard said gruffly. "She has earned her place," he added, looking at Abby with an intense stare.

"I should go with her," Sebastian said.

"Absolutely not," Wendy interrupted. "You have an infant son who needs his father. You may not like me, Vivian, but you know I can protect her. I'll go."

Vivian looked shaken but did not argue.

"So, will I," Fiona said. "I will go."

"No," Vivian said, giving her sister a silencing glare. "There are few of us powerful enough to cast the ritual to vanquish this Damnable spirit. With Margot still in the hospital, I cannot risk one of the most powerful witches in this Coven. You are a prime target for the Thanos. Losing you would weaken us beyond measure." Her voice was shaking with an emotion that refused any argument.

"I'll go," David said. Cordelia looked at her husband, terrified. "I know, dearest, but I can't let our son's murder go without recourse. I will make sure that Thanos bastard finds justice."

"Can you hold your vengeance in check, I wonder?" Lawrence stated. "We need him alive."

David shot him a hateful glare. "I said justice, not vengeance."

"Who else would go?" Cordelia questioned coldly, pointedly looking at Lawrence. "You?"

"Are you suggesting my husband should go?" Syble said, spurred into outrage. "He has a bum leg!"

"He's still a highly proficient witch," Gisela said. "In fact, you are quite well known for your biblical curses."

Lawrence looked somewhat mortified and quickly recovered with a surge of confidence. "I will go," he said confidently.

Abby couldn't tell if it was genuine familial duty or injured pride that urged him to volunteer.

"I'm not around all that often, it's time for me to remind everyone I am still a part of this coven," he added.

"I believe that's four," Gisela said pointedly.

"Lawrence, David, Wendy, and Abigail," Vivian said. Her voice was uncertain as she said the names. "You shall be the four." She was unable to hide her disappointment.

"I will follow them, and hole up somewhere nearby," Rodger said. "I am not the best in a fight, but I will bring my most powerful healing reagents in case anyone gets injured."

"I'll be there with you," Sebastian said. "A two-man extraction team." Rodger smiled, taking his husband's hand.

"I'll watch Little Evan, for you," Fiona offered. "He will be safe here."

"Very well," Vivian said, still making no effort to hide her displeasure. "The four volunteers will meet with me at midnight tonight. We will formulate our plans then."

"Why midnight?" Syble questioned.

"It's the witching hour, you daft twig," Bernard snapped.

Syble gasped in shock, then looked away in a huff.

"The rest of you should get some rest," Vivian said. "Once we have the blood components, this Coven will be performing some of the most complex magic we have ever done. It will no doubt be difficult, and will come at a cost." She speared each of them, one by one, with her most commanding stare. "Be prepared."

Vivian turned around to stare into the fire, dismissing all of them.

CHAPTER THIRTY-THREE

There was an electrical scent in the air. Abby looked up to see enormous metal towers extend into the sky, each with at least a dozen power lines disappearing over the hills to the next set of towers.

The sky was a dark gray with low clouds. A stiff wind brought a biting chill, and Abby thought perhaps it would snow. She looked over to see Wendy, David, and Lawrence standing in the tall grass.

"I feel like we should try to be more stealthy," Wendy whispered. Her words were barely audible over the howling winds.

"We should assume he uses spirits to stand watch for him," David said. "It's likely he has sentries everywhere. If that's the case, he already knows we're here."

"Remember, we only need a few drops of blood, no one needs to be a hero," Lawrence said nervously.

"It isn't too late to return to the fallback point with Rodger and Sebastian," David told Abby.

"No, I need to be here," Abby replied. "This is too important."

Wendy nodded. "Alright. Stay close, kid," she added with a wink.

"The abandoned water treatment plant should be located just over the hill there," Lawrence said, pointing to the map on his phone.

"Let's hope so," David said uneasily.

As they approached the crest of a hill, the four of them slowed down and began to move with more caution.

When they reached the top, they looked down at a sprawling industrial complex. From where they were, they could easily see a decaying water tower and several enormous pools of water, with an old metal catwalk connecting them.

The main building was in disrepair. The metal grate treacherously rusted. Next to the treatment plant was a small river with an angry current. The infamous Green River, Abby thought. The banks of the river were overgrown with sticker bushes and wild berries, all of which had browned in the cold of late fall.

"We should stick together," Lawrence said. "We could cover more ground if we split up, but he is far too dangerous, I think."

"I agree," David said, nodding.

"Abby, I want you to be very careful. He's going to target you once he knows you're with us," Wendy said affectionately.

"Don't worry, Aunt Wendy. I'm prepared to unleash holy hell on him, should it come to that," Abby said, as reassuringly as she could.

"I suspect you will," Wendy smiled.

"Just remember, we only need a couple drops of blood. No heroics," Lawrence reminded.

"We got it," Wendy reassured.

The four of them began descending the hill toward the old plant. The sound of the water lapping at the shore bounced off the valley walls, making it sound much louder than it really was. As they came to the bottom of the small hill, they encountered pavement that was slowly being reclaimed by wild plants. Most of the parking lot had been broken up by weeds and grass. Only fragments of the old concrete remained.

Abby looked up. At the far side between the main building and what had once been a parking lot, she saw the walls of a large concrete vat. It extended thirty feet into the air, and the smell of metal and rust permeated the air along with stagnant water. The whole place was a study in industrial decay.

A drop of moisture fell from the sky. Abby looked up to see low clouds threatening to unleash their rain.

The main building stood at least four stories into the sky. Its steel siding was corroded and falling apart. Several spots had rusted through completely. It looked anything but stable.

The cold rain began to fall, carried by a freezing wind. It pelted against the sides of the building, sounding like a metal drum with every drop.

Lawrence picked up his pace and swiftly approached a rusted-out doorframe. He gestured the others over. "This way," he said.

Abby and the others rushed toward the door, carefully avoiding clods of cement and bundles of weeds. David entered first. He put up his hand for Abby to wait a moment, as he checked to be certain the coast was clear.

Abby waited impatiently as he studied whatever it was on the far side of the door. After what felt like an eternity, David motioned for Abby to follow. Wendy entered right after, followed by Lawrence.

When Abby stepped in, she realized the entire building was one enormous room. In the center, taking up the majority of the structure, was an enormous boiler. The old metal boiler was nearly three stories tall with ramps, stairs, and a metal grate surrounding the entire rusted heap. It appeared there were water pools on the far side, though Abby couldn't see into them. From the smell of stagnant water, she imagined they were likely full, or at least partially filled, with murky water.

"No sign of him," David whispered. Abby could barely hear her aunt over the sound of rain drumming against the metal building.

"Let's move around the perimeter," Wendy suggested.

Wendy began moving into the building cautiously. She kept her hand up, ready to throw a spell at a moment's notice. With every step, Abby wondered if Atoro Thanos would suddenly appear from some hidden corner. The industrial boiler was enormous. There were more nooks and crevasses than Abby could keep track of. The open furnace doors and the metal grate and ramps provided all kinds of cover for some monster to lurk. Abby could only picture Atoro Thanos quietly watching their party saunter into his elaborate trap.

David approached the corner and stopped. He pressed his back to the edge of the boiler and motioned for Abby and the others to follow his lead. He poked her head around the corner, then quickly pulled it back.

"Looks clear," he said.

This is agonizing, Abby thought. *He may not even be here.*

David inched along the side of the building with the others close behind him. They hadn't moved more than thirty feet when he came to a dead stop. Abby looked up at her cousin, who stood frozen, staring at something inside the boiler. Abby followed his gaze and saw a thin foam mat with a sleeping bag.

"Is it his?" Abby asked. It seemed an unlikely bed for the prideful necromancer.

"It seems likely," Wendy answered. "I doubt he would let any vagrants live in here with him."

Abby backed up to the side nearest wall and walked down toward the large concrete pool a few yards away. A sudden chill washed over her. *We're being watched…*

Following her intuition, she let her gaze fall upon the rusted-out boiler. A long, grated-metal walkway wound up three stories above the vats. There, at the top, stood a motionless black form, looking at them.

They stood there, frozen, staring at one another. Each was waiting for the other to make the first move.

He raised one hand and pointed at Abby and the others.

"Hit the ground!" Abby yelled, flinging herself against the boiler and sliding to the floor.

A flurry of sparks rained down, fizzling as they hit the walls.

David and Lawrence threw themselves to the ground, while Wendy stepped into the large tube where they had found the bedding.

"He's at the top of the boiler," Abby called out.

"Got it!" Wendy shouted determinedly. "Don't touch the boiler."

David, Abby, and Lawrence quickly stepped away.

Wendy placed her hand against the rusted metal. "Ilium Ivokkus Fulgur!" An electrical spark danced around her hand and fingers, and then jumped onto the boiler, crawling up the large, dormant machine and disappearing near the top.

A loud yelp echoed down from above, followed by a thud.

"You got him!" Abby yelled, excitedly.

"I wouldn't count on it," Wendy said. "Without a line of sight, all I can deliver is a nice little shock. He's still dangerous, but hopefully on the defense."

"Let's go!" Lawrence said, leading them back toward the front of the boiler where they had seen a set of stairs leading up.

Lawrence cautiously climbed each step, testing his weight as he went. Once he made it to the second level, Abby approached the steps. When she reached the top, she saw Lawrence had made his way to the north end of the walkway. He turned toward Abby and pointed in the other direction. Abby headed cautiously to the south end, as Wendy and David made their way up the steps.

Abby reached the south edge of the boiler and quickly glanced around the corner. The walkway was clear, save for another set of stairs leading up to the top of the boiler. "That's the way up!" She pointed.

The wind howled, and rain pelted the metal structure.

"Abby get down!" David's voice broke through the deafening sound.

Without hesitation, Abby dropped to the ground. Her body crashed against the unrelenting metal grate beneath her. A black, snakelike figure was coiling down one of the metal supports slithering toward her. She pulled back, uncertain what horrible spell inched its way toward her.

"Aurum Regentus!" David called out. A blast of wind rushed from his hand, slamming against the smoky form. The wind caught the snake figure and carried it away.

Abby rose, pressing herself against the boiler. She looked up and saw a pair of feet retreating along the top grate. She began inching her way toward the staircase that would take her to the top.

Suddenly something touched Abby's arm. She yelped and turned to face the unimaginable horror lurking behind her. "Wendy!" she said breathlessly.

"Come on, kid," Wendy said with a grin. "Let's go topside and take this fucker out!"

Abby nodded and made a dash for the nearest staircase. Wendy stepped out to the edge of the grating and gave Abby cover as she climbed toward their prey.

When she reached the top, Abby looked out over a wide platform covering the top of the metal structure. On the far side of the boiler, near the back, a dark figure was waiting for them.

There he was. Atoro Thanos. He was a tall, menacing figure, wearing all black. A large knife was tucked in his belt. *That damn knife!* Abby thought as rage filled her. She thought of all her loved ones that blade had cut into, Margot, Gus, Rodger, her parents… she promised herself she would take it from him, permanently.

There was a bandaged stub where his right hand should have been, and his black eyes glowed with hatred. For a brief moment, she felt like they were portals into hell, dragging her in. *No, not this time!*

She pulled herself away and ducked down below the top of the boiler. Wendy approached the top of the stairs, and Abby motioned her to stay down.

Wendy crawled over to Abby and quickly popped her head up to locate Atoro. "I don't see him."

"He's probably coming around one way or the other," Abby said, pointing to the walkway circling the top of the boiler. "I'll watch in this direction, and you check that way."

"Alright," Wendy said, putting her back to Abby and watching in the direction Abby had indicated.

Abby waited, growing unsteady and impatient. Her whole body was rigid with tension. At any moment, she was certain Atoro Thanos would turn the corner and direct some necromantic curse directly at her. She waited… and waited… *he could have circled the boiler a dozen times by now,* she realized. *He's waiting for us…?*

Abby started to crawl along the harsh metal grating. Its sharp edges cut into her knees and the palms of her hands.

"What's happening," David asked, reaching the top of the stairs.

"Get down," Wendy said. David immediately dropped onto the catwalk, pressing himself flat.

Abby paused and quickly poked her head around the corner. A large figure was hunched down, leaning against the boiler. *He's there!* Abby began whispering a binding spell. If she could hold him in place long enough, they could get the blood they needed.

Suddenly the steel bar lining the edge of the grate broke loose and began writhing in the air. Abby looked up to see the wild railing coming straight at her. She rolled out of the way, barely avoiding being impaled as the metal crashed against the old boiler.

The railing pulled back, like a cobra preparing to strike. Abby dodged out of the way, as the metal crashed against the boiler again, her spell wholly forgotten.

"Astosis Terrumus Imperious!" David chanted. The rail began to rattle and shake. It recoiled, about to strike again, but it stopped. Instead, it shook violently. Coming loose from the walkway, it fell three stories, crashing against the cement below.

The grate tipped slightly, its worn fitting breaking loose from the boiler.

Abby screamed, suddenly sliding. She caught herself on the metal lip where the railing had once been and pushed herself against the boiler. Securing her handhold, she shifted her weight on to the stable portion of the platform.

Intuition triggered in Abby, and she instinctively moved her head to the left. A steel blade struck the side of the boiler where her head had been only a millisecond before.

"Kane bitch!" Atoro growled.

Abby rolled toward Wendy and David, who watched in horror as Atoro Thanos followed her around the corner. Abby kicked out with her feet.

Atoro brought his blade down into Abby's shoulder as her right foot connected with his chest. He stumbled back and swung again.

She closed her eyes, awaiting the sharp pain she knew was coming. The blade missed, deflecting off of something just inches from her flesh. Abby glanced back and saw David chanting something under his breath.

"Borrius Calamitus!" Wendy cried out, pointing her finger at Atoro. A strange string of light whipped out of her finger, striking his hand, and causing him to release the knife. It fell between the grating to the concrete floor below.

Atoro looked down at Abby, his eyes wild and frantic. "You die now!" He screamed in broken English. He pulled back slightly, and took a deep breath, puffing out his cheeks. Black smoke blew from his lips and slammed into Abby's chest. It knocked the wind out of her and sent her flying backward into the wall of the boiler.

Abby turned her head, trying to hold her breath. She didn't know what the smoke was, but she did not want to breathe it in. A gust of wind dissipated the smoke almost before Abby could finish the thought.

The rattling and screeching sound of metal-on-metal echoed through the building, drowning out the sound of rain and wind. Abby looked down as chains began crawling up Atoro's legs. The coiled around his midriff, pinning his arms against his torso.

Abby saw Lawrence come around the corner, directly behind Atoro. He was chanting steadily. All his concentration was on controlling the chains binding their enemy.

Atoro howled in frustration. Both David and Wendy came to their feet. Wendy quickly moved forward and helped Abby up.

"We got him!" Wendy said.

"Grab the knife!" David shouted to Abby.

Atoro's frustration turned into a smile. Abby's heart sunk as he began laughing.

"Be careful," David warned.

"Get what we came for!" Lawrence barked. "We only need a little. Do it, and let's get out of here!"

Wendy reached into her pocket and pulled out a small blade. She stepped forward and grabbed his arm.

A ghostly sound echoed through the building. The metal siding rattled as the spectral noise grew louder.

"Do it! Now!" David yelled louder.

Wendy brought the knife to the exposed flesh of Atoro's arm. Just as she was about to cut, the small blade flew from her hand and crashed against the side of the building. It fell, clattering the three stories to the cement floor below.

David's body crashed against the boiler. Abby snapped her head up, trying to see what had struck her cousin.

A cacophony of ghostly voices cried out all around them. They rattled the ground below and sent a chill down Abby's spine.

"Imperious Terranus!" Lawrence yelled. The chains began constricting around Atoro, causing the necromancer to cry out in pain. "Stop, or you will die!" he yelled.

"I do not fear death, you imbecile," Atoro growled.

The ghostly voices grew louder, echoing through the large metal building. David stirred from where he lay atop the boiler, dazed. Wendy covered her ears as the sound grew louder and louder.

Ghostly apparitions emerged through the metal walls and from the grate below. Atoro wore a big toothy grin as the spirits began to flood the building.

Lawrence lost his balance and fell to the ground. Spirits clawed at him, pummeling him with their fists. The chains coiled around Atoro's body fell to the ground, releasing him from his bondage.

"No!" Abby shouted.

Wendy pointed and began unleashing a spell when apparitions swarmed her. One wrapped his hands around Wendy's throat, cutting off her spell.

Abby turned to face Atoro. The necromancer raised his hand and pointed at Abby. "Silisario Sanguinentus," he shouted.

"Oblatus!" Abby said, holding her arms out, crossed in front of her. She winced in pain, as small cuts tore into her arms.

"Kantero Bombustia!" David shouted from the top of the boiler.

The metal grate beneath Atoro's feet burst, throwing him into the air. The necromancer slammed into the ceiling and fell. There was a sickening sound as his body crashed into the railing. A crack of bone and a cry of pain. As he began to slip over the edge, he grabbed the railing with his single remaining hand, trying to break his fall.

Abby rushed forward. He was dangling over one of the pools. There was water below, murky and brown, but she couldn't tell how deep it was or if he would survive the fall.

"Get his blood!" Wendy shouted, pulling herself to her feet.

Abby pulled a knife from her pocket. Atoro grunted in pain, as he dangled above the cesspool. She flicked open her blade and moved toward him.

Atoro let go of the railing and grabbed Abby.

Before she could react, they were both tumbling down, away from the boiler.

There was an enormous splash as they slammed against the surface of the water. Completely submerged, Abby could only see a pale light above her through the murk. She kicked her feet, fighting to reach the surface.

With a gasp of air, Abby filled her lungs. She looked around, treading water to keep her head out of the slimy brown sludge. Food wrappers and trash floated on the surface. There was no sign of Atoro Thanos. She pushed a bundle of rubbish away as it floated by. The corpse of a rat bumped up against her arm. Abby wretched.

"Abby!" Wendy cried from above.

"I'm all right," Abby called back.

"Thank God!" she shouted.

"Where is he?" David yelled down.

"I don't know," Abby said, looking around her for any sign of the man who pulled her into the murk.

"Hold on! We'll get you out of there!" Wendy shouted down to her before disappearing back over the edge of the pool.

"We're coming," Lawrence reassured.

"I'll stay here and provide cover. We still have no idea where he is!" David yelled.

Abby continued to tread water. She kicked her way to the edge closest to the boiler. It wasn't more than a few feet below the second landing surrounding the rusted metal machine. There was no ledge for her to cling to or a ladder to climb. Instead, she stayed near the edge and watched for any sign of the fiend they were hunting.

"Here," Wendy called out.

Abby turned to see Wendy and Lawrence hovering over the edge of the second-story landing. Wendy was coiling a rusty chain around the railing and extended one end into the pool. Abby reached out and grabbed the chain. It was a relief to have something to hold on to.

"Hold on tight," Margot said.

Abby wrapped the chain around her wrist to be certain it didn't slip out of her hands.

"We're bringing you up," Wendy said.

"Regentus Terranus Bleese." Lawrence began chanting over and over under her breath, concentrating on the chain.

The chain began moving, commanded by Lawrence's spell. Abby was pulled from the mire to the safety ladder on the inside of the pool. Water sluiced to the ground below as she pulled herself the rest of the way free of the sludge.

Wendy gave her a hand, pulling the rest of the way up. "You stink kid," Wendy said dryly as Abby plopped onto the metal grate.

"There he is!" David yelled from above.

Abby stood quickly and began searching for whatever it was David saw. When she reached the far end of the metal walkway, she saw Atoro. He was running toward the backside of the building, away from the pool. Only a rickety catwalk separated him from David.

Her cousin shouted something. A flash of light came from above, and a bolt of fire slammed against the side of the building missing Atoro by inches.

"This is for my son, you bastard!" David shouted, readying a new spell.

Atoro turned and raised his hands. Black smoke blew from his lips again and surged across the open space between them. It struck David squarely, knocking him backward. He lost his footing and tripped.

Abby watched in sickening slow motion as David stumbled, falling backward over the railing. "David!" she shouted.

He fell, tumbling thirty feet below. With a terrible crack, he hit the unyielding concrete and stopped moving.

"Aquarius Regentum Bombardius!" Abby yelled at the top of her lungs, extending her hands. The water sloshed forward over the edge of the pool, forming an enormous wave of murky water. It smashed against the steel walls and washed over the catwalk. Atoro Thanos disappeared in a wave of brown filth.

Abby began running for the stairs. The wave would not likely stop Atoro for long. She could hear her aunt's footsteps behind her. "Go help David!" she shouted.

When she reached the stairs, she began running. The grate shook under her. Abby flew along the rust-covered boiler toward the back of the building, past the massive concrete pools. She rounded the corner, and she saw him.

Atoro was scurrying to his feet. Abby tried to get off a spell, but he leaped through the doorway into the night.

She ran after him, pausing at the door to see where he'd gone. When she looked through the doorway, there was only darkness. A few yards away, she heard the Green River lapping at its banks. It was a still, quiet night, and Atoro was nowhere to be seen.

Abby's intuition told her to be cautious. She took a step forward and watched closely for any sign of Atoro Thanos.

"Where is he?" Wendy asked, running up behind Abby.

"He made it through the door," Abby said, uncertain if he escaped or if he was lurking out of sight, ready with a surprise attack.

Wendy made a run for the door.

"No!" Abby yelled.

As Wendy burst through the doorway, a large hand reached out and grabbed her arm. She crashed to the ground pulling Atoro Thanos with her.

Wendy struggled, wrestling with the larger man. "Do it, Abby!" Wendy yelled, trying to keep Atoro engaged so he could not escape. "Hurry!"

Atoro pulled her backward, taking, both of them just out of Abby's reach.

Wendy waved her hand and pointed her finger. A crash of thunder clapped from her fingertip. The world rumbled, and a bolt of lightning flashed through the darkness. It struck a moss-covered rock mere inches from Atoro's head. The moss sizzled in the rain.

Atoro arched his back, slamming Wendy against a rock. There was a heavy, cracking sound, and Abby watched in horror as her aunt went limp.

"Wendy!" Abby cried. Atoro quickly got up and ran.

Abby hesitated, torn between helping her aunt and chasing down the man who murdered her parents–the man whose blood would serve as the key to their salvation.

"Go! I'll look after them!" Lawrence yelled, coming up through the door.

Abby stood and ran after Atoro.

The man was a few yards ahead, running toward a line of trees near the river. She flung a spell. A wave of icy water washed over the bank of the rived, splashing over Atoro's feet. The necromancer kept running.

Abby put everything she had into running. The moss-covered river rock made her footing treacherous, but she didn't care. There was no way Atoro Thanos was going to slip through her fingers again.

She was gaining on him, as he dodged through the underbrush. Abby was inches from being able to reach out and grab him. A physical brawl was not something she could win, but she could hope to preoccupy him long enough to get a spell off. She only needed to daze him long enough to get his blood.

Abby was about to lunge at him, when the necromancer dipped between two trees. Abby screamed in frustration and continued after him. She chased him into a thick grove in the dense forest. Abby slowed her pace though the underbrush but kept running.

She lost sight of him. The trees blotted out the moonlight. Only the sound of Atoro's retreat offered any indication where he was. Abby ran in the direction of the footsteps, holding her hands up to push away the branches and leaves.

"Abby!" Someone called out. It might have been one of her uncles, but she couldn't stop to respond. Abby could not let Atoro get away. She continued to follow the sounds of his footsteps in the forest.

A root caught her foot. Abby fell, hard, to the ground. She pulled herself onto her knees and realized the sound of running was gone.

She looked up and saw nothing but the darkness surrounding her.

"Ignatatus Orbulum," Abby said, concentrating. A small orb of flame appeared in the palm of her hand. Orange light illuminated the area around Abby with a warm glow. There was nothing more than trees and roots.

She stood slowly, listening carefully for any sounds that might lead her to Atoro Thanos. She heard footsteps coming from her left. Abby turned. Sebastian stepped out from behind a tree.

"Where is he?" he asked.

"I don't know. Rodger?"

"With Wendy," he answered. "Search for his footprint, some kind of trail he left behind." He began scouring the ground, and Abby wasted no time doing as he said.

As every second passed, Abby grew more frantic. They were giving him too much time. Madness was taking over as she frantically rifled through the underbrush for some sign of passage.

"Over here!" Sebastian called out. Abby rushed to his side and looked at the ground at her feet. There it was, a large bootprint settled into the damp earth. She looked ahead, but couldn't find any more.

Sebastian knelt and placed his hand over the boot print. "Salumentus Luminous Confoustus." The footprint began to glow with a soft, blue light. A few feet away, another footprint began to shimmer, and then another, and another. He had left a trail.

The blue glow guided the two of them deep into the forest. As they trekked forward, Abby listened carefully for any sound indicating Atoro was near. Instead, she heard the rain and the wind rustling the trees above.

Abby hurried along at a faster pace. She didn't stop to wait for her uncle. They were beginning to ascend a small hill. Abby grabbed trees to help pull herself up the steep incline. The blue glow led them over the crest of a hill and down into a steep ravine.

She began limping in the direction of the glowing footprints. She was only just becoming aware of the pain from her earlier fall. Sebastian caught up to her and took her arm for added support.

"There's a cave!" Sebastian pointed.

A man-made opening in the earth, supported with wooden beams, became visible as they approached. An old rusted chain-link fence was sprawled across the opening to the cave. A small portion of the fence, large enough for a man to crawl through was bent up, allowing access. The footprints led into the darkness.

An ancient-looking, rusted sign dangled from the fence. "Property of Black Diamond Coal Company," Sebastian read. "It's an old coal mine?"

"Let's go," Abby persisted. She got down on her hands and knees and crawled through the opening in the fence.

The two witches crept along the mine tunnel following the illuminated footsteps of Atoro Thanos. At every turn, Abby wondered if the blue glow would come to an end and they would see the man himself staring back at them.

They passed several tunnels as they made their way deeper into the old mine. They approached a sharp turn to the right and followed it to its end. The passage opened into a small cavern. There was a wooden table set up against the back wall with several glass beakers and a small cast-iron cauldron.

Sebastian moved forward and pointed to the glowing footprints on the floor. Abby followed the tracks. They ended at a built-up door frame, protruding from the wall. A plain wooden door was set into it.

"It looks like he has a makeshift laboratory here," Sebastian whispered.

"What's that door?" Abby questioned as they moved in closer.

"I don't know, but be careful, Abby. There is no place more dangerous than a witch's sanctum."

Abby approached the door. She reached down and took the knob in her hand. She glanced back to see Sebastian was standing right behind her, ready to cast a spell. She took a deep breath and opened the door.

She peered into the dark. There was nothing more than a stone wall with veins of coal. "He's not here! There's nothing here!" Abby screamed in rage. She scoured the entire sanctum, patting the walls, looking for a secret door–anything that would lead them to the necromancer.

Nothing.

Sebastian was examining the door frame closely. "Abby," he said, his voice trembling.

Abby quickly came to his side. "Look here," Sebastian pointed. There were several sets of archaic runes etched into the wood of the door frame.

"What do they mean?" Abby asked.

"These symbols are used with translocation spells," he said. The disappointment in his voice was gut-wrenching. Sebastian fell back, resting his full weight on the door.

"Teleportation," Abby whispered. She sunk to the floor, unable to hold herself up. "He escaped…"

CHAPTER THIRTY-FOUR

The scent of fresh flowers wafted past Abby's nose as she poked her head out from under the covers. She waited for her bedroom door to close and looked to her left. The staff had placed a bouquet of white roses on her nightstand.

Abby pulled herself up and sat on the edge of the bed. She glanced at her phone. *Two in the afternoon... twenty missed calls... thirty-two text messages...* She tossed the phone back on the nightstand and fell back on the bed.

There was nothing but numbness. The world felt stale, as though it was going to dry up and crumble away at any moment. Abby searched for something, anything, and found nothing inside. *Am I dead?* she wondered briefly. She pinched herself. *I guess not...*

She needed to start acting like she was fine, or people would start to worry again. Sitting up once again, she slouched on the edge of the bed. Abby tried to will herself to move, and nothing happened. She stared forward at the thin crack of light at the bottom of the blinds. It permitted just enough sun into the room to vanquish the darkness completely.

Abby coughed and wrapped the comforter around her shoulders. There was a soft knock at the door. She remained silent, hoping whoever was at the door would move along if she remained silent.

The door cracked open slightly, and then all the way. Moments later, someone sat next to her on the edge of the bed. Abby didn't look to see who it was. *I don't care, just leave me alone,* she thought.

"Darling, it's time to pull yourself together," Vivian said softly.

"Because you decided its time?" Abby asked harshly.

"Because it's time," Vivian responded in kind.

Abby rolled her eyes, an effort that felt exhausting. "I'm not in the mood," she said. "I'm going back to sleep."

Vivian stood and pulled the comforter off her and tossed it on the ground. Abby grabbed the pillows and held them close. Vivian reached down and pulled them away, tossing them on the floor.

"Get out of bed!" Vivian yelled.

"Just leave me alone..." she whimpered pathetically.

"You aren't going to make me go through this by myself!" Vivian yelled, her voice riddled with emotion.

She looked up at her grandmother. Abby's jaw dropped. For the first time in her life, she saw tears in the old woman's eyes. Vivian Kane stood in front of her, a vulnerable creature. The indomitable matriarch of the Kane family was nothing more than a human–a fact she forever did her best to hide from the world.

"Get up!" Vivian yelled.

Abby stood and threw her arms up in exasperation. "Are you happy now? I'm up. What do you want from me?"

"I want you to fight! I want you to get out of bed and show me you haven't given up!" Vivian shouted, shaking with emotion. Then she collapsed onto the edge of the bed and buried her face in her hands, weeping.

Abby was frozen as she stared at her grandmother. She had never seen the old woman shed more than a single tear, let alone weep. Her anger and frustration began to melt away until there was nothing left but pain. She cautiously sat next to her grandmother and placed her arm around her.

Vivian leaned into Abby as she wept.

Vivian's tears invoked an emotional torrent within Abby. All the pain, grief, fear, and hopelessness of the last few days opened like a waterspout, rumbling to life with the turn of a valve. Her tears broke through the numbness she'd wrapped herself in, and Abby surrendered to it. The rawness returned, and the physical manifestation of emotions flooded her eyes and rolled down her cheeks. She sat, sobbing at her grandmother's side.

The two held one another as they wept. There was never a time she felt closer to her grandmother than she did at this moment. *She lost her son, I don't ever remember her crying before,* she thought as she held her grandmother close. *Not even at the funeral...*

There was a polite knock on the door, and Vivian quickly pulled away. She stood, diving toward the mirror over Abby's nightstand. She began wiping away any evidence of her tears.

Abby got up and moved over to the door, opening it only slightly. There on the other side, Lawrence stood, tapping his cane on the floor.

"Excuse me, but Mr. Greenly informed me Vivian was here. I have a terrible allergy to walnuts, and the cook says she can't change the menu without your grand-mother's approval," Lawrence stated, looking at Abby's red puffy face curiously as though he'd never seen anyone cry before.

"I'm sorry, she left a few minutes ago," Abby lied. "I think she was heading down to the library."

"Ah, very well," Lawrence said, making an abrupt turn and heading down the hallway.

Abby closed the door and turned to see Vivian take several deep breaths to reassert her well-fortified manner. The redness around her eyes was impossible to ignore; it was a blemish on a face impeccably maintained to hide any crack or insinuation of imperfection.

"How do I look, Darling?" Vivian asked, fussing with her hair as though it would fix everything.

"Like someone who's been crying," Abby admitted honestly. "Maybe that is what you needed," she suggested cautiously.

Vivian looked at her strangely, as though she had said something profane. "And what good did it do? My son is still lingering in limbo, tortured by that horrible spirit, along with your mother. My tears did not free them any more than yours have. Tears did not bring Augustus back to life, nor have they healed Margot or David. There is no magic in tears, Darling." she said. She glared into the mirror, searching for any other signs she had been ever-so-briefly vulnerable.

"Sometimes it makes me feel better," Abby said, moving closer.

"I can't imagine why," Vivian said. "I have never once had an occasion when letting myself get emotional provided any real help. All it does is distract me from what is really important. I should be in my laboratory researching, not wallowing up here in tears and feeling sorry for myself." She cleared her throat, removing any sign of the emotion lingering there. Her tone returned to its familiar coldness.

"I love you, Grandmother," Abby said, uncertain what else to say.

There was a sharp flinch on Vivian's face, a brief moment of uncertainty, and then the old woman swallowed her emotions. "A lot of good my love did your father," Vivian said her voice barely composed. She turned abruptly and walked to the door.

"Grandmother?" Abby called out.

Vivian paused at the door for a moment, but then left before saying anything, closing the door behind her.

She waited a few moments, hoping her door would open again and Vivian would return. It became obvious after several minutes her grandmother wasn't coming back. No doubt her momentary breakdown would never be spoken of again. Such were the ways of Vivian Kane.

Abby shuffled into the bathroom. She turned on the lights and quickly turned them back off after being bombarded by their brightness. She could hear her bare feet slap against the tile floor and stood in front of the sink. Abby didn't want to look up into the mirror. Instead, she brushed her teeth and disrobed in the darkness. She made her way to the shower, where she fidgeted with the knobs until she found the temperature she was looking for.

Stepping into the hot water felt like heaven. Abby let the comforting heat pound against her flesh, awakening her. Another swell of tears came, and Abby slid to the floor of the shower, weeping. She didn't care what Vivian said, there was magic in tears. It was a moment of emotional honesty, and it gave her release.

The tears were quickly washed away as she purged the hopelessness of the last two days. As the water disappeared down the drain, Abby imagined the tears being carried with it. All her fear, pain, and sorrow washed down the drain.

It was all she had left.

"Alright, thank you. Take care." Abby hung up the phone as she entered the sitting room off the library. She bounced Little Evan in her arms affectionately. "Aunt Wendy is doing better. She should be back home in a day or two."

"That is excellent news," Valorie Grace said, looking up from the book she had been reading.

"It is," Abby agreed. "I just wish Cousin David wasn't still in the ICU. With both him and Margot so badly hurt, and so soon after Gus..." Abby trailed off as her mind went blank. She was overwhelmed by the casualties this fight with Mother Damnable was causing.

Valorie shifted in her large, overstuffed leather chair, before asking, "How are the discussions going?"

Abby was grateful for the change of subject. "They're talking in circles now," she said, taking a seat in the chair across from her friend.

"I hear them shouting from time to time," Ms. Grace said cautiously.

"Yes," Abby said. "If I had to name one thing my family is good at, arguing would be at the top of the list."

"I can only imagine how frustrated everyone is. You and your family are under a great deal of stress," Ms. Grace said kindly.

"That's putting it mildly," Abby said. "I wish they would ask your counsel more. Lawrence and Syble seem convinced you are some kind of spy for the London Seven."

Valorie shook her head. It was an oddly relaxed gesture from the austere woman. "Their concern is somewhat warranted."

"Are you?" Abby asked, alarmed.

Valorie smiled and shook her head. "The Grace Coven is a member of the London Seven, but I, personally, am not in contact with them," Ms. Grace stated. "It is unfortunate your cousins mistrust me, but truthfully, Abigail, I don't know how much help I would be even if they did seek my assistance. Necromancy and the spirits of the dead are far from my area of expertise. You are far more fortunate to have the assistance of the Archibald Sisters."

Abby looked down at the sweet little boy sleeping in her arms. He looked so peaceful. She wished she shared his lack of concerns. She took a deep breath before returning her attention back to the conversation at hand. "It's not like the London Seven, and the Kanes are enemies," Abby suggested.

"No, but your family shares a long, strained relationship with the London Seven, dating back to the War of the Roses," Ms. Grace reminded her.

"It's been over three hundred years since they drove us out. There hasn't been so much as a harsh word exchanged between us since. You would think people could get over it," Abby said sarcastically.

"You might think so," Ms. Grace stated, raising her eyebrow in amusement. "Old rivalries have a tendency to linger, long after their relevance."

"It would seem witches hold grudges better than most," Abby said somberly.

"I could not argue with you on that point," Ms. Grace agreed.

Sebastian quietly poked his head into the room, trying not to intrude too much. "How's my son doing?"

"He's fine," Abby said, with a warm smile. "We're having a great time."

"Thank you for keeping an eye on him. Let me know when you get tired of it. I'll come out and take him back," Sebastian said.

"Don't worry. We're good," Abby said. "How's it going in there?"

Sebastian came the rest of the way into the room and stood next to Abby. "Unfortunately, it hasn't gotten any better," he said, sounding exhausted. "You haven't missed anything. Everyone is frightened. No one knows what we should do, so they are loudly complaining about everything else."

"I think I'll stay out here a bit longer," Abby said. "It's a bit intense for me right now."

"I don't blame you," Sebastian said. "I think we're at a dead end. We need to make another attempt at Atoro, but..."

"We're running out of witches strong enough to take him on," Abby said candidly.

He nodded soberly. "I'll check back in a while."

"Thanks," Abby said. "Good luck in there."

"I'm not sure there's enough luck in the world to get those people to agree on anything," Sebastian said, before closing the door to return to the library.

"How are you holding up?" Ms. Grace asked gently.

Abby didn't know how to answer her question. She was ready to fall apart at any moment, but she was also resigned. There was nothing more she could do. A small part of her had already accepted the fact that her parents would never be free.

She took a moment to compose herself before releasing the air from her lungs. "I'm not really sure," Abby confessed. "To tell you the truth, I haven't let myself think about it too hard. This numb plateau I'm sitting on seems like a safe little emotional oasis at the moment."

"Is it?" Ms. Grace questioned, seemly determined to knock Abby off her emotional ledge.

Abby gave her friend an uncertain look. "I've been trying to avoid it... it's just too much," she said, her voice cracking with emotion. Tears welled in her eyes, and she quickly batted them away and held firmly to her equanimity.

"I know it is," Valorie said kindly. "Why don't you leave that delightful little one with me and take a brisk walk outside. It stopped raining, and I don't think you've been outside of this house in the last couple of days."

Abby looked out the window. The dark gray sky was beginning to clear after the rain earlier that day. *Some fresh air does sound good,* she thought.

"Here, hand him over," Ms. Grace insisted.

There was a part of Abby that didn't want to be alone. She didn't want to face everything she was avoiding. She needed something else to cling onto, so she never had to face the turmoil brewing under the surface.

"Fine," Abby said with uncertainty. She handed the sleeping baby over to her friend and excused herself.

Abby moved down the hallway, and through the grand entry to the front door. The house grew quiet the further away she was from the library.

She stepped out the front door and down the few steps onto the circular driveway. The sun shone down on her face with a glimmer of warmth. It felt good. Abby drew in a deep breath, and fresh air filled her lungs. It was a cleansing feeling.

Abby walked along the driveway and did her best to focus on anything, everything else but what was nagging at her thoughts. After losing Atoro, she had done everything she could to avoid having to deal with the monumental setback. The pain, the agony… it was all too much to face. She tried to pull away from her own thoughts, only to be swarmed by them.

As she passed through the gate, she broke out into a fast run. She hadn't gone for a good run since before Halloween. Freedom washed away her worries as the old familiar movements carried her forward. She didn't pace herself, she didn't plan her route–she simply ran, leaving everything behind.

She ran faster and faster, farther from the house and its shouting matches, farther from the Coven and its secrets and intrigues, farther from the source of her pain.

Tears began to well in her eyes until they came flooding down her cheeks. Abby burst off the road into a small patch of trees and tumbled to her knees. Nausea swelled in her stomach, swirling with her unshed emotions. She wretched her breakfast into the pine needles beneath her. Pain stung at her very soul with such tenacity, Abby thought she would never feel the end of it.

The dark well of despair was growing larger and larger. There was no chance she could stop herself from falling in. The wet ground beneath her began soaking through her jeans, but Abby didn't care. There was no hope. Why did it matter? Nothing mattered anymore. She had nothing left.

She crumbled to the ground. All her strength had left her. *There's no hope for my parents... This is our fate... We'll all die and exist in eternal torment at the hands of Mother Damnable... Everyone I love will suffer... forever...*

Another wave of sickness clenched her stomach. Nothing but bile burned her throat as she heaved.

This isn't right... this isn't how it should be... Mom, Dad... why... Abby pulled herself up from the ground and felt a sudden unexpected wave rush through her. It wasn't pain anymore, it was something hotter–something she was becoming far more familiar with lately.

She stood and picked up an old fallen branch. Rage swept through her. Abby held the branch firmly in her hands and swung it as hard as she could at one of the trees. She swung again and again, unleashing a primal scream.

Again, again, and again she swung, slamming the branch against the tree with every ounce of her strength. She used her entire body to swing again, crashing the old dead branch against the large tree trunk. She swung until the branch broke in two. Abby looked down at the stub in her hand, useless to her now. With a deep, urgent scream, she hurled it into the forest.

Her entire body was sore from the rage that coursed through every muscle. Abby leaned against the tree to catch her breath, feeling drained and empty for a long time.

The cold seeped through her clothes, stirring her from her stupor. Abby slowly got up and began walking back toward her grandmother's house. It took several minutes to make it through the forest and back onto the main path. She was surprised by how far she had run in such a short time.

The closer she came to the house, the heavier the weight felt on her shoulders. Inside that house, she would find nothing more than tension, hopelessness, and grief. A part of Abby didn't want to return. *What would happen if I ran away? she thought. Would they even notice? Wouldn't it all be the same? I could play my violin and go to school, and stop worrying about magic and witches and wars…*

"Abby." She heard a familiar voice echo through her head. "*Help us, Abby!*" Her parents still needed her. The Coven still needed her.

She approached the front door and stepped inside the large white entry. Abby no longer heard the angry and frustrated tones coming from the library.

She entered the sitting room, where she had left Ms. Grace and Little Evan. She found them sitting in a chair, the sweet child asleep in her arms. Sebastian was standing next to her, getting ready to take his son.

"Are they done?" Abby asked. She sounded as drained as she felt.

Sebastian looked at her, worried. "For now. I don't know how much longer they can keep going in circles like this, but Vivian let everyone go for the night."

Abby nodded and walked toward a chair on the far side of the room, where Ms. Grace prepared to hand the baby over to his father.

"You are a very adorable young man," Ms. Grace said to the sleeping infant. She smiled up at Sebastian. "I know he is adopted, but I must confess he looks a great deal like you, Mr. Whitlock."

"Oh, thank you, Ms. Grace. He is ours in every way that counts." Sebastian said warmly.

Abby stood unmoving. Unblinking. She tried to chase a thought that hovered at the edge of her mind. It's slipped away when she tried to reach for it. *Adopted...*

"Is there something wrong?" Ms. Grace asked, leaning forward with a worried expression.

It can't be that easy...

She turned at looked at Evan, sleeping in his father's arms.

No... Is it possible? Atoro... blood....

"You turned white as a sheet just now," Sebastian added.

Abby stared forward, it took a moment for it to sink in that anyone had spoken. Her mind was racing with one thought after another. "No," she said, nodding her head. "I just... I just thought of something..."

"What is it? Ms. Grace asked, moving close enough to Abby to touch her forehead as if checking for a fever.

Abby shrugged her off, coming back to her senses. "Call Vivian," Abby said, trying to catch her thoughts before they ran away with her. "Call everyone back."

"Abby, are you all right? What is this about?" Sebastian asked.

Abby looked at him and started laughing. It was a real, genuine laugh, bordering on mania–the kind of laugh that bore all the relief, joy, and excitement that one person could feel.

Her eyes lit with life for the first time since they'd lost the necromancer. "We don't need Atoro."

"Abby, what–" Sebastian began.

Abby walked over to her uncle and stood beaming down her baby cousin's sleeping face. "We don't need Atoro, we have his blood right here."

Valorie looked at Abby, her eyes wide. "You mean..."

Abby nodded. "Evan is Atoro Thanos' son."

CHAPTER THIRTY-FIVE

"It's time," Vivian said, standing in Abby's doorway. She switched the light on.

Abby sat up. The light bounced off the white walls making it even brighter.

"Thanks for making sure I was up in time," Abby said, pulling herself from the bed and glancing at the time on her phone.

"Did you get any rest?" Vivian asked.

Abby shook her head. "Too nervous," she admitted.

Vivian came in and placed a loving arm around Abby's shoulder. "We all are," Vivian said. "Tonight, we put all this behind us, once and for all."

"I'm relieved," Abby said, feeling the emotions swelling inside. She took several deep breaths to ensure she stayed in control.

"What do you think will happen to them after this?" she asked.

"After the ritual?" Vivian asked. "They'll be free."

"Free to go where? Do what?" Abby asked.

"I don't really know, Darling," Vivian said. "There are so many people and religions that claim to know, but I couldn't begin to guess."

"Do you think it will be somewhere... nice?" Abby asked.

"Your mother and father were good people," Vivian said, a crack in her voice. Abby glanced at her grandmother and gave her a squeeze. "I... I can't imagine they would go anywhere but some place good."

"Is it..." Abby hesitated. "It is wrong of me to want them to stay?" she said quietly.

Vivian turned away, covering her mouth. "I would do anything to see my son again. Just to hold him one last time..." she said, her voice shaking with a desperation Abby had never heard from her grandmother before. "I was a terrible mother. But I loved him. I would give anything to be able to tell him that I loved him..."

Vivian collapsed onto the edge of the bed, consumed by the raw emotions she had buried for so long. They were unstoppable now. "I don't know if I ever told him..." she said, almost in a panic. "He said it to me so many times... I don't remember if I ever said it back..."

Abby sat next to Vivian Kane and held her as she sobbed. For a few moments, Abby felt sorry for her grandmother. She had so many regrets, and she would never be able to make up for them.

The sobs lasted for only a few minutes. Abby felt her grandmother stiffen and pull away. She watched Vivian pull a handkerchief from her purse and dab away tears.

"I'm sorry, Darling," Vivian said, standing.

"For what?" Abby asked, confused.

"That ridiculous display of emotions," Vivian said, visibly pulling herself together.

"You don't need to apologize. There's nothing wrong with letting yourself have a moment," Abby said. "We all need one from time to time."

"Not me, and for the second time in as many days," Vivian said, pulling a small flask from her purse and taking a healthy gulp. "Don't worry, Darling, it won't happen again. I'll see you downstairs. I'm certain everyone is nearly ready by now." She hurried toward the door.

"Grandmother?" Abby said.

Vivian paused a moment at the door. She glanced back. "You really should hurry along, Darling," she added. "It may be the Solstice, but even the longest night won't last forever."

Abby collected her coat from the closet and glanced at herself in the bathroom mirror. There was some puffiness under her eyes, and she looked gaunt and tired. *A little more. Just a little longer and I can rest,* she thought. She took a deep breath, tightened her ponytail, and zipped up her coat. She didn't bother wiping away her tears. She wore them as a badge of honor.

"Let's do this," Abby said and headed downstairs to join her family.

"Are you nervous?" Sebastian asked, reaching over to take Abby's hand.

Abby offered a weak smile as the car pulled up to her old home.

"A little," she confessed.

"It's all going to be over tonight." He squeezed her hand reassuringly.

Ms. Grace approached from a car that pulled up behind them. "It's time to head in," she told them.

Abby quickly stepped out of the car and gave her mentor a long and loving hug. "Thank you. For being here, for helping us, and for... everything," she whispered in Ms. Grace's ear.

"You are very welcome," Valorie said warmly. She extricated herself from Abby's embrace and made her way inside.

Abby glanced around at the neighboring houses as she stood next to the curb. The houses all looked the same. Nothing had changed in the last two years. It was the same sleepy old neighborhood. She turned in the direction of the park. On the far side was the cemetery, where Mary Ann Conklin was buried.

"Let's go in," Sebastian prompted.

Abby pulled herself back into the moment and smiled. "I'm ready," she said, taking a deep breath of fresh air.

They walked up the driveway to the main doors. Abby reached out and turned the knob. She pushed the door open and stepped into the main entry. A numb feeling settled over Abby. Weeks and months of research, anxiety, fear, and failures had culminated to this moment. Grief had crashed against her emotional shores for far too long. The emotional anesthesia was an unexpected merciful state.

Abby noticed several people standing at the bottom of the stairs. "Cordelia." She greeted the woman with a smile. She hadn't been certain she would come.

"Cordelia." Lawrence and Syble entered, greeting the other woman. The older gentleman looked down at the floor as if he was afraid to meet her eyes.

"Lawrence," Cordelia replied. "Thank you for saving my husband."

He blushed, looking flustered. "Have you seen your grandmother?" he asked, turning to Abby.

Abby shrugged. "A lot of people arrived before us. I assume they have already made their way upstairs," she explained.

He nodded once and fled upstairs, dragging his wife along.

Abby turned to Cordelia, offering her a smile. "This will be over soon. Gus will be able to rest."

"Yes." There was a steely rage in Cordelia's eyes as she started up the stairs. It was the look of a woman seeking retribution.

"Come along, Abby. It's nearly time," Fiona said, walking past Abby and up the steps.

"I'm coming," she said.

Abby took a single step when she heard a familiar voice from the doorway. "I'm here." Abby turned to see Hailey Westbrook walk through the front door. She was wearing a hoodie that nearly hid her beautiful face and black hair.

"Hailey?" Abby questioned nearly in a state of shock. The young woman opened her arms, and the two embraced warmly. Abby then held her at arms' length and gave her friend a thorough looking over. "Why are you here? I didn't even know you knew about this. Did Grandmother call you?" Abby asked.

"No, Madison did," Hailey said. "She told me about her mother... I'm sorry, Abby. You have lost so many good people to this specter. The Westbrooks want to help. I'm here to lend you my power.

"I'm so glad you're here," Abby said with a tearful smile.

"It's time." Vivian's voice rang down from above.

Abby looked up to see her grandmother standing at the banister looking down on them, drowning them with the disapproving look.

The girls hurried up the long sweeping stairs.

The altar was set up in the center of her father's old office. A red silk cloth was spread over the top of the small table, just as before. Five candles were set up in a half-circle, and a copper bowl sat in the center surrounded by herbs. Vivian stood near the altar next to the Archibald Sisters, who appeared to be giddy with excitement.

"It's time, kid," Wendy said, as she approached.

"Are you sure you're up to this?" Abby asked, noticing the healing bruises on the side of her head.

"I'm fine, in fact, I'm better than that. I'm ready to do this. This has carried on too long," Wendy said.

"You're right," Abby said. She noticed several coven members beginning to form a circle around the altar.

"Abigail," Two familiar voices said in unison. Abby turned to see Bianca and Inga Archibald approaching.

"Good evening," Abby greeted.

"We have a great deal—"

"Of work to do," Bianca said, a warm smile on her withered face. The two of them excused themselves and returned to Vivian's side.

As Abby watched them, her eyes were drawn to a small glass vial sitting on the altar. Several drops of dark liquid filled the fragile bottle. *Evan's blood,* Abby realized. *Thank God we didn't need him here for this.*

Gisela and Bernard made their way in, and it wasn't long before the room started to feel a bit crowded.

"Everyone, link hands. We are about to begin." Vivian gave Abby a hopeful glance.

Abby took a seat in the center of the circle, readying herself to open the Sight.

The room fell silent. A thick sense of anticipation lingered in every open space. Abby looked around at her family, and friends joined together for one common purpose. She tried not to think about the amount of power gathered here.

Vivian gestured toward the two elderly sisters hovering over their small altar. The Archibald Sisters began pouring reagents into a copper bowl. They lit the candles and ignited the incense.

The Sisters both looked at Abby. "You should begin," they said in unison.

With a deep breath, Abby looked the Soul Web. Anticipation coursed through her body. She closed her eyes and began the process of clearing her mind, holding every thought and emotion back.

Like a trickle of water, her mind began to fill with an image slowly coming together in her consciousness.

She stood in a vast, open plain, desolate and barren. It was just as it had been before. A dais stood a few yards away, and there, at the top, was a throne-like chair. Ash fell from the sky in small flakes.

The chair was empty. Abby had expected Mother Damnable to be there. She had been the last time they attempted the ritual. Abby looked around. There was nothing but forsaken ash-ridden plains for as far as she could see.

Abby looked up into the gray sky. A pale light broke through dark clouds, basking her surroundings in the faintest of sickly glows. A vein of lightning shot across the sky. It was chased by a thunderous rumble that shook the ground beneath Abby's feet.

Then there was a wild wail from behind her. Abby quickly turned to see two wolves only a few yards away howling to the sky. They were calling something. She cautiously backed away, and the wolves continued to howl, taking little interest in her.

There was another flash of lightning, followed by an enormous clap of thunder. Abby looked to the sky. The clouds grew darker. She felt a cool breeze spring up, swiftly growing into a storm. They were beginning the ritual.

A cackle rode on the wind. Abby took a breath, readying herself, and turned to face the throne. Mother Damnable was slowly climbing the stairs to the dais.

"Mary Ann Conklin," Abby said firmly. The spirit ignored her and continued her ascent to the throne. Faint cords extended from her ghostly form and disappeared into the sky.

The wolves quit howling. They licked their lips and began circling around the throne, coming to stand behind Abby on either side. They growled, baring their teeth in ghoulish dog grins, as Mother Damnable took her seat. She sat serenely as if she was getting ready to hold court.

Slowly, the specter turned her head and laid her eyes upon Abby. The old woman's withered face looked both angry and weary.

"Back to try again?" Mother Damnable asked.

"We aren't trying anything," Abby said. "We know what you are, Skugga. You are finished."

"Am I?" Mother Damnable grinned wickedly.

The two wolves began barking. The spirit of the old woman looked beyond Abby, where the wolves stood. She smiled at them curiously. "What have you brought with you?"

The wind began to blow even harder, and ash began to stir. Abby could barely see more than a few yards away; the ashen plains were obscured in darkness. Another flash of lightning. A rumble in the distance rose over the howl of the wind. The wolves continued to bark and growl. Abby glanced down to see they had moved protectively to either side of her.

"Your time is up," Abby said.

Mother Damnable studied Abby's face, searching for something. Some glimmer of doubt. The old woman leaned back in her chair and scoffed. "Go away, foolish child. There is no Ending me. Your ancestors couldn't do it, you think you can?"

"What price did you pay for your power? What spirit or demon will come to collect? What debts have you acquired for your revenge?" Abby asked.

Mother Damnable turned and gnashed her rotting teeth, spittle running down her chin. "You know nothing! Be gone with your dogs!" she yelled. Reaching back, her hand searched, grasping for the right cord.

The dogs lunged forward. They leaped from the ground, their teeth latching onto a long silver cord tethered to the old woman.

The wolves bit down, gripping the thread tightly in their teeth. They both thrashed their heads until the cord snapped. Mother Damnable screamed in fury and stood to face the wolves. She began backing away.

For the first time, Abby saw fear in the old spirit's face.

A single cord drifted behind Mother Damnable, floating loose in the air. The other end quickly disappeared, sucked into the heavens, and out of existence.

"You little whore!" Mother Damnable yelled. She lunged toward Abby but fell short. The wolves leaped on the spirit's backbiting and tearing away at the cords. As each cord snapped between the wolf's teeth, the ends began disappearing into the sky. "Get them off of me!" the old woman screamed.

The wolves continued to ravage the cords until there were none. Mother Damnable wept on the ashen-ridden ground. "I hate you! I hate you! I hate you!" she screamed as she pounded her fists on the ground.

The hysterics stopped, abruptly cut off as Mother Damnable brought herself calmly to her feet. Ends of silver cords floated like stubs from her back. Abby watched as they slowly withered and fell to dust.

"You're nothing more than a lowly spirit," Abby said, unable to hide the satisfaction in her voice.

Mother Damnable's mouth twisted into a menacing smile. "You are a clever little girl," she said, every word coated in venom. "You may have found a way to sever my power, but I still have claws, as you will soon see!" she yelled and leaped toward Abby.

There was a loud thud as Abby felt her body crash against the ground. She felt a heavy weight press on top of her and looked up to see Mother Damnable sitting on top of her. The old spirit wrapped her withered talon-like hands around Abby's neck, choking her.

Abby couldn't breathe. She paused for a moment, centering herself. She reached up and tried to pull the old woman's hands away from her throat. She was too strong; Abby couldn't budge them. She placed the palm of her hands on either side of Mother Damnable's head. Straining to reach around to her face, Abby gouged at the old spirit's eyes with her thumbs.

Mother Damnable let out a furious scream and released her chokehold. She clawed at Abby's hands.

Abby let go and balled her hand into a fist. She pulled back and punched the old woman in the face. Mother Damnable reeled back, and Abby knocked her off. She quickly rolled away toward the throne. She used the steps to pull herself to her feet and quickly turned to face Mother Damnable.

The specter slowly stood, as another flash of lightning lit the sky. The wolves were gone, and the wind was beginning to swirl around them.

"You haven't won!" Mother Damnable screamed. "You are all going to die!"

Mother Damnable stood. Her eyes were wild with fury.

Abby stepped back. The crazed spirit stared at her, poised to leap forward at any moment and tear her apart.

The wind began to pick up speed, whipping around them furiously. Abby reached for the throne to steady herself as Mother Damnable lunged forward and raked Abby's shoulder with her jagged talons. Abby fled to the far side of the throne and looked down to see blood seeping through her blue shirt.

"I will kill you!" Mother Damnable screamed.

Suddenly, the wind stopped. Silence descended as the sounds of the brewing storm abruptly ceased. Abby looked around to see the swirling wind was contained by the perfect circle of magic surrounding them. They stood in the eye of a tempest, cut off from the rest of the land of the dead.

She looked up. The twister opened a grayish-purple portal above them. "It's only a matter of time now," she said, watching the deranged spirit closely.

"You think I will give up so easily?" Mother Damnable growled.

"No," Abby said. "But I'm not scared of you anymore."

Mother Damnable stared at her with a glow of respect that melted away into pity. "You have no idea what lays ahead, do you?"

"I'm not interested in your lies, Mary Ann," Abby said, shaking her head.

"I've never lied to you, young one," Mother Damnable said sweetly, as though she were speaking to a child. "I never had to. Your grandmother cannot say the same, though, can she?"

"Don't waste your time," Abby insisted. "You're not getting into my head again."

"Tick-tock," Mother Damnable said, as she swayed to imaginary music. "Their voices are gone. What beautiful music they had. Their souls sang in agony," she said.

Mother Damnable began dancing at the center of the tempest, listening to a beautiful waltz played for only her by her chaotic magics. She amused herself for only a few moments before stopping abruptly and giving Abby a wicked grin. Her rotting jagged teeth were unsettling to look at. Suddenly, the deranged spirit winced as though she felt a sharp pain.

The once-powerful Skugga stumbled and stepped back. She quickly hid her worried look and began laughing maniacally. Her stone-like pallor began to fall apart. The gray specks covering the spirit's flesh flaked off and floated into the air. The fell up as though gravity didn't exist.

"There's still enough time to deal with you!" Mother Damnable cried out through her hysterical laughter.

She turned to Abby. The laughter stopped, and Mother Damnable stared Abby in the eye. She then reached out with both hands and lunged at Abby, screaming. "Die you filthy KANE!"

The spirit's hands grabbed Abby's throat again. Abby fell backward. Mother Damnable landed on top of her and quickly straddled Abby's chest, pinning her to the floor. Abby twisted her body, forcing the spirit to release her grip. Abby bucked her legs, and Mother Damnable tipped over.

"You'll be dead before long, little one," Mother Damnable growled, as specs of gray ash continued to drift from her body.

Mother Damnable raised her arms. The entire room filled with ghostly screams and mournful cries. They grew louder and louder in a deafening cacophony of horror. Disembodied spirits began swooping into the eye of the tempest. They began swarming around Abby, taunting and clawing at her.

Abby dropped to her knees. Terrible invasive thoughts of destruction and death began filling her mind. Her arms and legs became even more difficult to control as the maelstrom of death swirled around her.

There was no hope. Abby could barely control her body and crumbled to the floor. She was being violated by horrifying specters of death. She felt like she was trapped in a small room with a hundred other people pushing and shoving to make room. She was ready to surrender; let it all go and stop fighting.

"Not. This. Time!" Abby shouted. She let out a primal scream as she rallied her strength and resolve.

A wave of blue energy blasted from her voice. The spirits swarming around her body began to fizzle, and the voices shouting in her head began to recede until they fell silent.

A sense of relief settled in, as Abby realized she had won the trial of mental and emotional fortitude against the spirits trying to possess her.

Mother Damnable shrieked her rage. She gathered herself to make another lunge toward Abby. Suddenly, she stopped. She looked over Abby's shoulder, her gaze fixed on something.

Abby turned.

At least a dozen spirits stood behind her, framed by the edge of the tempest. There was a man in an old-fashioned suit with a brass pocket watch and a bushy beard. Marcus Kane. Abby recognized him from her vision. Next to him stood a tall, thin man with sharp features. A woman joined them, her face contorted in powerful rage. More and more of them stepped through the tempest until they were surrounding Abby and Mother Damnable. The spirit of a little girl pushed through the legs of those gathered around.

"Lily," Abby said. A healthy flush had returned to the little girl's sallow cheeks. She gave Abby a bright smile. Though Abby was uncertain who all the spirits were, she knew they were her ancestors, each trapped by Mother Damnable's insatiable desire for revenge.

The old hag scrambled to her feet, terror evident in her eyes. "I'm not done with any of you," Mother Damnable said, spitting her words like a curse.

"She can't hurt you anymore, Lily," Abby reassured.

"I know," Lily giggled. The spirits of her ancestors formed a circle at the edge of the tempest.

"I still have plenty of power!" Mother Damnable screamed.

Those she had tormented stood shoulder to shoulder, trapping Mary Ann in the center of their circle. She reached out and tried to grab Abby. With surprising speed, Abby stepped aside and avoided the spirit's attack.

"Not for long," Abby said. She made a fist. Pulling back, she punched Mother Damnable squarely in the face.

More spirits began appearing from the storm. One by one, they came forward.

Outside the circle, on the other side of the veil, Abby could hear her family chanting. The ritual was gaining strength as Mother Damnable weakened.

The loathsome spirit gave Abby an incredulous glare. "I've dealt with more than one Kane in my time. You'll be no different!" she barked.

"You've tried more than once to get rid of me. You have failed every time. Forgive me if I'm not impressed! None of us are," she said, gesturing to her family and ancestors united behind her.

She raised her hand and made a curse gesture with her fingers. "Celiata Franticus!"

A bolt of purple crackling energy shot from her fingertips, striking Mother Damnable in the chest. The deranged spirit cried out in pain as the magical energy engulfed her. The raw mystical force crackled through her body for a few seconds before it dissipated into nothingness.

Abby felt a weight on her shoulder. Abby looked at the hand, resting gently on her shoulder. She followed it up until she was looking into the warm, loving eyes of Evan Kane.

Her breath caught in her throat. He smiled.

Next, to him, a warm, smiling face, framed with flowing red hair, shined down on her with all the love only a mother could conjure.

"Mom," Abby cried.

The spirit nodded. "We are here with you, Abby." Behind them, a dozen or more faces she knew from her mother's old photographs stepped forward. A tear streaked down Abby's face as she watched the spirits of her mother's family link hands with her Kane ancestors.

One by one, each of the new spirits lifted their voices, joining the in the chant. The linked their hands. The power grew and swirled, combining with the force of the ritual outside. Abby watched as the souls of all Kanes, past and present, joined their Coven.

Abby stood and turned to face the evil spirit.

"Mary Ann Conklin," Abby shouted, standing between her parents. "You can't hurt us anymore. You have no power here!"

Mother Damnable took a step back. "You! Fiendish little witch!" she cried. Desperation was thick in her voice. Terror was written on her face as she leaned up against the foot of the throne.

Abby grabbed her parents' hands, joining her energy with theirs, and with a bittersweet determination in her voice said, "It's time."

She joined chant. Their voices cried out, carrying the anger and horror of lifetimes of torment. Abby could hear chanting coming from outside the swirling wind that formed the boundaries of the tempest. The shadowed forms of her living family stood shoulder to shoulder with those inside. As one, the Kane Coven lifted their voices against their enemy.

A purple haze started to form in the eye of the tempest. The gray stone flecks continued to drift away from Mother Damnable, faster than before. The spirit was beginning to look like a person of flesh and blood.

Mother Damnable stumbled, her face covered in pain. Then she began to fade. Slowly at first, then faster and faster. Her body faded, becoming more and more translucent.

The Coven continued to chant.

A sulfurous stench filled Abby's nostrils. The light above became blindingly bright, and Abby was forced to close her eyes.

Still, they kept chanting.

When she opened her eyes, Mother Damnable standing next to the throne. A mournful look stretched upon her withered face. "It isn't over," the crazed spirit uttered.

"It is for you," Abby said unapologetically.

Mother Damnable looked Abby in the eyes, her mournful gaze turned into something far more menacing. The deranged spirit began laughing and dancing around the room in a strange frenzy. "Soon... Soon!" she sang as though there were music playing all around her. "They will destroy themselves with their folly!" she sang out.

The crazed spirit stopped dancing abruptly, staring into the crowd of souls gathered around her. She locked eyes with the woman standing next to the soul of Marcus Kane. "You still lose, Angelica!"

With a frenzied scream, the crazed spirit buckled over. As she straightened, there was a panicked look on her face. A stream of gray smoke began to billow from her right shoulder. She howled in pain.

Mother Damnable stepped toward Abby, standing face to face with her. "It has only begun little one," she growled seething with anger. The spirit's body began to smoke, first from her chest, then her head. She stumbled and fell to the ground burning.

Abby watched as the smoke dissipated, leaving nothing of the old woman behind.

The spirit of Mary Ann Conklin was gone.

The wind howled through the realm of the dead as the sound of their chanting faded away. The storm began to scatter until there was nothing. Abby leaned up against the throne and watched as the shadows of her Coven disappeared. The spirits of her ancestors began to fade. Soon, Abby was alone.

She leaned back and sighed. Her first honest sigh in months.

It was over.

A faint glow radiated from the dais beneath the throne. Abby pushed the chair form the dais and uncovered the glyph.

The five-pointed star with the eye-like symbol in the center began to glow brighter and brighter. Abby watched as the seal that formed the Soul Web began to smoke. It grew brighter and brighter, turning to ash and flaking into the sky.

An unexpected scent filled the air in the land of the dead. Abby took a deep breath. Lilies? She looked around, there were no flowers nearby. A quiet settled over the area, a peace. Instead of the cold, muted world of death, there was now a bright, hazy glow.

Abby turned around. She was no longer in the desolate, gray land. She stood at the end of the long hallway. To her, right was a door, and as her eyes focused, she recognized the door to her old bedroom. Abby turned and looked toward her father's office. The door was slightly ajar, just like that day…

"Mom? Dad?" she whimpered as her body began to tremble. She took several steps toward the door. A blinding light shined through the window as she opened the door. Abby shielded her eyes until they adjusted to the light.

There, standing next to her father's desk were Jessica and Evan Kane. They stood with matching smiles, looking at Abby warmly. The love in their gazes was overwhelmingly bright. Abby wept openly at what she saw.

"Mom? Dad?" She questioned her own eyes.

Before she waited for a response, before she even realized what she was doing, Abby flew into her parents' arms. They pulled her into a tight hug and held her. Abby never believed she would ever feel them again. Their warmth, their scent, it was all just as it always was.

Countless times she had wanted this moment, cried for this moment, pleaded to any god who would listen for one last chance to have this very moment. Now she had it, and she wasn't sure she could let go again.

"Are you all right? Are you hurt?" Abby asked, looking at her parents over.

"We're fine, now," Evan said. Her father had the same sparkle in his eye he always had. "It's all over."

"Thank you, Abby," Jessica said, pulling her daughter in close and stroking her hair.

"Did she hurt you?" Abby asked.

"None of that is important anymore," her father said, reassuring her. He looked above at the bright light. "We have to go soon."

"Can't you stay?" Abby asked. "We could live here together again. I can use my gift, we can be together again."

Jessica and Evan shared a look. "That's not how it works, Abby," her mother said.

"I don't understand. We could still be a family," Abby pleaded.

"It isn't good for the dead to stay among the living," Evan said.

"And it isn't good for the living either," Jessica added lovingly.

"All we want for you is to be happy," Evan said.

"Don't be sad for us, my precious girl," Jessica said, holding Abby close. "Our suffering is over. You don't need to worry anymore."

"Do what you love, Abby," her father said, moving in and holding Jessica and Abby both. "Be happy. Do whatever it takes to find out what that is, and do it."

"We will be there," Jessica reassured. "As often as we can. It's your heart that draws us to you. It's when your heart sinks or falters that we will be there for you."

"Please don't go," Abby pleaded. Her heart broke all over again. The tears nearly blinded her as her parents' arms tightened around her. *I'll never let go,* she vowed, knowing it was a vain thought. She looked up into their eyes. "I love you so much," Abby managed to squeak from a throat thick with emotion.

"We know, and we love you," Evan said, kissing Abby on the forehead.

Jessica stroked Abby's hair. She kissed Abby on the cheek and gave her one last squeeze. "We love you more than anything," she told her daughter. "Live a long, good life."

Abby batted her eyes and wiped away the tears. It was a mere fraction of a second, and they were gone.

CHAPTER THIRTY-SIX

"They say I can get out of bed and walk around a bit tomorrow," Margot said, smiling warmly at her niece. She still looked frail and weak, lying there.

"We could go for a stroll on the grounds if you want some fresh air," Abby suggested. "I'll make Madison come too. It will be good to get her out of the house."

"I'd like that," Margot agreed. "I've been in this bed for far too long," she added.

"Remember, just because you are getting better doesn't mean you should push yourself too hard," Fiona reminded her, sounding every bit the mother.

Margot rolled her eyes and nodded.

"Listen to your mother, young lady," Fiona said, shaking her finger pointedly.

"I think I'm going to let you two work this out," Abby said, standing and heading toward the door. "I have to check in with my grandmother before I get ready for the concert tonight."

"I wish I could be there for you, Abby," Margot said sincerely.

"Don't worry. This one won't be my last concert," Abby said, with a smile. "I'm glad you're all right."

Margot smiled warmly at her and shooed her away.

As Abby disappeared into the hallway, she heard the rumblings of a loving argument in the room she left behind. Laughing, she headed down the hall.

There at the top of the stairs were Rodger and Sebastian, sorting through luggage. Wendy approached with Little Evan fussing in her arms.

"What's going on?" Abby questioned.

"We're taking everything back to the house," Sebastian explained.

"There isn't any reason to stay here now that things have been settled," Rodger agreed.

"Besides, we're all a bit tired of more than a few people still around," Wendy added with a wink.

"I don't blame you," Abby said. "When were you going to tell me?"

"We did yesterday. Remember?" Sebastian said.

"Oh, I thought you said after the concert," Abby stated. "I didn't realize you meant so soon."

"The concert is tonight," Rodger said. "And I don't know about you, but now that Lawrence and Syble have left, we have no problem escaping either."

"We figured we could have everything ready for you to join us tomorrow," Wendy added.

"I guess I can't really blame you," she said, chuckling and thinking fondly of her own bed.

"We were hoping you would understand," Sebastian smiled. "Will you say goodbye to Cordelia for us when you see her?"

Abby nodded. "She's at the hospital with David now, but I will tell her."

Wendy stopped swinging her nephew from side to side and looked at Abby. "How is he doing?"

"As well as can be expected, according to Cordelia," Abby said. "The surgery went well, and he's recovering. He'll be in the hospital for a while, but he should live."

Wendy sighed like she was releasing a held breath. "Thank goodness. He risked his life for us, I don't know what I would have done if he didn't pull through."

Abby nodded, and Wendy turned back toward her brother. "This is turning into a nice day. Let's go before I accidentally run into Vivian."

Abby waved goodbye and crossed the second-floor mezzanine to the east hall. The bouquets were fragrant, filling the room with the floral scent of white jasmine. Even the freshly cut plumage was white, to match the sterile décor her grandmother loved.

She came to the end of the hallway, where a set of double doors were closed. Abby approached and politely knocked.

"Come in!" a familiar voice called through the door.

Vivian's room was a palace. A large bed draped with white silk curtains rested on a raised platform in the center of the room. There was a fireplace on one wall and a bay of windows on the other. The magnificent room looked professionally staged, as though it had never been lived in.

"Good morning," Abby said. Her grandmother was seated at a small vanity. Vivian gazed into an ornate mirror, putting on a pair of diamond stud earrings.

Vivian glanced over. Upon seeing Abby, a smile crept across her face. "Darling, come," she said, extending her hand. "Come sit next to me." She made room for Abby to sit on the small bench beside her.

Abby sat beside her grandmother and gave her a hug. Vivian looked at her adoringly while she fussed with Abby's long red hair. For a brief moment, everything was at peace. Then she leaned over and gave Abby a kiss on the forehead.

"It's finally over," Vivian said, a sense of relief in her voice. "We can all finally be at peace."

"I haven't slept better in my life than I did last night," Abby said.

"Me too." Vivian smiled.

"You said you wanted to see me about something," Abby reminded her, a hint of curiosity in her voice.

"Yes," Vivian said with a sly smile. "I do. Wait right here, Darling," she added, before getting up and disappearing into the next room.

She returned a moment later with a large rectangular box wrapped in silver paper, with a sparkling white bow.

"What is this?" Abby asked.

"It's something your parents wanted to get for you," Vivian told her as if it explained.

"I don't understand, how could they have gotten me something?" Abby asked.

"I'll explain after you open your gift, Darling," Vivian said, placing the package on Abby's lap.

Abby slid the wrapping off the rectangular-shaped object. Inside was a heavy-duty stainless-steel case, with a handle and locked latches.

"Oh, Darling, I nearly forgot." Vivian retrieved a key ring with two keys attached and made a great show of handing them to Abby. "Here you go."

"What is this?" Abby questioned with uncertainty.

"Open it up and find out, Darling," Vivian prompted, as she handed her the keys.

Abby accepted the keys and unlocked the clasps. She slowly opened the case, fearing something would leap out and devour her.

Inside was a beautiful old violin, resting on a bed of velvet. The amber-colored wood had a hint of red, and the scroll work was masterful. It was unlike any violin she had ever seen. The same, yet somehow... more.

"This is magnificent!" Abby said, lifting the violin carefully from its resting place and holding it gingerly in her hands. She inspected the bridge closely. The intricate detailing was exquisite. "Who made this?"

"I really don't know much about it, other than your parents picked this one. It was created centuries ago by a man named Amati," Vivian stated.

"Nicolo Amati?" Abby squeaked, unable to believe what she was holding in her hands.

"Yes, Darling, that was his name," Vivian stated. "Do you know his work?"

"Of course, I do!" Abby said in amazement, her eyes welling with tears. "He was a master violin maker in the sixteenth century. He was Antonio Stradivarius' master. If you can imagine such an artist ever being a student himself. Amati is the one who taught Stradavarius everything he knew about making violins."

"Your mother and father did all the research. This was what they wanted to get for you because they believed in your talent," Vivian said.

Abby could not stop the tear that ran down her cheek. "I don't understand," Abby said. "How did they get this for me? They've been gone for almost two years now."

Vivian sat next to Abby and put her arm around her granddaughter. "There was an older gentleman, Lorenzo Feliz, from Lisbon. He had expressed interest in selling this violin a couple of years ago. When your parents started negotiations with him, he changed his mind. Then about a month ago, he reached out. Apparently, he has terrible arthritis in his hands, and playing was no longer feasible. He asked if our family was still interested in acquiring the instrument, so I got it for you... It is what your parents would have wanted," she finished evenly.

Abby looked at her grandmother in amazement. "This is really mine?" She asked. She was unsure how to believe it. This was too precious a gift.

"It is yours, My Darling."

"I have to go play it!" Abby hurriedly put it back in the case and latched it closed. She rushed to the door and paused. She set down her violin case, and turned around, rushing back for a big hug. "I love you, Grandmother."

Vivian returned the hug and quickly let go. "Run along now," she said, with a misty-eyed smile.

"Thank you," Abby said again.

"Get out, I have things to do," Vivian said gruffly, waving Abby away. She turned away, busying herself with nothing.

"I still love you," Abby said coyly, as she disappeared into the hallway with her new treasure.

Abby wore only a simple black dress with matching heels, despite her grandmother's attempts to deck her out in jewels. She refused to glitter like a treasure chest on stage and enlisted Ms. Grace to distract Vivian while she dressed. Like most classical musicians, she preferred to avoid anything that would distract from the performance; a concept surely lost on Vivian Kane.

Abby sat in the small dressing room they'd given her, nervously tuning her instrument. Her stomach was churning, and she was glad she ate very little for dinner. She focused on her breathing, trying to calm herself as much as possible. A polite knock came at the door. She gave herself a quick glance in the mirror as she got up to answer it.

"Are you ready?" Irene asked with a big smile. She wore a tasteful black gown with understated pearl jewelry and was looking sublimely happy.

"I'm nervous," Abby confessed. "The last couple days have been among the most challenging of my life. It's been a little hard to wrap my head around this performance." She smiled at her friend. "Actually, I'm trying not to freak out."

Irene gave her a kind hug. "You've got this," she stated. "You had this piece down before I even met you. Just stay cool, and when you get up there, imagine yourself at home practicing. You play this piece perfectly. Tonight is no different from every other time."

"Except there are a couple thousand people watching," Abby added dryly.

"There is that. However, the only effect that will have on anything you play this evening is the effect you let it have. You know how to focus, so use that tonight," Irene encouraged.

"I plan to," Abby said, trying to disguise the fear in her voice. While she was no stranger to performing in front of an audience, this was her first time in front of so large a group that did not consist mostly of parents and faculty.

"I'm going to take my seat," Irene said, glancing at her watch. "You're up in about three minutes, and I don't want to miss anything," She gave Abby another comforting hug. "You're going to do this, and you will be great." With another quick smile, she departed.

Moments later, a staff member knocked on the door and ushered her to her position stage right.

Abby was escorted to a small "x" constructed with tape on the floor. The bright lights shined down from the rafters, and she heard the beautiful piece being played on the other side of the thick red curtain. The audience clapped upon the conclusion of the guest artist. She leaned over and watched the young man take a bow and shake hands with the conductor before exiting the stage in the opposite direction.

"Our next artist is one of Seattle's very own, a talented young woman who will be attending Oxford University in the fall. Please welcome Abigail Kane!" Kristoff Schreiner, the conductor, announced, extending his hand.

Taking a deep breath and allowing herself no further time to think, Abby put on her best smile and stepped out on stage. Thunderous applause erupted, and she blanched. She was certain she could hear the prompting of several of her friends in the audience. She was incredibly grateful that the stage lights were shining in her eyes, preventing her from seeing anyone other than the conductor.

Abby politely shook Kristoff's hand.

"Do your thing, Miss Kane," he whispered, just loud enough for her to hear.

Abby took her position, and the audience fell silent, and the conductor raised his hands. Abby and the Seattle symphony brought their instruments to the ready. With a simple wave of his baton, Abby began playing her piece, leading the symphony into Vivaldi's beautiful concerto. She played the music as though her instrument was holding a conversation with the symphony behind her.

She closed her eyes and allowed herself to be a part of the music. The sound vibrated through her as the combined instruments created a harmony of sound. The energy of the music so beautiful, she lost herself to it completely. For one brief moment, she was part of a whole, and not a separate being.

As the last note was played, she felt herself drift back into her conscious body. She stayed with it until the sound faded. She opened her eyes. Abby blushed as the audience, mere shadows beyond the lighting, stood and applauded her. She knew she would carry the memory of that moment for the rest of her life.

For a moment, the faces of Evan and Jessica Kane floated into her mind. She wondered if her parents were here, in whatever way they could be. Her mother had said they would be there when her heart called them. She smiled and holding back tears. "I did it," she whispered solemnly, hoping they could hear her words.

Kristoff Schreiner took a bow and motioned to Abby, who followed his lead. He then stepped down from the platform and gave her a firm handshake. "That was incredible, Miss Kane, we would love to have you back," he said quietly.

"Thank you, Mr. Schreiner. I would love to," she said and exited the stage as the audience was still applauding her performance.

Abby breathed a sigh of relief. Though the performance was over, there was a great deal of adrenaline coursing through her body, filling her with nervous energy.

"Excellent performance, Miss Kane," several strangers commented, as Abby made her way back to her room. She thanked them politely and quickly sequestered herself in her changing room. Abby spent a few moments putting her instrument away and taking time to regain her composure.

Today was a day she had been preparing for since she first picked up the violin. Her parents had supported her every step of the way. She had always dreamed of them bursting into her dressing room and showering her with love and praise. Her mother would wrap her arms around her, crying over how talented her baby girl was. Her father would beam from the other side of the room, telling her how amazing she was, how precise and beautiful her articulation. Then they would all laugh at the exhilaration of the day.

Her parents should have been there. It wasn't the same. It would never be what she'd dreamed of. She looked in the mirror, imaging them beside her, and remembered what they'd told her. Don't be sad for us. We will always be with you. No, it wasn't the same, but it was all right too. "Mom, Dad," she said, through soft tears, "thank you for everything."

After a few minutes, Abby made her way backstage and waited for her cue to go on. When the time came, she and the others came out with the audience standing and applauding them. They each took a bow. The conductor handed Abby a bouquet of white roses. "Good luck at Oxford," he said, before moving on and giving the next performer a firm handshake. Abby bowed with the others one last time and exited the stage.

She headed off to the second-floor balcony, where she had a clear view overlooking the lobby. Her family would be waiting for her at the cocktail reception in the main hall, and this was the best place to spot them. After a few moments, she saw Wendy waving at her. Abby smiled and began making her way toward the stairs, before being stopped by several strangers who graciously complimented her. After thanking them, Abby continued the journey through the dense maze of people sipping on wine and cocktails. She joined her family, who were gathered around the entrance to the lounge.

Madison approached, giving Abby a warm hug.

"You were amazing!" Hailey said as she embraced Abby.

"I have heard the piece you performed many times," Ms. Grace stated in her usual stoic manner. "I must say this was among the best I have had the pleasure of hearing."

For the next five minutes, Abby blushed, embarrassed as her family and friends showered her with accolades. She was beaming in spite of her embarrassment. It was one of those moments in life when she truly felt the love of those around her as tangible and real as the people themselves. It was a feeling she wanted to hold on to for as long as she could.

Vivian looked over and gave Abby a knowing smile. For the first time in her life, she felt as though her grandmother was proud of her.

Sebastian was glowing with excitement and pride. Even Fiona, one of the most emotionally cautious people Abby had ever known, gave her a warm smile. Wendy and Rodger both hugged her and watched the jubilant celebration happening all around them.

For the first time in a long time, Abby felt genuine happiness. It was strange, an unusual sensation after the wrongness of the last year and a half. She allowed herself to revel in the feeling for a moment.

Abby caught herself getting emotional and excused herself. She didn't go far. She stepped around a corner near an emergency exit where she was mostly out of view of the people milling around. She pulled a handkerchief from her purse and pressed it to her eyes, careful not to smear her mascara.

Abby felt a hand on her shoulder and turned to see Sebastian standing behind her. "It still happens for me, too," he said. "Every time something good happens, I still wish my parents, or your mother, were here."

"I didn't realize it would hit me so hard," Abby quietly confessed, as she held her uncle.

"You're always going to miss them, Abby. Especially at times like this," Sebastian explained. "There will always be something missing, no matter how happy you are."

"How do you get through this?" Abby asked.

"I try to focus on the people who are here and appreciate them," Sebastian said. "It doesn't always work. Sometimes it does."

"I've been thinking about them a lot these last couple days," Abby admitted. "I feel at peace in some ways. I mean, I still miss them–miss them terribly–but I guess I thought it would be easier after the ritual. Lighter. You know?"

"It won't be," Sebastian affirmed gently. "The holes people leave behind when they are gone, never completely heal. Moving on is never as easy as we want it to be."

Abby looked at her uncle and gave him a warm smile. "You're kind of a smart guy," she jested.

"I've been around this block more than once, so to speak," Sebastian said, with a knowing smile. "Come on, let's join the others." He wrapped his arm around her shoulder.

Abby dabbed away a small tear forming at the corner of her eye as they made their way back toward the rest of the family. They welcomed her back into the celebrations without pause. She smiled at her loving family and friends.

Maybe I will be happy, after all, she thought.

LOOK FOR
THE EXCITING CONTINUATION OF THE HOUSE
OF KANE SERIES.

KINGDOM OF ASHES

HOUSE OF KANE BOOK THREE

✳ *Philip M Jones* ✳

COMING SOON

PUBLISHED BY FIRESONG ARTS
Changing the World, One Word at a Time
https://www.firesongarts.com/

PHILIP M JONES

Philip is a professional writer, known for his work with the the Irish Whip Podcast and the Prowrestling Post. When he is not writing, he sips tea and coffee while reading more than is typical of a 'normal human being.' He currently lives in Seattle, where he is a proud member of the LGBTQ community.

These books are a labor of love for him, and he hopes that you get as much enjoyment from reading them as he did from writing.

Listen to him in action as the co-host of
THE WORD NECROMANCERS PODCAST
available at https://anchor.fm/wordnecromancers

Be sure to join Philip's Facebook page,
https://www.facebook.com/AuthorPhilipMJones/
for more information on upcoming books, release dates, and other fun things that Philip finds interesting.

Liked This Book?

Please leave a review!

Reviews help books gain the recognition they deserve. By leaving a review you are helping to ensure that many more books from this author can be written and published for you to enjoy!

Submit reviews to prteam@firesongarts.com
Or visit https://www.firesongarts.com/reviews